About a Dog

Center Point
Large Print

Also by Jenn McKinlay and available from
Center Point Large Print:

Cloche and Dagger
Read It and Weep
On Borrowed Time
A Likely Story
Better Late Than Never

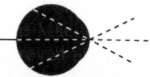

**This Large Print Book carries the
Seal of Approval of N.A.V.H.**

About a Dog

JENN McKINLAY

CENTER POINT LARGE PRINT
THORNDIKE, MAINE

This Center Point Large Print edition
is published in the year 2017 by arrangement with
The Berkley Publishing Group, an imprint of
Penguin Publishing Group, a division of Penguin
Random House LLC.

The text of this Large Print edition is unabridged.
In other aspects, this book may vary
from the original edition.
Printed in the United States of America
on permanent paper.
Set in 16-point Times New Roman type.

ISBN: 978-1-68324-499-8

Library of Congress Cataloging-in-Publication Data

Names: McKinlay, Jenn, author.
Title: About a dog : a Bluff Point romance / Jenn McKinlay.
Description: Center Point Large Print edition. | Thorndike, Maine :
    Center Point Large Print, 2017.
Identifiers: LCCN 2017024365 | ISBN 9781683244998
    (hardcover : alk. paper)
Subjects: LCSH: Large type books. | GSAFD: Love stories.
Classification: LCC PS3612.A948 A65 2017 | DDC 813/.6—dc23
LC record available at https://lccn.loc.gov/2017024365

For Kate "You Need More Conflict" Carlisle. From the day we met at a book signing at the Poisoned Pen, you have generously offered me your wisdom, advice, humor, encouragement, and the occasional kick in the pants when warranted. You are an amazing writer and an even better friend. I am so grateful to have you in my life and look forward to getting into way more shenanigans together! XO

Acknowledgments

This book would not exist without our Annie, a dog we discovered thrown away in an alley, who wagged her way into our hearts in a matter of minutes. As if she was meant to be ours, she immediately bonded with her schnauzer brother, Otto, and our two cats, Patsy and Loretta, until it was hard to remember a time when she was not in our pack.

There are so many people who played a critical role in the creation of this novel that I must start at the beginning so I don't miss anyone. My editor, Kate Seaver, sparked the idea when she said she thought I could write romantic comedies. That was all I needed to hear to revisit a genre that I adore. My mother, Susan McKinlay, encouraged my enthusiasm by spending a train ride from New York City to New Haven kicking ideas back and forth until we were both pretty excited by the raw story we'd created. My author friend Kate Carlisle endured a library conference in San Francisco, where she offered up a bazillion ideas to improve the conflict-light novel that I had in my head until it began to build substance. My agent, Christina Hogrebe, sealed the deal when I dropped the surprise manuscript on her and she devoured it with enthusiasm and delight. Finally, several longtime writer friends offered their support and encouragement with their willingness to read the early draft—Lori Wilde, Delores Fossen, Tanya Michaels, Holly Jacobs, and Nancy Warren. I feel so very fortunate to have all of these people in my life, most especially the crew at Berkley—sales, marketing, public relations, art, and all levels of editing, particularly on this manuscript, Amelia Kreminski and Yvette Grant—all of whom are so generous with their time and talent and make my books sparkle and shine. Thank you all! To the men who live in the frat house with me—Chris Hansen Orf, Beckett Orf, and Wyatt Orf—thanks for putting up with all of the take-out food I've been forcing you to eat. I will cook again someday, I swear. Love you forever!

About a Dog

Chapter 1

"Clearly, she hates us," Carly DeCusati announced from behind her dressing room curtain. "She must."

"Oh, come on, it can't be that bad," Mackenzie Harris protested.

Carly was the overly dramatic one in their group of friends, so Mac knew to ignore the paranoia in her friend's voice. She entered the curtained dressing room of the upmarket Boston bridal store and unzipped the cover on the bridesmaid dress that the shop assistant indicated had been chosen for her.

Mac pulled the garment out of the bag and flinched. She dropped the scratchy fabric and put her hand to her throat as if to ward off the ugly. There was no arguing it, the dress was hideous.

"Oh, ish, what color is this?" Jillian Braedon, another bridesmaid, asked from her dressing room.

"Cat sick?" Carly offered. It was clear from her tone she wasn't kidding.

"Maybe it's the lighting in here," Mac said. "Nothing ever looks good under fluorescent lighting."

"Yeah, no," Carly said. "The only place this dress would look good is in a blackout."

11

Jillian snorted and Mac sighed. As maid of honor, she knew it was on her to gently but firmly break it to the bride that they collectively hated the dress, which, with only four weeks to go until the wedding, was not going to go over well at all.

"Let's just try them on to be sure," she said.

"Really? Do we have to?" Carly whined. "I bet it gives me hives."

"I have a lotion for that," Jillian offered. As always, she was ever prepared for any situation, sort of like a Girl Scout minus the cookies.

"Listen," Mac said. "The sooner we try them on the sooner we can take them off."

The other two grumbled but she was reassured by the rustle of clothing that they were undressing to suit up as requested just like she was. Mac took the dress off the hanger and held it up in front of her. In a shade of brown green that looked like a bowl of guacamole gone wrong, the dress had padded shoulders and a puffy skirt the likes of which Mac had only seen at unfortunate eighties theme parties.

"Is it just me or does anyone else hear Madonna's 'Crazy For You' in their head?" Carly asked.

"Me, I do!" Jillian agreed. "I also have a sudden urge to rat up my hair in a lopsided ponytail and wear a lot of jelly bracelets."

Mac lowered the zipper on the side of the dress

and pulled it over her head. She shoved her arms through the holes and wiggled until the dress fell around her hips, landing somewhere at mid-calf. It took some maneuvering but she managed to pull up the zipper. She had to suck in her breath to make the snug middle actually fit, but she got it. Barely.

She closed her eyes and smoothed the skirt, hoping that when she opened them the dress would not be the nightmare she feared it was. She opened just one eye for a quick glance. Ew! She shut her eyes again. Surely, it couldn't be that bad.

Mac drew a deep breath and forced herself to face her reflection, trying to build up the nerve to look with both of her peepers. There had to be some mistake.

Emma Tolliver, the bride, had been her best friend since the first grade. Emma was a petite, pretty blonde with exquisite taste; surely, Mac was just missing something here, like maybe Emma was color-blind or had sustained a nasty head injury that Mac didn't know about. Seriously, there had to be some explanation for this fashion travesty.

She opened her eyes and pressed her lips together to keep from crying out. There was no getting around it. The dress was butt-ugly. Carly was right; Emma must hate them.

Mac noticed the others were silent and

wondered if they'd been rendered catatonic by the horror show of a dress.

"Hey, are you two all right?" she asked.

"I refuse to come out," Carly said.

"That sounds like a personal issue," Mac countered. "Jilly, how about you?"

"No, I don't think I can," Jillian said. "What if someone got a picture of this? It could go viral on the Internet. Oh, my god, we could be a bridesmaids-from-hell meme that would live on and on forever and ever."

"I can't get the zipper down," Carly said. There was the sound of some grunting and thrashing. "I swear to god if I can't get it off, I will burn this dress while wearing it."

"Stop the crazy talk, both of you. You can't take it off, Carly, you know Emma is going to want to see us in them," Mac said. "She'll be here any second."

"I love you all like sisters, really, I do," Carly said. "But I will eat a gun before I let anyone see me in this thing."

Mac poked her head, just her head, out of the curtain. She scanned the room. "There's no one here but us. I think we'll all feel better if we see one another. I don't want the image of me to be the only thing burned on my retinas for eternity."

The other two were quiet, until Mac said, "Well?"

"Fine, but I'm doing it under protest," Jillian said.

"Yeah, all right, but only because I need help with the zipper," Carly agreed. "On the count of three. One. Two. Three."

Mac shoved her curtain aside at the same time the other two did. They all stepped out and looked at one another. Mac felt her eyebrows rise up to her hairline. She knew how bad the dress looked on her, but the fact that the dress did nothing for Carly's short, curvy Italian va-va-voom figure, nor did it jive with Jillian's dark complexion and tall, slender wear-anything-and-look-amazing physique, told Mac that the only place the dress belonged was in the garbage.

The expressions on Carly's and Jillian's faces confirmed what Mac already knew; she looked as bad as they did. She glanced at the mirror. She was somewhere in the middle of the other two, as in average height and average build with shoulder-length brown hair that she hit with expensive copper highlights on a somewhat regular basis.

Really, it was a halfhearted attempt to be fashionable, given that she mostly wore her hair in a ponytail because although she paid a premium for the color, she was weak on the whole maintenance thing. She glanced back at her friends.

They looked like survivors from a train wreck.

It could have been the horrified expressions on their faces or maybe it was the poofy shroud of a dress making them look sickly and anemic. A second glance at the mirror and Mac confirmed that she looked as if she'd been belched out of the wreckage with her friends. Or worse.

"We look like floaters in a rest stop toilet," Mac said. Then a laugh burbled up out of her before she had the presence of mind to stop it.

"What are you giggling at? This is a crisis!" Carly cried. "Unless you think we could actually flush these dresses down the toilet?"

The three of them glanced around the room but there wasn't a commode in sight.

"I hate to even suggest this, but do you think Emma is doing that bride thing, you know, where the bride picks the ugliest dress possible for her bridesmaids so that she looks even better on her special day?" Jillian asked.

"No!" Mac shook her head. "Emma isn't like that."

"I don't know," Carly said. "She's the first one of us to make it legal. Maybe she's going a little bridal banana balls on us."

Jillian gave Carly a bug-eyed look and Carly bit her lip and stared at Mac, looking regretful as she said, "Sorry, I didn't mean to bring up . . ."

"No," Mac said and held up her hand to stop Carly's gush of apologies. "The past is the past. No worries. Let's just focus on the crisis at hand."

"How could she do this to us?" Jillian asked. "We're her Maine crew and have been for the past twenty years."

"Maine crew, ha, like main crew but we're from Maine!" Carly snorted. "I see what you did there."

"Yes, very clever," Mac said. "Now, focus."

She gestured at the triple mirror in front of them. And they all turned to take in their reflection with varying levels of alarm.

"You know when you find the perfect dress, the sort that makes you feel like a sexual goddess who wants to touch herself?" Carly asked. "Yeah, this dress is not that dress. This dress makes me want a vaccination and a full body condom."

"We'd be sexier in full body condoms," Mac said.

"A shot of tequila or four is the only thing that could make this dress palatable," Jillian said. "Wait here. I might have some in my purse."

Jillian ducked back into her dressing room, and Carly and Mac exchanged a bewildered look. When Jillian returned she was clutching several tiny bottles of Jose Cuervo. She met their stares and shrugged.

"What? This is our prenuptials girls' weekend to be spent out on the town in Boston. I packed for any unforeseen emergencies," she said. "Believe me; telling Emma we hate the dress is an emergency. But I suppose I could whip up a

17

soothing batch of chamomile tea if you'd rather."

Mac snatched one of the tiny bottles out of her friend's hand. She had just put it to her lips when the main door to the dressing room opened and Emma walked in.

"Oh, you found the dresses," she said and clapped her hands together. "Yay!"

"Yay?" Carly asked. She looked like she was going to take a swing at Emma. It had been known to happen, although usually only in bars late at night toward people who had seriously pissed her off. Mac stepped between the two women.

She thrust the small tequila bottle at Emma and said, "Cheers!"

Maybe if they got her drunk it would be easier to tell her the dresses were a no-go. Emma smiled and took the bottle, although she didn't drink.

"Celebrating?" she asked.

"Er, more like medicating," Mac said.

She glanced at Emma, her oldest friend. They had been through it all together; braces, first dates, thin envelopes from their dream colleges, even the sudden death of Emma's mother when they were teens. There was nothing Mac wouldn't do for her dearest friend except wear this dress. There was no way to finesse this, none at all.

"By any chance, and I ask this purely from an information gathering place and not as an accusation, are you mad at us?" Mac asked.

Carly and Jillian closed ranks around Mac and they all stared at Emma with varying looks of concern and worry. Emma tipped her head to the side and gave them a hurt and confused look. Her eyes looked sad and she pressed her lips together. Mac thought she was trying not to cry, but Emma shocked her by busting out a belly laugh as if she just couldn't hold it in any longer.

"Gotcha!" she cried. She winked and pointed at them with both index fingers.

Mac, Carly, and Jillian exchanged confused glances and then Jillian, the quickest on the uptake, asked, "You punked us?"

Emma nodded and then bent over as she laughed with abandon. "You should have seen your faces! That was the best."

"I hate you," Carly said with more respect than heat. Then she started laughing. Mac and Jillian joined in, although Mac felt it was more from relief than actual amusement.

"Ow, can't breathe, dress too tight!" Carly gasped. Jillian hurriedly unzipped her and Carly sucked in a few deep breaths before announcing, "Well, this was fun but I'm changing. Now!"

"Wait!" Emma said. "Look behind the garment bag in your dressing room, that's your real dress."

Jillian and Carly darted excitedly into their changing rooms, but Mac paused beside Emma and said, "Explain."

"Simple. You know what a pain Carly is about

19

clothes; I mean she is a fashion buyer so I get it, but still, she never likes the first thing she tries on, ever, so I figured if you all thought the dress I picked was truly hideous, then she would be thrilled with the dress I actually picked." She gave Mac a devious smile. "Bet you a fiver I'm right."

Mac raised her hands in a sign of surrender. "That's a sucker's bet. You didn't actually have some poor sap sew these eyesores, did you?"

"Nah, these dresses were some rejects from last season that the shop hasn't been able to unload."

"Shocker," Mac said.

"When I saw the sizes were close to yours, I asked my dressmaker Suzanne if I could borrow them." Emma shrugged. "I figured it would be a hoot, and it was, it totally was."

"I've got to give it to you; that was genius."

Emma grinned. Then she shooed Mac back into her dressing room. "Hurry up, go change, I want to see."

Mac ducked back behind her curtain to change. Sure enough, behind the first black garment bag was another one. She unzipped it and her breath caught.

A simple Windsor blue chemise, in a delicate chiffon with a matching silk lining, peeked out of the bag at her. Relief almost made her knees buckle. She pulled it off the hanger and saw it had a V-neckline, with a thin blue ribbon tied in a small bow right below the bodice and a matching wide blue ribbon at the hem, which landed just above her knees.

The dress was perfect and lovely and when Mac pulled it over her head, it felt like diving into a cool blue pool of water.

"Now this is what I'm talking about," Carly said.

"Amen," Jillian echoed.

"Count of three?" Carly asked.

"I'm ready," Mac called.

"One. Two. Three."

As one they stepped out of their dressing rooms to find Emma beaming at them.

"Do you like them?" she asked. She looked nervous. "Really like them?"

Carly opened her arms and initiated a group hug. "Sweetie, they are perfection."

As Mac was enfolded into the group, she couldn't help but think how much she had missed this over the past few years—the closeness, the camaraderie, the pranks, and the love. These women were her oldest friends, her people; how could she have run away from them for so long?

Chapter 2

Four more skinny margaritas," Carly ordered from the waitress who paused by their table. "And now, I must dance."

Carly looped her arm through Jillian's and dragged her to the dance floor. Mac watched them as they swiveled and gyrated to the DJ's thumping beat. They were clearing a nice chunk of floor space for themselves but not in a good way.

"Dang, Carly looks like a chicken being electrocuted out there," Emma said as she slid onto the stool beside Mac.

"And is completely unaware of it," Mac agreed. She glanced at Emma, who was tucking her cell phone back into her clutch. "How's Brad?"

"He misses me desperately, natch," she said. She tossed her blonde hair over her shoulder.

Mac smiled. Emma and Brad had met the old-fashioned way, in a bar, when he had tackled her to keep a drunk who happened to be his best friend from throwing up on her. The drunk had thrown up on Brad instead. Ah, the romance.

"Listen, I'm sorry I haven't been more available for wedding stuff," Mac said. "I mean we're just a few weeks out and you had to have the dresses made up off of our measurements, because I couldn't get back here for fittings . . ."

"Carly couldn't make it either," Emma said.

"Yes, but I'm the maid of honor. I'm supposed to be at your beck and call, you know, helping with the cake and flowers and all that junk."

"Okay, the fact that you just called it junk is exactly why being one thousand miles away in Chicago makes you the perfect maid of honor. No interference, no second guessing, really, you're good," Emma said. She picked up her glass and took a healthy swig.

"Ugh, see? I can't even feign enthusiasm. I'm the worst. If you want to replace me with Carly or Jillian, I will totally understand," Mac said. She knew she was a little loose lipped from the drinks but she was also as serious as a heart attack.

Emma waved her off. "Shut up, you idiot. You're my oldest friend. I could never replace you; besides, you're here now and you're actually going to set foot in Bluff Point for the ceremony, so how can I complain?"

Mac felt her heart lurch and her palms get damp at the thought of going home. It had been years since she'd set foot in her hometown of Bluff Point, Maine, and only for Emma was she willing to go back.

She had met Emma Tolliver in first grade when they arrived wearing matching Little Mermaid backpacks and decided they were twins. They quickly bonded over a love of Polly Pocket dolls

23

and a hatred of Jessie Peeler, the meanest girl in their class. By sixth grade their ranks had filled out to include Carly and Jillian.

Some of the best days of Mac's life had been spent in that small coastal town, hanging out at the beach with her gal pals and dreaming about the future. But then the very worst day of her life had been spent there as well and she hadn't returned since.

Emma put her hand on Mac's arm. "Are you sure you're okay with coming home?"

"Huh?" Mac shook her head, trying to clear away the margaritas and bad memories. "Yeah, I'll be fine. I mean, it's been seven years; surely, everyone is over the drama by now."

"Of course they are," Emma said. "In fact, since Tilda Curtis left Doc Curtis for their babysitter Hannah Bishop, who was barely of age at the time, well, let's just say the lesbian affair eclipsed you being left at the altar by Seth Connelly by a mile. They're all anyone ever talks about now."

Mac didn't even cringe at the words "left at the altar." So, progress, right? She would have patted herself on the back for such personal growth but she was afraid her last skinny margarita might cause her to fall off her stool in an indelicate heap.

"I'll have to be sure to send Tilda and Hannah a thank-you note," she said.

Emma laughed. She threw her arm around

Mac's shoulders and hugged her hard. "That's my girl. So, is Trevor definitely not going to make it to the wedding?" she asked.

Mac glanced at Emma. She knew this was the moment she should come clean about her and Trevor. Emma asking about him made it a natural segue in the conversation, but she just couldn't do it. She knew her bestie was not enamored of her boyfriend of the past few years. The few times Emma and Brad had come to see Mac and Trevor in Chicago, the visits had been awkward at best and downright hostile at worst. To tell Emma that Trevor had asked to take a break from seeing her would just fuel the fire of Emma's dislike of him and when they did get back together, Emma would be even less happy than before, if that was even possible.

Mac and Trevor were neighbors who dated, split everything down the middle, and while they enjoyed a robust social life together, they also retreated to their separate domiciles afterwards. Being an accountant, the relationship suited Mac as it was easily quantifiable in a profit and loss sense. She profited by having a date when she wanted one and she lost the risk factor of having her world decimated by Trevor since she maintained a healthy boundary between them.

Emma did not approve. She felt that in a relationship, a person should be all in or why bother and she had no qualms about sharing her feelings on the subject, especially when they were all together. Trevor taking a break from Mac would be inconceivable to Emma. It didn't help that his being unable to attend Emma and Brad's big day was undoubtedly not going to foster any additional warm fuzzies for him. Mac had no desire to make it worse.

"He is so sorry he can't make it," Mac lied. "He really tried to get the time off from work, but they're negotiating a big deal in London and he'll be gone for weeks. There was just no way he could get back here."

"Yes, I'm sure he's quite distraught," Emma said. Her tone was as dry as a hot wind.

"Really—" Mac began but Emma shook her head.

"It's fine," she said. "In fact, it might be for the best."

"What do you mean?" Mac asked. She didn't like the gleam in Emma's eye. Their friendship was based upon a lifetime of one of them having a really stupid idea and the other one agreeing like a dope. Sometimes she was amazed they had even survived to adulthood, and now whenever she saw that glint in Emma's eye she got nervous.

"This isn't like that time you thought it would be a great idea to dress up in gowns and follow Tim Tucker and Kyle Richards to their prom because you were hoping they needed dates, is it?" she asked.

"That plan totally would have worked," Emma protested.

"Yeah, if they hadn't actually already had dates that they were on their way to pick up, but they did," Mac said.

"My intel was bad," Emma admitted. "But, hey, we hung out at the Frosty Freeze all evening and met those cute guys from Portland."

"Who were in college."

"It wasn't my idea to go to Belmont Park with them. That was all you," Emma said.

"When your dad found us . . ." Mac said. She hissed a breath through her teeth; the memory still made her toes curl and not in a good way.

"And he brought your dad for backup," Emma said with a laugh. "I didn't think we'd ever see daylight again."

Mac laughed. It was true. Her father, the mildest man who ever lived, had been so outraged he couldn't even speak. It had been days before she was allowed to leave her room unsupervised.

"Well, we were only fourteen and we did sneak out of our houses," Mac said. "We can't blame them."

"Still, totally worth it." Emma held up her fist for a bump. Mac frowned.

"Is that still a thing?" she asked.

"Come on, give me bones," Emma cajoled.

Mac bumped her knuckles into Emma's with a smile.

"Okay, so here's the deal," Emma said. "I'm

pairing you up with Gavin for the wedding."

Mac felt her insides spasm. She picked up her drink and tried to look casual, although she feared she looked like she was about to get sick, which was not far off the mark. She took a healthy swig, because that would surely help, before speaking.

"Oh, okay, I didn't realize he was Brad's best man," Mac said.

"He's not, Brad's brother Bobby is," Emma said. "Gavin is more the second in command of the ring, but since he just went through that nasty breakup, I thought it would really cheer him up to be paired with you."

"Okay," Mac said. She wanted to slap herself. This was not okay. There was nothing okay about this. She drained her glass.

"I figure we'll just have Bobby stand with Brad and then Gavin can walk you into the wedding and be your escort at the reception and all of the other wedding events. That way you won't have to feel self-conscious about being solo, especially when you're coming home for the first time in forever. Perfect, right?" Emma asked.

Mac nodded. She had no other choice since her powers of speech had vanished in one swallow like the booze in her glass.

"Are you sure?" Emma asked. She squinted at Mac. "You know I wouldn't ask but the beyotch who broke Gavin's heart ran off with his business manager who absconded with most of Gavin's savings before departing. Honestly, I've never seen Gav so depressed, and I just thought since he's had a crush on you for forever—"

"No, he hasn't," Mac argued.

"Uh, duh, yes he has, like since he was eight," Emma said. "It's really so adorable. So, you're good with this?"

"Yeah, of course I'm good, really good," Mac said. She bobbed her head in what she hoped looked like an affirmative motion and not the panic-induced seizure it actually was.

"Yay!" Emma clapped and then hugged Mac in a hold that strangled. "Oh, and do me a favor and don't mention to Gavin that I asked you to pair up with him or that you have a boyfriend."

"You want me to lie to Gavin?" Mac asked. Despite the fibbing of the past ten minutes, she was the world's worst liar.

"No!" Emma insisted. "Just, you know, don't tell him everything."

"Yeah, that's lying by omission."

"Maybe, but you do owe me one."

Mac lifted one eyebrow and looked at her friend in surprise. They had never tallied the favors between them before and she couldn't believe Emma was doing it now.

"I hate to mention it, but when you blew out of town after your aborted wedding, who cleaned up the mess?" Emma asked. "Who wrote a million thank-you notes and returned all the gifts? Who made peace with the photographer, the caterer, the band—do I need to go on?"

"No," Mac grumbled. "I know you did all of that for me and I am forever grateful."

"And you always said if there was anything you could do to pay me back, all I had to do was ask. Well, I'm asking," Emma said.

Mac let out a sigh. She had always known this day would come, but she had thought it would entail babysitting Emma's kids while she and Brad took off for a romantic weekend. She had never envisioned this exacting of a payback.

"Of course, I want to help out anyway I can. It's just I don't think I can hide the truth from . . . oh, no, don't you dare," Mac ordered. It was too late.

Emma was looking at her with big, blue imploring eyes. This was the best weapon in Emma's how-to-bend-people-to-her-will arsenal. She could do the sad puppy eyes like no one else and she had employed this very trick to get the two of them out of several sticky situations over the years.

"No." Mac shook her head, trying to ward off the look. "Sad puppy eyes will not work on me. I'm immune. Seriously, I am not some ticket agent at the airline that you can bamboozle into upgrading you to first class for free."

Emma ducked her head as if she was about to cry and Mac felt the twist in her gut that indicated she was going to lose this contest of wills. She had to fight it.

"I mean it, Emma," she said.

At the sound of her name, Emma glanced up with sad puppy eyes fully engaged and she added the quivering lip. Boom.

"Oh, hell!" Mac snapped. "Fine, I'll do it, but if Gavin straight-out asks me if I'm seeing anyone, I am not going to lie to him."

But, of course, if she told Gavin she was seeing someone then technically she would be lying since she and Trevor were on a break. Oh, man, this was why she hated lying, suddenly everything was so complicated!

Emma's face cleared like a blast of sunshine through a cloud. "I knew I could count on you, Mac. Everything is coming together just like I hoped. This is going to be the best wedding ever."

Mac forced her lips to curve up. It must have looked better than it felt because Emma continued to beam at her.

"Come on, let's go dance," Emma said.

"You go ahead." Mac gestured at the table. "We have drinks coming so I should wait."

"Come out when they get here," Emma ordered. She skipped off to the dance floor and Mac watched as she tapped in and Carly tapped out. She didn't think she was imagining that as Carly walked, she listed to the side like a leaky little boat.

"I think I got a hitch in my get-a-long," Carly said. She stretched out her back and sat down

31

just as the waitress arrived with fresh drinks. "Ah, timing, as they say, is everything."

Mac resisted the urge to knock back all four drinks in front of her. Instead, she paid the waitress and tipped her generously, hoping that it would give her a positive karmic boost of which she was suddenly in desperate need.

"Spill it," Carly said.

"What? My drink? Where? On my dress?" Mac asked. She glanced at the front of her outfit to see if she was sporting a wet spot.

"No, tell me whatever it is that has you looking like you're facing a death squad," Carly said. She sipped her drink and looked at Mac through half-lidded eyes.

Mac knew there was no point in lying. As soon as Carly heard the news, she was going to freak out.

"Since I'm going stag to Emma's wedding, she just asked me if I'd mind being paired up with Gavin for the festivities," Mac said.

The lids on Carly's eyes snapped up. "Gavin, as in her little brother Gavin? The boy she raised as her own since their mother died? The same man-boy you slept with in a singular lapse of good judgment when you got dumped at the altar seven years ago? The one man in your personal history that Emma does not know about, that Gavin?"

"Yep," Mac said. She lifted her drink to her lips and downed it. "That Gavin."

Chapter 3

Mac lugged her suitcase, carry-on, and garment bag off the passenger car and onto the platform in Portland, Maine. The Downeaster train had brought her up from Boston, which had been her first stop after flying in from Chicago as she'd had to do a final fitting before picking up her dress at the Boston bridal shop on her way to Maine for the wedding. Now she just had to find Emma in the station and they would set out for Bluff Point, which was a half-hour drive up the coastline.

The two-and-a-half-hour train ride had given Mac plenty of time to think about the next two weeks. Emma, being Emma, had planned a wedding that was not just the celebration of two people uniting their lives. Oh, no, it was more like a two-week hostage situation where there was a daily itinerary of endless activities designed to milk every magical matrimonial moment out of the event. Just reading the five pages of detailed instructions that Emma had emailed everyone exhausted Mac.

Despite the intensity of the agenda, Mac planned to participate fully. She understood that the over-the-top celebrating was a part of who Emma had become when her mother passed away so young. Emma was always the one who made every birthday, Christmas, or Valentine's Day one to be remembered since she had a deep-seated fear that each one might be the last.

Since it was an Emma extravaganza, there were a million picky little details to nail down, and Mac had made a personal vow that she would be the perfect maid of honor for Emma. She would do whatever Emma asked of her and serve it up with a smile on the side. She hoped this would alleviate the guilt she felt since she had been such a no-show as a maid of honor thus far.

Mac wheeled her suitcase beside her as she entered the station, narrowly missing a mom and her two sons who were on their way out. One of the boys gave her the stink eye and Mac gave it right back. The boy's eyes went wide with fright—Mac gave a really good stink eye—and then she winked at him, letting him know all was forgiven. He grinned before he scampered off to catch up to his mom.

Mac entered the station and scanned the large room looking for Emma. Her friend's long, straight blonde hair usually gave away her location at a glance, but Mac did a quick visual sweep and didn't see her. She searched again thinking Emma might have her hair in a topknot or a ponytail, but no. There was no petite blonde anywhere to be seen.

Mac shrugged and hauled her bags over to a

seat. Maybe Emma was running late. She dug in her purse for her cell phone to see if there was a text she had missed, but as she moved her hand around the voluminous bag, she couldn't find her phone. She sighed.

She loved her big bag, she really did. It was one of the many reasons she'd let her gym membership lapse, besides the fact that she never actually went, as she figured carrying around twenty pounds of stuff kept her fit enough, but at times like this, which were frequent, she thought she really needed to downsize.

A buzz sounded from her bag and Mac held it open wide, hoping the display screen would light up so she could see it. Ha! There was a blue glow coming from the bottom. She snatched up her phone and answered it without pausing to look at the number.

"Emma, I'm here, where are you?" Mac asked.

"I'm right behind you," a man answered.

Seven years. It had been seven years since Mac had heard his voice, which was much deeper than she remembered, but still she would know Gavin Tolliver's voice in a crowded room loud with conversation and laughter. His was the sort of voice that wrapped around you like a hug. It was deep and masculine but full of warmth and kindness with a self-deprecating humor to it that Mac had always found charming even when Gav was a gawky teen just learning how to talk to girls.

Mac closed her eyes and braced herself before slowly turning around, still holding the phone to her ear. Her heart was pumping hard in her chest and when she looked at the man walking toward her it stopped for a solid three beats before it resumed its rhythm with a thump to the chest that felt like a closed fist to the sternum. Oomph!

"Hi, Mac," Gavin said into his phone, bringing his voice intimately into her ear while she stared into his baby blues. A woman could drown in eyes that pretty. How had she forgotten? Mac yanked the phone from her ear and ended the call.

"Gav," she said on a shaky exhale. He stopped in front of her right on the periphery of her personal space. She forced herself to smile with teeth, which felt like more of a snarl. "I wasn't expecting you. How are you?"

"Better now that you're here," he said.

Mac gave him a wary look. What the hell did that mean?

"I'm pretty sure if I misplaced my sister's maid of honor, I'd have to flee the state or possibly the country," he teased. He smiled at her and Mac felt it all the way down to her toes.

"Oh, yeah, huh," Mac stammered. She resisted the urge to do a face palm. She sounded like a moron.

"Come here," Gavin said. He tucked his phone into his jeans pocket and held out his arms. "A proper greeting is required for the return of the prodigal Mac."

"Oh, right, of course," she said.

In her state of shock at seeing him, Mac's legs were refusing to follow the basic one foot in front of the other protocol and she lurched forward into his arms, forcing him to catch her before she took them both down.

It was a good bracing squeeze, the sort cousins shared at annual family reunions. But it was enough for Mac to catalog the fact that this was not the man-boy she had fumbled around in a pickup truck with all those years ago. Oh, no, this was a man who stood well over six feet tall, with broad shoulders, a lean waist, and powerful arms. Gavin Tolliver had grown into a hottie when she wasn't looking.

Amazingly, his scent was the same and it struck Mac in the olfactory system like a lightning strike. The warm citrusy cedar smell that was uniquely Gavin blew open the locked door of her memories, and Mac was hit like a two fingered poke to the eyeballs with a mental picture of the man in her arms sans clothes holding her close and going in for a bone-wilter of a kiss. Ack!

She jumped out of his arms so fast she tripped over her suitcase and landed in a heap on the bench seat behind her. She cracked her hip on the wooden edge and the pain rocketed up her back but she refused to let it show. Instead, she quickly crossed her legs and threw her arm over the seat back, pretending that she meant to do that.

Gavin looked surprised and then he grinned at her as if he found her adorable and not freaky, which she clearly was. Mac wondered how she could have forgotten the dimple that dented his right cheek when he smiled or the girlishly long, thick lashes that framed his eyes so becomingly. Then he winked at her and she felt as if everything she had ever known to be true had just hopped on the Downeaster train back to Boston.

This was not the Gavin Tolliver she remembered in his grubby Little League uniform who thought it was hilarious to stick whoopee cushions under her sleeping bag when she spent the night at Emma's, for that was the only image of him she had ever allowed herself to recall after their one night together. It had worked like a charm to banish the memory of what had been the most amazing sexual encounter of her life. She had even convinced herself that their night together had only been spectacular because she had just been left at the altar and had been as emotionally charged as a hair dryer tossed into a bathtub.

But now, this man standing in front of her in his well-worn jeans and work boots was making the past seven years of her carefully crafted revisionist history an utter mockery. This guy had charisma and sexual magnetism to the tenth power. When he smiled at her, she actually felt her skin get hot and when he winked, well, her girl parts almost overheated. Dang, this guy could probably unhook her bra just by looking at it!

There was no doubt about it, Mac was screwed. Or maybe, she just wanted to be. Gah! Mac shook her head, trying to dislodge that thought. No, no, no! This was Emma's little brother! She tried to picture him in his Little League uniform. Sadly, she could not shove the man body in the form-fitting gray T-shirt in front of her into a dirty eight-year-old's baseball uniform. Damn it!

"Mac, are you okay?" he asked. "You look mad."

"What?" She glared at him. Then she glanced away, trying to avoid his gaze. "I'm fine, just tired."

"Long day of travel," he said. His voice was kind and understanding, which Mac found unreasonably annoying. "I'm parked right outside. Come on, let's get you home."

Without waiting for her answer, he took her hand and pulled her to her feet. Then he grabbed her bags as if they weighed nothing and wheeled them toward the door. Mac had no choice but to grab her purse and her garment bag and follow. She wished she had worn a better travel outfit than jeans and a T-shirt, then berated herself for even thinking about her outfit, and then she cursed Emma for not warning her that it was Gavin who would pick her up. Forget hostage situation; suddenly, the next two weeks looked more like an incarceration than a celebration and Mac did not have a get-out-of-jail-free card.

Gavin hefted Mac's bags into the back of a big black pickup truck. So, he still drove a truck, a different truck, but still a truck. She went to open the passenger door but he got there first, holding it open for her to climb in. Mac squeezed by him, trying not to brush up against him as she went. Healthy boundaries were going to be scrupulously maintained if a mere smell memory had her picturing him naked. Oh, horror!

He shut the door and jogged around the front of the truck. She turned on her phone and toyed with the screen, pretending to be doing something other than avoiding looking at him, which was really what she was doing.

Gav pulled out of the parking lot and turned onto the road that would take them home. Mac glanced out her window, wondering if the silence felt as awkward to him as it did to her. She supposed she should say something, but she had no idea what.

Why couldn't she be like Carly, who in her usual blunt fashion would just give his ass a squeeze, crack a bawdy joke about the last time they saw each other, and move on? Or like Jillian, who would say something kind but distant, which would effectively put up a barrier as daunting as razor wire between them, letting him know they were not going there. Ever.

Sadly, it was neither of those two who had slept with their best friend's little brother. Oh, no, that was Mac, who as a corporate accountant who operated in numbers and facts and bottom lines had zero capacity to navigate life's layers of innuendo. Damn it!

"So . . ." Gavin said. He gave her a sideways glance when she turned to look at him. "Are you hungry?"

"Nope," she said. "Not at all. Not even a little. I'm good. Thanks."

She pressed her lips together to shut herself up and turned away from him. Ugh, she couldn't even look at him. She could be half starved to death and desperate for a ham sandwich and she wouldn't do anything that would prolong their time together for even a nanosecond. Seriously, if she had to go to the bathroom, she would risk peeing her pants before she'd extend this trip to include a pit stop. Thankfully, she did not have to go.

"Okay," Gavin said. Again, his voice was gentle, as if he were talking to an injured baby bird. "Let me know if you need anything."

"Will do," Mac said. "Roger that, you betcha, by golly wow."

Okay, now the urge to punch herself in the

temple and knock herself out was almost more than she could stand. Being unprepared to see him again had reduced her to a babbling idiot.

He on the other hand did not seem to be suffering from any awkwardness. Obviously, Gavin either didn't remember what had happened between them seven years ago or he was so completely over it that it didn't occur to him that being thrown together after seven years of radio silence was weird. Now didn't that just fluff up her ego?

Still, if he had forgotten all about that night, it was most definitely for the best and it made her relax just the teensiest bit. Perhaps all of her worry had been for nothing and everything was going to be just fine over the next two weeks.

She stole a look at him, then glanced back out the window and then back at him. His hair was cut short on the sides and longer on top. It was several shades darker than his sister's, almost brown but not quite but not really blonde either. His bangs fell over his forehead in a casual way that could have been created with a lot of product and artful arrangement but Mac suspected was more the result of a quick towel dry and a distracted manner.

Despite the fact that Mac hadn't seen him in years, she knew the highlight reel. Emma had kept her apprised of all the main events in Gavin's life. He had gone to veterinary school, graduated at the top of his class, and had returned home to work at old Doc Scharff's practice. Doc was in semi-retirement and was training Gavin to take over the biz fully when he was done. Emma was so proud of her brother; she practically glowed when she talked about him.

Although she never admitted it, Mac knew that Emma had put her life on hold until she knew Gavin was settled. She always said she and Brad were saving for a house before they got married, but Mac suspected that Emma had been waiting to make sure Gavin could stand on his own two feet before she started a family of her own. Mac had a feeling Gavin didn't realize it and would be pretty unhappy if he ever figured it out.

Maybe that's just how big sisters were with little brothers. Mac didn't know because she didn't have any siblings. The only person who had ever been like a younger sibling to her was Gavin, and, oh, yeah, she had slept with him. Even thinking about it made Mac feel dirty.

Emma hadn't only shared Gavin's accomplishments, she had also kept Mac informed on his love life even though Mac had never asked and really didn't want to know. The last girlfriend, Jane, had never been a favorite of Emma's. She had dubbed her Jane the Pain, which had been shortened to "The Pain" for the duration of their relationship and had then morphed into "The Beyotch" after Jane ran off with Gavin's business manager.

Mac didn't like knowing all of the sordid details about Gavin's personal life, but she had never been able to stop Emma from oversharing without giving her a solid reason why. Now she was uncomfortable knowing as much as she did and not knowing what to say to him about any of it. The silence in the cramped cab of the truck was becoming excruciating, however, and she didn't think she could take it anymore as they crossed over the Presumpscot River, heading north on Route 1.

"So, it looks like they'll have a nice day for the wedding," she said. She grabbed for the old New England mainstay of talking about the weather like she was reaching for a life preserver in a choppy sea.

Gavin looked at her and grinned. "She speaks, and about the weather, too. I guess you can take the girl out of Maine but you can't take the Maine out of the girl."

Mac felt herself blush, which was alarming as she was pretty sure she hadn't had a case of the face hots in years. So, there was one more reason to avoid this man. No self-respecting thirty-two-year-old woman wanted to walk around looking rashy.

"Ayuh," she said, intentionally using an old Maine expression for agreement. Gavin smiled at her, which had been her intent but it also made her face heat up again. She resisted the urge to cover her cheeks with her hands and instead asked, "Er, so what's new with you?"

Gavin glanced from the road to her. He gave her a look with one eyebrow raised that said *Seriously?* before turning back to the road.

Mac blew out a breath. She was pretty sure she'd had pelvic exams that were more fun than this, and that was with the doctor saying "Scooch down" repeatedly until her ass cheeks felt like they were hanging on nothing but air.

"I'm guessing Emma has already given you the four-one-one on my life," he said. "Correct?"

"She might have mentioned some stuff."

"Well, in answer to your question, I'm fine."

He clenched his jaw and forced a closed-lip smile that flashed at her as if to prove he was A-okay, but when it didn't reach his eyes, she knew he was far from it. He turned back to the road, and Mac saw the muscle in his jaw tighten repeatedly. So, not fine then.

Chapter 4

That's good," she said. She knew it sounded lame but better that than nothing, she supposed. "I'm glad you're doing okay."

Gavin turned off Route 1 and wound his way down an old back road pockmarked with potholes that twisted and turned its way through the thick woods that skirted the edge of town. Mac bounced in her seat as they traversed the uneven pavement and smiled. How many times had she and her friends driven on this old road, trying to hit the potholes and make their car bounce?

When they broke through the trees, she was greeted by Spencer's Orchard. The sight of the roadside stand with the big white house and huge red barn in the background surrounded by rows and rows of apple trees hit Mac with a sense of nostalgia that made her misty-eyed. There had never been an autumn that she didn't spend at least one weekend picking apples at Spencer's Orchard right up until the year she left.

It was early June so the trees had bloomed just weeks before. She could still see some of the pink blossoms that had yet to close up into little fists of green that would plump out into juicy red Macintosh or Macoun apples by September. When she closed her eyes she could almost taste the sweet, tangy, crisp bite of the first apple of the season.

"You all right?" Gavin asked.

"Me?" Mac opened her eyes and glanced at him. "I'm fine, why?"

"You sighed," he said. "You sounded a bit forlorn."

"No." Mac shook her head. "Just nostalgic, I guess."

"You've been away a long time." It was a straightforward observation not giving Mac any inkling as to how he felt about her absence, if he felt anything at all.

They left the orchard behind and passed several farms. When they reached a large fenced field with a gray horse in it, Gavin flipped on his signal and pulled over to the side of the road.

"Sorry, I have to make a quick business stop, if that's all right?" he asked.

"Sure, no problem," she said. She glanced at her big bag on the floor. Why, oh, why didn't she carry around tequila like Jillian had on their girls' weekend? If ever there was a time for a covert shot of liquid courage this was it.

Gavin reached into the small space behind their seats and grabbed a paper sack. He glanced at Mac and then down at the bag.

"I know you said you weren't hungry, but it just didn't seem right to welcome you home without some Maine staples."

Mac watched as he pulled a paper-wrapped whoopie pie out of the bag. When he handed it to her, she grinned. The label on the wrapper read *Making Whoopie*, which was the name of Jillian's small whoopie pie store in Bluff Point.

"You know you can't get a decent whoopie anywhere except Maine," he said. Then he handed her a bright red can, and said, "To wash it down."

"Moxie soda?" she asked. Then she laughed, hard. "Wow, I haven't had a whoopie pie or a Moxie in years." When she said years, she made sure she twisted the "r" into an "uh," tapping into her old Maine accent.

Gavin chuckled. Then he pulled an apple out of the bag.

"Wait. Are you kidding me?" Mac asked. "You're handing me two fistfuls of sugar and you're going to eat an apple?"

He shook his head and then jutted his chin toward the farm. "Nah, the apple is for my girl-friend."

Mac's head whipped in the direction of the field, expecting to see some gorgeous farm girl, dancing barefoot across the high grass in a floral dress. Instead, the pretty pewter horse she had seen in the distance was moving toward the fence at a clip.

Gavin popped out of his side of the truck and went to the fence to meet her. Mac put the soda down but took her whoopie pie as she went to join him.

The horse tossed her silver mane and pawed the ground. Mac didn't speak horse, but judging by the happy nickering, the mare was pleased to see Gavin.

He gave a low whistle and she trotted right up to him and put her head over the top rail and pressed her long nose into his shoulder. Gavin put his hand on the side of her face and she whinnied. Clearly the affection between these two was mutual.

"How are you doing, Star?" he asked. She stepped back and tossed her head. "Let me see you run."

Star neighed and shook her head. If Mac didn't know better she'd swear Star understood him.

"Fine, no treat for you if you don't want to gallop for me," he said. He crossed his arms over his chest, hiding the apple.

Star backed up and pawed the ground.

"I guess I'll just go home then," Gavin said.

This time, Star pawed the ground and then pushed off with her forelegs and spun around. She did a short gallop around the field and Mac watched as Gavin's eyes narrowed as he observed her running.

"What are you looking for?" she asked.

"Star slipped on some ice and suffered a bone bruise about six months ago," he said. "She's better now but I still like to check on her and make sure there is no recurrence. It's a beautiful thing, watching her run again."

He took a small jackknife out of his pocket and deftly sliced the apple in half. As if sensing her treat was being prepped, Star bolted for them. Watching the wind whip her mane and the sun shine on her glossy silver coat, Mac could see what Gavin meant. She was beauty in motion.

"Want to feed her?" he asked.

"Me?"

Gavin looked around them as if checking to see if there was someone else there. Mac wondered if she should just shove the whole whoopie pie in her mouth and hope for a swift death from sugar shock. Why did this man make her feel so awkward? It was galling.

"You," he said.

He took her free hand and tugged her forward. He positioned Mac so she was standing in front of him and he took half of the apple and wrapped her fingers around it and then put his hand under hers. Together they held the apple out to the horse.

Star's enormous lips snuffled around Mac's hand, making her giggle. Then the horse gently took a bite of the apple, leaving half of it behind in Mac's hand.

"She's so careful!" Mac cried.

She turned to face Gavin, and realized too late that his face was just inches from hers and he was watching her with an affection that made her feel ridiculously warm and fuzzy inside. A nudge against her other hand made her whip back around just in time to see Star going for her whoopie pie.

"Oh, no, you don't," Mac said. She moved her arm out of the horse's reach. "The whoopie pie is mine."

She pressed the remaining bit of apple into Gavin's hand and stepped away from them.

"You should probably take over," she said. Then she took a huge bite of the whoopie pie to keep herself from saying anything stupid like, *OMG, you're hot!*

While she chewed the soft chocolate cake filled with delectable vanilla icing, she made herself think about Trevor. Her boyfriend—well, her boyfriend on hiatus. The guy she had been seeing for years. The one who had convinced her to start dating again when she was so broken and beat down she was sure she'd never let anyone into her life ever again. He was perfect for her. He caused her no grief, no strife, no heartache, which was exactly what she'd always wanted in a boyfriend. Period.

She turned away from watching Gavin and Star. She needed not to be thinking about Gavin in any way but as her best friend's little brother. She shoved another bite of whoopie pie into her cakehole.

A movement in her peripheral vision caught Mac's attention. Something was moving in the high grass at the edge of the field. She walked toward it, wondering if it was a cute little bunny or maybe a bushy-tailed squirrel.

Instead the big, blocky head of a brown and black brindle dog popped up out of the grass. It saw Mac and its brown eyes went wide. Its ears were floppy and its gaze scared. Mac got the feeling that it was just a puppy.

"Hey, it's okay," Mac said. "I won't hurt you."

The dog let out a yip and took off across the field at a low-to-the-ground run that made it look like a brown bullet just skimming the grass.

She supposed it belonged to the same farmer who owned Star, so she turned back to Gavin and his girlfriend who were still canoodling by the fence.

With a final pat on the neck, Gavin said good-bye to Star and they headed back to the truck. Mac held out the remaining half of the whoopie pie to Gavin, and he took it with a smile.

"You're out of practice," he said. "I remember when you could eat three of those and still make room for dinner."

"Only so I wouldn't get busted for eating three whoopie pies," she said. "Is this still the Dillmans' farm?"

"Yeah, why?" He polished off the whoopie pie in two bites and Mac had to force herself not to study his gray T-shirt to figure out where the sugar and fat could possibly go since there wasn't an extra ounce on him.

"Do they own dogs?" she asked.

"They have an old hunting dog, a vizsla named Tucker," he said.

"I saw a puppy in the field," she said. "You don't think it's a stray, do you?"

He shrugged. "Hard to say. I'll tell Mr. Dillman to keep an eye out for it though."

"Thanks."

Gavin shut her door and circled around the truck. In moments, they were back on the road. They passed another farm, a plant nursery, and a lumberyard, before the traffic got thicker as more neighborhood streets connected to the main road. Gavin slowed down to accommodate the other cars.

"I know I've been gone a long time," Mac said. "But the town looks amazingly unchanged."

Gavin turned the truck onto another main road. This one led them closer to the shoreline. Mac could smell the brine on the air and off in the distance she could see the top of the Ferris wheel at Belmont Park, which took up four acres at one end of the boardwalk that ran the length of the town's five miles of beach ending at the Bluff Point lighthouse. The big white beacon had looked over the town for more than two hundred years and Mac's heart lifted in her chest at the sight of it.

"Not much changes in Bluff Point," Gavin agreed. "Unless you look really closely."

Mac glanced at him and then back at the town. What did he mean by that? What had changed since she'd left?

They could have followed the road they were on all the way to the beach, but Gavin turned onto a smaller road that led to the center of town. Bluff Point had a traditional town green, with its two main churches sitting at each end as if keeping an eye on each other. In the middle of the green was an oversized gazebo, which was used as a bandstand for the Veterans of Foreign Wars brass band on Saturday nights in the summer.

Local businesses lined the streets that framed the town square, giving the town a busy, buzzy feeling as people moved from shop to shop like worker bees circling the hive. If there was a picture postcard for the perfect New England town, Bluff Point was it.

Mac studied the familiar buildings, looking for anything that was new or different. A few buildings had fresh coats of paint but that was about it.

She craned her neck to see Jillian's bakery *Making Whoopie* on the corner. Jilly did a bang-up business in the summer as Bluff Point's population easily tripled with tourists during the hot months. If Mac were with Emma, she would have asked to stop in to say hello but since she wanted to be clear of Gavin as swiftly as possible, she didn't.

"I'm looking closely," Mac said. "But I'm not seeing anything different."

"You're assuming I'm talking about the buildings," he said.

"Well, yeah," she replied. "Weren't you?"

"I was referring more to the people," he said. Mac had no time to ponder this as Gavin turned right onto a road that ran parallel with the town square; it was Elizabeth Street, the street where Mac had grown up.

The houses were old, built mostly in the late eighteen hundreds. The stately row of old Victorian homes lined each side of the street like a proper group of gossipy old dowagers. Mac remembered walking home from school on this sidewalk, her hair in braids, her knee sporting a scab beneath the hem of a dress her mother had foisted on her, as she dragged a stick along the wrought iron fences she passed by because it made such a delightful racket on the normally quiet street.

Halfway down the street, Gavin turned into the familiar gravel driveway. Mac glanced up at the large white house, with the deep green trim and the mansard roof that looked like a hat pulled low over its brow. Home!

Gavin had barely parked the truck when Mac popped out and jogged up the steps onto the wide front porch. She didn't have to raise her fist to knock because the screen door was shoved open and there stood her two aunts, Charlotte and Sarah Harris.

"She's here!" Charlotte shouted.

"I know, I can see her," Sarah said. "I'm hard of hearing, not blind, you know."

Charlotte got to Mac first and hugged her tight. She stepped back and pinched Mac's cheeks just like she did when Mac was six and Charlotte caught her foraging for snacks in the pantry, which usually ended with Charlotte cutting her a nice thick piece of cake.

"My turn," Sarah said. She elbowed Charlotte aside and took Mac's hands in hers. She scrutinized Mac's face as if looking for signs of illness and then released her hands after a hard squeeze. Sarah wasn't much of a hugger. "You look healthy."

"Healthy?" Mac asked. "Is that a euphemism for fat?"

Charlotte laughed and Sarah frowned. They were twins but the years and personal style caused them to look nothing alike. Charlotte wore her white hair in tufted waves and preferred dresses and dainty shoes, while Sarah was more pragmatic and wore her equally snowy hair in a sleek bob and was all about the pants, jeans being preferred. Except at the moment, they were dressed identically in white jumpsuits, sort of like prison uniforms, that covered them from top to bottom.

"Well, you're just as sassy as ever," Sarah said. "So that's something."

"Aunt Sarah, you just saw me in Florida a few months ago," Mac said. "Surely, you didn't think I'd changed that much."

"No, but you're home for the first time in years, and I just want to be sure you're handling it as you should," she said with a sniff.

Even though Aunt Sarah wasn't a hugger, Mac stepped forward and gave her a quick squeeze. "I'm fine, really I am."

Aunt Sarah gave her a brisk nod, signifying that the display of emotion was over.

Charlotte and Sarah were Mac's father's older sisters. Since he had come late in life to their parents, the sisters had taken a hand in raising him, and Mac knew that they doted on their little brother like the child they never had. When he married, they had extended that love and concern to Mac's mother and then to Mac.

No one knew why neither of the sisters had ever married or left Bluff Point, or if they did, they didn't speak of it. For Mac, the aunts were just woven into the fabric of her life. She couldn't imagine growing up without them. Because the family house was so large, when Mac's father married, the two sisters had continued to live in the family home with him and his family. There ever been a thought that they wouldn't, ven from Mac's mother, who loved her husband's sisters as her own.

When Mac's parents had retired to Florida several years ago, they had tried to get Charlotte and Sarah to come with them, but the two sisters could not be budged. Although they traveled quite a lot, neither sister had any interest in calling any place but Bluff Point home.

Mac was selfishly grateful for even though she'd suffered a self-imposed banishment from her hometown for the past seven years, it had always comforted her to know that the aunts were here, keeping the home fires tended.

"So, what's with the flight suits?" Mac asked. She gestured to their outfits and the sisters exchanged a look as if trying to decide how much to tell her. "You're not under house arrest are you?"

"If you must know, we are studying to be apiarists," Sarah said.

"Api-what?"

"Beekeepers, dear," Aunt Charlotte said.

"Huh." Mac had no idea what to say to this new development.

"Gavin Tolliver, aren't you a dear to bring Mac to us," Charlotte said. She was the flirtier of the two sisters and gave him a coquettish look through her lashes as he stepped onto the porch with Mac's bags.

"My pleasure, Miss Charlotte," he said.

"I'll bet it was," Sarah muttered. She was the feistier and more suspicious of the two.

"Sarah, be nice," Charlotte said. Sarah just waved her off like she was a housefly buzzing by her face.

"I'll take these up to your room, Mac," Gavin said. "If you'll show me the way."

"Oh, that's all right," Mac said. "I can take it from here."

"Mackenzie Harris, let the gentleman help you," Charlotte scolded. "You could fall trying to get those upstairs by yourself."

"She's right," Sarah said. "And he looks like he might be strong enough."

Gavin grinned. "Miss Sarah, if ever I start to think too highly of myself, I will be sure to come by and spend an afternoon with you."

"Bring me your grandma's lobster bisque recipe and you'd be welcome," she said.

Gavin raised his eyebrows. "She'd skin me alive for giving away her most prized recipe. That's a pretty steep fee to have my ego checked."

Sarah shrugged. "That's my price."

"Who are you kidding?" Charlotte asked. "You'd whittle him down to size just for the fun of it and you know it."

Sarah glanced away, making no comment, which Mac took to mean she conceded the point without having to actually say so.

"I'm sorry, you were saying something earlier about people changing?" she said to Gavin. She gave him a pointed look to let him know the sisters had not changed one iota over the years.

He grinned at her and Mac couldn't help but return it. The man's smile was infectious and she was pleased to have been the one to make him look, well, happy. She tried to shake it off but her smile would not be budged; best to get the man away from her ASAP.

"Follow me, please." She grabbed her garment bag and her carry-on and strode into the house, leaving Gavin to follow with her suitcase.

"I'll make some iced tea," Charlotte called up the stairs after them.

"Thank you," Mac called back.

She glanced over her shoulder to see Charlotte head toward the kitchen while Sarah watched Mac and Gavin from the foot of the staircase with a speculative gleam in her eye. Oh, that couldn't be good. Sarah never missed anything.

Mac's room was the third on the right, overlooking the side yard and the short wooden fence that separated their property from the neighbor's. At some point in her post-college years, Mac had come for a visit and transformed her teenage lair into a grown-up's room.

She sighed with relief when she entered and found the room looking very utilitarian, with its white furniture and soft green bedspread and matching curtains. There were no boy band posters on the wall or stuffed animals anywhere to be seen; absolutely nothing to be embarrassed about. Thank goodness.

She dropped her carry-on on the wooden floor and gestured for Gavin to park her bag beside it. She hung her garment bag in the closet and turned to find Gavin checking out her room as if trying to get a sense of the girl who used to live here.

"Thanks for the ride, the whoopie pie, and the help with the bags," she said.

She walked to the door but Gavin strode over to the dresser in the corner. On top of it were some of her favorite pictures of her parents, the aunts, and several of her with her Maine crew at various events in their lives.

Gavin reached out and picked up one from their high school days. Emma, Jillian, Carly, and Mac were standing on the boardwalk at the entrance to Belmont Park; they were holding cotton candy and popcorn, standing with their arms draped around one another's shoulders, and they were laughing.

Mac moved to stand beside him and he said, "Emma has the same picture on her dresser."

"Does she?" Mac asked. She traced her finger over the faces of the four young girls in the picture. "We were so young."

He put the picture back and turned to face her. "See? Some people do change."

Mac looked at him and frowned. "Are you trying to tell me I've gotten old?"

"No, I wouldn't say old," he said. "Grown-up, maybe, and you aren't the only one."

His blue eyes were steady on hers and Mac had a sudden epiphany about where he was going with this conversation. The intense look on his face told her more than words that he most definitely remembered their one night together, every single second of it. Uh-oh!

Alarm bells began to clang in her head so loudly that she had a hard time hearing what he said. She saw his lips moving, but it was like his sound card was broken and all she could get were random words and static.

"I'm sorry, what?" she asked.

"I asked you if we're ever going to talk about—" he began but she interrupted.

"No!"

"I think we should—"

"Dut dut dut."

"Mac, we need to—"

"Dut dut," she said. She raised her hand in a *stop* motion. "No, we don't."

Gavin clenched his jaw and she could tell she was infuriating him. Too bad. If they talked about that night then it was real, but if they never talked about it, she could at least pretend that it had never happened, which was about the only way she was going to get through the next two weeks, especially with this hot guy standing in place of the man-boy she had been expecting.

He took a step closer, putting him well within the periphery of her personal space. She knew she should mind, but sadly she didn't. She didn't back up or flinch and when he leaned in close and was just a whisper away from her, she had to fight the urge to rise up on her toes and close the gap.

"Pretending it didn't happen doesn't make it so," he said. Then he leaned in even closer and whispered in her ear. "Besides, don't you want to find out if that night was as sexy as you remember? I know I do."

Chapter 5

Gavin put his truck in reverse and started to back out of the driveway. For reasons he chose not to examine too closely, he stopped halfway down the drive and turned back to stare at the porch.

Smooth, Tolliver, really smooth. From the look on Mac's face when he'd mentioned wanting to see if the memory of their night together held up, he knew he'd either embarrassed the shit out of her or terrified her or both.

What had he been thinking? He should have stuck to playing it cool, taking his cues from her, and just seeing where the next two weeks led them. But that was the problem, two weeks was not enough time. It wasn't as if she had come back to stay. She would be leaving again, and soon.

After seven years Mac was finally here, but it was too damn short of a visit for him to figure out where her head was without actually out-and-out stalking her.

Miss Charlotte had broken up their moment by calling them to tea. Mac had run from the room like she was afraid he was going to devour her, smart girl, and when they arrived downstairs, he realized the polite thing to do would be to let Mac visit with her aunts alone. Plus, he needed some distance to regroup. He had known seeing her again would affect him, but he hadn't really been prepared for how much.

Through the windshield, he could see Miss Charlotte and Mac sitting on the porch swing, enjoying their iced tea as they rocked back and forth. He watched Mac push off the floor with the toe of one pink sneaker. Her jeans were snug and accentuated the slender curves his hands had itched to get ahold of. Her V-neck white T-shirt was simple but clung in all the right places, and she wore several strands of pretty blue beads on her left wrist, giving the outfit a bohemian style he liked.

Miss Charlotte said something funny and Mac tipped her head back as she laughed, exposing the column of her throat while her soft brown hair fell past her shoulders to the middle of her back. Gavin remembered being curtained by that hair when she had lain on top of him, smiling down into his eyes all those years ago.

Her hair had smelled of coconut and ginger, and from then on, he'd always associated those two scents with her. He'd gotten a whiff of it when he hugged her at the train station and again when he'd stood beside her in her room just now. Like a trigger, it had shot him right back to that night, that crazy unforgettable night, and like an idiot he'd decided to mention it to her. What a dumbass.

It really shouldn't have surprised him that he hadn't managed to keep his libido in check. Mackenzie Harris had been scrambling his brain since before he'd even had his first hard-on. She'd been a feature in his mental porn since his voice had cracked and after that one night together, it had only gotten worse. Oh, sure, he'd crushed on other women, sometimes for one night and sometimes for many months, but it was always Mac, the memory of her, that brought him to the razor edge of pain and pleasure.

After so many years, he'd been positive that the real Mackenzie couldn't possibly outshine the fantasy he'd created. But he was wrong, so wrong. From the second he saw her cross the train station and heard her husky voice come through the phone he'd held to his ear, he knew he was doomed. If he were Superman, Mackenzie was his kryptonite.

For a second, Gavin almost shoved the truck into drive and charged the house. The thought of storming the porch, grabbing Mac, and planting one on her just to see how she'd respond was more than a little tempting, but the "dut dut dut" she'd thrown at him like a ninja star made him pause.

It could be that she didn't feel the same way he did, and wasn't that a blow to his male pride? He didn't like to think it, but he had to respect it. When Emma had told him that Mac was coming alone to the wedding and had asked if he'd mind being her escort, Gavin had felt like he'd just been dealt the winning poker hand. But now, he wondered. Why was Mac alone? She was bright and beautiful and could have any guy she set her heart on, so why was she without the plus one?

He wondered if she'd had a relationship implode on her recently. If so, he was going to have to tend her just like he did the abused animals that showed up at his practice: with gentle, patient concern and care. He'd already been the man she'd turned to once in a state of extreme emotional distress. This time, if he could get her to give him another chance, he wanted her with him not because she was running from a place of pain but because she wanted him. Just him.

He was going to have to play this very carefully. They had Emma's wedding to get through together, and he didn't want to do anything that would take away from his sister's big day. He was pretty sure that hitting on the bride's best friend might just do that. Fine. He'd hover in the friend zone until he got any indication that there might be more. And by indication, he meant he'd be watching for even the flicker of an eyelash from Mac giving him the go-ahead. He was determined that he was not going to lose her again. Not if he could help it.

Gavin stepped off the brake and continued to

back out of the drive. Two weeks. He had two whole weeks to see where things stood with Mac, and he planned to take full advantage of every second.

"Did you read this thing?" Carly asked. She burst into Mac's bedroom without knocking, without warning, and without any sort of greeting, just like she had back when they were in high school.

Carly was the fourth in a family of five sisters, so she ate with gusto, moved at light speed, and could outshout just about anyone when she needed to be heard. Survival skills, she called them. Having eaten dinner at her house a few times, Mac knew this to be true.

Mac was lying across her bed, staring at the ceiling while thinking over, or rather over-thinking, the moments she had spent in here with Gav. Aunt Charlotte had called them to tea, halting whatever Mac would have answered to Gavin's question about their encounter seven years ago, which was a good thing because Mac's brain had shorted out and she was pretty sure she would have keeled over at his feet if they hadn't been interrupted.

"Mac, are you listening to me?" Carly demanded. She was holding the itinerary Emma had sent them with two fingers at arm's length as if it were a poopy diaper. "You have to do something about this."

Mac lifted her head and stared at her friend. "Why me?"

"Maid of honor," Carly said. "It's in the job description."

"I'm pretty sure shotgunning the über-bride's agenda is not in the maid of honor manual," Mac said. "I believe I am supposed to be a facilitator of all things bridal."

"Well, that's just wrong," Carly retorted. She flopped onto the bed beside Mac. "Have you read this thing?"

"I tried, but she lost me at shuffleboard on the pier at dawn," Mac said. "Speaking of which, aren't we supposed to be going somewhere right now?"

"Jillian's shop," Carly said. "To help make wedding favors."

"Oh, yeah," Mac said. "It's just the bridesmaids, right?"

"Meaning, are the dudes excused from stuffing organza bags with scented candles for three hundred guests?" Carly asked. She glanced at the itinerary. "Yes, they are playing pool at the Bikini Lounge."

"Oh, wow, that bar is still around?"

"Yes, and it will likely outlive us all. I should have been a groomsman. I'm much better at pool than bag stuffing."

"It's for Emma," Mac said.

"I know, but I hate girly stuff," Carly whined.

"Says the woman who buys lingerie for a living."

"Please, I buy big-girl panties for middle market department stores," Carly said. "It's not the glam career people like to think it is."

They were silent for a moment, both staring at the ceiling now. Mac was trying to picture what she was going to do the next time she saw Gavin. Considering the fact that when he had mentioned revisiting their past, she had bolted from the room like someone had torched her booty, she had to imagine their next meeting would be awkward at best.

What if he brought it up again? How was she supposed to handle it? Laugh it off? Pretend to get mad? Jump him? Okay, the last one wasn't really an option, but it definitely had the most appeal.

"Hello, Mac, hello." Carly waved her hand in front of Mac's face. "Where are you? I've been complaining for several minutes and I didn't even get a grunt of acknowledgment out of you."

Mac turned her head and glanced at her friend.

"Sorry, I was awake napping," she said. She rolled up to a seated position. "We should get going so we're not late."

"Yeah, we could do that, or . . ." Carly paused while she sat up and gave Mac a mischievous look. "You could tell me what happened between you and Gavin when he picked you up."

Mac gasped. "You knew? You knew he was picking me up and you didn't run interference?"

Carly gave her a look. "Oh, so sorry, I was stuck in a car with my oldest sister Terry, who lectured me all the way from New York about how my eggs are going to dry up and blow away and I'll never have children because I am over thirty. Next time I'll be sure to swing by the train station so you can join in the fun, too."

"Ugh, I'm sorry," Mac said.

"Thank you, but seriously, how did it go with Gavin?" Carly asked.

"It went fine," Mac said. The lie flew out of her mouth before it was fully formed in her head, sort of like a preprogrammed response of politeness to an uncomfortable social situation that she didn't have to think about.

She loved Carly dearly and she knew she could have told her the truth, but she did not want this silly thing between her and Gavin to become the focus of their two-week vacation. If she told Carly how truly awkward and weird it had been then it would be a thing and it would overshadow Emma's day and Mac couldn't have that.

"Really?" Carly asked.

"Yeah, I mean it was initially awkward for a minute because we haven't seen each other in years, but then it was like no big deal," Mac said. Being crap at lying, she made sure to make eye contact and hold it and not make any sudden hand gestures that might be construed as a tell. She felt like a mannequin but it must have worked because Carly nodded.

"Huh," she said. "I always thought the big dope would be hung up on you forever, but maybe Jane the Pain did enough damage that he's sworn off women or something."

"Yeah, probably." Mac blew out a breath and looked away. "He did seem a little different."

"Well, it's been seven years. Surely, you noticed what a fine hunk of man he's turned into," Carly said. "I mean if he wasn't one of my best friend's little brothers I'd start licking him at his . . . oh, sorry."

"Yeah," Mac said. "Been there, did that."

Carly laughed. She threw her arm around Mac's shoulders and gave her a quick squeeze.

"Listen, as the only person you've ever told about the whole Gavin thing, I know how much you enjoy feeling ashamed of yourself, but seriously, honey, it's time to let it go."

"You think?" Mac asked.

"Yeah, if he's over it, then you really should be, too," Carly said. "I mean why have angst if you don't have to?"

Angst, well, wasn't that an interesting euphemism for the pure unadulterated lust that had been coursing through Mac since Gavin leaned in close and whispered in her ear? She'd have to remind herself of that the next time they were thrown together.

She glanced at the itinerary in Carly's hand. Oh, goody, it looked like that would be tonight at the Bikini Lounge after candle stuffing. Yay.

Chapter 6

The Bikini Lounge was a ramshackle dive that had been in existence in Bluff Point for decades. It perched on the end of the town pier, hanging over the ocean with the stubborn tenacity of a barnacle on the side of a boat.

The breeze blowing in from the water was cold, and Mac hunkered into her hoodie as she walked down the pier toward the bright blue building at the end. The wooden planks bowed and creaked when she walked on them, and Mac wondered exactly how many people it would take to make the pier collapse.

"Stop thinking about it," Carly said.

"What?" Mac asked.

"The same thing you always think about when we come here," Emma said from in front of them. "That the pier is going to collapse on us and we're all going to die."

"I don't think that," Mac protested.

"Yes, you do," Jillian argued. She was walking beside Emma. "We all know how much you hate deep dark water."

"It's bathophobia, and it's a real thing," Mac said, as if that made it any less unreasonable.

"Which I would understand if you couldn't swim," Carly said. "But you can."

Mac glanced at the boards below her feet. A knot in the thick wood allowed her to see the churning water below. She felt her hands get slick with sweat. She really only liked the Bikini Lounge at low tide and in daylight; high tide and nighttime made her edgy.

"Who's buying the first round?" she asked.

"Me," Jillian answered.

"Cool, make mine a double," Mac said.

Emma opened the door and ushered them into the dark bar. The smell of stale beer and popcorn filled the air. The bouncer recognized Emma and Jillian and waved them in. He held up his hand in front of Carly and motioned for her and Mac to show their ID's.

"Dude, seriously?" Carly asked.

He gave her a hard stare and she scrounged in her purse until she found her license. Mac had ditched her bag for the evening and pulled hers out of her pocket. He checked their ID's under a flashlight and then waved for them to enter.

"Are we at an age yet where we should be flattered to be carded?" Carly asked Mac.

"No, I think that's forty," Mac said.

"So my desire to kick his butt is justified?" Carly asked.

She glanced over her shoulder at the big, burly doorman. "Eh, maybe I'll just sleep with him."

"Don't do that," Jillian said. "I have it from very reliable sources that his man parts do not match."

"Meaning what exactly?" Emma asked. She led them across the bar to the pool tables in the back corner, where Brad and the boys were hanging out.

"Big hands, big feet, and big nose do not necessarily mean big thrill drill," Jillian said.

"What?!" Brad Jameson, Emma's fiancé, gave them a feigned look of shock. "Jillian Braedon, did you just call a penis a thrill drill?"

"Oh, yeah, she did," Carly said. "It's Emma's fault. We told her not to talk about you."

Brad scooped Emma close and planted a kiss on her. "Aw, honey, I thought we agreed to call it the pillar of creation."

Emma laughed and said, "Or more accurately, *sleepus interruptus.*"

They pressed their heads together and shared an intimate look that in any other couple Mac would have found annoying, but if there really were such things as soul mates, Emma and Brad were it.

"What's this, a conversation about alternate names for man junk?" Zachary Caine, Brad's longtime best friend and Bluff Point's resident man whore, joined them. He was holding his pool cue and spoke into it like it was a microphone. "Count me in. Pulled pork."

He held out the cue to another groomsman, Sam Kennedy, who flashed a grin and said, "Trouser snake."

76

The girls all groaned. Then Zach held the pool cue out to Gavin. He'd been standing in the shadows against the wall but stepped forward and flashed a rueful smile. "One-eyed Jack," he said. Zach hooted with laughter and they exchanged a complicated handshake.

Mac noted that Gavin didn't look her way, so she kept her gaze averted, not wanting to risk eye contact. Maybe after her embarrassing escape this afternoon, he had gotten the message that she really didn't want to discuss the past and he was respecting her wishes and giving her space. Excellent.

She refused to acknowledge any pang of regret she might feel. Obviously, being home on the old familiar ground was wreaking havoc with her common sense.

"Hey there, Mac," Zach said. He stepped up close and gave her a thorough once-over. "Long time, no see, but now that I do I must say you are looking goooood." He grabbed her in a quick hug and then held the cue out to her. "So, what do you have for me, baby?"

Mac tried not to laugh, but Zach was the eternal twelve-year-old goofball. With his shaggy blonde hair and sloppy, devil-may-care charm, he could work a room like no one else. He was also the reason Brad and Emma had gotten together as he was the one who almost threw up on Emma, but fortunately Brad had put himself in the path of the puke. Ew.

Mac leaned close to the cue and cleared her throat. "Um, how about the south pole?"

Zach tipped his head back and cackled. Then he snapped his head in Carly's direction. He sidled up close to her, gave her a hug, and said, "It's all on you, sister."

"Oh, please," Carly said. "Just one?"

Zach drew himself up to his full height and gave her a sidelong look. "Is this a challenge, Miss Carly?"

"Loser buys a round of shots for us all," she said.

"Game on." Zach wiggled his eyebrows at her.

"Oh, boy, this could get ugly," Sam said. He elbowed his way around Zach and Carly and gave Mac and Jillian a quick hug. "Good to see you, ladies. There is entirely too much testosterone in here."

"You, too, Sam," Mac said.

Zach and Sam had come into Emma's life the moment she started dating Brad as the three men were business partners in a local brewery. Bluff Point Ale had begun in their college dorm room and the three of them had spent years perfecting it and selling it locally until they finally had enough capital to launch their own brewery, which they did two years ago.

"Hey, Mac, you should come by the brew house

and check out the operation," Sam said. "As chief brew master, I can hook you up."

Mac smiled at him. "I'd like that."

"Cool, it's a date." Sam turned back to the pool table and gestured to Gavin with his cue. "Hey, Gav, you should come, too. Brad told me you haven't seen the new eatery we're building."

"Sure, that'd be great," Gavin said. He didn't look at any of them, but leaned over the table and took his shot. Mac saw his jaw clench twice and she knew he was brooding about something.

"Wangdoodle," Carly said.

"Love sausage," Zach retorted.

"Gross," Jillian said to Mac.

Emma and Brad had shuffled off into a dark corner and were whispering together as if they hadn't seen each other in weeks instead of mere hours.

"Come on, I'll help you get the drinks," Mac said to Jillian. "I think Carly's going to be here awhile."

"Ba-donk-a-donk," Carly said.

"The best of three legs," Zach returned.

"Knobgoblin." Carly's voice was drowned by Zach's laughter.

As they walked to the bar, Mac glanced around the room to see if there was anyone else from town that she knew. There was not. She wasn't sure how she felt about that. Relieved, mostly, but also a little displaced. A part of her had geared up to run into someone, anyone, who had been at her catastrophe of a wedding seven years ago, but there was no one.

Before she had left Bluff Point at the age of twenty-five, this had been one of her hotspots to hang out on the weekends with the Maine crew. At the time, she couldn't have imagined a day where the bouncer wouldn't know her name or she wouldn't recognize any of the people seated at the bar.

"Curtis," Jillian called the bartender, another person Mac didn't know, and ordered four pints of Bluff Point Ale, natch.

"Why do you suppose the two of them never got together?" Jillian asked Mac as they leaned against the bar and watched Carly and Zach, who were still going one for one in the name game.

"Maybe they're too much alike," Mac said. "You know, that whole extroverted commitment-phobic thing they both have going."

"They'll be fun at the wedding though," Jillian said. "Carly can keep him in check and if not, I'm sure she'll have no problem hog-tying him and shoving him in a closet somewhere."

"And you're paired with Sam?" Mac asked. She glanced over at the lean man with the neatly trimmed goatee and head of dark hair. He was the tallest of the groomsmen, which suited as Jillian was the tallest of the girls.

"Yeah," Jillian said.

"Is he still single?" Mac asked.

"Why, are you interested?" Jillian asked. "Emma told us you were single for the next few weeks. I asked if you and Trevor had split and she said to ask you."

"Oh," Mac said. She wondered briefly if she should tell Jillian that she and Trevor were taking a break, but since Jillian was no more of a fan of Trevor's than Emma, she decided not to as it would only complicate things since she hadn't told Emma about their break. "The timing was bad for Trevor. He has business in London and can't get away so Emma paired me with Gavin for the festivities. As for Sam, I was thinking of him more for you."

"Oh, no," Jillian said. "I am not dating anyone until I get to Paris."

"Excuse me?" Mac said. "Did I miss something? You're going to Paris?"

"No, I just want to go to Paris," Jillian said. She had tied back her shoulder-length curls with a pretty purple scarf and she fussed with the ends of it while they talked.

"So go," Mac said.

"I will," Jillian said. "When the time is right."

"What's wrong with right now?"

"Emma's wedding."

"After the wedding."

"The bakery."

"Is always going to be there."

"You don't understand," Jillian said.

Mac looked at her friend. Her brow was furrowed and her mouth was pinched. She looked like a person wrestling with some inner demons. That, Mac understood.

"You're playing the 'what if' game," Mac said.

"Huh?"

"You want to go to Paris, right?"

"Yes."

"But in your head, you keep asking yourself 'what if' and then you fill in the blank with a random worry that seems legit at the time but is really just keeping you from doing what you want, which is to go to Paris," Mac said.

"No, I'm not. Okay, well, maybe a little, but still, flying to a country where you don't speak the language is a huge undertaking and it's not something a person should do lightly," Jillian said, but she didn't meet Mac's eyes.

The bartender put four tall pints in front of them and Jillian paid the tab. Mac wondered if she should say any more but she didn't want to risk annoying her friend. They had time to talk about Paris, no need to hash it all out in one evening.

Jillian took two beers and Mac took the other two. They arrived back at the group just in time to hear Carly shout, "And it's the homewrecker for the win!"

"Lovely," Mac said. She handed Carly a glass and toasted her with her own.

"All right, smarty pants, winner carries the shots," Zach said to Carly and he led her to the bar.

Jillian delivered Emma's drink to her and Sam joined her with Brad and Emma. Mac wasn't sure if she should crash that group or follow Carly to the bar. She knew she needed to move quickly before—

"Mac, how about a game?" Gavin asked.

Too late.

Chapter 7

Sure," Mac said after just the slightest hesitation. She pointed to the pool table. "Rack 'em up."

Gavin gave her an amused glance. "Yes, ma'am."

Mac frowned at him. Did he really just call her ma'am? Was that his way of being funny about her being five years older than him? Or was he just being polite? She was pretty sure ma'am was only polite when a woman was old enough to have gray hair south of her equator; before that, it was just rude. Now she felt the need to whup his butt at pool. It was a matter of principle.

She took a long sip of her beer and put it on a nearby table. Then she headed over to the rack to select a cue. She had spent an awful lot of nights right here, shooting pool and flirting shamelessly with whoever came near the table. She had some skill. She'd show Gav who was a ma'am.

The upside was that if they were busy playing pool then things couldn't get too hot and heavy in the conversational sense and there would be no need to revisit their talk from earlier. Or so she hoped.

"Do you want to break?" Gav asked but Mac gestured for him to go ahead.

She watched him lean over and study the table.

He had put on a gray and black plaid flannel shirt over his T-shirt and she liked the way it fit his shoulders. As he lined up his shot, she glanced away, not wanting to be distracted by his hands, which looked big and strong and a little bit wicked as he slid the cue through his fingers.

Mac quickly turned her back and reached for the chalk and tended the end of her cue, although it didn't look like it needed it. There was absolutely no reason why she had to be looking at Gavin's hands. None at all.

Crack! Gavin's shot was true and balls scattered all over the table, sinking two stripes and one solid. He moved into position to hit a combination to send another stripe into the corner pocket.

He moved in front of Mac and she was pushed back up against the wall as she tried to look anywhere but at the derriere in front of her. He missed his shot and she exhaled a huge breath when he moved away from her around the table.

"Your shot, Mac," he said.

"Speaking of shots." Carly joined them carrying a tray of drinks. "Bottoms up."

Mac and Gavin both took one and then Carly delivered the remaining ones to the rest of the group.

"To the happy couple," Zach shouted over the other conversations in the bar. "Long may you honk the magic goose."

Emma laughed and they all raised their glasses in a toast to Brad and Emma. While the others downed their drinks, Mac took a sniff of hers to determine what she was in for.

"It's Zach's shot of choice called the Three Wise Men," Gavin said. He tossed his back and put the empty glass on the table by her pint of beer.

"Three Wise Men? As in Larry, Moe, and Curly?" she asked. She took a sip and felt it burn like a ball of fire down her throat into her chest. It made her ears ring and not in a bad way.

Gavin grinned and said, "More like Jim, Jack, and Johnnie."

Mac puzzled it out for a minute and then blew out a breath and said, "Jim Beam, Jack Daniels, and Johnnie Walker?"

Gavin nodded.

"Oh, hell, no," she said and put her glass down. "That's the sort of drink that makes a girl do really dumb things."

"Really?" Gav asked. He leaned on his pool cue and studied her with a look of fascination. "Such as?"

It was on the tip of her tongue to say *sleep with her best friend's little brother* but Mac held it in, gave him a closed-lip smile, and instead said, "Drunken texting leaps to mind."

She lined up her shot and struck the cue ball, knocking a solid into a side pocket.

"And who would you be drunk texting?" he asked. He had his arms crossed over his chest and his head tipped to the side as he studied her.

You, Mac thought. She shook her head. What? Why was she thinking that? Thoughts like that were not helpful, not at all. She lined up her next shot and then paused. Wait. This was perfect.

This was her moment to admit she'd drunk text her boyfriend and tell him how much she missed him. She had told Emma that if Gavin asked her outright if she was seeing someone, she wouldn't lie. This would put an end to anything between them once and for all.

She opened her mouth to say "Trevor" when Zach staggered in between them, pointed at the shot Mac had abandoned, and shouted, "Party foul! You have to drink to the happy couple, Mac, it's a rule."

"No, it isn't," she protested.

"Yes, it is," he insisted. Then he put his hand on his chest and gave her a half bow. "Unless, of course, you want to donate the shot to the noble charity of Zach."

Mac laughed at his silly smile. She glanced at Gavin to see if he thought Zach could handle any more and he gave her a small nod.

"It's all yours, my friend," she said.

"Woot!" Zach scooped up the shot and bounced back over to the rest of their group.

"He's a lovable idiot," she said.

"Agreed." She was about to take her next shot when Gavin put his hand on her cue and said, "Hey, about before."

Mac felt her stomach drop. She did not want to have this conversation. Not here. Not now. Okay, not anywhere. Ever. But especially not here in front of Emma.

"Listen," he said as he pulled her away from the table and back into the shadows against the wall. "I didn't mean to freak you out earlier."

"You didn't—" she protested but he interrupted.

"Yeah, that's why you ran like a tsunami was coming to get you," he said.

Mac smiled. She had to give him that one. He returned her smile and the dimple in his cheek deepened.

"It's been a long time since we've seen each other," he said. "And my most recent memories of you are, well, let's go with unforgettable." His voice had that note of self-deprecating humor that she always found so alluring. She found herself leaning toward him when she really needed to be backing away.

Mac suddenly wished she had her Three Wise Men back. Was it hot in here? Why was she sweating? She pulled the neck of her T-shirt away from her skin and considered shedding her hooded sweatshirt.

"That being said," Gav continued. "I get it if you just want to be friends. This whole event is about Emma and Brad, and we probably shouldn't let things get complicated by revisiting the past."

Mac glanced at him out of the corner of her eye. Was he serious? He looked as honest as a Boy Scout. Sweet, delicious relief flooded her as she realized everything was going to be okay, followed by a surprising jab of disappointment.

Just like that he was letting it go? He wasn't going to pursue discussion of their one night together anymore? Huh.

Mac forced herself to nod. He was standing too close to her and it was causing her hormones to try and stage a coup and jump him. She inched away from him under the guise of turning to face him.

"Yeah, that's a good idea," she said. "You're right; we really want to keep it all about the wedding. We'll just leave the past in the past and be friends."

Gavin's gaze moved over her face and Mac couldn't tell what he was thinking. He looked remote, as if he was shutting himself away from her, and she found she didn't like that. But that was good, right? That was what she'd wanted, right?

"So, we're good?" he asked.

"Yeah, good," Mac agreed. "Really good."

"Okay, then." He gestured to the pool table. "Let's do this."

Mac won the first game. Gavin won the second. After their conversation, Mac had expected them to find new footing as old friends, but it didn't seem to take.

She felt Gav's eyes on her when she was lining up her shots, and it was not her face his hot stare was regarding. She caught her own gaze lingering on places on his body that she had no business looking at, but still she did.

Their conversation was light, how-about-them-Red-Sox type of stuff, and Mac found that she felt frustrated by it.

She wanted to know more about Gavin the man. She wanted to know how his practice was doing, whether he was happy in Bluff Point, and what his plans for the future entailed. But she couldn't ask any of that because they had agreed to be just friends, but not really friends, she realized; more like acquaintances.

But the reality was that's all they were destined to be. Once the wedding was over, they'd go their separate ways the same way they had seven years ago. It seemed less satisfactory than she thought it would be. After the second game, they hung up their cues to join the others.

The popcorn machine in the corner of the bar was churning out fresh hot buttery goodness and Gavin went to grab a bowl, while Mac took a seat at a tall table to watch the show. Carly and Zach had taken over the tiny dance floor, not leaving enough space with their wild gyrations for anyone to join them.

Emma and Jillian joined Mac where she sat watching their friend. Emma nested her arms on Mac's shoulders and propped her chin on her forearms while they watched Zach and Carly bust out moves that Mac was pretty sure could only be seen on a cable channel about wild animals mating.

"Are you having a DJ at the reception?" Jillian asked.

"Yep," Brad answered as he took the seat beside Mac. "We've told the videographer just to film those two when they hit the dance floor. I am pretty sure they could be an Internet sensation."

Mac laughed. "Carly would kill you."

"There is that," Brad said. "But we might make enough money in ads to pay off our mortgage."

Emma held up two hands like a scale. "Lifelong friend. Mortgage. Hmmm. Tough one."

Gavin and Sam rejoined them with popcorn for everyone, and as if the smell lured them in, Carly and Zach jogged over from the dance floor to partake.

"Well, kids, I hate to break up the party, but I have to be up and baking whoopie pies early in the morning," Jillian said. She glanced at Sam, and added, "You're coming by to pick up the wedding favors, yes?"

"I will be there," he said. He turned to Zach. "And you're coming with me."

"What?" Zach protested. "What time?"

"Eight," Jillian said. "Before the shop opens."

"Eight?" Zach looked outraged. "No one gets up at eight on the weekend."

"You are," Sam said.

Zach began to mutter as Sam led him to the door. Jillian and Carly joined them, with Carly commiserating with Zach about the evils of sunrise. Brad and Emma fell in behind them, leaving Mac again with Gavin.

They walked down the pier with a gap between them wide enough for two people to fill. Mac was beginning to think their acquaintanceship was actually more awkward than talking about their one-night stand. Who'd have thought?

The wood creaked beneath Mac's feet and she tried not to think about the churning water below the flimsy planks. She picked up her pace as the distance to solid ground seemed like it was getting farther away instead of closer with each step, although she knew it was probably just her panic kicking in.

A wave crashed against a piling below, and Mac jumped and made a little yip.

"Mac, are you all right?" Gavin closed the gap between them and took her arm, causing her to slow down. "Did you twist an ankle or something?"

"No, I'm fine," she said. She refused to look down and fastened her gaze on his shirt buttons instead.

"It's the water, isn't it?" he asked. "I forgot you hate the deep dark."

"I blame *Shark Week*," she said. She heard him chuckle but kept her gaze on his shirt. He was standing too close and eye contact at this juncture could only lead to more impure thoughts, which she was trying very hard to avoid since they now seemed to have this frosty pane of glass between them.

Well, Gavin smashed that. He pulled her close and tucked her into his side. "I promise I won't let you fall in and if you do, I won't let anything grab you in its powerful jaws and pull you under."

"Not helping," she said, although his solid strength beside her did calm her down just a little.

"All right, Mac?" Carly called from the front of the pack.

"Yeah, I'm fine," she said. "Okay, that's a lie, but I'm working through it. How freaking long is this pier anyway?"

Zach glanced over his shoulder at her. His face was kind but also full of alcohol-fueled mischief.

"You know what always helps me when I'm afraid, Mac?" he asked.

"The Three Wise Men?"

"Ha! Yes, but even better is singing," he said.

"Oh, please, no," Mac said.

She felt Gavin's shoulders start to shake as Zach wrapped one arm around Carly and the other around Jillian and began to belt out "Don't Stop Believin'" by Journey.

"Sweet peanuts," Mac said. "We are so getting arrested for disturbing the peace."

"Possibly," Gavin said, "but on the upside, a voice like that is sure to scare away anything that might lurk in the deep dark."

"Good point."

When they were two-thirds of the way in from the end of the pier Mac felt the wobble in her knees start to stiffen. The panic passed and she took a deep breath and leaned away from Gavin.

"Thanks," she said. "I've got this now."

She didn't think she imagined that he let her go with just a hint of reluctance, but she refused to dwell on it. When they were back on land, Mac resisted the urge to kneel down and give Mother Earth a big smooch. Barely.

A buzzing noise sounded and Gavin reached into his shirt pocket and took out his phone. He glanced at the screen and then typed something before putting it back in his pocket.

"The Walkers' golden retriever is in labor," he said. "Gotta go."

"Puppies!" Zach cried. "Hey, that would make

a swell wedding gift. Ask them how much they want for one."

"No, it most certainly would not," Emma said. She glared at her brother. "Don't you dare."

Gavin raised his hands in innocence. "Just hoping for a healthy litter here."

Hugs were exchanged as their group split up. The boys headed out in one group, while the girls were another, the only exception being Brad and Emma who were going to their new home, which they'd just moved into last month.

As Mac hugged everyone good night, she refused to feel weird about hugging Gavin. They had worked it out. Despite any lingering curiosity, they were solidly friends so there was absolutely no need for her to feel self-conscious about hugging him just like she hugged Sam, Zach, and Brad.

Except when she hugged the others, she didn't feel the same need to twine herself around them like a vine on a trellis as she did with Gavin. Muscle memory, she told herself. It had to be her muscle memory kicking in, remembering their erotic gymnastics the last time they'd been together. Right?

Yeah, that was it. She stiffened her spine and gave him a quick squeeze but when she would have stepped back, Gavin blew her muscle memory theory right into the wind when he held her close longer than necessary and whispered in her ear, "Oh, about our talk earlier, I forgot to mention one little thing. I respect your feelings one hundred percent, but I fully intend to try and change your mind about the friend thing."

Uh-oh!

Chapter 8

Gavin released her and Mac was positive her surprise showed on her face as he winked at her and then departed, off to help a mama dog bring her puppies into the world. Now why did that suddenly seem like the most honorable thing any man had ever done?

"Are you sure you girls want to walk home by yourselves?" Brad asked. He gestured to the other guys and himself. "Any of us would be happy to escort you to your door."

Mac hooked her arms through Carly's and Jillian's. "No, we're fine. We're just going up the road. The night air will do us good. Right, ladies?"

Carly and Jillian gave her curious looks and Mac knew she was overselling it, but this was an emergency. She needed a girlfriend consult immediately.

Carly must have seen something in her face, because she nodded and said, "You kids go on home. We're good."

"Text me when you all get home, so I know you're safe," Emma said.

They agreed and then stood under a streetlight watching as the rest of their pack wandered off into the night.

"Ouch!" Jillian pulled her arm out of Mac's. "Is there a reason you felt the need to cut off the circulation to my wrist?"

"What happened?" Carly said. "You two seemed to be doing fine and then you looked all bug-eyed like he made a play. Did he make a play?"

"Let's not talk here," Mac said.

She broke away from the other two and began to stride in the opposite direction from their friends.

"Where are you going?" Jillian cried. "This isn't the way home."

"Shortcut," Mac lied.

She heard the other two hurrying behind her, but she didn't stop until she had crossed Main Street and was striding across the town green, which was mercifully empty.

Carly was gasping and panting and when they reached a park bench she threw herself down onto it in a heap.

"That's it," she declared. "I can't go another foot. Now tell us what the hell is going on?"

"Gavin is refusing to be friend zoned," Mac said.

"What? I thought you said everything was copacetic between you two," Carly said.

"I lied," Mac said. "It's been weird and awkward since the get-go. I just thought if I pretended that everything was okay that it would magically become okay, but it's not going to be okay, is it?"

"Wait! Back up. I am totally lost. Since when don't you and Gavin get on?" Jillian asked. "I always thought you were close. I mean you've always adored him like a little brother."

"Oh, god, I'm going to hell." Mac collapsed onto the bench beside Carly and dug her hands into her hair. This was a nightmare.

"Yeah, it's not really a brotherly relationship that Mac shares with Gavin," Carly said to Jillian. "It's more like *Big*."

"Big how?" Jillian asked, clearly confused.

"Like *Big* the movie," Carly said. "You know, older woman defiling a younger man."

"I did not!" Mac protested. "I'm only five years older, sheesh, it's not like we're Harold and Maude."

Jillian gasped as it all came into focus. "No way! You're sleeping with Gavin?"

"No! Past tense," Mac said. "I slept with Gavin."

"What? When?" Jillian cried. "And how do I not know this? Does Emma know? Oh, my god, this is her Gavin. He might as well be her firstborn. Oh, she's going to kill you. You remember when he had his first girlfriend and she thought the girl was moving too fast. Emma made us run interference until the girl finally broke up with him."

"And there's the dilemma," Mac said. "Not so much my death as that might be a relief right now, but yeah, Emma finding out about Gavin and me is a concern."

"You think?" Carly asked.

"But I still don't understand," Jillian said. She paced in front of the bench as she talked. "You haven't been back in Bluff Point in seven years. When did you and Gavin hook up?"

"You might as well take it from the top, Mrs. Robinson," Carly said.

"Shut up," Mac said. She looked at Jillian, which was difficult because she was afraid of the judgment and derision she was going to find there. But this was Jillian; there was no judgment, just concern.

"The night of my wedding, or rather my aborted wedding," Mac said. "I was pretty distraught."

"Rightly so," Jillian said. She eased onto the bench beside Mac and put her arm around her shoulders.

Mac swallowed hard and glanced at the church sitting on the east side of the town green. Spotlights lit up the spire that reached to the sky, illuminating the tower where the big brass bell chimed every Sunday to call the worshippers to service.

It had happened right there in front of god and every person she had ever met in her life, or so it had seemed at the time.

The arched wooden door was closed now, but on that day, a brisk day in May, it had been wide open. Ribbons had festooned the pews, flowers had poured off of the dais in a riot of pink and white—it had been the perfect setting for her wedding. Mac's bridesmaids, Jillian, Carly, and Emma, had walked down the aisle to Pachelbel's "Canon in D" while Mac stood with her dad in the vestibule waiting for the traditional bridal march to start.

But then a car horn had blasted through the anticipation, and Mac had turned her head to see Jessie Peeler, her nemesis since she'd cut off Mac's braids in the second grade with a pair of children's scissors, sitting in a zippy red convertible, honking the horn repeatedly and staring at the front of the church. Mac had been livid that Jessie was trying to cause a distraction and ruin her day—typical—but then Seth Connelly, her groom, came bolting down the aisle, running toward the door.

She had thought he was coming to save the day and chase Jessie off but no. He never stopped or slowed down or broke his stride, he just shouted, "Sorry, Mac, I just can't do it. I don't love you." Then he jumped into Jessie's car and she sped off with Mac's man, leaving Mac rejected and alone in all her bridal finery on her wedding day.

She and her father had stood stupidly staring after the car as it disappeared around the corner.

Sensing catastrophe, Emma, Carly, and Jillian had run back down the aisle to get to Mac. Before she knew it, she was being shoved into a pickup truck and Gavin was driving her away from the chaotic scene at the church, away from everything she had thought her life was supposed to be.

"I didn't plan for it to happen," Mac said. "I just—my whole world had imploded, and I reached for the first source of comfort I could find and it was Gavin."

Jillian nodded. "I remember now. Aunt Sarah went after Seth's parents and had to be subdued. Aunt Charlotte couldn't stop crying. Your poor parents were in shock. And we were all so worried about you that we decided the best thing we could do would be to get you out of there and eradicate any vestige of wedding anything at the church, the house, the venue, all of it. Your dad and Aunt Sarah wanted to go after Seth with a shotgun."

Mac laughed. "Dad's a pacifist. He doesn't even know how to shoot. Aunt Sarah though— she could probably manage it."

Jillian snorted.

"I think your dad was feeling sufficiently motivated to learn," Carly said. "We all were."

"Emma told Gavin to take you away and let you cry it out all over him if need be," Jillian said.

"She cried something," Carly said. Mac gave her a death glare.

"It's not funny," Mac said.

"Oh, come on, it's a little funny," Carly said.

"No, it isn't," Jillian said. She gave Carly a quelling look. Then she turned to Mac and gave her a hurt look. "I just can't believe you never told me."

"I was never going to tell anyone ever," Mac said.

"But you told Carly," Jillian pointed out.

"No, I didn't," Mac said.

Carly leaned around Mac to talk to Jillian directly. "It's true; she didn't share her sordid story with me. I figured it out when I caught her in the midst of her walk of shame. Not a pretty picture: her wedding dress was wrinkled and torn, she was carrying her bra in her handbag—really, it was about the gnarliest walk of shame I've ever seen, and I've seen my share."

"So glad you enjoyed it," Mac said. She tipped her head back and looked at the dark sky. She could only pick out a few stars, the brightest ones, behind the glow of the old-fashioned lampposts that lit up the town square at night.

"Oh, Mac," Jillian said. "You should have told Emma at the time."

"I know," Mac said. "But I didn't want to embarrass Gavin, and I was so raw from Seth's betrayal. I just packed a bag and bolted to the first job I could find, which happened to be in Chicago. I would have preferred Australia."

"Well, I for one am glad you didn't go that far," Carly said. She sounded uncharacteristically sentimental and Mac reached over and squeezed her hand.

"Okay, I can see where this is a pickle," Jillian said. "But it's hardly a crisis. I mean, you have a boyfriend. You're not available so even if Gavin is curious about what could happen between you, all you have to do is play the relationship card and he'll back off."

Carly and Mac both shook their heads.

"You don't have a boyfriend anymore? You and Trevor broke up? But I thought you said he was just working in London," Jillian said. Her eyes lit up with hope.

"No, we didn't break up, exactly, but even if we did, it's very uncool of you to sound so happy about it," Mac said.

"Oh, sorry." Jillian cringed.

"Don't be," Carly said. "He's an ass, no one likes him."

"I like him," Mac argued.

"No, you don't," Carly said. "And that's why you're with him."

"That's the dumbest thing I've ever heard," Mac said. "Why would I be with him if I didn't like him?"

"Because, Little Miss Number Cruncher, you don't want to be with anyone you actually like, or god forbid, love," Carly said. "Back me up, Jilly."

Mac turned from Carly to Jillian. "Explain."

"It's nothing," Jillian assured her. "It's just that you're an accountant."

"What does that have to do with anything?" Mac felt as if her temples were contracting as she tried to follow their reasoning.

"Your life is all about loss and gain, right?" Jillian asked.

"And profit margins, acceptable risk, and tax laws; so what?"

"Because, dummy, getting involved with someone you actually care about, for you, is a solid loss since the last time you were burnt so badly," Carly said. "And that's why you're with Trevor in a going nowhere relationship—because the risk of loss is minimal emotionally, financially, and I'd wager physically."

"How many times have you two analyzed my love life?" Mac asked.

"Every time you make us hang out with Mr. Stick Up His Butt," Carly said.

"We've just been worried," Jillian said more diplomatically.

"And bewildered," Carly said. "What do you see in that guy?"

"He's nice," Mac growled.

"So are granny panties," Carly said. "But you don't want to wear them every day for the rest of your life. Besides which, he is not nice!"

"Yes, he is."

"Puhleeze," Carly snorted. "You cannot be that deluded. He's a manipulative jerk, or did you forget that he lied right to my face when I was sent to Chicago last-minute and showed up on your doorstep to do an impromptu girls' night? He said you were out when you were in the shower just to get rid of me. He's an asshole."

"Carly, that was over a year ago and it was just a misunderstanding. Gah, I can't talk to you," Mac said. She was beginning to regret confiding in her two friends. Who needed the psychoanalysis? All she wanted was help with the immediate situation.

"I still don't see why you can't just mention Trevor to Gavin," Jillian said. "Whether we like it or not, he is your boyfriend, and Gavin would have to respect that."

"Because Emma asked me not to mention him," Mac said.

"Huh?" Jillian asked. "Why?"

"She seems to think that, given his recent breakup, my playing single girl to Gavin's lonely boy will cheer him up," Mac said.

"Oh, it'll cheer some part of him up," Carly joked. Jillian and Mac glared at her and she huffed out a breath.

"This whole thing is a recipe for disaster," Jillian said. "You realize she asked you to pair up with Gavin specifically because she trusts you so much and with the most important person

106

in the world to her save Brad. Does she not see you two as consenting adults? Whatever was she thinking?"

"She's got bridal brain," Carly said. "She wasn't."

"Well, why didn't you say no, Mac?" Jillian asked. "Or better yet, why don't you just say you changed your mind?"

"She blindsided me," Mac said. "And now I feel like it's too late. It's so close to her wedding day. I don't want to do anything that will bum her out."

The three of them were silent while they mulled over the situation.

"You know you could have told me, right?" Jillian asked.

"I know," Mac said.

"You didn't not tell me because you think I'm a 'good girl,' right?" Jillian asked. She made air quotes when she said "good girl," letting Mac know it was a sore point.

"Um, last I checked you carry tequila in your purse," Mac said. "I think any hold you had on the good girl rep is dusted and done."

"Sorry, being a pastor's daughter leaves a girl with issues," Jillian said.

Pastor Braedon, Jillian's dad, was the minister who was going to marry Mac and Seth. He was a good man, but even he had wanted to punch Seth in the face for what he'd done. Mac smiled at the memory.

"Listen, I think the simplest way to get through

this is to just run interference," Carly said. "Jillian and I will make sure over the next two weeks that you and Gavin are never alone."

Jillian nodded. "All of Emma's activities are for the whole group, minus the bridesmaid stuff, so it should be easy-peasy to Velcro ourselves to you and make it impossible for Gavin to revisit the past."

"Of course there is an alternative to this plan," Carly said.

"What's that?" Mac asked.

"You could just sleep with him again."

"Hello? Trevor. Boyfriend." Mac stood up from the bench. She was more irritated with Carly than she should be. She knew that. Carly was just being her usual bawdy self, but at her suggestion, Mac had felt a flash of heat that was impossible to ignore. She could not think of Gavin that way. She simply could not and any suggestion otherwise left her rattled.

"Fine," Carly said. She rose to her feet and pulled her jacket tight about her body. "It was just an idea, you know, to put the whole lust thing between you and Gavin to bed, as it were."

"Stop," Mac said.

"Okay, but you might want to sleep on it." Carly tried for an innocent look but failed miserably.

Mac turned to Jillian. "I'm going to choke her out. You're my witness. Tell them I was provoked."

Jillian stood up and shook her head. "Stop it, both of you. We have a plan now. Everything will be okay unless, of course, you do sleep with him again."

Mac said nothing. In fact, she was pretty sure her brain shut down in self-defense as she did not want to risk picturing Gavin or a bed or Gavin in bed or any variation on that theme whatsoever. Too late.

Like a movie loop in her head, she remembered the night in the back of his pickup truck as if it had just happened. Gavin drove her to a field on the edge of town and they'd parked between two old copper beech trees.

While Mac had cried and cried and cried, Gavin had opened up the back of the truck and tossed down a blanket so they could look at the stars while they drank from a bottle of Jack Daniels he had swiped from his father's liquor cabinet when he'd stopped at home to grab her a box of tissues.

Mac had cried until she was sure she was dehydrated. Gavin hadn't said a word. He'd listened to her cry. He'd kept one hand on her back as if just by touching her he could ease the pain and humiliation that was shredding her from the inside out.

When she'd finally run out of tears, she'd turned toward him to thank him, but the words never came. Instead, she'd been caught by surprise by the way the full moon shone on his hair, making the lighter strands glow. His gaze on hers had been steady, full of compassion and concern, and something else, something she wasn't ready to see but which felt like a balm on her wounded heart.

Mac grabbed him by the front of his dress shirt and pulled him close and then she kissed him. Gavin was still for just a breath, as if trying to grasp the fact that her lips were on his and he was deciding what he should do about it. Mac would have ended the kiss right then and there and apologized, but Gavin shoved his fingers into her elaborate hairdo and held her still while he took over the kiss, plundering her mouth with his as if he had been planning to do this very thing for years.

It had been the most amazing kiss, the most amazing night of Mac's life, and now she had to make very, very sure that it never happened again.

Chapter 9

"What was I thinking?" Emma cried. "How could I have thought I could pull this off? It's going to be a disaster! That's it! We have to cancel the wedding!"

Mac didn't bother to glance up from the Library Lover's murder mystery she was reading while sprawled on a lounge chair on Emma's back deck. This was, after all, the fourth time in as many days that Emma had threatened to cancel the wedding.

"Breathe," she said. "In through your nose for eight seconds, hold it for four, now let it out through your mouth for eight."

Emma did as she was told and then said, "But the wine . . ."

"Do it again," Mac said. When Emma was about to start talking, she added, "One more time."

Emma did as she was told while glaring at Mac at the same time.

"I'm sorry, is my crisis interrupting your reading?" Emma asked when she was finished.

Mac glanced over the top of the book at her. "Are you calmer now?"

Emma huffed out a breath. "Yes."

"Okay, good." Mac put her book aside and sat up. A movement along the bushes that formed a natural fence between Emma's yard and the neighbor's caught Mac's attention. She stared past Emma at the thick hedge. Could it be a deer or a moose? She hadn't seen either of those in the seven years she'd been gone from Maine.

A long tail stuck out of the hedge. It was brown and wagging. Mac stood and moved closer to the railing. Soft brown ears and a black nose poked out of one of the bushes.

"I thought you and Brad weren't going to get a dog just yet," she said.

"Dog? What dog?" Emma joined her at the rail just as a floppy brown puppy rolled backwards out of the bushes. "That is not my dog."

A fat, fluffy white cat pounced out of the bushes with a fierce hissing noise and her claws extended.

"And that is Mrs. Gruber's cat Snowball," Emma said.

"Really?" Mac asked. "She looks more like Satanball."

The furious white cat chased the puppy, who yelped and fled all the way across the yard until the brown and black blur disappeared into the woods beyond.

The cat stopped at the edge of the trees and paused to lick its chest, looking quite pleased with itself.

"I'm sure I've seen that dog before," Mac said. "I just can't remember where."

"Sorry for your mental collapse," Emma said, not sounding sorry at all. "But can we get back to me now? I am the bride."

Mac could tell she was only half kidding.

"Sure, what's the problem this time?"

"Wine," Emma said.

"I am not whining," Mac protested. She pushed back her Red Sox baseball hat and gave her friend an irritated look. "I have been at your beck and call for four days and I have not even sniveled, not even when you made me help you with the seating chart and place cards, not even once."

"No, not whine, wine," Emma said and made a drinking gesture with her hand.

"Oh, good idea, I'd love some," Mac said.

"Fabulous, are you willing to drive down to Portland to get it?"

"Come again," Mac said.

The back door to Emma's house banged open and Gavin stepped out onto the deck. Mac had a sudden urge to cover herself, which was ridiculous given that she was in a tank top and shorts, perfectly respectable, but the hot stare Gavin sent her when he saw her made her feel practically naked.

"Gavin, your timing is perfect," Emma said. "I need your truck."

"Okay, why?" he asked.

"Mac needs to go to Portland to pick up eight cases of wine, because the winery guy who told me he could get it delivered here in time is a big fat liar," Emma said. "This is what I get for buying local."

"Harsh," Gavin said.

"Okay, so his driver had an emergency appendectomy, still," Emma said. "I need to have it picked up today so that Brad can store it in the brewery before the wedding stager takes over the brewery to clean it up and decorate it for the reception. Believe me, we are going to need every minute of the next week and a half to get it done."

"I got like three words out of that," Gavin said. "Portland. Wine. Today."

"Good enough," Mac said. She stood up and wiggled her fingers in front of him. "Keys, please."

"Do you even know where you're going?" he asked. He held his keys just out of reach.

"GPS is my friend," Mac said. "Emma, address."

"And how are you going to lift eight cases of wine?" he asked. "Each case has, what, twelve bottles in it?"

Mac raised her arms and clenched her muscles like she was a power lifter. "I'm stronger than I look."

Gavin tapped the brim of her hat, knocking it over her eyes. "No, you're not. Come on, I'll drive."

"Oh, will you?" Emma cried at the same time Mac said, "No!"

They both looked at her and she said, "I mean, don't you have to be at work, healing sick animals and stuff?"

"Doc Scharff is covering the afternoon so I can be on call tonight," he said. "We have a goat that's about to kid out at the Peaberry farm and dollars to donuts, it will happen at three in the morning, so I'm free this afternoon."

"Perfect," Emma said. She pulled out her phone. "Okay, Mac, I'm texting you the address and then I'll text David at the winery and tell him to expect you."

She kissed Gavin's cheek and then Mac's and practically pushed them out the door, shoving Mac's big bag into her arms as they went.

"Drive safe!" she called and slammed the door shut in their faces.

Mac followed Gavin to his pickup truck with the same enthusiasm of a criminal about to be hanged. How could this have happened? She and the girls had been managing the situation so well. Four days, four, had passed and Mac and Gavin had not been alone together, not once.

What was worse, she hadn't washed her hair, thus the hat, she had no makeup on, and she was a little afraid her deodorant had worn off. She did a quick check. Nope, she was good. Well, that was something anyway. Then again, seeing her in her natural state, especially if she was smelly, might work as a repellent. Now she wished her deodorant had worn off.

She wondered if she could send an emergency text to Jillian or Carly and have them arrive in time to provide buffer. Probably not. Damn it.

Gavin drove, trying to keep his eyes on the road and not on the woman in the passenger seat beside him. It was a losing battle.

Out of the corner of his eye, he could see her plugging the address Emma had given her into her GPS app. Without makeup and half hidden under a baseball hat, she looked like she was twelve, which made him feel like a pervert for the lurid thoughts he was having about her. Clearly, it had been entirely too long since he'd been on a legit date.

The way she fussed with her phone, he could tell she was trying to avoid talking to him. He wasn't an idiot. He got it. He just wasn't going to make it easy for her.

"Turn right onto Main Street in one mile," the robotic voice of the app instructed.

"I'm pretty sure I can get us to Portland," he said. "It's once we're there that we'll need an assist."

"Oh, right," Mac said. She fumbled with her phone. "I'll just mute the bossy britches."

"Thanks," he said.

He wondered if this would be as uncomfortable as their last car ride together. Maybe he should have respected her obvious desire for space.

Why hadn't he just given her the keys? Oh, yeah, because letting a woman haul eight cases of wine seemed kind of rude and because it was the first time he'd gotten her alone in four days.

Despite his obvious ulterior motive to get her to consider him more than a pal, he was wondering how she was holding up being back in the town she hadn't set foot in since, well, that night. Yeah, he definitely didn't want to think about that or he'd start picturing her naked again.

"How is it going?" he asked. "Being back in town?"

"Fine, good, great." She nodded like she was trying to talk him into believing it.

"Did you want to pick one?" he asked.

She flashed him a smile. "Fine, it's fine."

So, she didn't want to talk about coming home. Okay. He supposed they could go back to the weather, always a safe bet, or he could nut up and confront the situation between them. He went with the latter.

"So, I almost didn't recognize you without your mushrooms," he said.

"Come again." She gave him a look.

"Carly and Jillian," he said. "They seemed to have sprouted on you like fungus."

"We're very close."

"Uh huh, I know a block when I see one."

She turned her head to look at him and opened her mouth to say something but seemed to change her mind. Then she narrowed her eyes at him.

"Carly would definitely kick your ass for calling her a fungus," Mac said.

Gavin laughed, then he frowned. He could totally see Carly whupping his behind.

"That's okay. I know you have my back. Right, buddy?" he asked.

Mac's eyebrows lifted, tipping her hat brim back just enough so he could see her warm brown eyes regarding him with . . . suspicion. Yes, it was definitely suspicion. Smart girl.

They passed through town and he turned onto Route 1. It was a mild day so he had the windows halfway down and the breeze blew into the cab of the truck, whipping the ends of her hair until she was forced to wind it into a quick braid, which she tied off with a band from her big purse.

He glanced at the voluminous bag. How much stuff did a woman need to carry for a wine pickup in Portland?

"Were you planning on spending the night?" he asked.

"I'm sorry, what?" she asked.

He pointed to her bag.

"Oh," she said. "I know it's a little bigger than normal."

"Little bigger?" he asked.

"Okay, a lot bigger," she said. "But I like to know that I have everything I need when I'm going to need it."

"Such as?"

"You want to know what's in my purse?"

"Just to make sure you're not smuggling a dead body out of town," he teased.

"I don't know. That's kind of personal, don't you think?"

"More personal than other time we've spent together?" he asked. Her eyes went wide and she looked flustered. Well, at least she wasn't immune to him. Cold comfort, but he'd take it.

"Fine," she said. She lifted her purse onto her lap and unzipped it. "Let's see; pencils, pens, hairbrush, girl stuff, wallet, sunglasses, an extra workout shirt—hey, that's where that went. I've been looking for that."

She looked at Gavin and he lowered one eyebrow in disbelief. She really carried around all of that stuff, every day? It boggled.

"Don't look like that," she chastised. "I need all of this. I also have sunscreen, a first aid kit, a blow-up neck pillow, an umbrella, my accounting calculator—"

"Stop!" Gavin said. "You have an accounting calculator in your purse?"

Mac hefted it out of her bag so he could see it. It was the size of a paperback book but looked like it weighed quite a bit more.

"I always have it with me," she said. "You never know—"

"When you're going to have to bust out a math equation?" he asked.

She dropped it back into her bag.

"Geek," he said.

"I'll have you know the preferred term is nerd," she said. Her cheeks warmed to a faint pink hue and he decided he liked being the one to make her blush.

"My apologies," he said. "Nerd, then."

"Much better," she said.

"Well, nerd girl, make with the gadget because we are arriving in Portland," he said.

Mac fumbled to turn the volume up on her phone. As the GPS commanded where to turn and when, Gavin followed its directions, trying not to get distracted by the woman beside him.

Judging by the way she'd had Jillian and Carly running defense around her the past few days, he knew he needed to let her off the hook about the two of them, even though it about killed him not to see if any of the magic that had been between them before was still there.

"You have reached your destination."

Gavin parked his truck in front of the small local winery. Before Mac could hop out, he caught her hand in his and held it until she turned to look at him.

"Listen," he said. "I just want you to know that

it's okay if you don't want to revisit the past. I shouldn't have teased you the other night and told you I was going to try to change your mind. Just friends is fine, it's better than fine. Okay?"

Mac stared down at her hand in his and then glanced up at his face. The look in her eyes made his breath catch. She looked just as fragile and vulnerable as she had all those years ago. It took every bit of self-control Gavin had to keep from pulling her close and kissing her until she didn't look so scared, until she looked at him with the same heat and longing he remembered when he'd finally made her his.

He dropped her hand and jumped out of the truck.

Chapter 10

Mac watched him through the windshield. The look on his face. Wow, just wow. If she had any doubt that there was a spark between them that look removed it. Gav looked like he'd wanted to . . . no! She wasn't going to go there.

She shoved open her door before he reached it and hopped out of the truck. The winery was located in an old brick building off of Monument Square. Wanting to put some space between them, Mac didn't wait for Gavin but hurried into the shop. Maybe she'd get lucky and the guy would offer samples.

The bells chimed on the door when Mac pushed it open. The storefront was small with only a handful of tables and counter seating along the window overlooking the street.

Bottles of wine were stacked floor to ceiling all around the room and a blackboard sign announced the specials of the day. A man in a red flannel shirt with a matching lumberjack beard was assisting a customer behind the counter. Despite his Gentle Ben appearance, he seemed to know what he was talking about in regard to wine.

"If you're serving duck, you want pinot noir, always pinot," he said to the woman in front of him.

She was tall, thin, and blonde, wearing an outfit that screamed she had paid too much for it at Nordstrom's. Her purse was a clutch, nothing like Mac's bag of tricks, and the diamond sparkler on her wrist announced her social status from three blocks away.

Mac could only see her back but even from there she knew the poor wine guy was dealing with one of those Real-Housewife-wannabe types. Someone who thought she was living a glam life while lusting after her pool man and finding drama in her kids' ballet lessons. Poor bastard.

Gavin fell in beside Mac while they waited. The bearded man glanced past the woman and smiled to acknowledge them and Mac smiled in return. The woman, clearly unhappy at losing the man's attention, glanced over her shoulder at them.

Mac gasped. She knew it had to happen sooner or later. Why not later, universe, why not later? But here it was. The woman staring at Mac like she was a wad of gum stuck on her Jimmy Choos was Jessie Peeler—correction, Jessie Connelly— the woman who had snatched Mac's groom right out of the church and drove off with him in her sporty little red convertible.

Mac wasn't sure if she was going to faint or throw up or both and not in that order. Her heart was pounding in her chest, and her breath was coming in rapid little gasps. Good grief, she was panting like a dog. She closed her eyes. She had to get a grip on herself.

She cracked one eye open. Jessie looked amazing. Her hair was perfect, her skin flawless, her outfit was the season's latest, nothing from last year for the ever fabulous Jessie Connelly. Mac glanced around the shop. The only thing that could complete this horror was if Seth was with her.

As if reading her mind, Gavin leaned down and whispered in her ear, "Don't worry. He's not."

Mac would have sagged with relief at that, but then Jessie turned all the way around. She looked Mac over and not in a nice way. "Excuse me, do I know you?"

"I don't think so," Mac said. As in all times of great stress, she opened her bag and began to root around looking for something, anything, a magic wand, a sword, really, she wasn't picky, to make the woman go away.

"No, I'm positive that I know you," Jessie persisted.

Mac wondered if she could knock her out if she crunched her on the head with her calculator. That didn't seem subtle enough. Mac kept digging.

"Gavin," Jessie said. "How good to see you. I swear you get more handsome every day. Now help me out, do I know your friend?"

Gavin coughed into his hand but Mac didn't know if it was because the woman had just called her his friend or because he was dying inside at the thought of having to introduce Mac to her own archenemy. Poor guy, she would have felt sorry for him but all of her pity was being taken up by her own needs at the moment.

"Uh, no—" Gavin began but Jessie interrupted with a gasp.

"Oh, my god, Mackenzie Harris, is that you?"

Mac thought about jumping into her bag feetfirst, then she wondered if she could knock her own self out with a punch of her calculator to the temple. Even better, maybe she could fake an urgent phone call, which she would totally do, yeah, if she could find her phone. Damn it!

"Mackenzie?" Jessie asked again.

Mac looked up. Ah, yes, here it was. Jessie Peeler Connelly was talking to her. Jessie with her designer dress and shoes, her perfectly styled blonde hair in big, bouncy waves, her makeup, which looked like a pro had spackled it on, and, of course, she still had her cute little button nose and arching eyebrows. Mac wanted to punch her in the throat.

"I'm sorry, do I know you?" Mac asked. Yeah, because she could be bitchy like that.

Jessie put her hand to her throat. She looked Mac over, taking in her bedraggled grungy state with a look in her eyes that was actually worse than scorn; it was pity.

"I am so sorry," Jessie said. "I had no idea."

"What are you talking about?" Mac asked.

Jessie gestured to Mac's big bag. "I had no idea that you were so down on your luck. Here, let me help you. It's the least I can do after what I did." Jessie opened her clutch and grabbed a wad of bills that she held out to Mac. "Please take this and use it for whatever might bring you some joy."

Mac had never actually seen anyone's head explode but judging by the pressure in her temples she was pretty sure she was about to have *brainus eruptus,* or a seizure. Hard to say. She glared at Jessie and then turned to Gavin.

"Make her go away before I do something that lands me in jail for the duration of Emma's wedding."

"Got it," Gavin said. He took Mac's arm and led her to the far corner. "Wait here."

He then headed back to the counter. Mac turned her back to them and pretended to read the labels on the bottles while she blatantly eavesdropped.

"Jessie, Mac isn't down on her luck," Gavin said. "She's fine. We're just running errands for my sister's wedding."

"Oh," Jessie said. "But she looks so . . . unkempt."

"Yes, as running errands and prepping for a huge event will do to a person sometimes," Gavin said. His tone clearly indicated that she should let it drop. "Excuse me, are you David?"

"Yes, I take it you're here for Emma Tolliver's order. So sorry about my delivery guy. Appendicitis—what can you do? I have it waiting by the side door," David said. "If you'll just sign here."

"Thanks," Gavin said.

Mac could hear the shuffling of papers and she expected Gavin to call her back, letting her know they were going now. She was more than ready.

"Oh, one more thing Jessie," Gavin said. "Mackenzie Harris is right at this moment and has been for every second that I've known her the single most desirable female walking the face of the earth. Just so you know."

Mac felt her jaw drop. Oh, no he didn't!

Before she had a chance to pull herself together, Gavin grabbed her hand and pulled her toward the side exit where two handcarts were loaded with their cases of wine.

David excused himself to Jessie and helped Gavin wheel the cases out to the truck, where Mac climbed into the bed and arranged the boxes for optimum secure transport. She couldn't look at either Gavin or David for fear that she would drop dead of mortification. She had never been sure that it was possible before, but at this moment, yes, she was sure.

When David took the carts back into the shop, Gavin climbed up into the bed of the truck with Mac.

"You okay?" he asked.

He stood next to her at the back of the truck and the look of concern in his eyes was almost Mac's undoing. She refused to crack, however. She had no more tears to shed over Jessie Peeler and Seth Connelly.

She took her baseball hat off and ran her hand through her hair as if she could wipe away the bad memory of the past fifteen minutes.

"Yeah, I'm okay," she said. "Honestly, it's good that it's finally over. I was dreading running into Jessie more than anyone else, even Seth."

"Why?" he asked. Gavin looked utterly perplexed.

"Because Jessie has been able to make me feel insecure since we were five," Mac said. "She was always poised and polished, whereas I . . ."

"Look unkempt?" Gavin teased. The dimple in his right cheek winked at her and Mac couldn't help but smile in return.

"Shush," she said. "You know, I've pictured running into her a million times. I knew it had to happen at some point. Of course, when it did, I thought I'd be, oh, *showered* leaps to mind, with hair and makeup a bonus."

Gavin laughed and Mac felt the steel bands of anxiety that had laced themselves around her chest at the sight of Jessie ease. She was actually going to live through this thanks to Gavin.

"Thank you for what you said in there." She

put a hand on his shoulder and gave it a squeeze. "That was very kind of you."

Gavin looked at her hand and then her face. The look in his baby blues scorched. Mac took her hand back and forced a laugh. She had to steer this ship back on course. Now.

"I had no idea you were such an accomplished liar," she joked.

She went to hop off the truck but Gavin grabbed her hand and spun her back around.

"I meant every word," he said. His gaze locked on hers and Mac knew there was no escaping him even if she wanted to, which she didn't.

Out of the corner of her eye, she saw a head of blonde hair, but she didn't pay any attention. Gavin pulled her in close and fast and before she could even register what the heck was happening, he was kissing her.

With one hand he cupped her face while the other spread across her lower back, pulling her in tight. Mac had no choice but to grab onto his shoulders and hang on while he slanted his mouth over hers and kissed her with a thoroughness that left her breathless and longing for more.

The smell of him, citrus and cedar, hit her low and deep like a flashpoint. Gavin, the feel of his strength against her softness and the firm press of his mouth where it met hers, wooed her into yielding to him just as it had before. She had forgotten none of it. Seven years should have dulled the memory but it was as fresh and crisp as if she had been with him just last night.

As quickly as he'd grabbed her, he released her and Mac was relieved that he seemed a little light on oxygen as well.

"What was that?" she asked, panting and trying not to.

Gavin jerked a thumb in the direction of a black Mercedes convertible that was screeching away.

"A little show for Jessie; I didn't want her to doubt me, too," he said. He cupped Mac's face and stared into her eyes as if willing her to understand that he really did consider her the most desirable woman ever. Then he grinned at her with a wicked twinkle in his baby blues. "Don't worry, we're still just friends. I get it."

He hopped to the ground and held his arms up to her. Mac was too rattled to resist and let him catch her and put her on her feet. She took a couple of shaky steps forward but managed to become fully mobile; well, at least she didn't fall on her face and make a complete ass of herself.

As Gav opened her door for her, Mac climbed back into the truck, knowing she was in deep, deep trouble.

Chapter 11

Whcried. "There's not supposed to be any kissing!"

"Yeah, that's a big no-no," Jillian agreed. "You're not even supposed to be alone with him. How did that happen?"

"Emma had a wine crisis and asked us to go to Portland to pick it up for her but whatever. Did you miss the bigger part of this?" Mac asked. "Jessie thought I was 'down on my luck' and she insinuated that it was her fault." She made air quotes with her fingers when she spat the words. "As if she and Seth could have that much of an effect on me."

"Okay, that's just funny." Carly chortled.

Mac looked to Jillian for backup, but she was obviously struggling to keep a straight face.

"I hate both of you," Mac said.

"Mackenzie Harris, is that any way to talk to your dearest friends?" Aunt Charlotte asked. She entered the room, carrying a tray of tea and jam tarts.

"I have my reasons," Mac defended herself. She rose from her seat on the sofa, took the tray from Aunt Charlotte, and set it on the large coffee table.

"But thankfully, being unkempt is not one of them," Carly said.

Mac sent Carly a blast of stink eye, which Carly ignored.

"Save a raspberry tart for me," Aunt Sarah cried as she walked past the open doorway of the sitting room carrying a guitar case. She was dressed in jeans and a T-shirt with a black leather vest and black biker boots.

"Okay. Um, you look lovely, by the way," Mac called after her.

Aunt Sarah made a shooing motion at her with her hand and never broke her stride.

"Where is she off to?" Carly asked.

"Guitar lessons," Aunt Charlotte said. She smiled. "Her teacher is a pioneer of the surf rock music sound from the early sixties."

"She's learning how to rock?" Mac asked. At least that explained the boots and the vest.

"She's rocking something," Aunt Charlotte said with a mischievous smile.

Mac was speechless. Carly, however, not so much.

"Go, Aunt Sarah, go!" Carly hooted and Mac and Jillian frowned at her.

"So, what's this about you running into Jessie Peeler?" Aunt Charlotte had always refused to use Jessie's married name of Connelly. She said it was the principle of the thing and at the moment she was making a face like she tasted something bad.

Mac explained about the encounter, leaving out the part about Gavin saying nice things about her and kissing her. No need to get Aunt Charlotte all aflutter.

"Well, I am so glad you had Gavin with you to help you through such a touchy situation," Aunt Charlotte said.

Carly sputtered her tea back into her cup and Mac gave her a warning look.

"What?" Carly said. Then she grinned. "Are you feeling touchy?"

Aunt Charlotte glanced between them, which was the only thing that prevented Mac from telling Carly off. She knew her friend was just trying to make light of the situation but to Mac there was nothing light or funny about it. When Gavin had kissed her . . . ugh, she had promised herself she wouldn't think about it. Ever.

She glanced at the food in front of her and chose a strawberry tart. She stabbed it with her fork and chewed her first bite as if it had done something to offend her. Quite the contrary, Aunt Charlotte's tarts were legend and Mac forced herself to slow down and savor the flaky crust, the creamy custard, and the sweet strawberries piled on top.

When her plate was clean, she felt infinitely better. With Aunt Charlotte in the room, the conversation veered away from the Gavin situation and Mac actually began to relax as Jillian told them stories from the bakery and Carly shared some of her adventures in underwear buying that had Aunt Charlotte in stitches.

"Men in black lace, really?" Aunt Charlotte asked. She fanned herself with a napkin. "I just can't picture it. I can't."

"Lucky you," Carly said. "I had a male model's junk right in my face as he strutted down the runway in a stretchy black lace boxer brief thing."

"You are making that up," Jillian accused.

"Hand to god," Carly said. "Lace underwear for men, it's a thing."

"We should get some for Brad as a joke," Mac said. "You know Sam and Zach would be all over that."

Carly tapped her chin with the tip of her finger. "I may have some connections."

"Oh, goodness." Aunt Charlotte blotted her eyes with her napkin. "I haven't laughed that hard in forever, but I'm afraid I have to skedaddle."

"You're going out?" Mac asked. It was already past eight o'clock. The aunts were usually in bed by now.

"Well, of course, dear, it's poetry slam night at The Grind," Charlotte said.

"Poetry slam?"

"Uh-huh," Charlotte said. "I've been working on my riff for a week."

"Your riff?"

Mac stared at Charlotte as if she'd never seen her before. It was then that she noticed Charlotte was dressed all in black, with a fitted knit top, skinny pants, and black flats. She looked like Mary Tyler Moore from *The Dick Van Dyke Show*.

Aunt Charlotte started snapping her fingers, and then she spoke in a clear chant. "I'm seventy-two—I ain't no fool/But the clock's winding down—No time for school/What I am—Ain't what I've been/So I'm living now—Before it's the end."

Carly was the first to start snapping her fingers as applause, and then Mac and Jillian joined in. Charlotte gave them a small bow and waved to them as she trotted out the front door.

"It's like I don't even know them anymore," Mac said. "Beekeeping, guitar lessons, poetry slams; I need to call my dad."

"I, for one, think it's awesome," Jillian said.

"Me, too," Carly agreed. "Way to grab life by the balls."

"Please do not use that expression in regard to my aunts," Mac said. Then she shuddered and the other two laughed.

Mac walked her friends to the door and they loitered on the porch chatting for a while when Aunt Sarah came striding up the walk with her guitar in hand. She looked flushed and had a spring in her step that Mac had never seen before. Once again, Aunt Sarah didn't break her stride as she blew past them on the way inside.

"Night, girls," she said as the door banged shut behind her.

Mac frowned after her.

"Well, at least someone around here is getting some," Carly said.

"Ack! Carly, that's my aunt," Mac said.

"Yep, and she's having a helluva lot more fun than us; well, except for maybe you," she said.

"You have to get out of the underwear industry," Mac said. "I swear all you see is sex everywhere."

"Whatever," Carly said. "I know what I saw."

"Focus, people," Jillian said. She looked at Mac. "Since Emma and Brad are meeting with my dad for their final counseling session, this is our last free night on the itinerary. We need to make a plan."

"To do what?" Carly asked. "She's already blown the operation. How was the kiss with Gavin anyway?"

"Fine, normal, okay, I guess," Mac stammered. Her heart was pounding and she could feel a telltale heat creep up her neck into her face.

"Oh, man, that means it was amazeballs," Carly said to Jillian. "Remind me again, why are we trying to cock block the poor guy?"

"Because Mac has a boyfriend," Jillian said. She wrinkled her nose, leaving no doubt as to what she thought of Trevor.

"Actually, I don't, exactly," Mac said.

"What?" Carly and Jillian cried together.

"But you said . . ." Jillian began but Carly interrupted.

"I knew it!" she crowed. "That night on the green you said 'we didn't break up, *exactly,*' and I knew something was weird. So, who did the breaking up? You or him? Please tell me it was you."

"It wasn't me," Mac said. "And we're just taking a break while he's in London, it's not even a breakup, really."

"That prick!" Carly shouted. "How could he? Does he not even realize how lucky he is that you put up with his bullshit?"

"You don't understand." Mac pressed her palm to her forehead. She loved her friends, dearly, but this was exactly why she hadn't told them about taking a break with Trevor.

Both Jillian and Carly just stared at her and she got the feeling that in their minds they understood all too well.

"Wait, if you aren't technically with Trevor, what is the problem with you and Gavin?" Carly asked.

"The problem is that Gavin is Emma's little brother," Mac said. She thought she should get points for not adding "duh" to her comment. "Emma is so protective of him; she'd be so pissed if we hooked up. How could I do that to her?"

"You don't know that she'd be pissed," Jillian said. She sounded doubtful but she forged on. "I mean maybe she'd be happy that her brother and her best friend are hooking up."

"But what if she isn't?" Mac asked. "Her wedding is in a matter of days. Can I really risk ruining it for her by getting involved with Gavin?"

Both Carly and Jillian looked pensive. Clearly, no one knew how Emma would take it and that proved to Mac that it was definitely not worth the risk.

"All right, I see your point, but I have to ask, what happened after you kissed him?" Carly asked. She looked eager for details.

"He said we were still just friends, that he did it because of Jessie," Mac said.

"Do you believe him?"

"Yes, mostly," Mac said.

"Okay, for the next week and a half, you have to maintain the perimeter," Carly said. "Be friendly but not too friendly, be nice but not too nice, you get the picture."

"Got it," Mac said.

"And absolutely no being alone with him, call us for backup," Jillian said. "Even if it's awkward—agreed?"

"Agreed," Mac said.

She hugged her friends and waved as they headed down the driveway. It occurred to her that she hadn't talked to Trevor since she'd left Chicago. Even though they were technically on a break, that seemed wrong. She went inside to call him but then did a quick time change in her head and calculated it would be the middle of the night in London. She'd call him tomorrow.

She realized she was relieved that she didn't have to talk to him. Again, that seemed wrong and she wondered if it was guilt about the kiss with Gavin that made her want to avoid Trevor. No, the kiss had been a spontaneous thing done by Gavin to tweak Jessie. It hadn't meant anything.

Mac pressed her fingertips to her lips. Okay, so it had rocked her world. So what? She had a history with Trevor, a life together in Chicago that she valued. Gavin was still her best friend's little brother. And while Emma wanted Mac to cheer Gavin up, it was a far cry from what Mac wanted to do to him when she allowed herself to think about it, which was why she didn't allow it.

She cleared away the plates from the sitting room and tidied the kitchen. As she was climbing the stairs to her bedroom, she thought about the day's events and knew that her friends were right, the best offense was to keep her distance from Gavin.

Mac knew that if anything more than a spur of the moment smooch happened between them, it would be like letting out a genie that she couldn't shove back into the bottle. And this genie was a wrathful djinn who would likely destroy Mac's relationship with her best friend and that was too high of a price to pay no matter how good of a kisser Gavin was. She felt a flash of heat cook her from the inside out. Yeah, it was time for a cold shower.

Mac closed the door to her room and thought about what to say to Trevor when she talked to him. Was she obligated to mention kissing Gavin? She didn't think so; after all, they were on a break. Besides, she had told Trevor that she was paired with Emma's little brother for the wedding.

Trevor didn't know about their past encounter; it hadn't seemed relevant before, but Mac had confided in him about feeling uneasy about Emma's request that she bolster her baby brother's spirits by being his quasi date. Trevor had thought it was hilarious that her role as maid of honor included a babysitting stint. Now she wondered if she should have confided in him more fully. Would he have cared enough to be here? She honestly didn't know.

Twelve more days. She just had twelve more days until she was back in Chicago, riding the L back to her corporate job in the Loop. Usually, just the thought of riding the elevator to her corner office would have filled Mac with a surge of excitement, but at the moment she wasn't feeling it. It had to be anxiety, numbing her usual workaholic buzz. She just had to get through the wedding without damaging any of her relationships and all would be well.

She flopped onto her bed and stared up at the ceiling. Surely, she could manage that. Right?

Mac was running late. She hadn't been able to sleep and when she finally did, her dreams had been full of naughty images of Gavin that made her feel hot and dirty at the same time. Clearly, she was losing her mind.

She threw back a cup of cold coffee and grabbed a granola bar out of the pantry. She had promised to meet Emma at the hairdresser's on Main Street to help Emma pick the hairstyle that would go best with her veil. Jillian was working in her bakery so it was left to Carly and Mac to help Emma. Because Carly tended to like extreme styles, Emma was counting on Mac to be the voice of reason.

"You look terrible," Aunt Sarah said as Mac banged out of the front door. Sarah was reading the paper and enjoying her coffee while relaxing on the porch swing.

"Thanks," Mac said. "I was going for awful, but terrible works."

"Again with the sass." Aunt Sarah tutted. "Slow down before you trip and break your neck."

Mac paused to tug on her tennis shoes. "I have

a feeling a broken neck is the only excuse that will be accepted if I am late for Emma's hair appointment."

"Well, you won't be of much use to her if you're damaged," Aunt Charlotte said.

Mac wanted to ask them both about their evenings out, but then she thought about what they might share and realized, no, she didn't. With a wave, she bolted down the steps to the driveway.

She shoved the granola bar in her bag and hurried down the street. She knew the hairdresser's was on the far side of the town square, so she took a shortcut in between two houses that led to an alley that would cut her trip in half.

Mac turned into the alley and was striding quickly down the uneven pavement when she heard a fierce growl that made the hair on the back of her neck stand on end. She stopped and slowly turned to her right.

There, behind a Dumpster next to the shattered remains of what looked like several pots of tulips, was a brown dog, baring its teeth and looking like it wanted to rip Mac's throat out.

Chapter 12

Easy, boy," Mac said. Her heart thumped hard in her chest and she glanced at the end of the alley to determine if she could escape if she ran. She had visions of trying and having the dog chase her down and clamp its powerful jaws on her leg or her throat. She'd never make it.

She glanced back at the dog. It growled, keeping low to the ground. Only its big, blocky head was visible from its spot behind the Dumpster, and she couldn't tell how big the dog actually was except that it definitely wouldn't fit in her purse and that was saying something. Oh, man. Why couldn't she be snarled at by a Yorkie or a Shih Tzu?

She took a cautious step away and the dog growled, deeper and meaner. Then Mac heard a thumping sound. The dog crept forward and she noticed it was brown and black with a white chest. Was it wagging its tail? What was that supposed to mean?

Mac had never had a dog for a pet. Growing up she'd had a cat, an orange tabby named Chubby who lived happily in the family home for seventeen years. When he'd died, she knew she could never love another pet as much as him so she'd never gotten another.

With her limited knowledge base on canines, she knew that growling was bad but wagging was good. Or so she thought. Maybe the dog was wagging because he planned to make her his lunch. Yeah, that settled it. Mac took another step away. The dog growled and it rumbled low and deep from its chest.

Okay, so the stepping away thing wasn't really working for the dog. She stood still and studied the face staring at her from its hiding spot. One of its ears flopped down across its head and Mac recognized the puppy she had seen in Emma's backyard.

"Oh, hey, I know you," she said. The dog wagged, thumping its tail against the side of the Dumpster. "Are you all right?"

The dog whimpered and she felt her heart clutch in her chest; maybe the poor guy was hurt.

"Listen, I don't speak dog," Mac said. She knew she sounded nervous and she suspected that was bad form. She glanced around her, looking for anyone to help. There was no one, just her, the dog, and a bunch of smashed tulips.

Mac took a deep breath and willed herself to calm down. If animals could sense fear then she needed to get a grip on hers. She noticed the dog hadn't moved. Maybe it was injured. She had to get a better look. She slowly crouched down, watching how it reacted to her.

"It's okay," she said. She kept her voice soft

and kind, hoping the dog could sense she meant no harm. "I'm not going to hurt you."

The dog whimpered and then wagged. Mac studied the dog's face. Despite the very canine teeth, the dog had pretty brown eyes, a stubby black nose, and now that Mac was close enough, she could see the faint black stripes in its brown fur, making it a brindle. It also had a collar. Excellent.

If it had an owner, it could be friendly. Mac wondered how long it had been in the alley; maybe it had been lost since she'd seen it at Emma's. No, wait. Her memory clicked and she remembered seeing the dog in the horse field on the very day she had arrived in town.

Mercy! Had the poor thing been lost all this time? It was probably starving. She wished she had a dog treat, but then she remembered her granola bar. Maybe some food would make the dog trust her enough to come out from behind the Dumpster.

She carefully reached into her purse and pulled out the granola bar. She took off the wrapper and noticed that the dog never looked away from her.

"Are you hungry?" she asked. "It probably tastes like rocks and sticks to you, but it is food, I swear."

Mac held out her hand with a bit of the granola bar in it. The dog stared at her. She moved closer and the dog lowered itself to the ground, making Mac tense up, and then it wagged.

"You're really giving me mixed signals here," Mac said.

She inched closer, stopping a couple of feet short of reaching the dog. She didn't know what she'd do if the dog attacked her at this point. Die, she supposed. With that in mind, she redoubled her effort to get the dog to trust her.

"I promise I'm not going to hurt you," she said softly. She kept her hand steady, holding the food out. "I just want to make sure you're okay and I'll try and get you back to your people. I won't hurt you. I promise. You're going to be okay."

Mac's legs were beginning to cramp and she was sure she and the dog were going to be in this stalemate until nightfall when the dog moved. It belly crawled toward her just a few inches and stopped.

"Good dog," Mac said. "That's right. You can trust me. Come on. It'll be okay."

The dog crawled forward again, stopping just in front of Mac's hand. Mac waited and watched. The dog's tail was still wagging and its ears were flopped to one side. The warm brown eyes never left Mac's face. She really wished she could tell what the puppy was thinking.

She swallowed, trying to stay calm while waiting to see what the dog would do. To Mac's surprise, the dog nudged the granola bar aside with its cold nose and pressed the top of its head into the palm of her hand.

"Oh," Mac said softly.

The dog's head felt like warm velvet beneath her fingers and it looked up at Mac from beneath her hand with big brown eyes that seemed to have witnessed a world of hurt.

"It's okay, baby," Mac said. "You're going to be okay."

The dog made a deep shuddering sigh as if it was psyching itself up for something, then it cautiously climbed into Mac's lap. The dog's posture was rigid as if bracing for rejection. There was no question it was taking a huge leap of faith in trusting her. Mac felt her throat get tight and as she looked into the dog's earnest face, she could see the pretty eyes imploring, *Please don't hurt me!*

"It's okay, you're safe now," Mac said. She cautiously hugged the dog close until she felt it relax against her. She gently stroked the dog's side, giving it a minute to adjust to her. When Mac glanced down at the dog in her arms, its pink tongue flicked out and caught Mac on the chin. Mac smiled as she wiped the spit away.

Okay, now what? Mac carefully checked its collar for tags. Naturally, there were none. She did a mental assessment of what she had in her purse. Amazingly, there was nothing she could use as a leash. She didn't want to risk losing the dog, or worse, having it run out into traffic, so she figured she'd have to carry it.

Mac hefted the dog and her bag up into her arms. The dog had to be a solid twenty-five pounds but it let Mac lift it without protest. Great.

Mac glanced down at the end of the alley. Gavin's veterinary clinic was one street over from here. Surely, she could make it there, and with any luck at all it would be Dr. Scharff on duty and not Gavin. Mac supposed she could turn around and take the dog home, but if anyone would know who it—she glanced down at the dog—okay, who *she* belonged to, it would be Gavin or Dr. Scharff.

By the time she got to the office, her arms were shaking and she was afraid she was going to drop the dog. Mercifully, the automatic door slid open when Mac stepped onto the mat and she entered the waiting room, which was empty.

She passed several chairs and approached the high counter at the end of the room. She couldn't see anyone behind it, but she forged on.

"Hello?" she cried.

A gentle snore was the only answer she got. Huh?

The counter was wide so Mac used it to set down the dog, who immediately leaned into her. Mac wrapped her arms around her so she would feel secure.

"Hello?" Mac called again.

She glanced over the counter and found Gavin, dead asleep on the desktop in front of him. He'd made a pillow out of his arms and his pale brown hair flopped over his forehead. His lips were slightly parted and Mac thought she spotted a tiny bit of drool in the corner of his mouth. He was snoring very quietly. His face was relaxed in sleep, making him look like the innocent little boy she had once known.

She figured the Peaberry's goat had kidded in the wee hours of the morning as Gavin had predicted. Mac didn't want to wake him. She wondered if she should just take a seat and let him have his power nap.

A sudden shrill chime sounded from her bag, making Mac jump, the dog growl, and Gavin snap awake all at the same time.

"Sorry," Mac cried. "I'm sorry."

"Huh, what?" Gavin blinked at her. "Mac? A dog? Am I still dreaming?"

"No," Mac said. She kept one arm around the dog while she searched her bag for her phone. She grabbed it and held it up to her ear. "What?"

"Mac, where are you?" Emma cried. "You were supposed to be here fifteen minutes ago."

"I know, I'm sorry," Mac said. "I found a dog."

Gavin stood, rubbed his face, and then held

his hand out to the dog. She thumped her tail on the counter and pressed her head into his hand, welcoming his attention.

"A dog, what? Here, talk to Carly," Emma said. "My hairdresser needs my scalp."

"Mac, what are you doing?" Carly asked. She sounded amused.

"I rescued a dog," Mac said.

"Let's take her into an exam room," Gavin said as he lifted the dog out of Mac's arms. "I can give her a proper once-over there."

"Ooh, a proper once-over sounds naughty," Carly said.

"Shut up," Mac said. Gavin frowned at her and she cringed. "Sorry, not you, Carly."

He nodded as if this made perfect sense and led the way into a small room off of the lobby. The puppy popped her head over his shoulder as if looking to make sure Mac was following.

"Listen, I have to go," Mac said.

"Wait," Carly said. "You aren't supposed to be on your own with you know who."

Her voice was low and Mac imagined she was trying not to let Emma overhear their conversation.

"I know, but there are extenuating circumstances," she said. "Besides, technically, I'm not alone."

"Whatever," Carly said. "I hope you know what you're doing."

"I do," Mac lied. "It'll be fine. Tell Emma I'll get there as soon as I can."

"All right, smell ya later," Carly said and hung up.

Mac went into the exam room and found Gavin sitting on the floor with the dog. She was hunkered low to the ground and looking very nervous. Mac dropped her bag on a chair and got down on the floor, too.

She glanced at Gavin as the puppy wiggled into her lap. "Sorry we woke you. I was just going to grab a chair and wait while you got some shut-eye."

"Nah, it's fine," he said. He looked exhausted and it was all Mac could do not to offer to let him rest his head in her lap. Good thing the dog was already there. "So, what do we have here?"

"I have no idea," Mac said. "I found her crouched in the alley that runs between First and Third Streets. She was sitting in a pile of broken flowerpots that once had tulips in them, half hidden behind a Dumpster."

Gavin made a concerned face. "Tulip bulbs are poison for dogs. Any chance you noticed if she ate any?"

"No, it looked like she'd gnawed on some of the flowers and stems, but I don't know about the bulbs."

"If she did, she could have an upset stomach, drooling, depression, tremors, or heart problems," he said.

Mac lifted the dog's chin and looked her in the eye. "Did you do that?"

The dog wagged her tail and licked Mac's chin.

Mac looked at Gavin. "She's not talking."

He smiled. "After I examine her, you can show me where you found her. We might be able to tell if she ate anything bad or not."

"Thanks," Mac said. "I really appreciate this."

"No worries," he said. "It's what I do."

He stood up and opened a cabinet. He took out a stethoscope and a thermometer. Then he crouched back on the floor with Mac and the dog.

"She seems to trust you," he said. "Can you hold her and talk to her while I check her over?"

Mac nodded. Gavin ran his hands over the dog, checking her legs and paws. He then checked her sides, her back, and her neck. When he leaned close to examine her ears, she turned her head and licked his face. Gavin smiled at her and gave her a gentle scratch beneath the chin.

"You're a sweet girl, aren't you, love?" he asked.

His voice was so gentle and kind, it made Mac want to climb into his lap and have him scratch her under the chin. She glanced at the puppy and noted she was staring at Gavin with a look of worship. Apparently, his charm was not limited to females of the human persuasion.

Mac wondered if she'd looked at Gavin like that when he'd run his hands over her all those years ago. Then she cleared her throat and glanced away. She had to get a grip. There was no point in going there, none at all.

"She's young, maybe three months old judging by her teeth. She hasn't been spayed, and she doesn't seem to have any injuries, so overall she's looking good," he said.

Mac nodded, not trusting herself to speak.

Gavin continued his examination. The stethoscope portion went fine, but the dog did not like the rectal thermometer, not at all.

"I know it's very rude of him, isn't it?" Mac asked the dog, who had begun to growl. "But it's just to make certain that you're okay. Gav's a good guy, I promise."

"Huh, I don't think I've ever had a person vouch for me to their animal before," Gavin said. "Thanks for that." The thermometer beeped and he checked it. "Her temp is fine. She's a little on the thin side but otherwise okay."

"Good." Mac sighed. The dog, sensing her exam was over, flopped onto her back and gave Mac a decidedly sassy look.

"She likes you," Gavin said. "What are you going to do with her?"

Mac frowned. "I don't know. Call a dog shelter, I guess. I mean, the aunts are too old to take on a puppy, and I'm not going to be here much longer."

Gav didn't say anything, but Mac could tell there was something on his mind.

"What?" she asked. "What are you thinking?"

"I don't want to tell you what to do," he said. He dropped the disposable thermometer sleeve into the biohazard bucket and put the thermometer and stethoscope on the counter.

"But?"

Gavin sighed. "You might want to foster her for a while and see if you can find someone to adopt her as an animal shelter may not go well for her."

"Why?" Mac asked. "She's so cute. I'm sure she must have a family who loves her and is looking for her."

"Maybe, but she doesn't have a microchip or tags," he said. "She's awfully young, so I'm thinking . . ."

He hesitated and Mac wondered what he was holding back.

"Out with it," she said. "What aren't you telling me?"

"Since you found her in an alley," he said. "I suspect that she might have been thrown out."

"Like with the garbage?" Mac gasped and hugged the dog close. "Who could do such a thing? She's adorable."

"Some people do shitty things to animals," he said. He looked so much older than his twenty-seven years. Mac wondered how many times he'd seen a dog thrown out or worse.

"But Tulip is so young, she's just a baby," Mac protested.

"Tulip?"

"Seems appropriate." She shrugged.

He grinned, then he looked sad. "Here's the other bit of bad news. She's a mutt so it's not like someone lost an expensive pedigree dog and will want her back. She's got the big, blocky head and broad shoulders of an Amstaff, an American Staffordshire terrier, and the shorter nose of a Boxer, but whatever else is in there, I have no idea."

"Wait. She's part 'pit bull'?" Mac asked. She looked at the adorable goofball in her arms. She had heard stories of pit bull attacks and she remembered how she'd felt when Tulip had first growled at her. Scared.

"Yes, it's a pretty umbrella term that covers a couple of breeds, but her head and shoulders are definitely from that lineage," Gav said. "If she goes to a shelter she has a one in six hundred chance of being adopted, which means she'll likely be euthanized."

"As in put to sleep?" The words squeezed around Mac's insides like a giant fist, making it hard to breathe.

"Yeah," Gavin said. He looked grim.

Chapter 13

No, just no," Mac said. She stood and Tulip pressed herself against Mac's leg as if to make sure Mac didn't forget her. She reached down and scratched Tulip's head. "That's not happening to you. Not on my watch."

"Mac, I can keep her here and try to find a home for her," Gavin said.

Mac knew that was the practical solution. Gavin was tapped into the local dog lover community in ways she never would be, but when she glanced down at Tulip she just couldn't do it. She couldn't foist her off like she was a nuisance or a burden.

"Thanks, but if you have a leash I could buy or borrow, that'd be great," Mac said.

"If you're actually going to take her, you're going to need stuff," Gavin said. He led the way out of the exam room to a display of pet care items on the wall in the lobby. He handed Mac a leash.

She bent over and clipped the leash onto Tulip's boring beige collar. "Such as?"

"Food, bowls, a bed, toys, and treats for bribing good behavior out of her might be a good idea," he said.

Mac fished through her big bag and pulled out her wallet. She took out her bank card and handed it to him. "Can I buy it all from you?"

Gavin shook his head. "I'm not taking your money."

"Uh, yes, you are," she said. "Come on, I need this stuff and you have it."

"But you are . . ." He paused as if he didn't know what to call her and an abrupt awkwardness fell between them with all the subtlety of a cartoon anvil.

"A client," Mac said assertively.

Gavin looked as if he'd argue, but the door opened and Mrs. Carson walked in carrying two large cat carriers. Judging by the yowling coming from the carriers, the cats were not happy about their confined situation.

Gavin hurried forward and took the carriers from her hands. "Good morning, Mrs. Carson."

"Thank you, dear, you're—"

Whatever Mrs. Carson had been about to say was interrupted by Tulip as she began to bark and jump at the carriers in Gavin's hands. Mac dug in her heels and held Tulip back while Gavin set the carriers up onto the high counter out of Tulip's reach.

"Oh, my," Mrs. Carson said. She put her hand to her throat as if she were afraid Tulip was going to go for it.

"Don't worry," Mac said, using all of her strength to hold Tulip back. "She's just an exuberant puppy."

Thankfully, Tulip was wagging as she hopped up on her back legs, trying to get to the cats.

"I'm off for lunch soon," Gavin said. He scooped Tulip up in his arms. "How about I drop off what you need at your house then?"

Mac dropped her credit card onto the desk behind the counter. "Thanks and be sure to bill me."

Gavin looked like he'd argue but Tulip began to wiggle in his arms so he had to hustle her out the door with Mac trailing behind holding the handle of the leash. Once outside, he set her on the ground and Tulip immediately began to sniff the area around the door.

"Are you sure you can handle her?" he asked. Mac made a muscle with her free arm and Gavin smiled. "Yeah, I know you're stronger than you look."

"And don't you forget i—" Whatever Mac had been about to say was lost as Tulip decided it was time to go and dragged her up the side-walk.

"I'll be by at noon," Gavin yelled after them.

Mac barely had time to wave before Tulip hauled her around the corner and out of sight. The walk back to Mac's house wasn't a walk so much as a drag, with Tulip dragging Mac up the street and Mac having to redirect Tulip from going in the wrong direction.

When Mac decided to cut back through the

alley, Tulip planted her haunches on the ground and refused to budge. Mac tried coaxing her past the Dumpster where she'd found her, but Tulip was having none of it. When Mac stroked her back to calm her, she discovered Tulip was trembling. She immediately crouched down on Tulip's level.

"Hey, there, baby girl," she cooed. "It's okay. We're just walking by. I need to check and make sure you didn't eat anything bad."

At the word *bad,* Tulip dropped to her belly and looked like she wanted to scuttle away. Mac realized the poor dog had heard the word before and not in a good way. She knew she couldn't force the dog any closer to the smashed flowerpots, so she tied her to another porch rail and quickly hurried across the alley to check out the refuse.

There wasn't much left of the flowers and Mac suspected that Tulip had climbed onto the back steps of the real estate office and accidentally knocked the pots off the stoop.

She searched through the soil and found several bunches of roots. It didn't look like any of them had been gnawed; still, she'd keep an eye on Tulip and make sure she didn't show any symptoms of distress.

Mac knocked on the back door, but the office appeared to be empty. She highly doubted that the Realtors who worked in the office had tossed a puppy in the alley, but maybe they had seen someone or something. Mac decided she would pop in later for a chat.

Mac crossed back to the dog and untied her. Tulip pressed against her and Mac scooped her into her arms. She knew the only way Tulip was going to get past the Dumpster was if Mac carried her.

She walked to the end of the alley before she put Tulip down and when she did, Tulip rose on her back legs and licked Mac's face, catching her right on the lips.

"Oh, ugh!" Mac laughed. "We're going to have to discuss some boundaries, Miss Tulip, let's start with no open-mouth kisses, m'kay?"

Tulip's tongue hung out the side of her mouth and one of her ears flopped over the top of her head. She bounded forward, eager to leave her traumatic past behind.

"I hear that," Mac muttered as she hurried to follow her.

They sped up the gravel drive to home to find Aunt Sarah puttering in the front flower bed while Aunt Charlotte was exactly where she'd been before, reading the newspaper while relaxing on the porch swing.

Seeing new people to love, Tulip leapt and twisted, trying to break free of Mac's hold. At the commotion both sisters looked up and although they generally looked nothing alike, they now wore matching expressions of dismay as Mac and Tulip approached.

"What is that?" Sarah asked.

"This is Tulip," Mac said. "She's going to be staying with us for a while."

"A dog?" Charlotte asked. "You got a dog?"

Tulip went to jump on Sarah, who frowned at her and said, "No!"

Tulip immediately sat down, her tail thumping the ground as she looked at Sarah for approval.

"How did you do that?" Mac asked.

"Sarah is a natural alpha," Charlotte said.

Tulip glanced up at her and jumped toward her.

"No," Charlotte said and Tulip leapt at her again, forcing Mac to tighten her grip on the leash.

"You have to say it like you mean it," Sarah said. She stepped in front of Tulip and said, "No."

Tulip immediately sat back down. Sarah held out her hand and Mac put the leash in it. Sarah reined Tulip in tight and led her up the stairs to meet Charlotte.

"I didn't know you knew anything about dogs," Mac said.

"Duh," Sarah said. Mac blinked. When had Sarah picked up the vernacular of a middle schooler? "I have friends with dogs."

When they approached Charlotte, Tulip tried to jump onto the swing with her but when it moved,

Tulip hit the ground like a bomb had just gone off.

Mac crouched down beside her. "It's okay. It's just a swing."

She sat on the top step of the porch and Sarah sat beside her. Tulip wriggled across the floor until she was wedged in between them. Then she glanced up at them with her tongue hanging out, looking ridiculously happy.

"Poor thing must be thirsty," Charlotte said. "I'm going to get her a bowl of water."

She eased off of the swing and slipped inside. Mac's phone began to chime in her purse. She glanced at the display and saw it was Emma and that Emma had already called her five times, in fact.

"Weren't you on veil duty?" Sarah asked.

"Tulip put the kibosh on that plan," Mac said.

"Tulip? She didn't bite you for that?" Aunt Sarah asked.

"Trust me, it fits," Mac said. She thought about the broken pots in the alley and hoped she was right that Tulip hadn't eaten any of the bulbs or roots or whatever it was Gavin was worried about.

Aunt Sarah shrugged. "It's your dog."

"What? No," Mac said. "I just found her tossed out in an alley. I'm only fostering her until we find her people or a forever home."

"Uh-huh," Sarah said.

The screen door opened and Charlotte arrived with a big plastic bowl full of water. She put it down on the side of the porch and Tulip watched her as if she hoped it might be for her.

"Come on, doggy," Charlotte said.

"Her name's Tulip," Sarah corrected her.

"For real?" Charlotte asked.

Mac rolled her eyes. "It's just temporary. I can't call her Dog."

Tulip didn't move so Mac got up and led her over to the bowl of water. Tulip slurped up a bellyful and then flopped down onto a patch of sunlight. Mac marveled at the way the darker stripes of hair gave her coat a tiger stripe–like look to it. She really was a beautiful dog.

"So, what's the plan?" Sarah asked. Mac resumed her seat beside her and Charlotte joined them.

"Gav is bringing some supplies over on his lunch hour," Mac said. "Then I guess I need to figure out if she belongs to anyone and if not find someone who wants her."

"Because you don't?" Sarah asked.

"It's not that I don't so much as it's just not practical," Mac said. "How would I get her back to Chicago? And that's just for starters."

"Yeah, blah, blah, blah," Sarah said. "You could make it work."

"Maybe," Mac said. "But I don't know how Trevor feels . . ."

"Who cares how he feels?" Sarah interrupted.

"Sarah!" Charlotte chided her sister.

"What? It's not like they live together," Sarah said. "I don't think he has any say if she wants a dog."

"His opinion matters to Mac," Charlotte argued.

"Why?" Sarah asked. She gave Mac a searching look. "Why do you care what he thinks?"

Chapter 14

Whoa, whoa, whoa," Mac said and held up her hands. "This has nothing to do with Trevor or what he thinks. We're jumping way ahead here. First, we need to see if she belongs to anyone."

"I thought you found her thrown out in an alley?" Sarah said.

"Possibly thrown out," Mac said. "I took her to see Gavin, and he says she's a puppy so she could have escaped her yard and then got lost."

"What else did Gavin say?" Charlotte asked.

"He thinks if she goes to a shelter, she'll be put down because she is a mutt with an undesirable breed in the mix," Mac said. "That's why I have to find a home for her. I mean look at her. She's a perfectly lovely dog."

They all glanced over to where Tulip was napping. She was ridiculously cute.

"Mac, why haven't you answered my calls?" Emma cried as she strode up the gravel driveway with Carly at her side. "I must have called like six times."

"Sorry," Mac said. "I found a dog."

"Told you so," Carly said to Emma as they stopped below the steps.

"Dog?" Emma asked. "What dog?"

Mac pointed to the passed-out puppy at the end of the deck.

"Oh, she's adorable," Emma said. "Did you have Gavin check her out?"

Mac could feel Carly's beady-eyed stare on the side of her face, but she ignored her and focused on Emma.

"I did," she said. "He thinks she's in good health, though I have to keep an eye on her in case she ate anything funky while she was on her own."

As if sensing she was the topic of conversation, Tulip roused herself and ambled across the deck to wedge herself tight against Mac's hip. She lifted her head and plopped it in Mac's lap before she dropped back into dreamland. Mac had the feeling Tulip had been checking to make sure she was still there, like she was just making sure of her. The thought made her heart hurt.

She put her hand on Tulip's head and said, "I guess I have to make some flyers with her picture and post them in town to see if anyone is missing their dog."

Mac wondered if everyone heard the reluctance in her voice or if it was just her.

Carly rubbed Tulip's head and said, "I can help."

"Me, too," Emma said.

"Don't you have wedding stuff to do?"

"Nah, Carly picked the perfect hairdo to go

with my veil; she convinced my hairdresser to do a half-up half-down sort of thing," Emma said.

"Cool," Mac said.

She felt the teensiest bit displaced by Carly but then she was relieved. The wedding thing really wasn't her bag as she had avoided any and all things to do with nuptials since her own imploded.

She often thought if she could have back just a few of the hundreds of hours she had spent picking invitations, flowers, music, cake—yeah, she could have learned to play an instrument or have a solid first draft of a novel done.

"Good, you're here," Gavin called through the open window of his big black pickup truck as he pulled into the driveway.

Tulip, who had been dead asleep moments before, heard his voice and rocketed off the deck and galloped straight for her new best friend. Gavin opened the door of the truck and crouched down, letting her love all over him.

"What is it about a handsome man with a dog that gets my heart all aflutter?" Charlotte asked.

"I hear that," Carly said with an appreciative sigh.

Mac looked at Gavin and noted the way his biceps bunched beneath his T-shirt sleeves when he picked the puppy up for a hug. His large hand was ever so gentle as it caressed Tulip's head.

Mac felt a flash of heat and she cleared her throat as if she could cough it out.

"Tulip," Mac called the puppy. "Come here, let the poor man alone."

Gavin put the puppy down and grabbed a large bundle out of the back of his truck. He carried it over to the porch and put it on the steps at Mac's feet. Then he reached into his back pocket and handed her the credit card she had left with him.

"For services rendered?" Carly asked, making it sound tawdry. Mac gave her a dark look but Carly didn't look the least bit repentant.

"How has she been?" he asked.

"She drank water and napped and has seemed very happy," Mac said.

"She's a little rambunctious," Sarah said. "But nothing a good obedience class won't cure."

Gav gave Mac an intrigued look. "Planning to take her to school?"

"Not me," she said. "That will be up to her forever people."

"Ah," he said. He pressed his lips together as if to keep from saying anything else. Then he turned to Emma and said, "Hey, Sis, maybe you can adopt her."

Emma's eyes went wide. "I'd love to, really, but Brad and I will be gone for a month on our honeymoon. So, you know, sorry."

Mac looked at Carly, who shook her head.

"No dogs allowed in my building in Brooklyn."

Before Mac could even look their way, Charlotte spoke up.

"No," Charlotte said. "She'd probably outlive us which would be unfair to her."

"Speak for yourself," Sarah snapped. "Although, in all fairness, she'd probably be happier with a younger family."

"Okay, then, 'found puppy' posters it is," Mac said. She tried not to look at Tulip when she said it as it made her feel guilty.

"Make sure you drop one off at the office," Gavin said. "I can put it up and see if anyone recognizes her."

"Thanks," Mac said. She gestured to the bundle that Tulip was sniffing. "For everything."

"No problem," he said. "I'll call to check on her later."

"Hey, don't forget tonight we all have dance lessons at Ms. Poole's," Emma said. "Seven o'clock sharp."

This was one of the many items on the itinerary that Mac had been dreading. Dance lessons for the wedding party? Had Emma gone completely insane? She glanced at her friend. Yes, it was clear from the crazy light in her blue eyes that she had.

Mac had been trying for days to figure out how she was going to get out of it. Dancing cheek to cheek with Gavin for two hours; yeah, like that wasn't going to kill her. She'd even contemplated faking a sprain.

Tulip pawed the bag at her feet, and Mac had a sudden flash of brilliance. She was so relieved she almost hugged the puppy to her chest. She resisted, barely.

"Yeah, about tonight"—she paused to gesture at Tulip—"I don't think I'm going to make it. I mean I have to hang the 'found puppy' signs and I can't leave her alone on her first night here. She'll freak out."

"But you have to come," Emma said. "It's the whole wedding party. We're going to learn to waltz so we don't look like tools at the reception. It'll be fun."

Mac glanced at Gavin and felt her insides spasm. Fun was not the first adjective that leapt to mind when she thought of being in his arms.

"Sorry but puppy," Mac said. She noticed Carly wasn't backing her up, so she gave her a meaningful look and her friend got the hint.

"That is too bad," Carly said. "Maybe we should cancel. I mean I've got my sick dance moves down and Zach seems to be able to keep up with me. Do we really need lessons?"

Emma looked horrified and Mac couldn't blame her. Having the electrocuted chicken owning the dance floor at your wedding would terrify even the mellowest of brides, which Emma was not.

170

"No, you all should definitely go on without me," Mac said.

She forced herself to look at Gavin in an effort to appear casual. He was looking at her with understanding, which made her feel like a heel for using the puppy to avoid being close to him. Here he thought she was devoted to the dog and she was really just using her as an avoidance tactic. She was a horrible person.

"Don't be ridiculous," Sarah said. "I don't have any plans tonight, I can watch the puppy."

"And I can help," Charlotte chimed in.

"Oh, no, I couldn't ask that of you, I mean she's so active and you're . . ." Mac's voice trailed off.

"If you say old, I swear I'll tan your backside," Sarah said.

"Uh, no, I was thinking more like, um . . ."

"You should probably stop talking now," Charlotte said.

Mac closed her mouth.

"Excellent," Emma said. "Don't forget to wear a dress and your shoes for the wedding. We can break them in." She turned to look at her brother. "That goes for you, too."

"A dress?" he asked. "I don't really think I have the legs for that. Knobby knees, you know."

Mac chuckled even though there was truly nothing funny about the situation. She noticed the others did as well. Good looking and charming and kind to animals—why couldn't Emma's brother have the manners of a bridge troll and look like reanimated roadkill? Truly, the whole situation was utterly unfair.

"Why don't Emma and I help you with the 'found puppy' signs now?" Carly offered. Mac gave her a look and she shrugged.

"Yeah, we can totally do that," Emma said.

"There's not enough time to do that and then get to—" Mac began but Gavin interrupted her.

"If it will help you out time wise and put your mind at ease, I can pick you up on the way to Ms. Poole's. You'll have time to hang your signs and I can give Tulip a once-over before we go," Gav said.

"No, that's not—" Mac refused but Emma was louder when she said, "That's wonderful. Thanks, bro."

"No worries," he said. "See you tonight."

They all called good-bye after him and watched as he drove away. Tulip looked from the truck to Mac and back as if concerned that he was leaving.

"Don't worry," Mac said. "He'll be back."

Tulip thumped her tail on the porch and looked delighted. Mac rubbed her ears and tried to squelch the part of her that was also eager to see Gavin again.

Like an itch she refused to scratch, desire lingered just under her skin. She had to ignore it, she knew that, because if she gave in, then the itch would become an all-consuming fire and she couldn't let that happen. It wasn't right for Gavin, for Trevor, for her, or even for Tulip.

Gavin arrived promptly at six forty-five. Mac was wearing the silver sandals that Emma had chosen to go with their bridesmaid dresses and a rose-colored sundress that was fitted on the top and flared about her knees. She'd put her hair up in a simple twist and wore silver earrings and a silver cuff bracelet. Her makeup was light as she didn't want anyone to think she'd put any effort into her appearance. She was just dancing with her best friend's little brother, no big deal, or so she kept telling herself.

When she opened the door to Gavin's knock, she felt her heart sink. He wore dark gray dress slacks and a white dress shirt, open at the throat and with the sleeves rolled back, revealing his powerful forearms and giving him a look of barely polished masculinity that made her breathless. His light brown hair hung over his forehead in careless disarray and he looked freshly shaved.

He looked her over, taking his time as if savoring every inch, and then wolf whistled. "Looking good, Mackenzie Harris."

"You clean up okay, yourself," she said.

"Where's my girl?" he asked.

As if she knew she was his girl, Tulip came

racing into the foyer, wiggling as she walked. She jumped up on her hind legs as if she could throw herself into his arms, and Gavin laughed as he scooped her up and let her lick his face.

Goop. Mac felt her insides turn to mush at the ridiculously adorable picture the man and dog made together.

"Oh, honestly," Sarah said as she came into the room. "How is she ever going to learn any manners if you encourage her to behave like a wild animal."

Gavin squeezed Tulip tight and then he put her down.

"You're right, Miss Sarah," he said. "But she's just so cute; I can't resist her big brown eyes. I've always been a sucker for pretty brown eyes."

Chapter 15

Mac's throat was suddenly dry. She could feel Gavin's gaze upon her but she refused to acknowledge that he might be talking about her, lest she throw herself into his arms like Tulip had. Not only would it be beyond embarrassing, but the fact that she wanted to so badly scared the snot out of her.

"So, I should be back in a couple of hours," Mac said. "If anything comes up, if she needs me, feel free to call me immediately. I can be home in fifteen minutes. Really, don't hesitate."

"Oh, pshaw," Sarah said. "What could we possibly need? Charlotte is setting up our chick flick movie. I requested a Matthew McConaughey where he's more shirtless than not, and we're going to enjoy popcorn and milkshakes. She'll have a great time."

"McConaughey, huh?" Gav asked.

"Don't be a hater," Sarah said. "The boy can act and be shirtless at the same time and that takes genuine talent."

"Hater?" Mac asked. She looked at Sarah as if she didn't recognize her. "Who are you and what have you done with my aunt?"

"Have fun, kids," Sarah said. "Don't do anything I wouldn't do—then again, that doesn't leave much." Sarah winked at them and patted her leg for Tulip to follow her as she exited the room.

Mac looked at Gavin and noted that her face felt hot. She shrugged as if she had no idea what to say, all true, and he laughed.

"I'm sorry," she said. "I have no idea what has gotten into the two of them lately. It's like I suddenly have two teenagers living in the house in the bodies of two seventy-two-year-old women."

"That's awesome," Gav said. "Everyone should be that young at heart."

"You wouldn't say that if it was your aunts," Mac said.

Gavin opened the door for Mac and she led the way outside. It was still light out but the evening air was cool against her face for which she was thankful.

On the drive to Ms. Poole's dance studio, Gavin asked her questions about Tulip, thank god, as it put them solidly back in friendship mode before class.

Gavin talked about the vaccinations that Tulip might need and Mac agreed that if they didn't find her owner soon, she would go ahead and have her vaccinated.

"It's too bad you can't keep her," he said as he helped her out of the truck. "You'd make a great puppy mama."

Why this made Mac's heart tap-dance with pleasure, she had no idea. She suspected that coming from Gavin it felt like the highest sort of praise, but also, way down deep where she refused to go, she knew she would really like the chance to be Tulip's mom.

Ms. Poole's studio was housed in the remodeled barn on her property on the outskirts of town. She had kept the big rolling barn doors and opened them wide while she was giving a class to keep the air moving.

Mac could see that she and Gavin were the last to arrive. They picked up their pace as they crossed the gravel lot, and Gavin took her elbow in his hand as he helped her navigate the uneven terrain in her high-heeled sandals.

A waltz was playing from an iPod set in a speaker stand and Emma and Brad were working their way around the shiny wooden dance floor while Ms. Poole followed them, adjusting their hand positions and counting their steps.

"One, two, three, that's right," she said. "Sway and glide, move together as one."

Mac eased into the room, not wanting to interrupt, and Gavin followed. Jillian and Sam, and Zach and Carly, were slouched in chairs along the wall with another couple Mac hadn't met but figured was Brad's brother Bobby and his wife Linda.

Bobby looked like an older version of Brad,

and Linda looked pregnant. Very, very pregnant.

"Bobby and Linda," Carly said. "This is Mac, maid of honor."

"Nice to meet you," Mac said as she shook hands with the couple.

"You, too," Linda said. "We've heard so much about you."

"That can't be good," Mac joked.

Bobby smiled. "On the contrary, Emma raves about you. We're so glad you're here. It meant the world to her to have you in her wedding."

Mac nodded. She was glad she was here, too, even if it meant dealing with the big guy at her side and their sordid past. Emma was worth it; being with all of her nearest and dearest, totally worth it.

"Mackenzie, darling, how good of you to join us," Ms. Poole said as she crossed the room toward them.

Mac glanced at her watch. Shoot! They were five minutes late. Ms. Poole never appreciated nuances in the space time continuum if it meant her student was late to class.

"Sorry, Ms. Poole," she said.

As her former teacher approached, Mac marveled that Ms. Poole did not appear to have aged a day since Mac had last taken ballet lessons with her twenty years ago.

Tall and slender, with a regal bearing, the woman never slouched, seriously, and she still wore her usual long black leotard with an animal print skirt draped around her hips. Her black hair was scraped into its ever present bun, making her arching eyebrows and red lips as striking as ever.

Mac took great comfort in the fact that of all the things she remembered about Bluff Point, Ms. Poole her ballet teacher had not changed one iota. And then, Ms. Poole clapped and Mac almost raced for the bar with the mirror and assumed the first position, with heels touching and toes pointed out.

Ms. Poole caught her eye and smiled. "It's good to have you back, Mackenzie."

"It's good to be back," Mac said and she meant it.

Ms. Poole addressed the group, "Welcome, everyone, let's have you all join our bride and groom on the dance floor, shall we?"

Jillian sidled up to Mac as they migrated to the dance floor. "You got this?"

Mac glanced at Gavin where he was joking with Sam.

"Yeah, I mean we'll be swaying back and forth like high schoolers for an hour or so—how intense can it get, right?"

"Good point," Jilly said. "See you on the other side, hopefully without any broken toes."

Mac moved to the far side of the dance floor. She could feel her palms beginning to sweat and felt overly aware of her heartbeat. Nerves, lovely.

Gavin strode across the floor toward her, looking way hotter than any veterinarian she had ever met. She tried to picture him as the scrawny, brace-faced kid who used to sneak up on her when she was wading in the ocean and grab her leg in an attempt to pull her under, scaring the dookie out of her every time.

But the man in the dress shirt was blocking that image with his broad shoulders, lean hips, and wide, wicked smile. Oh, dear. Mac swallowed. This was Gav, her best friend's little brother, who her best friend had raised like a son, Mac reminded herself. She had to maintain healthy boundaries for her friendship's sake, for her relationship's sake, for goodness' sake.

Gavin stopped a foot away from her. He looked amused when he held out his left hand as if he knew what she was thinking. Mac put her hand in his, too aware of how his fingers wrapped gently around hers. He put his other hand high on her back, right below her left shoulder blade.

Mac could feel the heat from his palm through her dress, scorching her skin. She put her left arm on top of his, resting her hand on his shoulder. She didn't look up at him, afraid that her face would give away her über awareness of his nearness. Instead, she stared at the button at his throat.

The position felt very formal, which was excellent. She had been a bit worried that his scent would distract her and she'd trip and land them both on the hardwood floor in a heap, but this distance was doable.

"Very nice," Ms. Poole said to them as she walked by. "You have a lovely form."

Gav leaned close and whispered in Mac's ear, "I think she's talking about me."

She jerked back from the feel of his soft breath caressing her skin and gave him a one-eyed squint.

"Really?" she asked. This was good; a little trash talking would reestablish the sibling-like relationship between them. "Done much dancing, have you? Don't tell me, let me guess— you can bust out the Dougie and you think you're dancing."

"What's wrong with the Dougie?" he asked. "I'll have you know I also do a mean Soulja Boy."

"Uh-huh," Mac said. She gave him an unimpressed look, which was totally bogus because, honestly, any man that could dance even a little was pretty cool in her book.

"So full of doubt," he said. He shook his head at her and Mac had to fight her smile, because if she smiled at him that might be construed as flirting and she was most definitely not flirting. Not at all.

Ms. Poole instructed the group on the basic box step, using Emma and Brad as models, but

Mac wasn't listening. Now that she had made the unfortunate move of looking at Gavin, she found it difficult to look away.

He was just a whisper away from her. When he met her gaze, the dimple in his right cheek deepened, and his long lashes fluttered down as he looked at their feet. She could see the smooth line of his jaw and wondered if there'd be any end-of-the-day stubble if she traced his chin with her fingertips.

Suddenly, Mac wanted to press up against him and just sway. She didn't care if they danced a step. She wanted to feel both of his arms around her and the press of their two bodies together. She wanted to step up on tiptoe and kiss the curve of his mouth from corner to corner.

"Okay, people, let us begin," Ms. Poole said. She clapped and broke the spell that Mac had been falling under.

Mac shook her head. What had she been thinking? This was Gavin! She had to get her head together. Healthy boundaries!

Ms. Poole pointed a remote control at the iPod in the corner and the sound of a waltz swelled out of the small speaker and filled the room.

Mac braced for Gavin to step on her toes, to lean from side to side on the offbeat, to flail around like a man signaling that he was drowning, to hold her too close, push her too far away, or to careen out of control right off the dance floor.

She was not prepared for him to execute a perfect box step around the dance floor that he ushered her through with the gentlest pressure of his hand on her back. Nor was she ready for him to spin her out and pull her back in or to pick her up and twirl her before putting her back on the ground while never missing a step.

"I'm sorry," she gasped when he resumed the box step. "Are we auditioning for *Dancing with the Stars*?"

Gavin laughed and sent her back out into a spin, then caught her in his arms after pulling her close.

"Surprised?" he asked. His breath tickled her ear and she shivered, and not in a bad way.

"More like stunned," she said.

"Dude, quit it, you're making the rest of us look bad," Zach hissed as he and Carly galumphed by like two water buffalo caught in quicksand.

Mac pressed her face into Gavin's shirtfront to keep from laughing out loud. When she looked up, Gavin was smiling down at her and she felt happy, purely happy. She smiled back, thinking this was one of life's perfect moments. Then she remembered it was all based on a lie and she took a step back and resumed the proper posture.

As they waltzed, she asked, "Where did you learn the snazzy dance moves?"

"An ex-girlfriend from my college days," he said. "She was a dance major."

"Oh." Mac nodded. She felt an inexplicable spurt of jealousy. Emma had never told her about any dance major girlfriend of Gavin's. Mac would have remembered. So, yes, she had to pry. "Emma never mentioned that you dated a dancer."

"I don't tell Emma everything," he said. Then he gave her a look that seared her soul. "As you should know."

Mac's eyes went wide with alarm. He was going there. She didn't want to go there. He was talking about them. She knew he had never told Emma about that night, because she was quite sure Emma would have said something, or, you know, shanked her. Mac hadn't said anything either. Did he know that? Did he want to know that? Was it relevant? Mac felt her breath hitch.

"I don't tell her everything either," she said, just in case that was what he wanted to know.

"So I gathered," he said.

Mac searched his face. What was he looking for from her? Acknowledgment of that night? An interest in revisiting it? At the mere idea, her internal body thermometer spiked and she felt scorched from the inside out. She stumbled on her feet, but Gavin caught her and steadied her as easily as if it was his purpose for being. Oh, boy.

Chapter 16

When he smiled at her, it was full of warmth and affection. As he held her gaze into a turn, Mac was surprised to find that she didn't feel shame anymore. Instead of a dirty little secret, that night between her and Gav suddenly felt more like a special moment in time that they shared. It wasn't terrible, awful, or ugly, but rather, it was magical and lovely and smokin' hot.

"All right, that's it, you show-offs," Emma said as she and Brad waltzed by them. "You two are not allowed to dance together at the reception until after Brad and me. Clear?"

Mac glanced at her friend and just like that all of the shame and horror about defiling her best friend's baby brother came crashing down upon her. She stepped back from Gavin, widening the space between them, and stiffened her back.

"Of course, we won't," she said. "In fact, probably, we should split up and help the others."

She let go of Gavin in midstep and turned away. Grabbing Zach and Carly, she broke into their dance and pushed Carly at Gavin while she stepped into Zach's arms.

She saw Jillian and Sam go by. They were well suited and had mastered the basic step but were not bold enough to try anything else. Jillian sent her a concerned look and Mac forced a smile that she knew looked a little manic; still, she grabbed Zach and began to haul him around the dance floor.

"Whoa, easy there, killer," Zach said as they careened toward the corner. "I think I'm supposed to lead."

"Oh, yeah, sorry," Mac said. She relaxed her grip and took a deep breath.

"And one, two, three—oh, sorry, damn," Zach said as he went the wrong way, kicked Mac's instep, and then tripped.

Mac caught him before he fell and they both started laughing.

"I swear I can walk across a room without falling," he said.

"And by the end of this, you'll be able to dance across the room without falling," Ms. Poole said as she joined them. She glanced at Mac. "Great idea to pair up the good dancers with the . . . er . . . less good dancers."

"Thanks," she said.

"All right, Zachary, we're going to try something different with you," Ms. Poole said.

"Story of my life," he quipped.

"Mackenzie is going to dance the lead and I want you to put your hands on her hips and stand behind her and mimic the steps she takes," Ms. Poole said. "Once you get that down, I'll let you have a partner again."

She arranged Mac in front of Zach, who stood behind her and put his hands on her hips.

"Just follow Mac," she said. "And one, two, three."

Mac felt a bit like an idiot with her arms up, holding no one, but at least she wasn't in Gavin's arms thinking impure thoughts. So that was something.

Zach kicked her heels a couple of times but after making it around the floor once, he started to get the rhythm of things.

"Hey, check me out," he said and Mac glanced over her shoulder and smiled at him.

"Looking good, Zach," she said.

They passed by Gavin and Carly, who seemed to be doing well. Gavin held her in the proper position, leaving plenty of room between them, which was good because Carly had her head down with her eyes glued to her feet as if to make sure they didn't go where they weren't supposed to.

"Carly, look at me," Gavin said. "I promise I won't step on you."

"It's not you stepping on me that I'm worried about," she said. "It's me stepping on you. I don't want to cripple you. I'm not exactly a size two. More like a size six times two. I mean, these curves cannot be contained, which is awesome, but they might prove deadly if they crash into you at full speed."

Carly glanced at him quickly, looking so vulnerable that Mac felt her throat get tight. Her curvy Italian friend was clearly feeling self-conscious about her robust figure, which never happened, and Mac desperately wanted to go over and hug her.

"You won't crash, I promise," Gavin said. His voice was firm but gentle, and then he picked Carly up and twirled her in the air and set her back on her feet, never missing a step.

"Holy crap!" Carly squealed. She looked at Mac and asked, "Did you see that? You need to take a picture of that shiz, because I am going to Instagram the hell out of that. Hot damn!"

Mac burst out laughing and she noticed that the other couples did, too. Meanwhile, Zach stopped dancing behind her and shouted, "Way to set the bar too high for the rest of us, Gav."

Ms. Poole joined them and gave Zach her fierce look. "You will be able to do that before you leave this class."

"You're in trouble now," Mac said.

Ms. Poole took Zach's hand and separated him from Mac, so Mac took the opportunity to take some pictures. She even got one with Carly in midtwirl. She looked radiant. For that alone, Mac wanted to go over and kiss Gavin on the mouth; okay, not just for that but it sounded much better in her head when she blamed her longing for a lip-lock on his kindness instead of her own lust.

She watched him as he took Jillian for a spin while Carly danced with Sam. He laughed at something Jillian said and then he twirled her, too. Mac snapped a pic and marveled at how Gav managed to make everyone feel at ease.

She was reminded of how gentle he had been with Tulip when she was sad and scared. Then she remembered how kind he had been to her the night her life had unraveled completely. There was so much more to Gavin Tolliver than the fact that he was her best friend's little brother. And yet, she really couldn't get past that, could she?

So far, she had lied to Emma about the true nature of her relationship with Gavin. Yes, it was a lie by omission but still a lie. She had been vague about the status of her status with everyone, not a total lie but not exactly the truth either. And then there was Trevor; were they still a couple? Would they be one again?

She had no business looking at any man while she was still kind-of-sort-of with him. She knew her friends didn't care for his inflexibility, but it was an undemanding relationship that worked for Mac. She had companionship when she wanted it and she didn't when she didn't.

Theirs had always been a relationship that worked because neither of them suffered the day-to-day compromises that strangled the life out of other relationships. Trevor was a good man and Mac was happy with him. It was unfortunate that Emma had asked her not to mention him to Gavin, because that really would have cleared up most of Mac's problems. Then again, if she told Gavin they were taking a break, he'd probably look at it as a green light to make a move. She could only imagine how Emma would react if Gavin made a serious play for Mac.

She glanced at her friend and saw Emma, who was now dancing with Brad's brother Bobby while Brad danced with the very pregnant Linda, watching Gavin with a happy smile. How many years had Emma put her life on hold to fuss and worry over her little brother? Too many. Mac didn't have the heart to take that away from her right now.

Fine. For Emma, she would continue to play the single girl to Gavin's sad boy, although, she had to admit he really didn't seem that sad to her. But maybe that was because she was only seeing what he wanted her to see. Maybe Gavin was suffering a lot more than she realized because he was pushing it all aside for the sake of his sister. That did seem like something he would do. Man, when did life become so complicated?

"All right, everyone, let's go back to our original partners," Ms. Poole said. She looked a little weary after her time with Zach.

Mac put her phone on the bench and crossed the floor to Gavin. He held open his arms and she stepped into him, feeling a comfortable familiarity sort of like coming home.

Ms. Poole cranked up the music and they began to glide across the floor. Gavin's gaze caught hers and Mac found she couldn't look away—didn't want to, in fact. There were no spins and twirls this time. It was just the two of them, studying each other, seeing the changes the seven years apart had wrought and bridging the time and distance with simple acceptance and understanding.

Suddenly a funky beat sounded over the waltz and everyone's attention was drawn to the bench where Mac had left her phone. She noted the screen was lit up and vibrating while "Uptown Funk" cranked out of its speaker.

"Is that your ringtone, Mac?" Zach asked. "Now that's what I'm talking about."

He let go of Carly and busted out a dance move that involved squatting and flailing his arms. Ms. Poole stepped forward, grabbed him by the back of his shirt, and hauled him to his feet.

"No, just no," she said. She turned and frowned at Mac.

"Sorry," Mac said. "I'll just get that." She stepped away from Gavin and hurried across the room. She snatched up the phone and noted the display read Aunt Sarah. What?!

"Aunt Sarah?" She held the phone to her ear.

"You need to come home, right now, and bring

Gavin with you," Aunt Sarah said in her usual brusque manner.

"Why? What's wrong? Aunt Charlotte—"

"Is fine," Sarah said. "It's Tulip."

"Is she—"

"She's as sick as a dog, as they say," Sarah said. "So hurry."

Sarah ended the call and Mac looked up at Gavin.

"It's Tulip," she said. "She's sick."

Chapter 17

Let's go." He charged across the floor toward the door.

"Thank you, Ms. Poole," Mac said. She looked at Emma. "Sorry! I'll call you later."

"Do!" Emma said.

Whatever else Emma had been about to say, Mac missed because she was jogging after Gavin, who was already halfway across the parking lot. He opened her door and hurried around the front of the truck, letting her pull her own door shut.

He fired up the engine and shot out of the driveway and back onto the main road. It had taken them fifteen minutes to get here earlier but Mac had a feeling they'd make it back to her house in half of that.

"What did she say exactly?" he asked.

"Nothing much, just that she's as sick as a dog," Mac said. "What do you think it could be?"

"I won't know until I see her," he said. "Try not to worry."

She ignored his advice and went into full-on worry mode. "Oh, no, what if she did eat some of those tulip bulbs?" Mac asked. "I thought I checked carefully but what if I missed something?"

"We'll make her well," Gavin said. "I promise."

"She's just a baby," Mac said.

Gavin reached over and took Mac's hand in his. He squeezed her chilly fingers in his warm grip and Mac felt reassured.

"Let's save the panic until we have something to panic about," he said.

"You're right. Thanks."

Mac leaned over and rested her head on his shoulder for just a moment. Gavin rested his cheek on her hair in what Mac took as a gesture of comfort. Then he kissed her forehead and drove on.

When they pulled into the driveway, Mac hopped out of the cab of the pickup while Gavin reached behind the seat for his medical bag.

Aunt Charlotte was waiting on the front porch. "Oh, good, you're here. They're out back."

Gavin joined them on the porch and Charlotte led them into the house, down the hallway, through the kitchen, and out the back door. The backyard spotlight was on and there in its glow were Aunt Sarah and Tulip, standing beside each other in the yard next to a pile of throw up.

"About time," Sarah said. She patted Tulip on the head and said, "Mom's here." Then she looked at Mac and said, "She's all yours."

"What happened?" Mac asked as she reached down and rubbed Tulip's ears.

The aunts exchanged an uneasy look. Gavin

crouched beside Tulip. He began to talk so sweetly to her that Mac was momentarily distracted. Tulip was looking shaky and tired but she leaned up against his side and stared at him with her big brown eyes as if she trusted him above all others. Mac got that.

A movement caught Mac's attention and she noticed that the sisters were trying to sneak back into the house. Oh, but no.

"Stop right there," she said. "What happened?"

"Shirtless Matthew McConaughey," Sarah said.

Gavin looked up from the dog. "Excuse me?"

Charlotte looked mortified, so Mac decided to spare her from having to explain in front of Gavin.

"I'll be right back," she said. She and the aunts moved up onto the porch. "Explain."

"I don't want to," Charlotte said. "You're going to think we're terrible babysitters and then when you have children you won't let us watch them."

"It's not our fault the dog clearly has food issues," Sarah said.

"Aunt Charlotte, I won't think you're terrible," Mac said. "Since I don't have babies, let's not worry about the babysitting thing just yet, okay? Now why is Tulip so sick?"

Sarah took a piece of cardboard out from behind her back and handed it to Mac. "That's why."

Mac turned it over in her hands. It was the box from the granola bars they kept in the pantry; well, it was the corner of the box at any rate.

"She ate the box?" Mac asked.

"The box, the five granola bars inside in their wrappers," Sarah said. "She was just moving on to the saltine box when we noticed she was gone and caught her."

Mac glanced back at Tulip, who was sitting on the grass, staring up at Gavin with adoring eyes while he checked her over. Her tail was thumping on the ground with every nice word he said to her. It was ridiculously adorable and Mac had to look away because for some reason it made her uterus hurt.

"So, McConaughey's pecs came on the TV, you two got distracted, she got into the pantry and ate the whole box of granola bars," Mac said. "That sound about right?"

"Yes," Sarah said. "Let's blame the pecs. It's always the pecs' fault."

Mac closed her eyes for a moment to calm her mind. "All right, I'll let Gavin know."

"Could you not mention the pecs, dear?" Charlotte asked.

Mac nodded.

"Thank you." Charlotte looked relieved. "Okay, this is too much excitement for me. I'm going to work on my poetry. Good night."

Sarah went to follow her sister and Mac said, "Hold up there, Bruno Mars. How did 'Uptown Funk' become my ringtone for you?"

Sarah glanced from side to side as if looking for an escape hatch or for someone else to step forward and take the rap.

"You had an old-style telephone ringing for my ringtone," Sarah said. "So lame. I wanted something with a little pep."

"And you know how to change a ringtone?" Mac asked.

"I'm not a Luddite," Sarah said. "Now go tend your dog and your cute veterinarian."

"He's not—" Mac protested.

"Sure, he is," Sarah said. "That's your dog, isn't it?"

"For now," Mac said.

"Then he's your veterinarian, for now," Sarah retorted. With a toss of her white bobbed hairdo, she strode back into the house, humming her ringtone.

That was it. Mac was calling her dad tomorrow to find out what the heck was going on with the aunts. "Uptown Funk," seriously?

She shook her head and hurried back down the stairs and across the lawn to Tulip and Gavin.

"Apparently, this happened," Mac said. She handed Gavin the corner of the box. He took it in one blue gloved hand and turned it over.

"Well, this explains the foil wrapper in her puke," he said.

"Oh, poor baby." Mac crouched down and reached for Tulip. The dog immediately left Gavin, climbed into Mac's lap, and leaned against her. Then she licked Mac's mouth.

"Blerg." Mac wiped her lips. "Why is it always on the mouth?"

"She loves you," Gavin said.

Mac rubbed Tulip's chest and tried not to think about the dog becoming attached to her. "Do you think she'll be okay?"

He glanced back at the box. "Yes, there aren't any raisins or chocolate in these so she should be just fine. If there are any more wrappers inside her, they'll pass one way or another."

"Oh, joy," Mac said.

"Are the aunts all right?" he asked.

"Charlotte is embarrassed, but Sarah is not at all," Mac said. "I'm not sure what's going on with her. You know she's the one who changed her ringtone on my phone? It's like she's an adolescent again."

"Maybe she's in love," Gavin said.

"What?" Mac gave him a look like he was talking crazy. "She's seventy-two."

"There's an age limit on falling in love?"

"No, but . . ."

Gavin met her gaze and quickly looked away. Mac narrowed her eyes at him.

"What do you know?"

"Me? Nothing, not a thing, not one silly little thing," he said.

He jumped to his feet and pulled off his latex gloves, dropping them into a ziplock bag before stuffing them into his medical case.

"Huh," he said. He looked at his wrist where there was no watch. "Look at the time. Gotta go."

Mac kissed Tulip's head and set her on the ground.

"Gavin Tolliver, don't you dare try to evade me," she said.

He snatched up his bag, patted Tulip on the head, and strode toward the back door.

"Call me if Tulip takes a turn for the worse, but truly, I think she'll be fine," he said.

He stepped up onto the porch but Mac was right behind him and closing in fast. Tulip was right at her side, bounding up the steps as if she suspected there was a game afoot. Gavin slid through the back door and hustled through the house.

"Gav," Mac said. "I will tackle you to get the information I want. Don't think I won't."

"Promises, promises," he said.

He shot out the front door and down the steps. Mac couldn't move as fast as she wanted; cursing her high-heeled sandals she slid out the front door leaving Tulip inside.

She was too late. Gavin was in his truck and backing down the driveway as if a hellhound was chasing him. Mac plopped her hands on her hips and glared.

"You can't escape me, Gavin Tolliver!" she shouted. "I know where you work!"

Gav honked and turned out of the driveway and onto the road, leaving his taillights to wink insolently at Mac as he disappeared around the corner.

Mac turned around and stomped back into the house. This conversation was not over. She hunkered down next to Tulip.

"What do you think, baby girl?" she asked. "Shall we pop in for a checkup with Dr. Gavin tomorrow?"

Tulip barked. Then she thumped her tail on the floor.

"I couldn't agree more," Mac said.

Chapter 18

As if one of his sheet-rumpling hot steamy dreams had conjured her out of the early morning fog, there was Mac striding down the sidewalk toward him. Gavin resisted the urge to rub his eyes in case he was seeing things. If he was, it was a helluva good way to greet the day, so why mess with it?

He unlocked the front door to the clinic and stepped on the rubber mat, making the automatic door whoosh open. Without breaking her stride, Mac trotted into the office with Tulip at her side.

She was wearing mint green Converse sneakers paired with denim shorts and a body hugging pink tank top that about stopped his heart. Her straight brown hair was loose and swayed across her shoulders with each step she took. Tulip pranced beside her, looking up at Mac like she was the sun. Gavin knew exactly how the puppy felt.

He couldn't remember a time in his life when seeing Mac didn't lift him up, make him smile, and make him try harder at whatever challenge he was facing. Man, how he had missed her.

When he was ten and his mother passed away from a sudden aneurysm, leaving his family shattered, everyone treated him like a little baby who lost his mommy. Pity poured down on him in a suffocating goop that made it impossible to breathe or to grieve. But not Mac; she didn't try to reduce him to being a baby. She knew, just like he did, that his childhood as he'd known it was over and she never tried to pretend it wasn't.

On the day of his mother's funeral, she was there all day with Jillian and Carly. The three fifteen-year-old girls took care of them all; fetching and carrying, organizing the food, the guests, even the parking. But when the last guest left and everyone was emotionally drained and out of comfort to give, it was Mac who found Gavin hiding out beneath his tree fort.

She didn't say a word. She picked up his spare baseball glove and played catch with him until the fireflies had gone to bed, the crickets had packed up their evening symphony, and Gavin's arm had given out. When he collapsed to his knees and wept for the first time since losing his mom, it was Mac who wrapped him in her arms and held him tight.

She never said a word. She never made him false promises about how everything was going to be okay. She never diminished his pain by saying she knew how he felt. She just let him cry it out. She never let go and she never pushed him away. And when he fell asleep with his head in her lap, she leaned back against the old maple tree and let him sleep until his father came out around midnight and picked Gavin up and carried him to bed.

Gavin had never forgotten that night. He wasn't sure if that was the night he'd fallen in love with her or if it had been as far back as when Emma brought Mac home with her from first grade to play; of course, he had just been a toddler then. Still, it seemed to him that he had been in love with Mac as far back as his memories could take him.

He crouched low and let Tulip waggle her way into his arms.

"How are you today, princess?" he asked.

"Lighter," Mac said.

When Gavin looked at her, she said, "She passed the rest of the wrappers this morning."

"Ah," he said. He scratched Tulip's ears. "Good girl."

"This is for you as a thank-you," Mac said. She was holding two paper cups full of hot coffee and she handed one to him as he rose to his feet.

The heat of it filled his hand and he looked from it to her. How had she known? His night had been blown to heck by an emergency call from one of his patients who tended to see the specter of death hanging over her cats every time she got overly lonely. He'd been lucky to clock in four hours of sleep last night after that emergency visit that was not, and he was feeling the loss of every minute.

"I could kiss you for this," he said. He saw her face grow warm with embarrassment and he thought he might kiss her anyway. "But just so you know, if this is about Aunt Sarah, I am not bribable. I am much more afraid of her than I am of you."

"Is that so?" she asked. She gave him a speculative look that was way hotter than it should have been.

"It's so," he said. He took a big gulp of the bitter brew and almost moaned. Life might be worth living after all; then he caught her smile and he knew life was worth living for sure, because Mac was here.

He turned and led the way into the clinic. The lights were on and the equipment was humming. He glanced at the clock on the wall. Doc Scharff was due in later that morning, thank goodness, because since his ex, Jane, had run off with Carl the bookkeeper, they hadn't had a chance to hire anyone to take their places, so Gavin was acting as pencil jockey and veterinarian in training and it was getting old.

He had taken the breakup with Jane pretty hard. Partly because she'd blindsided him by running off with Carl but also because he'd felt like his life was finally falling into place. He'd finished veterinary school, had a cute girlfriend, and was settling back into his hometown, where he hoped to have a family of his own.

Then poof! She was gone, taking the book-keeper with her. At first he'd thought it was because he was in love with Jane, because he had cared for her very much, but then Mac came home, and now he was having a hard time remembering why he had been so bummed about losing Jane. When he thought of her and their relationship, he was left with the feeling that it had been . . . fine. But looking at Mac, he realized he wanted so much more than fine, and it was her.

"Well, it just so happens I have other business with you," Mac said.

That got his attention in more ways than one. "Do tell."

"I checked my bank account," Mac said. "You didn't charge me for services rendered or for all of the stuff you gave me for Tulip."

"She's a stray that you found," he said. "I'm not going to charge you for fostering a dog. That isn't right."

"Of course it is," she said. "She's my responsibility so I need to pay for her."

He sat in the chair behind the counter and waved his hand at her. He was not arguing about this.

"Okay, we can table that discussion, but we will be discussing it," Mac said. "But since we're here, I want Tulip to get vaccinated. I'm guessing she didn't have the best care as a puppy and I've been reading up on parvo and distemper. I can't let that happen to her."

"I think that's wise," he said. He reached down and rubbed Tulip's head. "Better safe than sorry. Bring her into the exam room, and I'll—"

Whatever he'd been about to say was cut off as three people arrived one after another, looking to have their pets vaccinated. Gavin gestured for Mac to head into the exam room, since she'd gotten there first, but she shook her head.

"Maybe I can help," she said.

She watched what paperwork he gave the first patient and then she joined him behind the counter with Tulip at her side. She muscled him out of his spot at the computer and began to process his patients. Just like that.

"Go," she said and gestured for him to leave the processing to her. "I got this."

"What about Tulip?" he asked.

"She's cool here," Mac said.

Gavin stepped away and watched her behind the counter as she greeted the people and their pets. Tulip, sensing they were in for the long haul, circled the floor until she found the perfect spot to lie down with her chin resting on Mac's feet. The two of them looked just right sitting there.

Unclear as to what had just transpired, Gavin shook his head and led the first patient into the exam room. He realized his only regret on the whole morning was that he hadn't taken the opportunity to kiss Mac like he'd wanted to, but then, he reminded himself that he was playing the long game.

He wanted Mac, there was no question in that, but he wanted her to want him, too. For that, he had to be patient and win her affection just like he did with his furry people.

Before he shut the exam room door behind the mastiff with the runny nose, he glanced at her just one last time. Yes, she looked right here in his world and in his life. Man, at the end of two weeks, he had no idea how he was going to let her go—again. He really hoped he didn't have to.

Mac glanced at the clock. Emma's itinerary did not leave her much wiggle room. Today was the day they were supposed to meet the pianist at the church and listen to him play, so Emma could pick the march she wanted for the wedding. Jillian was working and Carly had texted to say she had strained something the night before at dance lessons and was currently lying on an ice pack, so that left Mac.

Given that it was the same church where Mac had been so unceremoniously, or rather quite ceremoniously, dumped, she wasn't really looking forward to walking through the arched wooden door to hear the pianist play wedding tunes. Been there, done that. Truly, the only thing she wanted to hear in that space was a dirge. Still, it was for Emma.

Since she had to be at the church at ten thirty, she figured that would give her the morning to stalk Gavin and coerce him into telling her what he knew about Aunt Sarah's transformation.

Mac had noted before going to bed last night that on the website, Gavin's office hours started at seven in the morning with a one-hour vaccination clinic for walk-ins. She figured she might as well start the vaccination process for Tulip. Since the puppy hadn't been microchipped and didn't even have tags on her collar, odds were she hadn't been vaccinated either.

The walk through town had been brisk and quiet. Mac had stopped at The Grind, Bluff Point's coffee shop on Main Street, for a large steaming cup of java. On impulse she picked one up for Gavin, too. She hadn't even known if he drank coffee but it'd seemed rude not to bring him one if he did.

In her head, she had justified all of the reasons why she needed to visit Gavin at the ass crack of dawn. But when the doors had opened and she saw him standing there, she knew it had all been a lie.

She was here because she wanted to see him, plain and simple. With that realization, she had almost thrown the coffee at him and bolted, but then she really would be the crazy stalker she was trying to convince herself that she was not.

Instead, she hid behind Tulip getting vaccinations as her excuse for being there. She had to admit for an excuse it was a damn good one, but then the people started pouring in. How had Gavin been managing all this since Jane the Pain had left?

After watching Gavin sign in the mastiff with the sniffles, all of Mac's accountant skills had been fully engaged and she had happily stepped in to give him a hand. As she met each patient, she noted that some of them had no charges on their accounts. Cheryl Benson, for example, appeared to have had four of her cats treated over the past month and had not paid one red cent.

Mac happened to know from the aunts' gossip that Cheryl Benson was loaded. She had been three years ahead of Mac in school and had reigned over them all as the head cheerleader and homecoming queen. She married the captain of the football team, and when that investment didn't pay out, she had gone on to divorce him and marry an older rich guy, three times in all, and was now newly divorced from the latest oldster and living in one of the mansions in the historic district in town.

According to the aunts, all Cheryl had to do was go out and shake the money tree, which in her case was a small orchard of ex-husbands paying her a chunk in alimony probably so she would go away, so she was more than capable of paying her vet bill.

As she approached the counter with her cat carrier in her arms, she looked Mac over. She did not look happy to see her.

"You're new, aren't you?"

Clearly she didn't recognize Mac, which was more than fine.

"It's my first day," Mac said, not a total lie.

"Tell Gavin Cheryl Benson is here, please," she said.

"Certainly, Ms. Benson," she said.

"Gavin calls me Cheryl," she said. "We're very close."

Mac was betting they were not nearly as close as Cheryl would like. It was clear from Cheryl's outfit that she was trolling for a man, namely Gavin. Wearing an off-the-shoulder eyelet blouse with a push-up bra beneath it on top of leggings with platform pumps, Cheryl was strutting her stuff. Add to that the full-face makeup and artfully tousled pixie cut of her dark hair and she was clearly a woman on the prowl.

Yeah, not on Mac's watch. She glanced at Cheryl's record. It seemed she came in twice a week to visit Gavin with one cat or another and she never paid for her visits. Knowing Gavin, he didn't want to charge her because there was nothing wrong with her cats, but for Mac, she was eating up his professional office time so if she wanted to stalk him, argh, she was going to have to pay for the privilege.

"How nice that you're friends," Mac said. "If you could just give me your payment information, I'll go ahead and send you into an exam room."

"Excuse me?" Cheryl asked.

"Your payment information," Mac said. "I'm afraid I'll need that before you can see the doctor. Judging by my records, and I'm doing quick math here so forgive me if the actual cost is higher, but I believe you owe the doctor somewhere in the vicinity of about four hundred dollars. Now, will that be debit or credit?"

"How dare you," Cheryl snapped. "I told you we are friends. He doesn't charge me, you idiot, now tell him I'm here."

"Sorry, he's with a patient," Mac said. "You see, here in the office this is business, and if Dr. Tolliver is seeing your pet here, you have to pay him. Now, friends meet outside of the office to spend time together, so if you're such good friends, I'm sure that's where you'll be doing your socializing with him." Mac held out her hand. "Your card."

Cheryl looked like she wanted to spit in Mac's hand. Instead, she said, "I don't think so. I'll be talking to Gavin about you. We'll just see if you have a job after today."

"Oh, I'll have a job," Mac said. "And I believe it will entail calling a collection agency to pursue any outstanding debt of, oh, let's say over one hundred dollars. That seems reasonable, don't you think?"

Cheryl looked like she wanted to reach across the counter and rip Mac's hair out. Instead, she slapped her credit card onto the counter and fumed. Mac ran the charges and had Cheryl sign the slip.

"Did you want to see Dr. Tolliver now?" Mac asked. "We can run that bill after your visit."

"No, thank you," Cheryl snapped. She clutched her cat carrier to her chest and stormed out of the office as her cat yowled all the way.

And so went the rest of the morning with a nonstop parade of furry patients and a couple of scaly and feathered ones as well.

"Ooph!" Mac slumped down into her seat in an exhausted heap. The lobby was clear and suddenly all she wanted to do was put her head on the desk and take a power nap.

"Call me if you don't see any changes in Pip's condition," Gavin said.

Mac straightened up as Gavin walked Mrs. Whitaker out with her Yorkshire terrier in her arms. She was an elderly lady, who lived in the center of town and her dog Pipsqueak was her constant companion.

"Thank you, Dr. Tolliver," she said. "I don't

know what we'd do without you. Say good-bye, Pip." She waved Pip's paw at Gavin and Mac before she exited through the door.

"Holy bananas," Mac said. "Is it always that busy?"

"No," he said. "Usually, it's worse."

Mac laughed and Gavin smiled. He sat on the edge of the desk and Tulip came out of her sleeping spot and began to sniff his legs to see who all he had been spending his time with. Gavin reached down and rubbed her ears.

"I suppose we missed the vaccination clinic," Mac said.

Gavin glanced at the clock. "By a little more than two and a half hours. It's okay though; I'm sure I can fit you in."

"Two and a half hours?" Mac shot a look at the clock and then jumped to her feet. "Ack! I'm late. I'm supposed to meet Emma at the church to listen to music. I don't have time to get Tulip home and get back. I'm the worst maid of honor ever. Emma's going to kill me!"

"Mac, relax," he said. He caught her arms and held her still. "Tulip can stay with me and I'll get her shots done. You go listen to music and come back when you're done. Okay?"

"Are you sure?" Mac asked. She gave him a warning look. "She gets into things."

"After all the help you gave me this morning, it's the least I can do," he said. "Go."

213

He released her arms and gave her a gentle push toward the door.

Mac grabbed her heavy bag and draped it across her body. She kissed Tulip's head and said, "Be good."

Tulip thumped her tail on the floor, which Mac took as a solemn promise of good behavior, or at least the promise that she'd try. Good enough.

Chapter 19

Mac had expected the time spent in the church to be an ordeal, and at first it was. They listened to so many classical pieces that they all blended together and Mac felt like she was no use at all. Of course, it didn't help that a part of her spent every second in the church looking for an escape hatch.

Finally, when Emma had winnowed it down to two classical pieces, Mac called Brad at the brewery and had him weigh in on the decision. He wasn't jazzed about either, then he asked the pianist if he knew the piano version of "Falling in Love at a Coffee Shop" by Landon Pigg.

When the music director started to play it, Emma let out a soft sigh and they all knew it was the one. When she turned to look at Mac, Emma's eyes were watery and Mac felt her own throat get tight.

"It's going to be the most beautiful wedding ever," she said. She hugged Emma close as they both smiled through their tears.

Mac glanced up at the vaulted ceiling and the pretty stained glass windows that colored the sunbeams that flooded into the sanctuary. She had thought being in this space would be hard, that it would bring back all of her humiliation and shame, but instead, as she stood beside her best friend, she felt uplifted.

She realized it was easy to be here for people that she loved. This wedding wasn't about her. In fact, it had nothing to do with her at all. So she was going to be just fine standing at this altar as maid of honor and watching two wonderful people commit their lives together. After all, what could be better than that?

She parted company with Emma on the church steps, feeling more optimistic about the wedding than she had since Emma had asked her to stand up for her.

Mac was halfway across the green when she saw them. Gavin was holding the end of a chew toy rope and Tulip was galloping after him trying to get it. He started to go one way and then faked her out and went another way. Tulip tried to hit the brakes and turn around but ended up rolling tail over floppy ears in a comical wipeout that made Gavin laugh.

It barely slowed the puppy down and she jumped to her feet and gave chase again. Gavin was ahead of her but when Tulip put on the speed, she got tangled up in his feet. As Mac watched in horror, Gavin flailed his arms in a desperate bid to gain his balance, which failed spectacularly and he went down hard on his back.

"Gav!" Mac shouted and sprinted across the green grass toward him. She dumped her bag and dropped to her knees beside him. "Are you all right?"

Tulip was standing on his chest and licking his face as if she could kiss it better. Mac grabbed her collar and pulled her off, handing her the chew toy rope that had been abandoned on the ground.

"Gah, it's always on the mouth with that one," Gavin said and he wiped the dog spit from his face.

Having been on the end of Tulip's kisses, Mac couldn't help but laugh.

"Are you hurt?" she asked as she leaned over him, looking for scrapes or contusions.

"Depends," he said. "Does bruised dignity count as an injury?"

"It won't get you any boo-boo kisses," she teased. "But, yeah, it does smart."

"Really?" he asked. "There has to be blood loss for boo-boo kisses? That doesn't seem fair. Wait! I'm pretty sure I've got a scrape. Here?"

He pointed to his forehead. It was fine. Mac shook her head at him.

"How about here?" He pointed to his cheek.

Again, Mac shook her head, but she felt a seductive heat swelling within her when she caught the wicked twinkle in his eyes and she was sure it showed on her face. She felt locked in by the heat in his baby blues, and she couldn't look away even though she knew she should.

"How about h—?" Gavin began but was interrupted by the arrival of Zach and Sam.

"What's up, kids? What are you two doing, taking a siesta?" Zach asked. He sprawled out on the grass next to Gavin. "Hey, look! That cloud is in the shape of a pair of boobies."

"Lady present," Sam reminded him. He kicked Zach's shoe and then plopped down onto the grass beside him.

"Sorry, Mac," Zach said.

"Oh, wow, it really does look like a pair of palookas," Sam said. He glanced at Mac. "Sorry."

"It's fine," she said. She felt Gavin's eyes on her face and she turned to see him staring at her with an intensity that made her insides spasm. Her throat went dry and her voice was hoarse when she said, "Well, I'd better go."

Gav's eyes narrowed and he was looking at her lips as if all he could think about was kissing her. Mac was pretty sure she was going to combust on the spot. Her phone chimed in her bag and she jumped to her feet and grabbed it.

"I'd better take that," she said. She picked up the end of Tulip's leash and rose to her feet. As she ran away, because there was no way to pretend that wasn't exactly what she was doing, she called over her shoulder, "See ya, fellas."

She was ten steps away before she could get her brain to command her fingers to answer her phone.

"Hello?" she said.

"Mac, babe, how are you?"

Trevor! Mac almost dropped her phone. Instead she looked down at the dog beside her and tried to ground herself.

"Uh, hi," she said. She quickened her pace, trying to put distance between her and Gavin.

"Are you all right?" he asked. "You sound weird."

"Yeah, I'm fine, must be the international cell connection," Mac suggested.

She was so not fine! She had been moments away from kissing her best friend's little brother in front of the entire town of Bluff Point. And the real pisser was that a small part of her, a teeny tiny part, still wanted to. She must be losing her mind.

She brought Trevor's image to mind. She had to get a grip. Clearly, coming home had rattled her more than she realized. She blew out a breath. Thank goodness Trevor had called to get her head back in the right space.

"Long distance on cell phones is the worst," Trevor said. "So, how goes Emma's wedding extravaganza?"

"Really well," Mac said. She told him about picking the music and how the aunts were faring. "How goes the business venture?"

Trevor told her about the negotiations. He was in his element, loving every bit of the battle for each clause and amendment to the contract. Mac could just see him in his hotel. His tie would be loose at his collar, his jacket would be thrown over a chair, his dark brown hair would be rumpled from his fingers plowing through it, and he would be contemplating the room service menu, wanting to order a steak but opting for the healthier chicken instead.

"But enough about me," Trevor said. "What else has been happening? It's not weird that I'm calling, is it? I just wanted to know how you're doing, you know . . ."

"With us taking a break and all?" Mac asked. They both knew that the break had not been her choice.

"Yeah," he said. "You're not mad, are you?"

Mac took a moment to think that over. Trevor hadn't mentioned taking a break until the night before he left. She had stopped by his apartment to wish him a good trip and while she watched him pack, he had proposed that they take advantage of his absence to be single for a while. Mac had been stunned. She had acquiesced mostly because she was too surprised to do anything else.

"No, I'm not mad," she said. That was true. She'd never been angry about their separation, just confused.

"Oh, good," he said. "So, it's going okay?"

Mac could hear the anxiety in his voice and she

wondered if he was reconsidering their break. Well, since he was the one who had proposed it, he'd have to be the one to end it, too. A girl's pride could only take so much waffling.

"Yeah, it's okay," she said. "And you?"

"Good," he said.

An awkward silence filled the line that had nothing to do with a bad cell connection. Mac finally took pity on them both.

"I found a dog," she said as she turned onto Elizabeth Street. As if she knew she was the topic of conversation, Tulip looked up at Mac with her tongue hanging out of her mouth and her mouth curved up like she was smiling. Mac rubbed her soft head and felt her heart melt.

"What do you mean?" Trevor asked.

"I was walking through an alley and there she was," Mac said. "She's young; about three or four months, a brown and black brindle with the funniest swirls of color on her forehead. She's quite adorable."

"But you're not keeping it, are you?" he asked.

"Well, no, I wasn't planning to," Mac said.

"Good. You know I'm horribly allergic and it would make it impossible for me to come over to your place," he said.

"They make allergy medicine for that sort of thing," Mac said.

She resisted the urge to point out that since they were taking a break, he might not have to worry about coming over to her place. Then again, if he was thinking like that, maybe he was also thinking that their break was not a permanent thing. A week ago, she would have been so relieved but now, well, now she wasn't sure.

"Babe, in my position, I can't take anything that might make me drowsy. You know that, Mac," he said. His tone was reproachful and Mac sighed. She knew he never took anything that might impair his abilities in the board-room.

"I'm just taking care of her while I'm here," Mac said.

He was silent for a moment as if processing this new development. "All right, but you should probably unload it as soon as possible. You don't want to get attached."

"I won't," Mac said. She knew her tone was belligerent but she couldn't help it. She really didn't like his bossy tone.

"Mac, think," he said. "You're a career girl who works sixteen-hour days, how could you possibly care for a puppy. It wouldn't be fair to it."

"It's a she," Mac said. "And she's part pit bull so she's tougher than you'd think."

"A pit bull? Good Christ, Mac, they're vicious beasts," he said. "For your own safety, you need to get rid of it. Take it to the pound today and let them deal with it."

"But they'll likely euthanize her," she protested.

"Which is probably for the best," he said.

"I have to go," Mac said. She was standing on the curb in front of her house and she was so angry, it was taking all that she had not to throw her phone on the ground and curb stomp it into a million pieces.

"Listen, I'm not trying to be a jerk," Trevor said. His voice was placating. "It's just that you're thousands of miles away from me, with a strange dog, a pit bull, no less. Mac, hon, I'm just worried about you. Wouldn't you be worried about me if the situation was reversed?"

She could hear the concern in his voice and she knew it was legitimate. He was right. She would be worried about him if he was thousands of miles away and had picked up a stray dog; of course, that was mostly because she knew how he felt about dogs, but still.

"I'm sorry," she said. "You're right. This whole thing is silly. I posted 'found dog' notices all over town, so I'm sure her people will come and claim her any moment. Don't worry."

"Oh, that's good, really good," he said. "So, we're all right?"

"Yes, we're fine," she said. "It's just been more intense than I expected, coming home and all."

"You'll be leaving soon, just a few more days, really," he said. "When we get back to Chicago, we can revisit us and see where we stand. You'd like that, wouldn't you?"

Mac's mind went blank. Suddenly, she didn't know what she wanted anymore.

"Yeah, sure," she said. "That sounds good."

"Excellent. I'll call you in a few days," he said. "Take care."

"I will," Mac said. "You, too."

She ended the call, feeling like something had shifted between them. She wasn't sure what it was or if it was just the challenge of communicating long distance, but as she climbed the steps to the porch, she tightened her grip on Tulip's leash. Despite all of Trevor's valid points about her having a dog in Chicago, she didn't even like to think about the day Tulip's family came to claim her, and if she was honest, deep down she hoped they never would.

Chapter 20

"I am not wearing that!" Emma declared. She slammed the gift bag shut and scanned the restaurant to make sure no one had seen the horror that met her eyes.

"Oh, come on," Carly protested. "It's a bridal veil with little tiny penises on it—why wouldn't you wear it?"

"Shh," Emma hushed her. "That's our third-grade teacher, Ms. Lamont, in the corner. I will die, simply die, if she hears the word 'penis' come out of your mouth."

"Better out than in," Carly quipped.

Mac had been about to take a sip of her wine and managed to snort it right up her nose. Jillian thumped her on the back and said, "Maybe kicking off the bachelorette party at Bluff Point's finest seafood restaurant was not the best plan."

"Oh, pish," Carly said. "I don't see why she won't wear the veil. It's charming. I got the sparkly purple penises and everything."

"Maybe it's because she lives here and doesn't want anyone to see her wearing penises—purple, sparkly, or other," Jillian suggested.

"Stop saying penises!" Emma hissed. Against her fair skin the blush of embarrassment was bright red and blotchy. Mac felt for her, really she did.

"Mac, what's your vote?" Carly asked.

"No, a resounding no on the penises," she said. Emma gave her a death glare. Mac grinned.

"Buzzkill!" Carly cried. "This is supposed to be an off-the-hook bachelorette party and what are we doing?"

"Enjoying a nice dinner out," Emma said. She grabbed the waiter as he passed by. "Check please! And now we'll go for some drinks and a walk by the water."

"And then you'll wear the penis veil?" Carly badgered.

"No," Emma said. Her eyebrows lowered and she looked distinctly like Grumpy Cat.

"I love it when she makes that face," Carly said. "Usually, it only makes an appearance when she's talking about Jane the Pain, so it's a treat to see it now."

"Ugh, do not mention The Beyotch's name to me," Emma said. "I loathe, detest, and despise that woman."

"Don't hold back," Jillian said. "Tell us how you really feel."

Mac and Carly smiled at her teasing; Emma did not.

"She is a horrible human being," Emma said. "I swear I'll punch her in the throat if I ever see her again."

"Easy, Ronda Rousey," Carly said. "People break up. It happens. You can't go around assaulting your brother's ex-girlfriends. Besides, didn't they split like six months ago?"

"There's a time limit on punishing the woman who jilted my brother?" Emma asked. "I don't think so. Did you know I asked her to be a bridesmaid? And she said yes! She could be here with us right now."

Suddenly, Mac felt as if her skin was too tight. The thought of having to pal around with a girlfriend of Gavin's should not bother her as much as it did, should it? No, it definitely shouldn't.

"I'm sure she didn't mean to hurt Gav," Mac said.

"That's not the point," Emma said. "The point is that she did and here's how it works in my world: if you break my baby's heart, you are dead to me. Deader than dead, and I will happily bury you."

Jillian's eyes went round, making her look like an owl, and Carly bit her lip as if to keep herself from spilling state secrets, or, you know, telling Emma that Mac and Gav had a fling once. Mac noticed they were both trying not to look at her, so she did the only thing she could think of—she picked up her wine and chugged it. If she'd had any hope that a flirtation with Gavin was a possibility, well, that had just been returned to sender address unknown.

"So, back to the veil," Carly said. "I say we draw straws."

Mac had never loved her more. As they left the restaurant, with Carly walking beside Emma still beseeching her to wear the penis veil, they all giggled at the ridiculousness of the conversation.

For a moment, Mac felt as if she had traveled back in time. How many giggle fits had she shared with these ladies over the years? Too many to count. A feeling of gratitude filled her and when Jillian fell in beside her and hugged her close, Mac squeezed her back.

"So, word on the street is that you and Gav were caught canoodling in the town square," Jillian said. She kept her voice low so that Emma couldn't hear.

"Who said that?" Mac asked. Then she knew. "Zach or Sam?"

"Sam," Jillian said. "He stopped by the bakery this morning and said he got the feeling he and Zach interrupted something significant yesterday between you and Gavin."

"Men!" Mac huffed. "I swear they are way worse gossips than women."

"True that. Now tell me, what's happening between you two?" Jillian asked.

"Just friends," Mac said. Jillian's dark brown eyes were steady as they studied Mac's face and she almost squirmed. But really, minus Mac's salacious thoughts about Gavin, nothing had happened between them. She didn't think almost happened counted. "Tulip knocked him down and I was checking on him. That's it. I swear."

"All right, but if you need me to run interference, let me know," Jillian said.

Mac thought about the exotically lovely Jillian throwing herself at Gavin to distract him from Mac. Yeah, no.

"Really, it's all good," Mac said. "I talked to Trevor yesterday and he wants to talk when we both get back to Chicago. I think he's reconsidering this taking a break thing."

"But are you reconsidering it?" Jillian asked.

"What do you mean?"

"I mean is Trevor who you really want to spend your life with?" she asked.

"Yes," Mac said. "We have a really good life together." Jillian didn't say anything, so she added, "Look, after what Emma just said about Jane, I plan to keep a low profile and sail out of Bluff Point in a little over a week, having done no damage to any of my relationships."

"I'm going to miss you when you go," Jillian said. She glanced at Emma and Carly ahead of them. "Now that you've been back, do you think you might come back more often?"

"You mean now that I've finally come back to town and faced down my humiliation?" Mac asked.

"I was trying to put it delicately, but yes,"

Jillian said. "It hasn't been that bad, has it?"

"You know, it hasn't," Mac said. "In fact, other than being on the receiving end of Jessie Peeler Connelly's scorn, it's been pretty unremarkable."

"Well, except for the whole babysitting the little brother debacle you've got going," Jillian said.

"Yeah, aside from that," Mac said. "You know, I was thinking I may even come back for the holidays."

Jillian beamed at her and Mac felt it tug at her heart. She had never thought about how left behind Jillian and Emma might feel with Carly and Mac off on their own adventures.

"I'm going to hold you to that," Jillian said.

"Come on, you two," Carly called from the open door of Marty's Pub. "Hurry up!"

Whereas the Bikini Lounge was a tourist friendly place, catering to the summer visitors who loved their Maine lobster, tee times, and lighthouse tours, Marty's Pub was a local joint. Tucked away on a side street off the town green, this was where pints of Bluff Point Ale were copiously consumed, darts were played, and Red Sox were cheered.

Emma managed to snag a small table by the front window and had already ordered the first round of drinks when Mac and Jillian caught up. When Marty, the owner, saw it was Emma and her Maine crew out to celebrate her upcoming wedding, he sent over a complimentary round of shots. And so the festivities began.

Much of the conversation was about their previous adventures, like the time Jillian had deployed rescue one on a blind date only to have Carly misunderstand the call and send the actual fire department over to the restaurant where Jillian was suffering through her overcooked steak and an equally leathery banker.

Also, they reminisced about the time Mac had forged their chemistry teacher's signature on passes to the library and they got caught. Suspension had been pending until Emma pointed out to the principal how dumb it would sound if four of the high school's best students were suspended for going to the library.

When it was Mac's turn to buy the drinks, the waitress was nowhere to be found, so she decided to try her luck at the bar.

Carly grabbed her arm on her way, and said, "Make Emma's a double, I'm going to get her in that veil if I have to get her shnockered to do it."

Mac nodded but, of course, had no intention of doing any such thing. She was not going to be the party responsible for making the bride puke or wear sparkly purple phallic symbols.

She found a tiny opening at the bar between a lady in stylish business attire and a thickset man who had the beginnings of a bald spot on the back of his blonde head.

"Excuse me," she said.

They both ignored her. Mac tried to wiggle into the small space. The woman gave her a put out glance and shifted an inch closer to her companion. The man didn't acknowledge Mac at all. Not a big surprise since he seemed to have his sights locked on the bartender's hooters.

The bartender, a pretty brunette in a tight tank top, smiled at Mac and asked, "What can I get you?"

"Four lemon drops," Mac said. She figured as shots went they weren't as hard-core as Zach's Three Wise Men. She was already beginning to feel the effects of their carousing and she really didn't want to wake up with a hangover the next day.

"Coming right up," the bartender said.

"Hey, what about me, Tina?" the man to Mac's right asked the bartender as he leaned over the bar to get a better look-see at her front. "What about that question I asked you earlier?"

"Sorry, Seth, I don't hook up with married men," Tina said.

Mac felt a blast of icy cold start at the top of her head and work its way slowly down her scalp, over the back of her neck, until it swept down her body all the way to her feet. Seth? Her Seth? No, not her Seth! Jessie's Seth. Was it really?

She turned her head ever so slowly in his direction to find he was regarding her with beer-soaked, heavy-lidded eyes that looked just three sips away from passing out. Despite the bloated face and red nose, thinning hair and middle-aged paunch, there was no question that this was the man she had almost married. Holy crap!

Seth! Here he was in Marty's Pub, hitting on a bartender ten years younger than him while his wife—Mac checked his finger for a ring—yep, still married—while his wife was where? Home with the kids?

Suddenly, Mac thought she should send Jessie a cookie basket for taking this loser off of her hands. Why hadn't anyone told her what a sack of sleaze he had turned into? Oh, yeah, because every time someone had tried, she had shut them down. She had never wanted to hear his name mentioned ever again.

"Mac? Mackenzie Harris?" He frowned and blinked at her.

"Hey, Seth," she said. "Long time."

His gaze raked her from head to toe, taking in her low-cut, formfitting, black sleeveless blouse, her jeans, and her black stilettos with the silver spike heels.

"You look hot! What'd you do? Get some work done? A little nip and tuck? Are those inflatables?"

He reached out as if he was going to honk her boob and Mac slapped his hand away.

"Don't even think it," she said. She smoothed

her hand over her black top as if wiping her palm clean of him.

"Aw, don't be like that," he said. "We had something once. Don't you remember?" He lowered his voice as if it made him sound sexy and added, "We were almost husband and wife and, hoo, we sure did practice the horizontal mambo a lot."

Mac felt a shiver of horrified revulsion ripple through her as her gag reflex kicked in. This, she could have been married to this. Suddenly, the world seemed glorious, full of unicorns and rainbows and glitter bombs because she was not in fact married to Seth Connelly.

"'Almost' being the operative word there, chief," she said.

The bartender put the drinks down in front of Mac, who tossed a big bill at her and told her to keep the change. She'd certainly earned it, putting up with Seth the sad sack.

"Well, this was awful," Mac said to Seth. "See you around."

She went to scoop up her drinks but Seth grabbed her wrist and pulled her around to face him.

"Oh, what's this?" he asked. His lip curled in a mean look. "You think you're better than me now?"

"Not *now*, no," Mac said. "Truthfully, I was always better than you."

She tried to tug her arm out of his grip but his fingers tightened, digging into the skin. That was it. Mac had had enough.

When she had moved to Chicago and was on her own for the very first time in her life, she had enrolled in self-defense classes. They had been marvelous for working out the pain and hurt after her humiliation by Seth but as time went on and she was less angry, they had become her preferred method for working out. She now had a programmed response to any unwelcome touch and it involved pain for the toucher.

Instinct took over; she made a fist and rotated her arm in the opposite direction that his thumb was pointing. She was so fast he lost his grip on her wrist. He was pulled off balance and his face hovered just inches from her fist. Mac knew her sensei would have approved if she punched Seth right in the nose. Instead she opened her hand and used his face to shove him hard into his seat.

She leaned in close and said, "Don't. Ever. Touch. Me."

"Fine, whatever, you didn't have to go all aggro on me," Seth whined. He hunched his shoulders forward and turned back to his beer.

When Mac reached for her shots, the bartender handed back her money and said, "That was spectacular and those are on me. I insist."

Mac smiled at her, picked up the shots, and

turned around. Standing right behind her was Gavin.

"Oh, hi," she said.

He loomed like a thundercloud, glaring in Seth's direction like he was picturing exactly how he was going to tear him apart. That couldn't be good.

"Hey." Mac nudged him with her elbow, while trying not to spill her drinks. "You okay?"

Gavin looked at her, really looked at her, and then a slow smile spread over his face. He took the shots out of her hands to carry them for her, leaned close, and whispered in her ear, "What you did just now, yeah, that was totally hot."

Chapter 21

Mac was dazzled to have him so close, looking so powerful and strong. Honestly, how was a girl supposed to cope with that? She almost turned back to the bar to order an ice water except she didn't want to go near Seth.

"Thanks," she said. "I told you I was stronger than I looked."

"You did," he agreed. "Now can I take him outside and punch him until my arm gives out?"

"No, you may not," she said. She grinned. "But I love that you offered."

She led the way back through the crowd to their table. Not a big surprise, but there she found Brad, Zach, and Sam had made themselves at home at the table.

She looked back at Gavin and asked, "Are you guys stalking us?"

"Well, I can't speak for the others," he said. "But . . ."

The look he sent her stated quite plainly that his interest in her was picking up right where they'd left off in the park yesterday. It should have terrified her; instead it was ridiculously charming and felt as magical as spotting an unexpected shooting star in the night sky. This was so not good!

When they joined the others, Mac passed out the girls' lemon drops, making sure to maneuver so that the table was always between her and Gavin. She could no longer deny what was happening between them; well, she would deny it to everyone else, but to herself she had to be honest about the attraction that was snapping between them. She hadn't ever encountered anything quite like it before and she suspected it was as dangerous as a loose high voltage wire and she did not want to get zapped.

Maybe it was because they had that one night between them. Mac figured it made sense that when you knew a person in the most intimate way possible, you were forever on their radar. She glanced over at the bar and saw Seth. Maybe not.

Then again, it could be because she had abandoned Gavin in the bed of his pickup truck. He'd been asleep and she'd crept away in the wee hours of the morning and never looked back. They'd never had the morning-after conversation; did that mean there was unfinished business there? Was that it?

Carly lifted her shot up in the air and called, "May all your ups and downs be between the sheets!"

Zach let out a raucous cheer and the girls clinked their glasses and swallowed their shots down. Another round was bought but Mac knew when she'd had enough. She passed hers off to a couple at the next table and caught Emma doing the same. They shared a wink and went back to their group.

When the pub was crammed to bursting, Emma declared it was time for the girls to go for their walk on the boardwalk. Mac felt the sweet relief of knowing that she would soon escape Gavin with their healthy boundaries intact. Nothing had happened, she had made sure, and life was good.

"We'll come with you," Brad said.

Mac felt her hopes dash against the rocks. No, no, no!

"Shouldn't you bachelors be out dropping singles in strippers' G-strings or something?" Mac asked. She was desperate.

"We already did that," Zach said. "It's no fun when two of the bachelors spend all their time in the parking lot smoking cigars and talking about their feelings." He looked at Brad and Gavin. "Pathetic!"

Brad shrugged and hugged Emma close. "I just know what I want."

"Me, too," Gavin said.

He was standing behind Mac and he whispered it so that only she could hear it. Mac felt her heart clutch in her chest but she pretended she didn't hear him and let Carly grab her hand and drag her out of the pub.

"So, if I can't get Emma to wear the veil . . ." Carly said as they walked but Mac interrupted.

"No."

"You don't even know what I'm going to say."

"Yes, I do," Mac argued. "You're going to throw the maid of honor under the bus and make her wear the veil. No!"

"Just give it to Zach," Jilly said as she joined them. "He'll wear it."

"Genius!" Carly said and she dropped Mac's arm and hurried back to Zach.

Jillian and Mac exchanged a laugh when Zach squealed like a girl and slapped the tacky veil on top of his shaggy blonde head like it was exactly what he'd always wanted.

"I swear he will be a twelve-year-old boy forever," Mac said.

Jillian tipped her head to the side as she considered the big goofball. "I don't know. I think there might be some hidden layers under all the boisterousness. I get the feeling he's over-compensating for something, but what? I know, I'll go ask Sam."

She dropped Mac's arm and walked away. Judging by the wiggle in her hips, she probably should have passed on the last round as well. No matter; Sam looped an arm about her waist and the two of them led the way to the boardwalk. Carly and Zach joined them in the lead while Emma and Brad meandered behind the group, gazing into each other's eyes in a seriously sickening display of besotted bride and groom.

Mac wondered if she should ghost out of the party. The aunts were watching Tulip, and she was all too aware of how that had gone last time. They were forbidden from watching any movies with shirtless McConaughey or any other pec-worthy actor, but still it was getting late. She paused by a storefront that was closed for the evening and pretended to be looking at the window display. She tracked the group out of the corner of her eye until they disappeared around the corner, then she stepped back, planning to jet in the other direction.

She slammed into a hard body right behind her and her gaze shot up to the window to see Gavin's reflection behind hers in the glass. His hands were on her hips, keeping her steady on her ridiculously high shoes.

"Busted," he said.

"I have no idea to what you are referring," she said. She tried to sound haughty but it just came out guilt ridden.

"You were going to ghost right out of Emma's bachelorette party," he said.

Mac hung her head. She knew there was no denying it, so she went for vague. "Maybe."

She was aware that he had not let go of her hips and she was still pressed up against his back. That brought images to mind that had no business being in her head, so she stepped forward and turned around, putting some space between them.

"Are you worried about Tulip?" he asked.

She nodded. It was partially true; besides, it sounded so much better than telling him she was avoiding him because she was inappropriately warm for his form.

"Don't be," he said. "I texted Miss Sarah and she assured me Tulip is fine."

"You texted my dog sitter?"

"Tulip is my patient," he said. He took out his phone and showed her the texts—several of them—between him and Sarah. "I was concerned, you know, especially after last time."

It was about the sweetest thing she'd ever heard of a man doing and she wanted to hug him, really badly. She didn't. Instead, she handed his phone back and punched him on the shoulder. There, that was a boundary builder if ever there was one.

"Well, aren't you something?" she asked.

He opened his mouth to reply when there was a shout from the corner, drawing their attention that way. A shaggy blonde head covered in a mid-length veil appeared around the side of the building.

"Yo, what's taking you so long? We got tickets for the Ferris wheel! I'm going to try and puke off the top. It'll be epic!" Zach yelled.

"On our way," Gavin shouted back. He looked

at Mac as they began walking in the direction their friends had taken. "Looks like you missed your window."

"At least I know Tulip is okay," she said. "I didn't want to text for fear that they would think I didn't trust them, so thanks for that."

"Sure," Gavin said. He was staring straight ahead where the light from a streetlamp illuminated Zach's head. "Is he wearing . . . hmm . . . does it have . . ."

"Sparkly purple penises on it?" Mac asked. "Yes, yes it does."

They followed Zach and his snazzy headgear to the line at the Ferris wheel, where all of their friends were queued for the next ride.

"Where were you two?" Emma asked. "You almost missed it."

"Window shopping." Mac grimaced. "You know me when something shiny catches my eye."

"Like this?" Brad asked and he jerked his thumb in Zach's direction.

"Yeah, that's actually more of a repellent," Mac said. She glanced at their group, trying to figure out how she could land a seat with one of the girls.

"Oh, now you have to admit, he does wear it with a decided panache," Sam said.

"Only Zach could carry it off," Emma agreed.

"Tickets!" the ride engineer shouted.

"Here!" Emma slapped two tickets into Gavin's hand. "That's for you two. Go!"

She hurriedly passed out tickets to the rest of the bridal party and just like that Mac was climbing aboard a rickety metal bench with a clamshell-shaped canopy and a footrest beside Gavin. The gatekeeper fastened the bar across their laps and they set off up into the air.

Heights had never bothered Mac as much as deep dark water, but she wasn't a huge fan of them either. Still, it wasn't cruising up above the amusement park that had her pulse racing. No, it was definitely the man sitting beside her who looked too big to be contained by the narrow bench. He moved one arm along the back of the bench seat and rested the other on the lap bar as if he was trying to find enough space for his limbs but couldn't.

"You okay?" he asked.

"Yeah, I'm good," Mac said. She wedged herself into the corner to give him more room. "Oh, look, here come Zach and Carly."

Gavin leaned forward and set the bench to rocking, which made Mac grab the bar in her lap.

"Sorry," he said. "Man, I haven't been on this thing in years. I forgot how rickety it was."

"Not helping," she said.

"I didn't know you were afraid of heights."

"I'm not, but I do have a healthy fear of falling."

He smiled and took her hand in his. "Come here, it's better if you sit in the middle for more even weight distribution."

She gave him a dubious look. He ignored her and pulled her close so that their sides were pressed together and he had his arm around her shoulders, locking her in place. The swing swayed with their movements and Mac closed her eyes. Nope, that didn't help either.

"All right, let's take your mind off of it," Gavin said. "You ready? I spy with my little eye, the pointy part of a church."

Mac looked from him to the ground, swallowed hard, and then saw the two churches off on the town green. They looked very self-important with their nighttime spotlights illuminating their facades.

"Abiding Savior," Mac said and she pointed to one of the churches on the town green.

"Close but I was thinking of St. Stephen's," he said.

Mac gave him a look that said she didn't believe him and he shrugged.

"Your turn," he said.

Mac scanned the town from their perch. They were inching upward as each car was loaded with new passengers.

"I spy with my little eye, a big white tower," she said.

Gavin looked toward the rocky cliffs on the

north side of town. "That's easy, Bluff Point lighthouse."

They continued the game, making the chosen objects farther and farther away as they rose higher and higher into the sky. After a few more rounds, Mac realized she wasn't nervous anymore as she scoured the landscape for a flagpole that Gavin had referred to as sexy. Then she spotted it on the far end of the pier, hoisted above the Bikini Lounge. A bright yellow flag with a pair of pink bikini bottoms as an emblem flying high over the popular night spot.

She turned around, looked at him, and laughed. "I don't think I ever noticed that flag before."

Their faces were just inches apart, and Mac found herself longing to trace the outline of his mouth with a fingertip and feel the rough stubble on his chin graze her palm. She quickly looked away.

"I spy with my little eye a mermaid," she said. She could feel Gavin's gaze on the side of her face. Then she felt his hand move from her back to her hair. He ran the ends of it through his fingers, sifting it as if he was trying to learn its texture.

Mac glanced down. The Ferris wheel was still loading as more people climbed aboard. How much longer until the ride actually started? Would she be able to make it without ruining the healthy boundary she had been trying to maintain between her and Gavin? Maybe she should jump. The idea had merit except she wasn't one for self-inflicted pain.

"The mermaid is painted on the Belmont Park sign," he said.

Mac felt the breath she didn't know she'd been holding whoosh out of her lungs. They were back to the game. This was good, very good.

"I spy with my little eye"—Gavin paused as if he was searching for the perfect thing before he continued—"a patch of grass on a hill, beneath two old copper beech trees, where a pickup truck can park all night and no one will find it."

Chapter 22

Mac gasped and turned to look at him. His fingers were still tangled in her hair. His gaze was steady, full of affection, and heat, and cloudy with tender memories she had sealed away forever.

She knew she could no longer pretend their past didn't exist or that the night between them had been less than what it was. It wasn't fair to either of them.

"Oh, Gav." She sighed. "Don't . . ."

"Don't what? Remember? When I look at you, I can't do anything else. I remember kissing the tears off of your face," he said. His voice was a low gruff rub against her skin. "Following their wet trail from the corner of your eye, down your cheek, to catch them on the tip of your chin."

He let go of the lap bar and rubbed his thumb across the point of her chin. Mac stopped breathing.

"You shivered in my arms and I knew," he said. "I knew I would take you right there under the stars and make you mine."

She looked into his eyes and saw the possession in them. He still considered Mac his and way down deep inside a tiny part of her cried *yes*.

"I remember the smell of your hair, coconut

and ginger, the feel of your skin, so soft, and the curve of your hips when I gripped them and slid into you."

Everything went gray and Mac started to see spots.

"Breathe, Mac," he said.

She did, sucking in a breath like she'd been underwater too long and was about to drown.

"I only have one regret about that night." He moved in close and his breath tickled her ear. "I lost you. I never got over losing you, Mac."

The ride kicked into gear and they began to pick up speed. The lights below them whirled in a kaleidoscope of neon and Mac felt as if the colors were shooting out of her fingertips and the ends of her hair because that was how magical Gavin made her feel.

It was inevitable, she realized, as she leaned into him. This. Only this existed in this moment and time. She pressed her mouth against his. His lips were warm. The kiss was soft and lovely and not nearly enough.

She parted her lips and felt his hand release her hair and cup the back of her head, bringing her in closer, holding her in place while he deepened the kiss, pushing his way into her mouth while coaxing her out to meet him.

Mac grabbed the front of his shirt and pulled him flush against her. Then she twined her arms around his neck to lock him in place. She could taste whiskey and cigars on his tongue and it made her blood pressure spike as the familiar citrus scent of him filled her senses.

His hand slid under her shirt and she arched into his touch. He gripped her hip and a blast of heat rocked Mac's insides as she remembered that night together with his hands on her hips as he took her completely. He moved his fingers up her side to cup one breast and run his thumb over the achy tip.

Mac moaned and she felt him smile against her skin as he worked his way down her throat toward the nipple that had puckered for want of attention. He was tugging the neckline of her shirt down to gain access to her flesh when the ride began to slow.

"Damn," he muttered. He pulled her shirt back up and moved his mouth back to hers. Between kisses, he said, "I'll just have to be content with kissing you senseless . . . for now."

She wasn't sure how long they kissed; seconds, minutes, or several spectacular hours. But she felt it when the Ferris wheel slowed to a stop, and she had the presence of mind to pull her mouth away from his.

They stared at each other for a moment and then he grinned at her and it warmed her all the way through her skin to her core.

"What?" she asked.

"You."

"What about me?"

"So much better than a memory," he said.

Mac ducked her head. He was right. She had never allowed herself to savor the memory of their night together but the feel of his lips on hers had been so deliciously familiar, and provoked such a crazy heat inside of her, that she could no longer deny that their shared night so long ago had been something extraordinary.

But this, tonight, was fraught with danger. First, she had no idea how Emma would feel about her hooking up with her "baby" brother and, second, she didn't even know how to go about starting that conversation. But she needed to make a decision and quick before something bad happened.

It occurred to her that at the moment the most likely "bad thing" was going to be her, ripping off all of his clothes and having her way with him. And that would be very, very bad given they were in the middle of the amusement park— tempting as hell, but very, very bad. She had to talk to Emma.

"Hey, you okay?" he asked.

Mac forced herself to meet his gaze. He looked concerned and she really didn't want to be the one to turn it into a look of hurt by rejecting him. Mostly, because she realized she didn't want to reject him. Man, she had truly bollixed this one. Cripes, what if someone had seen them?

"I'm good," she said. She glanced around to see where the rest of their people were.

"Don't worry, no one saw us," he said. "I know you don't want to do anything that might impact Emma's big day. How about we keep this on the down low until we figure it out. Okay?"

Mac sagged in relief. He understood. "Yes, that would be great. Thank you."

When the ride engineer popped up the lap bar, Mac hopped out of her seat and hurried down the runway. She wouldn't feel okay until she saw the others and knew for certain that their make out session hadn't been witnessed by anyone else.

They found their people around a basketball arcade game. Brad was shooting to win Emma the giant panda bear. It didn't look like it was going his way. Zach took the spot next to him and prepared to shoot, giving Carly a double thumbs-up as he went.

In short order, they were rejected with no panda to show for it. Sam stepped up next and said to Jillian, "Don't worry, I won't let you down."

She put one hand on her hip and said, "I'm sorry, are we a couple? Because I don't remember us becoming a twosome."

"I'm your groomsman," he said. "I'm better than a boyfriend because after the wedding, you're rid of me. Plus, now I can waltz."

"You just stick to waltzing," Jillian said and gestured for him to step aside. "I got this."

Sam gave her an impressed look and stepped away from the booth. Jillian stepped up to the line, grabbed a basketball, and palmed it like a pro. Being almost six feet tall, she had played on the high school volleyball team all four years and had been team captain her senior year.

"Look at that," Zach said. "She has some serious ball handling skills."

Carly hooted with laughter and Jillian gave them both a look that said they were going to eat the ball if they weren't careful. She tossed the first one and it bounced off the rim; she tossed the second to the same result. Zach started to make a drumroll noise with his mouth and Sam started chanting, "Jilly! Jilly! Jilly!"

She stepped back, dribbled once, and let the ball fly off the tips of her fingers. Nothing but net!

Emma shrieked and jumped up and down, while Carly gave Jilly a high five. Mac hugged her tight and Jilly made a fist and pumped it into the air.

"Okay, sugar pants," she said to Sam. "Pick your prize."

Sam stepped forward and picked a huge lion. Then he looked at the boys and said, "I don't know about you all, but I am feeling somewhat emasculated by this, although I love my new friend."

He hugged his lion and they all laughed.

"Step right up, only one basket wins you the prize of your choice," the barker cried out.

"Come on, Gav, you have to win one for the team," Zach said. The group turned to look at him and he shrugged and turned to Mac.

"If I participate in this display of testosterone, what would you choose?" he asked her. She looked at the array of supersized stuffed animals and saw a big banana hanging on the end of the booth.

"The banana," she said. "Definitely, the banana."

Gavin stepped up to the line, with a five-dollar bill in hand. Mac grabbed his arm.

"No, I was just kidding," she said. "Don't do it! These things are rigged."

The barker and Jillian both gave her outraged looks.

"Except for you, Jillian," she said. "You hit that like a boss."

"Are you saying you don't think I can do it?" Gavin asked.

"No, I just . . . ." Mac didn't know how to say she felt uncomfortable having him win her anything, or even try to, after their sexy time on the Ferris wheel. Lines were getting blurry and she was feeling very confused.

"Don't be a doubter," Gavin said.

"Let him try," Zach said. He pushed his veil over his shoulder and plopped his hands on his hips.

"Come on, Gavin, win our self-respect back."

Brad looked Zach over and said, "Yeah, that ship sailed, princess."

Gavin went to the line and the barker took his money and gave him three basketballs. Whoosh. Whoosh. Whoosh. He went three for three.

Zach clapped his hands to his veil and jumped up and down. Brad laughed and slapped Gavin on the shoulder and the girls all stared at him like he was a demigod. There was just something über sexy about a guy who can make bank at an arcade and win a gal the big prize.

"One banana for sure," Gavin said. He looked at Emma and Carly and said, "And whatever you two want, because clearly Jilly doesn't need me to win her anything."

Sam looked at Jillian and said, "We can share custody of Leo."

"Leo?" she asked. "You named him already? I was thinking Simba."

"Oh, hell, no," Sam said, and the two of them began squabbling.

Mac took her big banana from the booth guy and hugged it to her chest. It was totally stupid, but she'd always wanted a guy who could win her silly stuff. Then she looked at Gavin, but she couldn't have him, not yet anyway.

When the group stopped to watch the men try to win the strongman competition by ringing the bell by hammering the lever with a sledgehammer, Mac took the opportunity to pull Emma aside.

"Hey there, bride girl," she said. She watched Emma's face to see if there was a hint that she knew about what had happened on the Ferris wheel, but Emma turned a slightly tipsy brilliant smile on her and hugged her hard.

"Oh, Mac, I'm having the best time, aren't you?" she asked.

Mac nodded. She was, or she would be, if it wasn't fraught with anxiety and inappropriate thoughts about Emma's little bro.

"I am," she said.

She stared at her friend, wondering how she should broach the subject of her and Gavin. Ugh, knowing how Emma felt about her sibling, Mac wondered if she expressed an interest in him Emma would think she was a pervert or, god forbid, a cougar.

"Here's the thing though." Mac paused to choose her words carefully before continuing, "When you asked me to hang with Gavin, you said he was really depressed about his breakup, but I have to say, he doesn't seem that bummed out about it like maybe he's moved on from his heartbreak and might even consider dating again."

She pointed to where the men stood and they both glanced at Gavin. He and Brad were doubled over laughing at Zach's antics as he tried to hit the lever that would send the puck up to the bell. Zach got tangled in his veil when he went to strike and managed to drop the heavy mallet on his foot and hopped around on one foot, howling.

"Honestly, I haven't seen him laugh like that in months," Emma said. "Come to think of it, even longer, maybe years. I think having all of us around him, you know, like family, has really cheered him up."

"Like family," Mac repeated. Oh, man, Emma probably thought they all viewed him as a little brother like she did. Awkward. "Or maybe he's met someone he's interested in?"

"No," Emma scoffed. "Mac, you didn't see him after The Beyotch left. He was a wreck. He lost twenty pounds, he never smiled, he wouldn't leave his apartment except to go to work, it was awful. I was literally afraid he was going to die of a broken heart."

"Really?" Mac felt her stomach twist. Oh, god, what if this whole flirtation between them was just Gavin getting his mojo back? What if— oh, horror—what if she was just his transition woman?

"Trust me," Emma said. "This is the first sign of life I've seen in him in ages. I really hope that before the wedding festivities are over my bro has got his groove back."

"Yeah, let's hope."

Mac looked at her friend with her bright blue

eyes so like her brother's. Emma had no idea the prurient thoughts Mac was entertaining about Gavin, nor did she know about their past or that it was clearly not completely in the past.

Mac knew she could take this moment to tell Emma, but what would that do to their friendship? What would it do to Emma's wedding? Especially given how protective of Gavin she was and always had been. Mac did a gut check. Could she handle having her oldest friend call her The Beyotch if she was unhappy about Mac and Gavin hooking up? Nope, she could not and she was not brave enough to do this to her best friend. Not now.

"You've been great about cheering him up," Emma said. "Thanks, Mac, I owe you for that."

Mac gave her a half smile. If she only knew; yeah, Mac suspected if Emma knew what was what and what had been Mac would be sporting a black eye and possibly a fat lip.

All right, so the talking to Emma plan was officially abandoned. Probably it was for the best. This would force her to keep her distance from Gavin and that was as it should be. She and Trevor were on a break, but it was just a break and they clearly had some things to work out, whatever happened to them in the end.

What was she supposed to say to Gavin at this point? Oh, hey, sorry for grabbing you and kissing you on the Ferris wheel, but, oh, yeah, my boyfriend and I are taking a break so I figured it was okay. Like there was any way she could work that into a conversation and not sound like a complete jerk.

The group meandered through the games, rides, and junk food, buying popcorn and cotton candy, and when it was time to leave as the park was closing for the night, Emma stopped them all under the Belmont Park sign.

"Oh, I know what I want to commemorate the night," she said.

"Because a giant unicorn isn't enough for you?" Gav asked. She crossed her eyes and stuck her tongue out at him.

"I want to recreate the picture we took here seventeen years ago," she said. She looked at her friends. "Remember?"

"Are you kidding?" Carly asked. "I keep it on my dresser."

"Me, too," Jillian said.

"Me, three," Mac joked.

"Ha! Me, four," Emma said. "Okay, same positions."

Without having to be told, they each stood in the exact spot they had stood in so many years ago and laughed at themselves for being able to remember exactly how they had all looked back then.

Brad snapped the picture and Zach said, "I may be biased but I think this is the best-looking group of women I have ever had the pleasure of calling my friends."

"Aw," Carly said. She reached out and pulled him into the group and as they all kissed his face, Brad snapped another picture.

When they released poor Zach he was covered in lipstick and wore a silly grin. "On that note, I am going home," he said. "I mean how could my night get any better than that?"

They all parted with hugs and promises to meet up at Brad and Emma's house for a cookout the next day. Emma had her list of final details to go over with the girls so it was going to be a working dinner.

Mac handed off her banana to Carly as they walked out of the park and dug into her purse for her phone. She wanted to be sure the aunts hadn't called as she never would have heard it over the sound of the amusement park.

Her phone showed that she had missed a call and there was a message. The number wasn't one she recognized so she stepped away from the group. The horrified thought that it might be her ex Seth—that he had somehow gotten her number—filled her with dread but then common sense kicked in and she figured that was ridiculous.

She held the phone to her ear with one hand and plugged the other ear so she could hear over the conversation around her. When she heard the stranger's voice on the message, she felt her stomach drop into her feet.

"Hi, um, this is Ralph Lester. I believe you have my dog."

Chapter 23

'm so sorry, Mac," Gavin said. "These papers look legit."

"They can't be!" she cried. Her throat was tight, she couldn't breathe, and her eyes were burning from unshed tears.

After listening to Lester's message, Gavin had insisted that Mac arrange to meet Lester at his clinic on the chance that he was just some pervert trying to hook up with a woman over a lost dog.

Mac only wished that was the case. Lester had shown up with papers certifying that he had gotten Tulip from a friend. When Gavin had called the friend to verify the description of Tulip, it had matched perfectly, a three-month-old brown and black brindle of undetermined parentage. Apparently the owner had a pure breed American Staffordshire terrier and had been less than thrilled with the surprise litter of half Boxers.

Mac was devastated. She had left Tulip in an exam room, refusing to let Lester see her until she knew beyond a shadow of a doubt that she belonged to him. With each moment that passed it was looking more and more likely that she would lose her dog.

Ralph Lester was sitting in the lobby of Gavin's

animal clinic in grubby jeans, a hooded sweatshirt over a stained white T-shirt, and a pair of tennis shoes that had seen better days. He sported the middle-aged man's requisite receding hairline and spare tire and smelled faintly of bacon and despair.

"I'm not letting him take her," Mac said. "I'm not even letting him look at her."

She crossed the lobby and glared at the man in front of her. He flinched when he met her gaze.

"Is there a problem?" he asked. He looked nervous. "My dog is all right, isn't she?"

"She's fine," Mac said. "In fact, I was wondering if you'd consider selling her."

The man considered her for just a moment and then shook his head. "No, I don't think so. I'm pretty attached to the little fur face."

"Really? So attached you lost her?" Mac snapped. "You never got her proper tags, she was underfed, and I'll bet she hasn't been vaccinated, has she?"

Lester looked irritated. Gavin put his hand on Mac's shoulder and gave it a squeeze. She didn't know if it was to calm her down or to remind her to keep her cool. It didn't matter. She wasn't calm and she wanted to kick Lester's backside right out to the curb.

"Listen, I don't need a lecture from you about how to take care of *my* dog. Can I have her now?" he asked. "Or do I have to call the cops?"

"I'll get her," Gavin said. When Mac would have argued, he squeezed her shoulder again.

Mac stared at Lester. "One thousand dollars."

"What?" he asked.

"I'll pay you a thousand dollars for her," she said.

Lester grinned. "No, I don't think so."

Gavin came out of the exam room with Tulip. She was straining at her leash to get to Mac. Mac knelt down and let the dog rush her. Tulip licked her face—got her in the mouth—which made Mac laugh and sob at the same time.

"Hey, there, girlie," Lester called. Then he knelt down and held out his arms.

To Mac's horror, Tulip broke away from her and rushed to Lester. She buried her face in his hands as if reacquainting herself with his scent and he enfolded her in an affectionate hug. Tulip wagged her bottom and licked his face. Mac felt like it was a punch in the chest. Her dog really did belong to this guy.

"Well, it looks like you took okay care of her," Lester said as he got to his feet and took Tulip's leash. "So, thanks for that."

He began to walk to the door and Mac felt like tackling him to the ground and snatching her dog back. Gavin must have read her mind because he grabbed her hand in his and gave it a squeeze.

"Two thousand dollars," Gavin said.

"I'm sorry?" Lester asked.

"I'll pay you two thousand dollars for her," he said.

Mac whipped her head in Gavin's direction. Was he really doing that for Tulip? She didn't think her heart could break any more than it had, but it did.

"Yeah, no," Lester said, looking at him like he was crazy.

"Three thousand," Mac said.

"Four." Gavin upped it again when Lester kept shaking his head.

"No!" Lester said. He smiled at them, showing his yellowed uneven teeth. "But thanks for the offers, crazy people."

He stepped on the mat and the door opened. He led Tulip out and Mac took a step forward as if she could stop them, but she knew she couldn't. If the man wouldn't take four thousand dollars for the dog, clearly there was no price that would change his mind.

Once outside, Tulip paused and looked over her shoulder at Mac with her big brown eyes. She looked sad and a little afraid. Mac cried out but Lester didn't even pause. He dragged Tulip away, and she scurried to keep up with her ears flattened back and her tail tucked between her legs.

"Did you see that?" Mac cried. "She's afraid. She doesn't love him. She doesn't want to go with him. And did you notice he smelled like bacon? I bet that's why she was so happy to greet him. What dog doesn't love bacon? I have to do something. I have to get her back."

The sob when it came from inside of her almost doubled her over it hurt so bad. Tears blurred her vision and she couldn't catch her breath. She was shaking so hard she thought she might break apart into a million pieces of pain.

Gavin pulled her into his arms and held her tight. Mac collapsed against him and sobbed all over his shoulder, until his shirt was soaked and her eye sockets were dry.

He never said a word. He didn't try to talk her out of her feelings. He didn't try to spin it or find some sort of positive outcome. He knew she was devastated and he let her be devastated. He ran his hand up and down her spine in a gesture of comfort that soothed like no words could.

When Doc Scharff arrived and found them standing in the lobby, he asked, "Grieving?"

"Yeah, something like that," Gavin said.

Mac stepped away from Gavin and glanced at the white-haired old man in the lab coat. She rubbed her face with her hands and took a steadying breath. "Sorry, Doc."

The kindly old veterinarian patted her shoulder. "It's all right. I've been doing this for over forty years and I still cry every time I have to let go of a patient."

Mac felt her throat get tight again and she nodded.

"Go get her a cup of coffee," Doc said to Gavin. "She looks like she could use it. I can handle this place on my own for a while."

Gavin nodded and put his hand at Mac's back to usher her out the door. Instead of walking to The Grind, however, he led her to the stairs that ran up the side of the two-story white building. At the bottom, he took her hand and pulled her up the stairs behind him.

Potted plants that looked like they were in the throes of suicide filled one corner of the small deck. Gavin unlocked the security door and gestured for Mac to go in. She stepped into an apartment that was compact but charming with a galley kitchen to the right and a large living room to the left.

Gavin moved around her and swept a pile of clothes off a nearby chair and tossed them through a doorway on the right, closing the door afterwards. He turned back to face her and shoved his hands in his back pockets. Now he looked like the little boy she remembered and, yet, still sexy.

"It's not much but you can't beat the commute to work," he said. She nodded, tried to smile, and failed.

"Can I use your bathroom?" she asked. "I'm pretty sure I need to deal with this." She pointed to her face, knowing full well that she had the post-crying jag, blotchy cheeks, swollen eyes, red nose, and pale lip thing going, always so attractive.

"Sure, I'll make coffee," he said.

Mac splashed cold water on her face until the red receded and she looked pasty pale. When she glanced in the mirror, her own sad brown eyes stared back at her and she remembered the last look Tulip had given her with her own dark eyes. Mac had thought she had no more tears left, but as one coursed down her cheek and she sniffled, she knew she was wrong.

There had to be something she could do, some way to get Lester to sell her dog back to her. She was a mutt, of no distinction, how could he have said no to four thousand dollars?

That reminded her, what had Gavin been thinking offering that much? She dried her face with one of his towels and the citrusy cedar scent that was uniquely his filled her up and comforted her. He was a good man, that's what he was thinking. And he deserved so much better than to get tangled up with a woman who was likely nothing more than a transition person for him— and his sister's best friend. It would complicate everything if they didn't work out. The best thing she could do for him would be to stay away. For good.

Newly resolved, Mac left the bathroom and

found Gavin standing in his small kitchen waiting for her. For the rest of her days, she would remember him exactly like that.

Leaning, with his back to the kitchen sink, he stood with one foot crossed over the other and his arms folded loosely over his chest. His caramel hair hung down over his forehead and his ruggedly handsome face looked equal parts sad and serious. When he saw her come toward him, one corner of his mouth tipped up, flashing the dimple in his right cheek as if he was trying to smile just for her, to help her, to make her feel better.

"You okay?" he asked. His deep voice rumbled out of his chest and smoothed over Mac's frayed nerves like a caress.

"Yeah, I'm good," she said. "In fact, I'd better go. You need to get back to work and I'm sure Emma needs me for something or other."

"Are you sure?" he asked.

Mac nodded. She knew she was in a weakened state and the sooner she put some distance between them the better, otherwise she might throw herself at him in an effort to feel comforted when in reality the only thing that could make her feel better was getting Tulip back.

"So, what are you going to do about it?" Aunt Sarah asked after Mac recounted the events of the morning.

They were sitting on the porch enjoying Aunt

Charlotte's frosty lemonade, while Mac silently plotted the death of one Ralph Lester. Okay, not really, but the idea brought her a bloodthirsty sort of comfort, which felt better than focusing on the flash of hurt she'd seen in Gavin's eyes when she bolted out of his apartment.

"I don't think there's anything I can do," Mac said. "If Tulip belongs to him and he won't let me buy her, I'm screwed."

The aunts exchanged a look. Charlotte looked concerned while Sarah looked annoyed.

"What?" Mac asked.

"Nothing." Sarah shrugged. "I just figured you'd give him a proper chin check before letting him make off with your dog."

"Chin check?" Mac asked. "As in punch him in the face? Okay, that's it, what is going on with you?"

"Just sayin'," Sarah said. She turned away to study her clematis vine, which was winding its way across the porch rail.

"I have to say, Mac, Sarah is right," Charlotte said. "You're usually much more of a fighter." She turned to Sarah. "Remember that time she socked Pete Turner in the nose when he wouldn't stop following her around saying he was going to marry her? That was epic!"

Epic? Mac was boggled. "Look, if I couldn't get him to take four grand, I doubt a beating will bend him to my will."

"Four grand?" Charlotte choked. "Where were you going to get that money?"

"Gavin and I got a little carried away," Mac said.

"Understandable. But more to the point, why wouldn't he take the money?" Sarah asked.

"That's a lot for a dog he didn't seem to be taking very good care of," Charlotte said. "Don't you find that curious?"

Mac looked at her two aunts. They were right. Something wasn't right in Lester land and she was going to find out what it was.

"If you two will excuse me, I need to go check something on my computer," Mac said.

As she got to her feet and crossed the porch, she heard Sarah say to Charlotte, "That's our girl."

Chapter 24

"Are you sure this is the right address?" Jillian asked. She pointed at the ramshackle one-story cottage rife with overgrown grass and a rusty chain-link fence running around the property.

The four women were in her Jeep parked across the narrow neighborhood street from the house that Mac had found listed as belonging to one Ralph Lester on the town's property records. He lived on the outskirts of Bluff Point, barely a resident of town as far as she could tell. How Tulip had managed to get seven miles into town to be found in that alley, Mac couldn't fathom.

"The property is listed as belonging to Ralph Lester," Mac said. "It has to be him, unless there is more than one of them, which is unlikely in our petite community of seven thousand residents."

"It's just that I'm surprised he turned the offer of money down," Jillian said.

"No kidding," Carly agreed. "If anyone ever needed four thousand dollars, it's this guy."

"I have a visual," Emma said. She was using her father's binoculars to spy on Lester from the back seat. "Oh, my eyes!"

"What is it?" Mac asked.

"He took his shirt off," Emma said and handed the binoculars to Carly, who was beside her in the back seat. "I didn't know shag carpeting was making a comeback."

"Oh, gross," Carly said. "Wax the back, dude."

"All right, whatever," Mac said. She was feeling anxious and antsy about her baby girl. "Do you see Tulip anywhere?"

Carly was silent for a moment. "No, no sign of her in the room with him."

"That's weird," Mac said. "She likes to be wherever her people are."

"Maybe she doesn't like him," Emma said.

"This proves he's not her people," Carly said.

"Or not," Jillian said. Her voice was grim.

"What is it?" Mac asked.

"Look behind the house to the right," Jillian said. "Is that—oh, Mac, I'm so sorry."

Mac leaned over her friend in the driver's seat and stared out the window so hard her eyes almost crossed. It was dark out as they had waited until after the cookout at Emma and Brad's to do Tulip recon. They had considered including the boys but Mac was afraid that much testosterone might cause problems, plus she was still trying to keep her distance from Gavin, so they fibbed and said they were going shopping instead.

She scanned the dark yard and then saw some movement in the back and a motion-activated spotlight snapped on. Mac gasped. Rage, red-hot and ready to explode like a supernova, pulsed through her entire being.

She pushed her door open and hopped to the ground. No one, but no one, tied her dog up in the backyard. She ran across the street. She heard her friends calling after her, but she paid them no heed.

She was getting Tulip out of there if she had to hop the fence and haul her out. She ran along the chain link, circled the yard to the back. Tulip must have smelled her coming, because she whimpered and her tail thumped on the ground.

"Hi, baby," Mac called softly to her. "I'm here. It's okay. I'm here."

Tulip barked a happy greeting, then rose from her crouched position in the dirt and ran at the fence. Her leash was too short, however, and when she got to the end of it, she was yanked off of her feet and slammed back to the ground with a cry of pain.

It was like a knife in her chest, and Mac was pretty sure she could rip the fence down with her bare hands.

"Son of a bitch!" Carly cursed as she joined Mac at the fence.

"We have to get her out of there," Mac said. "She doesn't belong there. Look at it, it's disgusting. She doesn't have food or water. There's no shelter, just broken down rusty old crap everywhere. She could get cut. I can't, I just can't . . ."

"Shh," Emma said. She wrapped her arms around Mac and hugged her tight. "It's going to be all right. We'll get her out of here. I promise."

Tulip was lying in the dirt, facing Mac. She was whimpering as if she could sense Mac's stress and wanted to comfort her. Mac forced herself to pull it together for Tulip's sake.

"Okay, what's the plan?" Her voice was hoarse from holding all of her rage in. She cleared her throat but it didn't help.

"A little snip ought to take care of the problem," Jillian said. Mac looked at her friend and noticed she was holding bolt cutters.

"I love you," she said.

"You know me, I like to be prepared," Jilly said.

"All right, Carly, come with me," Emma said. "We'll go to the door and distract him while you two get Tulip out. Whistle once you've got her and then we'll drive the car to the next street and pick you up on the other side of the woods."

"Okay, let's do this," Mac said. She enfolded all three of her friends in a quick group hug. "Be careful. I have a hinky feeling about this guy."

"This guy? Really? Between the back hair and the toilet in the front yard, I really thought I'd found my soul mate," Carly said.

Jillian snorted and kneeled down, getting ready to start cutting the chain-link as soon as Emma and Carly were in place at Lester's door.

Mac followed them and waited where she could see Lester answer them. Emma and Carly knocked and waited. Mac wondered what they were going to use for an excuse to voluntarily stop by this dump. Encyclopedia sales? Engine trouble? Religious messengers? What would Lester go for?

She heard the door open and Emma started talking. Mac beat feet back to Jillian, who started cutting the chain-link as soon as she saw Mac coming. The chain was thick and it took longer than Mac would have expected. She rocked on her feet, planning to dive into the backyard as soon as the opening was big enough.

"Okay, now!" Jillian said. She dropped the bolt cutters and curled the chain-link back. She'd managed to cut a hole large enough for Mac to wriggle through and Mac dropped to her belly and crawled through. When her shirt got snagged, she didn't stop but let it tear as she kept going.

Tulip's tail was thumping on the ground and her whimpering had grown even louder. Mac rose to her knees and hurried across the hard packed dirt.

Tulip pounced on her as soon as she was within reach. She licked Mac's face, on the mouth, and hit her like a cannonball with her front feet, knocking Mac to the ground, which was fine with Tulip because she could keep licking.

Mac laughed and rubbed her ears. "Okay, easy does it, girl. We have to get you out of here fast."

Mac had just unclipped the chain from Tulip's collar when a bright white beam of light slapped her right in the eyeballs.

"Hey, you there, what are you doing?"

Mac held up a hand to shield her eyes. From the authoritative sound in the man's voice, she knew this was bad.

She turned and glanced over her shoulder and hissed, "Run, Jilly, run!"

"I can't," Jillian said. She gestured beside her and Mac saw another cop standing there.

"Oh, crap," she said.

The back door to the tiny house opened and out walked Lester. He looked smug. "Did you really think I didn't notice you casing my place for fifteen minutes before these two showed up at my front door?"

Emma and Carly came out behind him with another officer at their back. Okay, so an inordinate amount of back hair didn't mean the guy was stupid. Mac had really felt there was a correlation there but obviously she'd been wrong.

"Officers, I can explain," Mac said. And she did, in the middle of the backyard with Tulip at her side. The three officers listened to what she had to say. They looked sympathetic to her plight but not enough to let her take Tulip.

"I'm sorry, ma'am," Officer Morgan said. He looked to be the senior of the three, but Mac doubted he had more than a year or two on her in age. "But you can't just take the dog. If you genuinely suspect abuse, there are procedures in place."

"But she has no food or water," Mac protested. "She's chained in a backyard. What sort of person does that?"

"Hey, hey, hey," Lester blustered. "How I take care of my dog is none of your damn business."

"Easy, Mr. Lester," Officer Polson said. "It is my business if I make it my business and you'd best keep that in mind."

Polson reached down to pet Tulip and Mac liked him for it. Maybe they could get out of this with the puppy after all.

"I'm sorry, but I felt it was important to take care of the dog first and follow procedure second," Mac said.

"It doesn't work that way," Officer Morgan said.

"Well, it should," Carly said. She moved to stand beside Mac, as did Jillian and Emma.

"I want them arrested for trespassing and for destroying private property," Lester said. "Just look what they did to my fence."

Morgan went over and examined the gaping hole. "I'm sure the ladies are willing to make restitution. Right, ladies?"

"Sure," Mac said. "As soon as he gives me my dog."

"She's not your dog!" Lester yelled. "You found her in an alley a few days ago."

"Yes, but I've been taking care of her and I got her vaccinated. Did you?" Mac asked.

Lester threw his hands in the air. "Get off my property."

"Fine," Mac snapped. "But I'm taking my dog with me."

Tulip's ears went back and she pressed herself against Mac's side. It was clear she didn't like the yelling. Mac felt bad and tried to rein in her temper.

Lester had handed his ownership papers to the third officer in the group. The officer shuffled through them and then handed them to Morgan.

"Everything looks in order," he said. He didn't sound happy about it. "It looks like the dog is his."

"I think it's time you ladies left the premises," Morgan said. He wasn't unkind about it, but he did sound firm.

"I won't leave without my dog," Mac said.

"Me either," Carly declared and linked her arm with Mac's.

Jillian and Emma joined the human chain and Officer Morgan squeezed his temples between his fingers as if he was warding off a headache.

"Okay, fine," he said. "But you're giving me no choice but to place you under arrest."

"I can't believe he really arrested us," Carly said. "I mean I thought he'd get a good laugh out of it and let us go, but look at us; we're actually in freaking jail!"

Mac sat slumped on the metal cot, leaning up against the cement wall. They were in a narrow cell made up of two cement walls with bars for the remaining two walls, one of which had a door, also made of bars. Quite the ambiance.

The Bluff Point jail had exactly two cells, one for boys and one for girls. The four of them filled the girl cell, while the boy cell was currently unoccupied. Thank goodness.

"I'm sorry," Mac said. "This is all my fault."

She dropped her head onto her knees, but then reeled back as the smell coming off of her clothes made her eyes water. One more thing about a dog being chained, they really didn't have a lot of options on where they went to the bathroom. Mac in her haste to get to Tulip had obviously rolled in something stinky.

"No, we're in it together," Emma said. "I really thought we'd be able to get her out of there. It kills me that we had to leave her with that . . . that . . . hairy troll."

"We'll save her, don't you worry." Jillian sat on the cot beside Mac and put her arm around her, then she sniffed the air around Mac. With a look of disgust, she checked the bottom of her shoes.

"It's not you, it's me," Mac said. She pointed to the mysterious brown stains on her pants and Jillian flinched.

"I'm just going to move back over there," she said.

"Understood," Mac said. She'd peel off her clothes if she could, but naked in jail just seemed so much worse than smelly in jail.

"Oh, man, I just had a horrible thought," Carly said. "What if they keep us in here and you miss your wedding?"

Mac looked at Emma. That could not happen. She would feel horrible, awful, devastated.

"Nah," Emma said. "They can't hold us that long; seriously, this is a misdemeanor at best. Besides, even if they did, Brad would come and save me."

"Like he is right now," a man's voice spoke and they all turned to see Brad striding into the jail with Zach, Sam, and Gavin at his back.

"Oh, girls, what did you do?" Zach asked.

"It's a long story," Jillian said. "How about we tell it over drinks after we get out of here?"

"Sounds good to me," Sam said.

Officer Polson arrived with the keys to the door. He unlocked it and let Emma, Carly, and Jillian go. When Mac went to follow, he held her back with a hand on her arm.

"Can I talk to you for a moment?" he asked.

Unaware of her plight, her friends headed out the door. Mac didn't call them back. She figured if she was going to get the verbal ruler across the knuckles, she'd take it for the team. Besides, if she had to, she'd do it all over again, but next time she'd get her dog out and hopefully not reek of poop.

"Listen, Ms. Harris—"

"Mac," she said. "Everyone calls me Mac."

He nodded. "Okay, Mac, here's the thing. I understand why you did what you did. Between you and me, I've got a bad feeling about that guy, and I plan on going back to Mr. Lester's house quite often and if I see anything that warrants my involvement, I will not hesitate. Does that help?"

Mac felt the hot spurt of tears fill her eyes. She nodded quickly. "Yes, it does, a lot actually. Thank you."

He looked away as if he was unsure of what to do with a woman's tears. He closed the cell door and led the way out of the room. Mac went to follow him and found Gavin standing off to the side waiting for her. She tried to look brave and strong and even forced a smile but it unraveled on her. Her lips wobbled and she started to cry.

Gavin opened his arms and Mac stepped into them. Again, he said nothing. He just held her while she fought to get ahold of herself.

"Hey, you two, we're all going—" Zach bounced into the room but stopped when he caught sight of Mac's sad face; or maybe it was the fact that she was in Gavin's arms, but she suspected it was the former given that she was such a pretty crier and all.

282

"I think I'm just going to take Mac home," Gavin said.

"Gotcha. Man, what is that stank?" Zach sniffed the air and did a quick check of the bottom of his shoes.

"Yeah," Mac said. "It's me."

"Oh." Zach cringed. He looked as uncomfortable as the officer had and Mac figured if she could bottle this blotchy face, runny nose, and whiff of dog doo-doo she'd have herself some damn fine man repellent.

Zach was made of tougher stuff than she gave him credit for, however, and he stepped closer and awkwardly patted her back. "It's going to be okay, Mac. We'll get her back somehow."

Mac stepped away from Gavin and gave Zach a watery smile. "Thanks, dude."

Zach winked at her. "I'll go get everyone out of your way, okay?"

"That'd be great," Gavin said.

"If you change your mind it's two-for-one pitchers of our very fine Bluff Point Ale at Marty's," Zach said. He paused and looked at Mac, and said, "But you might want to shower and comb that." He pointed to his head and then hers. "And maybe wash this." He circled a finger around his face and then pointed to her.

"Good night, Zach," Mac said. She used the hem of her shirt to wipe her eyes and when she looked up he was gone.

"You ready?" Gavin asked.

"Yeah," Mac said. "If you want to join the others feel free. You don't have to give me a ride home. I can call the aunts."

"Please, stop the crazy talk," he said. He picked up her bag where it sat beside him on the floor. "Officer Morgan let me collect your stuff for you. I think they all feel pretty bad about what happened."

"You should have seen it," Mac said as she draped her bag over her shoulder. "Lester's got her chained in the backyard. She didn't have food or water. There's no shelter. She looks sad and lonely and scared. I can't bear it, Gav. I can't bear to leave her there."

"I know," he said.

He put his hand on her lower back and ushered her through the door. The main room of the small-town police station was empty except for the officer on desk duty. He glanced up at them as they passed but one look at Mac's face and he glanced away as if desperately hoping for an emergency call on his radio.

Sheesh, did the women in these men's lives never cry? As Gavin led Mac out the main door, the officer looked infinitely relieved.

"Do I really look that bad?" she asked.

"There is no right way for me to answer that question," he said.

"Oh, my god, that bad?"

"See? No right answer." He opened the passenger door to his pickup truck, which was parked out front, and she climbed in.

Mac resisted looking at her reflection in the mirror on the back of the sun visor for about three seconds. Then she flipped it down and the built-in light switched on. Mac shrieked.

Chapter 25

Oh, you looked," Gavin said as he climbed in on the driver's side.

Mac turned to face him. "No one said anything. I was in a jail cell with my three best friends and not one of them suggested I try to spit shine the dirt off my face or finger comb my hair. Really?"

"Well, things were a bit chaotic," Gavin said.

"We were in there for two hours," Mac protested. "I need three new best friends. Oh, man, I can't go home like this. The aunts will think I've come back from the dead or worse."

"You can clean up at my place," he said. Not giving Mac any say in the matter, he drove through town and parked on the street in front of the clinic.

Mac would have argued or just bucked up and gone home but she didn't have an ounce of fight left in her and she really didn't want the aunts to see her like this, looking like she'd been hog wrestling in the dirt. Okay, the dirt they could handle no problem but the misery that seemed to be etched in the filth on her face, yeah, that would break their hearts and she'd rather see them when she wasn't feeling quite so raw.

When they walked into Gavin's she saw the remnants of the poker game the boys had been playing when Emma called them to be busted out of jail.

"I hope you weren't winning," she said.

"Nope." He picked up his hand and showed it to her. It was a random assortment of throwaway cards. "Your arrest probably saved me from losing my shirt."

"Well, there's that," she said.

"Go. I'll make some tea." Gavin handed her a towel and a robe and pushed her in the direction of the bathroom. "And throw your clothes in the hall so I can put them in the washing machine."

Mac dropped her bag on the floor and went without argument. The robe was huge. In a manly shade of charcoal gray, it was soft and fluffy and smelled like him. Mac wanted to climb inside of it and stay there until her heart healed but she feared that was going to be a long time coming and he might want his robe back before then.

She stripped down and dropped her clothes right outside the door. She couldn't blame him for wanting to get them in the washer as fast as possible. She imagined they could stink up his apartment in no time.

She turned the shower temperature to smoking hot as if she could fry the anguish right out of her pores, then she stood under the jets trying to get the image of Tulip being left behind out of her head. It didn't work and she started to cry, again. She figured this was it, the last time

287

she would let herself fall apart tonight, so she let it break her down all the way to a cellular level.

She sobbed, she wailed, she cried, and she didn't stop until she felt as if she'd wrung every bit of angry frustrated grief out of her system. She suspected there'd be more tomorrow but for now she was an empty vessel, a shell, with no purpose except to survive until she could figure out how to free Tulip from her prison.

Gavin sat on the couch, flipping through channels with the remote. His walls were thin, which with no neighbors wasn't usually a problem, but even with the steady beat of the water in the tile shower, he could hear Mac crying as if someone had reached inside her chest and ripped her heart out.

Twice he got up to go comfort her, but sanity kicked in and he realized charging into a bathroom where there was a naked woman working through her grief was awkward at best and creepy at worst. So he sat, nursing his beer and feeling like a little part of himself was dying with each sob that she heaved.

Finally, the crying stopped and so did the water. After a few minutes the door opened with a plume of steam and Mac stepped out. Gavin had his beer to his lips when he saw her and he froze, unable to remember if he was taking a drink or finishing a sip or what as his brain turned to mush at the sight of her.

She was towel drying the ends of her hair, which was wet and combed back from her face. Whether her cheeks were pink from the heat or scrubbing he didn't know, he just knew that she looked charming and alluring all at the same time. He shifted in his seat against the sudden tightness in his crotch and felt immediately guilty for thinking that she was hot when she was clearly still struggling with her emotions.

When she looked at him, he saw a flash of sad in her eyes but she soldiered on, not letting it take over. Her big brown eyes looked soft surrounded by her water-soaked spiky lashes and he had to resist the urge to pull her close and kiss each one.

His robe on her was huge. Given that her clothes were currently spinning in his dryer, the knowledge that she was likely naked or near naked under the robe did not help his sudden shortness of breath.

"Here," he said as he stood. "I can get you some tea, cocoa, warm milk, scotch?"

"I don't want to trouble you," she said.

"No trouble," he said, which was a blatant lie because her state of undress was causing him no end of serious freaking below-the-belt trouble.

He crossed the living room and went to pass her on his way to the kitchen, but when he got into the same breathing space as her, he lost his sense of purpose. He took the towel she held in her hands and threw it on the floor and then he backed her up against the wall and put his mouth on hers.

This. This was what he'd wanted to do since he'd seen her sad face at the jail. He wanted to hold her and comfort her, he wanted to kiss the hurt away just like he had all those years ago.

He wanted to strip her naked and he wanted to bury himself inside of her until they were one. But for now, he kissed her, slow, openmouthed deep kisses that made her hum in the back of her throat like a cat purring.

"Stop me now," he said. "If you're going to, do it now."

He was pretty sure that if she did, he was going to die, but at least he'd die in her arms with his lips on hers and his erection pressed up against her.

"Can't. Stop." Her breathy words rocked him like a one-two punch to the chest.

Gavin didn't hesitate. He shoved the robe aside and sucked in a breath when he saw she was just in a bra and undies. Pink. Silky. History.

He slid his mouth over her skin to the breast that had taunted him before and he pulled the delicate fabric aside and put his mouth over the hard bud and bit down. Mac moaned and her legs buckled, so he grabbed her hips and jacked her up against the wall, shoving his thigh between her legs to brace her.

Her hands gripped his shoulders and tugged at his shirt until he paused to yank it over his head. He unfastened her bra and it went the way of his shirt. Then he pressed his chest against hers and they both hissed from the contact. When his hands slid up her sides to cup her breasts and her head fell back on a grunt of pleasure, yeah, he was pretty sure he was going to die.

How many times had he pictured her just like this, coming apart in his arms? Her brown eyes looked smoky with a fire banked in their depths. He was determined to turn up the heat and make her feel the burn for him, just him.

He slid his hands down to her hips and hoisted her up against him so that her legs locked around his waist. His own knees almost buckled when her hot spot cupped his hard-on, making his heart thud in his chest and his ears ring. The connection was positively combustible.

He slanted his mouth over hers and kissed her as if she were as vital to his survival as the air that he breathed. He was pretty sure she was. She responded by digging her fingers into his hair and pulling him even closer.

It felt as if they couldn't ever be close enough. He cupped her bottom and turned away from the wall, striding over to the couch, where he dropped back in a free fall that pulled her down on top of him, making all of her girl parts line up perfectly with his boy parts. Bliss.

This was it. He couldn't take it anymore. He hooked a finger into her silk bottoms and pulled them down just far enough to give him access. Then he slid one finger right up and in, making Mac buck against his hand. He used his thumb to hit that deliciously sensitive nub, and Mac cried out in a hoarse shout as she began to convulse around his fingers, making him damn near come in his jeans.

When she finished riding out the orgasm and stopped grinding against his hand, Gavin planted a kiss on her that left her panting in his mouth.

That about destroyed him and he decided it was time for her to lose the undies completely. He grabbed the satiny string at her hips with every intention of ripping them off. And then his phone began to buzz and beep.

"Huh . . . what?" Mac broke the kiss but he had her by the panties and he wasn't letting go.

"Phone," he murmured against her neck as he reached for his cell on the coffee table.

He would have happily, oh so happily, ignored it, but it wasn't the ringtone for family or friends. Oh, no, this was his emergency vet number. Damn it!

He pulled Mac close and she sagged against him in the aftermath of his lovemaking like a shadow hugs the ground. How he wanted desperately to bury himself deep inside of her, but the text message on his phone ended that.

Gently, he pushed her hair back from her face and kissed both of her eyelids, her nose, and finally her lips.

"I have to go," he said.

Mac looked at him, her brown eyes unfocused and dreamy, and he remembered that look. He had seen it on her face just once before. It was his look. It belonged just to him.

"The Marcels' boxer just had a seizure," he said. "I have to go and check on him."

"Oh," Mac said. Then her eyes popped open wider and she jumped off of his lap. "Oh, I'm sorry. Go! You need to go."

"I want you to stay here and wait for me," he said. He cringed when he stood up. Vet with a raging stiffy, coming through.

She opened her mouth to protest but he kissed her, effectively stopping her argument. Huh. He'd have to remember that. Then he scooped up the robe from the floor and wrapped her in it.

"Make yourself at home," he said. He yanked on his T-shirt and grabbed his wallet, phone, and keys. "I'll be back as soon as I can."

"Okay," she said.

Gavin paused by the door for one last look. Her hair had dried in thick waves about her shoulders. Clutching the front of the robe together, she looked fragile and a little lost. Oh, hell.

He strode across the room with one purpose in his every step, to kiss away the vulnerable woman and bring back the hot siren who had tortured his unconscious for seven long years. His mouth took hers ruthlessly and when she grabbed his shirt and pulled him in close, he knew he had her.

When he stepped back, breathing hard and feeling like he was going to bust a seam on his jeans, he was pleased to see that she was looking at him like she was planning to eat him for breakfast. Yes, he'd let her.

"Wait for me," he said. He turned and left the apartment as fast as he could, knowing that if he looked at her for one more second, he'd have her naked in his bed riding his cock until he was completely drained, which judging by how hard he was at the moment, would take a week, possibly two.

Chapter 26

Mac stood in the center of Gavin's living room, feeling like she'd just jumped off of a high-speed train and it was not the aftereffects of the orgasm making her feel like that. Oh, no, it was the shame.

Shame cloaked her in an acid bath of self-loathing. She had almost gone full frontal. She glanced down; who was she kidding? She had gone full frontal with Gavin. Gavin! The guy she was only supposed to be cheering up, although in her own defense he'd looked pretty cheery there until the phone rang.

She slapped her hands to her face, which was suddenly eight shades of fiery hot embarrassment. What the hell had she been thinking? She had promised herself she wouldn't do this. If Emma found out . . . oh, god, she might oust Mac right out of the wedding party.

She let out a little shriek. She had to get the hell out of here, before Gav came back, before she slept with him, because she would. She knew that now. There wasn't enough willpower in the world to make her not crawl all over him if he crooked his little finger at her. Crooked his finger. Sigh. Mac dropped her head to her chest as the memory of the havoc his fingers had managed to wreak upon her invaded her brain space.

In seconds, she was dressed in her still damp clothes. As she pulled them out of the dryer, she didn't care that they were more wet than dry. She didn't even bother to put her bra back on but shoved it in her bag, which she threw over her shoulder. She hurried for the door, but then paused.

This was Gavin. She had run out on him once before. Could she really do that to him again? He had been very specific that he wanted her to wait for him.

A note. She'd leave him a note. Notes made everything better, right?

She hurried over to a small desk in the corner where he had his laptop. She searched the top, which was bare, and then opened the middle drawer, thinking it would be the place for paper and pens. Jackpot!

She grabbed a pen and then reached for a pad of sticky notes. The corner of a photo caught her eye. She knew she should ignore it, but, yeah, she didn't.

She pulled the photo out from under the pad and there was Gav, smiling not at her but rather lovingly at the woman in the picture with him. Her breath caught at just how handsome his profile was; truly, the man did not have a bad side. From the background, she gathered the picture was taken at his clinic and he was leaning against the front counter and a pretty redhead was tucked under his arm gazing up at him and he looked besotted with her. Mac frowned. She did not like this picture.

She flipped it over. Scrawled in a woman's hand were the words:

Gavin and Jane 2016

She flipped it back over. So, this was Jane. Mac moved closer to a light so she could really examine the woman's features. She had a prominent nose and chin and her eyes, which looked to be a very bright blue, were set far apart. Her red hair was long, covering what Mac suspected were sticky-out ears. Overall, she was okay. Nothing special.

Yeah, right. She glanced in the drawer and saw there was a whole stack of photos of Jane and Gavin: riding bikes, hiking a mountain, on the beach, and dressed up for a formal date. In every one, Gavin looked smitten with the redhead. Clearly, they had enjoyed each other's company quite a bit. Mac felt a clawing inside her chest and realized it was her old friend jealousy. She hadn't felt that since Jessie had made off with her fiancé.

If Jane hadn't been special to Gavin then why did he have all of these pictures, and why didn't he ever talk about her? She'd seen his face when

Jane's name came up; it was so neutral it was clearly not neutral. Oh, crud, that meant that Mac was most definitely his transition woman. Ack!

It was bad enough she was fooling around with her best friend's little brother; now she'd have to deal with all of the attachment that came with a person transitioning out of one thing and into another. She dropped the picture into the drawer and slammed it shut.

She tapped the pen to the pad and tried to think of what to say. It had to be nice without offering any possibility for the future. Thanks for the good time? No, too cold. Plus, it had been way better than good.

No, there really wasn't anything in Miss Manners that covered ducking out on a man and leaving him hard up because you're on hiatus from your own relationship, you suspect you're just his NER (nonexistent relationship), aka, friends with benefits, booty call, etc., oh, and your best friend will likely kill you if she finds out you're fooling around with her little brother.

Okay, then, blame it on someone else. Misdirection of fault, which always worked, right?

She scribbled:

The aunts called. Had to go. Sorry, Mac.

She debated a kinder, gentler closing but she couldn't write "love," "fondly" seemed wrong, and X's and O's were wildly inappropriate. "Sorry" would have to do, and at least it was honest. She was sorry; sorry for agreeing to be his buddy for Emma, sorry for going too far with him when he clearly wasn't over his ex, and sorry for not being stronger and letting things get out of hand, as it was, between them.

Leaving the note on the kitchen table, she grabbed her bag and darted out, locking the door behind her. She hurried down the stairs and up the sidewalk, putting as much distance between her and his place as she could without looking like a felon on the run.

She didn't slow down until she reached the cover of the trees that lined the town green. The night air was heavy and damp, cool with a briny tang to it, letting her know it must be high tide. It was almost midnight, but she felt no fear walking through Bluff Point this late at night. Even though she had been away for years, this was home and she knew every crack and crevice, every nook and cranny of its craggy familiar face as if she had never been gone.

The churches were lit up for their nightly sentry duty, and a light breeze ruffled the leaves of the maples overhead. The shops were all closed but the streetlamps, made to look like old-fashioned lampposts, kept back the gloomy shadows with their yellow light. Mac had missed this town, she realized. Walking along the sidewalk, she felt as if it was embracing her back into the fold. Too bad she couldn't stay.

The sound of a car engine cruising up on her made Mac turn and look over her shoulder. Her heart kicked into high gear, thinking it might be Gavin. It was not.

As the Jeep slowed beside her, the passenger window rolled down, and Carly leaned out and said, "For the love of all that is holy, please tell me this is not Walk of Shame, Part Deux."

"Okay, I won't tell you," Mac said as she opened the back door and climbed in.

"What?" Jillian whipped her head around to look at Mac from the driver's seat.

"I'm joking," Mac said. "What are you two doing out here?"

"Well, after jail we were going to go for drinks but we discovered being incarcerated really builds a girl's appetite so we all went to the diner on Route One and had blueberry pancakes, and now we're headed home."

Mac felt her stomach rumble. She could use a pancake about now.

"The more interesting question is why are you out here?" Carly asked. "Because I was under the impression that Gavin was taking you home."

"Yeah, well, that was before I got a glimpse of myself in the mirror," Mac said. "Thanks for telling me I looked like dog shit, by the way."

"Well, you already smelled like it," Jillian said.

"Besides, we figured you were too upset to care."

Okay, Mac could concede that point.

"So, you look freshly laundered," Carly said. "How'd that happen?"

"I took a minute to clean up and wash my clothes and was just walking home," Mac said. "So, see? NBD."

"No big deal?" Carly asked. "Where exactly did you do laundry and clean up?"

"Gavin's place," Mac said. She tried to make it sound as casual as she would say the library, or the post office, or a rest stop on the highway, but even she could hear her voice drop an octave and become raspy.

Jillian turned the Jeep into Mac's driveway at the same moment Carly squealed, "You slept with him, didn't you?"

"What?" Mac asked. "No!" Technically, it was not a lie; there had been no sleeping involved.

"You can tell us the truth," Jillian said.

"I am," Mac said. She tried to sound indignant, but she knew it came out as defensive instead.

"Uh-huh," Carly said.

"Whatever." Mac rolled her eyes. She opened her bag and rummaged around for her house key. Grabbing the big ring, she pulled it out of her purse and Carly shrieked and grabbed for the keys.

"Mackenzie Harris, if you did not fool around

with Gavin, what is your bra doing dangling from your keys?" she demanded as she held Mac's pink bra up as evidence.

Mac thunked her head against the headrest on Jillian's seat. "Would you believe me if I said it wasn't mine?"

"No," Jillian and Carly said together.

"It was worth a shot," Mac said. "Look, it's not how it seems. I took a shower at his place—"

"Before or after sex?" Carly asked.

"Before," Mac said and then clapped a hand over her mouth.

"Good," Jillian said, ever practical. "Because you needed one."

"No, no, no, that's not what I meant," Mac said. "Listen, emotions were running high, mostly mine, and we fooled around, really, it wasn't any more than that."

"Then why did you sneak out of his place?" Carly asked.

"What makes you think I snuck out?" Mac asked.

"Because this is Gavin," Carly said. "And if he was there when you decided to leave—no wait, if he was there, why would you decide to leave? I mean if you had access to that bod, you could start kissing his—"

"Stop before you overheat," Jillian said. Then she turned to Mac. "She's right; Gavin would have insisted on driving you home. So, if I accept that what happened between you is none of my business—"

Carly opened her mouth to protest, but Jillian spoke right over her and said, "And I do, then my concerns are now centered on Emma. Is what happened between you and Gavin going to impact her in any way?"

"No," Mac said. "In fact, that's why I left, so that no damage can be done."

"No damage?" Carly asked. "Or no more damage?"

Mac shrugged.

"Did you ever think that maybe you should just tell Emma about what happened between you and Gavin seven years ago?" Jillian asked. Her voice was gentle and not judgy, which Mac appreciated so very much.

"I've thought about it," she said. "But I feel like the timing is not ideal. Also, did you see how she talked about Jane? She hates her—I mean, really hates her. And speaking of Jane, yeah, I found pictures of her in Gavin's desk."

"What were you doing searching his desk?" Jillian asked.

"Snooping, obviously," Carly said. "What'd you find out?"

"I was not snooping," she protested. "He had to leave to go tend an emergency with a boxer, so I was merely looking for paper to leave him a note, because it's the polite thing to do."

"I know I always appreciate a sweetly penned note post-coital," Carly said.

"It didn't go that far," Mac insisted. "But the thing is when I found the pictures of her right in the top of his desk, it occurred to me that I'm probably his transition woman from that relationship, and we all know what happens to transition relationships."

"Oh," Carly said, making a bad face. "Kabloeey. Kablammy."

"Kaboom," Jilly offered.

"I know, right?" Mac said. "It won't work out between us, it'll end badly with hurt feelings, and then Emma will be stuck in the middle."

"Yeah, I can see how that would be a concern," Jillian said. "Okay, well, fooling around happens at weddings all of the time. There is no need to panic."

"Yeah, just keep from crossing the finish line, and you can flirt with him and head back to Chicago without worrying about being his transition boink or pissing off Emma."

"Okay, I can do that. Your word you won't say anything," Mac said. "Both of you."

"I promise," Jillian said.

"I've been zip-lipped for seven years, I'm not going to crack now," Carly said.

"Thanks," Mac said. "And thanks for the ride."

Carly gestured to the front door, where the

aunts were standing in the porch light. "You might want to put the bra away."

"Yeah," Mac said. She stuffed it back in her bag and zipped it closed. With a wave and feeling newly resolved to keep things casual with Gavin, she left the car and continued her walk of shame up the steps to the front porch.

Chapter 27

Mac was pretty sure she would have made a fine detective. So far, she had spent the better part of the past day and a half staking out Lester's house, doing drive-bys, and waiting for his piece of rust Buick to be gone from the premises so she could sneak under the fence, which had not been fixed, and snuggle Tulip, bringing food and water with her when she did.

Tulip was filthy and in desperate need of a bath, but Mac didn't care. She loved on her dog and let the puppy climb in her lap while she talked to her, letting her know that one way or another Mac was going to get her out of there.

It was on her first visit on the second day that the situation got complicated. Tulip sprang from Mac's lap and barked at the fence. A flash of panic hit Mac and she feared it was Lester coming to get her, but then why wouldn't he use the back door?

She glanced at the fence and her stomach flip-flopped when she saw the familiar tall, muscled frame of Gavin as he hoisted himself up over the top of the fence. He dropped onto his feet and strode forward but as soon as he was within reach of Tulip, she took him out at the knees, knocking him on his keister. Then she licked him right on the mouth.

"Oh, ugh." Gavin groaned. He wiped his mouth with the back of his hand while rubbing Tulip's ears with the other. "Always on the mouth, princess, really?"

The early morning sun shone on his light brown hair and Mac remembered how soft it had felt beneath her fingers. She glanced at his hands now rubbing Tulip's belly, and she remembered what they felt like against her skin. She fanned her face. Why was it suddenly so hot out here?

Gavin stood and walked over to where she sat in the dirt. He crouched down beside her and continued to pet the dog that trotted at his side.

"Why am I not surprised to find you here?" he asked.

"I'm predictable?"

"No, never that."

They were both silent and Mac felt the weight of their last time together pressing on her chest like a cinder block. She knew she had to say something, but what?

She tried to remember what Carly had said, that it was okay to flirt with Gavin but to keep it easy, keep it light, don't go too far. Yeah, easy for Carly to say, flirting was hardwired into her DNA. Mac wasn't like that. She wasn't even sure she knew how to flirt, and if she did it was usually unintentional and only happened because she didn't like the guy. A guy she liked? Yeah, those were the ones she hid under tables to avoid. She scouted the yard. No tables. Ugh.

She needed to be clear about it. There could be no mixed signals or unclear signs. She had to shut this shiz down between them before . . .

Gavin kissed her, swift and sweet but no less potent for its brevity. Boom! And just like that all of Mac's resolutions twirled away on the wind like dandelion fluff, which she was pretty sure was all that was in her frontal lobe at the moment.

He broke the kiss and leaned back on his heels. "You've been ducking me."

"No," she lied.

One eyebrow of his quirked higher than the other and Mac wondered just what it was that made that look so sexy. Was it because she had his full attention, or because there was some serious flirt behind it, or was it just because it kicked his already rugged good looks up a few notches? Hard to say.

"I wouldn't say ducking, exactly," she said. She had practiced this speech in her head five thousand times over the past thirty-six hours. She'd even said it aloud to Tulip, who had been singularly unimpressed.

"Avoiding, dodging, hiding from," he listed the possible adjectives.

"Tell me about Jane," she said. Then she wanted to slap herself. That had not been a part of her so carefully crafted speech. She was going off message. Nothing good ever came of going off message.

He tipped his head to the side. "What do you want to know?"

"Were you very much in love with her?" she asked.

"Jane?" He said her name as if he was trying to clarify that Mac was actually asking about her.

"Yes," she said. "The one who ran off with—"

She bit off the words but the damage was done as he said, "The bookkeeper Carl."

She gave him a sad look. "Yeah, listen, I'm sorry. It's none of my business."

"It's not *not* your business."

She gave him a bewildered look and he shrugged.

"Jane and I dated for a while. I thought we had something good going, but then she fell for Carl," he said.

"And?" she prodded.

"And what?"

"You were shattered and devastated and alone," she said.

Gavin laughed. He saw her face and tried to stop. He failed and then caught her dubious look and cleared his throat. "Yeah, no."

"But Emma said that Jane broke your heart," Mac said.

"Hmm, it was a swift kick in the ego to be

dumped like that, no doubt, and for a while I was disappointed, but I was never devastated." He shook his head. "She broke my bank account when she and Carl emptied it to fund their tryst, yeah, but my heart, no. I've recently remembered how much more all-consuming being in love is. It was never like that with her."

"Huh." Mac's brain scrambled to try and process what he was saying.

"Is that why you've been avoiding me?" he asked. "Were you worried that I was pining for Jane?"

"No," she said. "Maybe. Argh."

She face-palmed herself, and Tulip shoved her big brown nose against Mac's forehead to kiss it and make it better. This was not what was supposed to be happening! Mac shook her head.

"Here's the thing," she said. "While I acknowledge that there is undeniable chemistry between—"

"Oh, no, here it comes," Gavin said. He pursed his lips and gave her a look that said he had thought better of her than this. That stung.

"Here comes what?" she asked.

"Your prepared speech on why we can't be together. Let me sum up," he said. "Emma's wedding, me being her younger brother, you leaving town in a matter of days. Blah. Blah. Blah."

"It was way better than that," Mac said. "It was touching and poignant and heartfelt."

"I'm sure, but we're out of time," he said. Abruptly, he rose to his feet, dragging Mac up with him. He bent over and pet Tulip on the head. "See ya, girl."

Mac frowned and then she heard it. The distinctive rattle of Lester's muffler as he drove down the street toward them.

She bent down and kissed Tulip's head. "Later, baby girl, with treats."

"Come on, he's almost here," Gavin said.

They bolted for the fence. Mac slid under and Gavin hopped over it. They took off running on the path that led through the woods at the back of Lester's property. Mac heard Tulip barking after them and was relieved that it sounded like a happy bark, like she thought this was a game. Mac hoped she was right because this was a game Mac planned to win.

Halfway through the woods, they slowed down to walk. Mac's breath was sewing in and out of her lungs and she could feel the burn with each gasp. Gavin didn't seem to be suffering nearly as much; so annoying.

"I'm parked over there," she said and pointed to a narrow path in the woods.

"I know. Jillian's Jeep was a dead giveaway. I parked right behind you," he said.

Mac led the way out of the woods. She could hear the birds in the trees and feel the soft crunch of the pine needles under her shoes. The woodsy smell was rich and pungent and a small part of her wondered if they could just hide here in the forest where the past didn't matter and the sun played hide-and-seek in the leaves overhead, tempting her to while away the day flirting with the man beside her, but no. He might be dismissive about her concerns for Emma's wedding and her feelings about the two of them, but Mac couldn't be.

As she stepped onto the side of the road next to the Jeep, Gavin grabbed her hand. He pulled her back as if afraid that she was running away again; she was.

"Be steady," he said.

Mac looked at him curiously and he jerked his head in the direction of the police car parked on the opposite side of the street. Mac's mouth made an O of understanding.

Officer Polson waved to them from the open window of his car. Mac wondered if this was where she ended up in the back of the squad car again.

"Have a nice hike in the woods?" Polson asked.

"It's a good morning for one," Gavin said. He shoved his free hand in his front pocket, the picture of boyish innocence.

"Sure is," Polson agreed. "I trust you'd let me know if you saw anything of concern in the forest."

"Absolutely," Mac said. She pulled her hand

out of Gavin's, knowing full well that if she was going to make a getaway, this was her chance.

She opened the driver's side door and climbed into the Jeep. Gavin shook his head at her as if to let her know she was just putting off the inevitable. She flashed him a smile.

"Bye, boys," she said. She started up the engine and drove off without looking back.

"Emma, I need to talk to you," Mac said. Her conversation with Gavin had been grinding on her all morning and she wanted clarification before it drove her bonkers.

"Sure, what's up?" Emma asked.

It was midday and they were in Emma's bedroom, packing her suitcase for her honeymoon. Emma had laid out every possible outfit choice for her time in Europe and Mac was helping her with the final selection process.

Emma held up an adorable aqua lace chemise and Mac nodded. Then Emma held up a pair of ridiculously high-heeled sandals to go with it and Mac shook her head. Cobblestoned walkways in Old World cities were not kind to stilettos. Emma made a face and tossed the shoes back into the closet.

"I had a talk with Gavin about Jane," Mac said.

"Oh?" Emma glanced up from her suitcase, which was half full. "What did he say?"

"He said he wasn't that devastated about their

breakup," Mac said. "In fact, he seemed meh about it."

"Well, of course, he did," Emma said. "What guy likes to admit he's crushed and devastated?"

"I really didn't get crushed or devastated off of him," Mac said.

"That's because he's saving face," Emma said. She gave Mac a look. "You weren't here right after it happened. You didn't see him. He was a mess. But since you've been here, distracting him and making him happy again, he probably can't remember how sad he was. See? I told you he needed the boost."

"Hmm," Mac hummed.

She wasn't really sure what she'd wanted Emma to say, but it was definitely more along the lines of "Yeah, silly me, clearly Gavin couldn't have been in love with Jane the Pain."

Not that it was any of Mac's business but she found she really didn't like the thought of Gavin being in love—no, didn't like was too mild. It was more like she detested the idea of Gavin being in love with anyone and his assurance that he hadn't been had made her heart soar.

Okay, that was a little self-awareness she could live without. Why did she care who Gavin loved or didn't love? In a matter of days, she was going back to Chicago, a city she loved, to a career she loved, to a relationship that she had parked like a car in long-term parking—it had to be retrieved sometime. Oh, that was a telling metaphor, wasn't it?

She heard her phone chime in her purse. "Excuse me, I'd better take that."

"No problem, but be thinking about black capris versus blue jeans while you're gone," Emma said.

"You're going to Paris," Mac said. "Black is always good in Paris."

She grabbed her phone and left the room. She glanced at the display. It was Trevor. A spasm of guilt hit her low and deep. Images of her near naked self with Gavin flashed before her eyes like a fireworks display of *oh, wow*. There was no candy coating this. Whether anything more happened between her and Gavin, she had moved on from Trevor. Now how did she tell him?

"Hello," she said.

"Mac, how are you?" he said. "Or should I say pip pip, cheerio, and all that?"

She forced what she hoped sounded like a laugh and not like someone stepping on a duck, which is what it felt like.

"So, the negotiations are going well?" she asked.

This led to a very detailed monologue about his own legal prowess in the corporate proceedings that his company was undertaking. It sounded very complicated and, frankly, really boring, but Trevor was clearly enjoying every bit of the contractual dodgeball game so she listened until he got it all out of his system.

"But enough about me," he said. "Are you eager to be done with all of that wedding stuff? I imagine you are bored out of your skull in that tiny town with all of those provincial people."

"Surprisingly, not that bored," Mac said.

She thought about the orgasm she'd enjoyed at Gavin's hands and knew that boring was never going to be a word she associated with him. Then she shook her head. Just because Trevor was not as skilled as Gavin and it was usually a one in ten chance that she'd get where she wanted to go with him that was no reason to have mean thoughts, right?

"What about that dog situation?" he asked. "Did you manage to unload it?"

"More like she was taken from me," she said.

"I'm not following," he said. "I thought you wanted to be rid of it."

"*It* is a *she*," Mac said. Was Trevor always this obtuse and irritating or was she just being sensitive because of her fondness for Tulip? "And, yes, I did want her to be reunited with her loving family but that isn't what happened."

"No? Well, don't fret. I'm sure it's all for the best," Trevor said. "At least now she's off your hands and you don't have to worry about her anymore."

"Of course I'm worried about her," Mac said. She wanted to rail and wail and whine, but Trevor cut her off.

"Listen, I'm sorry, but I have to go," he said. "Big dinner with the board of directors tonight."

"Okay, um, I did have something I wanted to talk to you about," she said. She knew it was bad form to have a relationship discussion over the phone, but she really felt she needed to broach the topic of making their hiatus a permanent one.

"No can do," he said. "I really need to get ready for dinner. I'm hoping to grease the wheels for a promotion."

"Sure, I understand," Mac said.

But she didn't, not really. If the person you were involved with was upset about something, shouldn't that matter more than greasing wheels? Ah, but this was why she and Trevor had been together for the past few years. They never had to compromise what was important to them for the other person. They never had to put the other person first. That was what she'd wanted after her disastrous breakup with Seth and it had been perfect. But now it wasn't enough, not even close.

It was early afternoon when Mac drove back to Jillian's bakery from Emma's house and she was trying to decide which flavor of whoopie

pie she was going to stuff in her cakehole first. They had managed to get Emma packed for her honeymoon. The wedding plans were on schedule and Emma was beginning to glow with a radiance Mac had never seen in her before.

With the windows down, the radio up, the warm sun on her skin, and a cool breeze blowing into the Jeep, tossing her hair about her face, Mac felt as carefree as she had as a child.

Despite her worry over Tulip, her disappointment in Trevor, and her anxiety about the situation with Gavin, Mac felt her heart lift up. She was truly happy for Emma and Brad. It was an extraordinary thing to see two people so perfect for each other planning a life together. It gave her hope and the beautiful day made her feel as if anything was possible.

She was zipping along a side road when she saw a woman walking on the narrow shoulder. It wasn't unusual, except the woman wasn't dressed for a stroll on a Maine back road. She was in a tailored dress more suited to a garden party, carrying her high heels in one hand while she gingerly picked her way along the rocky side of the road.

Her blonde hair was mussed and as Mac slowed down she saw the woman raise her hand to her face and wipe away tears. Without overthinking it, Mac pulled over.

She leaned across the console and called out

the passenger side window, "Hey, can I give you a lift?"

The red, blotchy face that met hers made Mac start. Staring back at her was Jessie Peeler Connelly.

Chapter 28

W hat do you want?" Jessie snapped.
Mac pressed her lips together to keep from shouting a mean retort at the woman, who, like it or not, was obviously distressed.

"Just what I said," Mac said. "Do you want a lift?"

Jessie looked at her like she'd rather take a ride on a garbage truck. She glared at Mac, and Mac was about to shrug and tell her to suit herself, but she didn't.

She remembered seeing Seth staring at the bartender's hooters the other night—the pig—and she remembered that Jessie, with cruel intention or not, had saved her from marrying that loser. Maybe in the grand scheme of things, she owed Jessie one.

"Did Seth make you cry?" she asked.

Jessie paled and her eyes looked haunted. She glanced away and her voice was vicious when she asked, "You'd like that, wouldn't you? You'd like to see me suffer the same humiliation you suffered with everyone laughing at you behind your back."

Ouch! It was a direct hit and normally Mac would have stomped on the gas and let Jessie eat gravel, but she didn't. Hurt people hurt people, and it didn't take more than a teaspoonful of empathy to see that Jessie was hurting mightily.

"No," Mac said. "I wouldn't like that, but I would like to help you if you'll let me."

As if her kindness was the knife point that cut through Jessie's anger more effectively than any harsh words ever could, Jessie collapsed, falling to the ground in a heap.

"Oh, shit!" Mac muttered.

She quickly shut off the engine and leapt out of the car to run around the front and check on Jessie. The woman was curled up in a heap in the dirt and leaves on the side of the road. A low keening came from Jessie's mouth as she hugged her knees to her chest and rocked back and forth.

"Do you need me to call someone?" Mac asked. "If not Seth, someone else?"

"I don't have anyone else," Jessie cried. "He's made sure of that."

The agony in her voice made the marrow in Mac's bones freeze. Would Seth have done that to her, alienated her from all of her friends? She couldn't see that happening, and Jessie had been popular in school with loads of friends, so Mac had a hard time believing she had no one now. Maybe she was just being her usual diva self.

"Come on, there has to be someone," she said.

"Not when your letch of a husband tries to bang

every woman who walks into your house," she said. "Makes it hard to keep any friends."

"Oh," Mac said.

She didn't know what else to say. The last time she'd run into Jessie had been at the winery in Portland and Jessie had been, well, frankly, a bitch. But then, Mac had a curious thought. What if Jessie had been sincere?

Mac had been looking a bit rough, mostly in an effort to keep Gavin at bay, but maybe Jessie's offer of money had been genuine.

"Did you mean it when you offered me money to treat myself at the winery in Portland?" she asked.

Jessie lifted her head up and met Mac's gaze. She was the picture of misery. "Yeah, I really thought I'd ruined your life and you were down on your luck. I know it's horrible but as guilty as I felt, I was relieved that someone else had a crappier life than mine."

"Well, that's honest."

"Then I saw Gavin kiss you and realized that what he'd said was true." Jessie wiped her nose with the back of her hand. She gave Mac a bewildered once-over. "He really has the hots for you. You know you might want to up your game if you're trying to land him."

"And you were doing so well," Mac said.

"A comb or a brush," Jessie said. "That's all I'm saying; okay, and maybe some lipstick."

Mac rubbed her eyes and tried not to laugh. She figured if Jessie was back to critiquing her, she was going to be fine.

"Okay, enough about me, I'm not the one crying by the side of the road," Mac said. Jessie looked stricken and Mac felt bad. "I'm sorry, that came out wrong. What I meant was what are you going to do about you and Seth?"

"There's nothing I can do. I'm trapped," Jessie said. She started to cry again and Mac sat helplessly beside her, not knowing what to say. She let her cry it out.

"I'm sorry," Jessie said.

"Oh, it's fine," Mac said. "Take your time."

"No, I mean I'm sorry about before," Jessie said. Her voice was so soft Mac had to strain to hear her.

"Excuse me?" Mac said. It wasn't so much that she needed to hear it again—okay, maybe she did—but she also wanted to be sure that she'd heard what she thought she'd heard.

"I'm sorry that I ruined your wedding," Jessie said. "I'm sorry I was always mean to you."

Mac shifted on the ground beside her. "Why were you always so mean?"

"I don't know," Jessie said. "You just seemed so confident all the time, and everyone always liked you. I always felt like I had to work for it, and let's face it, most of my friends only liked me for my money. Your friends adored you just for being you. I hated you."

"I got that," Mac said. "If it evens it out, I hated you, too, especially after my wedding fiasco, but, wow, you really saved me."

They were silent for a while. No cars passed by and the stillness in the trees around them made Mac feel as if time had slowed. She wondered if it was mostly because the last fifteen minutes of conversation had blown her mind.

"He's been cheating on me from the first day we were married," Jessie said. She looked sickened by the admission and then she started to cry again. "Even on our honeymoon, he had a quickie with a cocktail waitress in the coatroom of our hotel. I found out when I got chlamydia but by then I was already pregnant with Gracie."

"Son of a bitch," Mac said. She didn't know what to do, so she put her hand on Jessie's back and just kept it there as a constant pressure point of compassion.

"I threatened, I begged, I pleaded," Jessie sobbed. "But he told me that my fat pregnant body disgusted him and he had needs. God help me, I believed him. After Gracie was born, I thought it'd be okay, I was so stupid, but he didn't stop cheating and then I got pregnant with Maddie."

Mac felt nauseated. All this time, all these years, she had been licking her wounds thinking Jessie Peeler had humiliated her and stolen the life that was supposed to be hers and she'd despised her for it. And all along, Jessie had unwittingly saved her.

"Why haven't you left him?" Mac asked, knowing full well that things were often more complicated than simply packing a bag and going.

"He told me if I ever tried to leave him, he'd take the girls away," Jessie said. "Besides, what would I do? I graduated with a business degree but never worked a day in my life. Seth blew through my inheritance within the first five years of our marriage. I have nothing. I have no one. He owns me, literally."

This was unacceptable. There had been a time when Mac would have happily seen Jessie suffer for the rest of her days, but looking at the woman now, she couldn't wish any worse upon her than she'd already suffered.

"Business major, huh?" Mac asked.

"Yeah, what a joke," Jessie said.

"Not necessarily," Mac said. "Where are your girls right now?"

"At a playdate," Jessie said. "They're getting dropped off at the house at five. Seth and I were on a lunch date but when I got mad at him for trying to pick up our waitress, he dumped me on the side of the road."

"What an asshole," Mac cursed and Jessie gave her a watery smile. "Get in the car. We need to get you cleaned up."

"What for?" Jessie asked.

"Job interview," Mac said.

"Huh?"

Jessie looked at her like she was crazy, but Mac had never been more sure of anything in her life. She grabbed Jessie's hand and pulled her to her feet. She opened the passenger door and then grabbed her big bag from the back of the Jeep and dumped it in Jessie's lap.

"I have no idea what's in there exactly, but I'm sure you'll find a brush somewhere," Mac said.

She hurried around to the driver's side door and climbed into the car. She turned on the engine and put it into drive.

"How are you not a hunchback, carrying around a bag this heavy?" Jessie asked.

"It has everything I need," Mac said.

Jessie held up her pink bra. "Yeah, I can see that."

"Listen, are you interested in getting a job or not?" Mac asked. She felt her face get warm but she refused to be embarrassed at having Jessie find her bra in her bag. There were bigger things happening here.

"Yes," Jessie said. But then she averted her face and glanced out the window. "But who is going to hire a thirty-two-year-old woman who has never held a job before?"

"Don't worry about that," Mac said. "Worry

about making yourself presentable in the next five minutes."

Jessie shot her an alarmed look and dove back into Mac's bag.

When Mac parked the Jeep in front of Gavin's clinic, she got out and gestured for Jessie to follow her. Together they approached the building with Mac looking confident and Jessie looking terrified.

"But I don't know anything about animals," Jessie protested.

"You don't need to," Mac said. "You're here to do the books."

"I am?" Jessie asked.

"If you think you want to," Mac said.

She stepped on the mat and the door opened. The two women froze in their tracks as an absolute barking, hissing, screeching, howling cacophony of chaos greeted them.

"Oh, my god," Jessie said. She looked like she was debating running away.

"You want a job?" Mac asked.

"Yes," Jessie said.

"Then let's show them what you're made of," Mac said.

Gavin was behind the counter, trying to take a payment while listening to another pet owner talk his ear off. Two dogs were snarling at each other in the corner while a cat had gotten loose and climbed on top of the shelf that housed the pet food and was hissing at anything that moved toward her.

Mac hurried behind the counter and took the payment out of Gavin's hands. When his eyes focused on the fact that it was her, he looked so relieved she thought he might weep. Instead, he kissed her forehead and glanced at Jessie.

"My helper," Mac explained.

He looked bemused and said, "Um . . . okay."

Jessie gave him a nervous smile and Mac pulled her over to the computer to show her what was what and how it worked.

"You, go," Mac said to Gavin. "I'll get them sorted and send them in to you. Do you have anyone waiting?"

"Just Cheryl Benson and Jiggles in exam room one," he said.

"Really?" Mac asked. "Did she pay for this visit?"

Gavin shook his head. "I haven't seen the cat yet, so I don't know what's wrong."

"I do," Mac said. "It has a case of horny-owner-itis." She turned back to Jessie and handed her the sign-in clipboard. "See who's here and who's been waiting the longest and then start sending them in. We have four exam rooms. Gavin will be starting in room two."

"I will?" he asked.

"You will." She glowered and then she went to

kick Cheryl Benson's sneaky behind out to the curb.

Three hours passed in the space of a blink. By the time the lobby was sorted and patients were seen, payments were processed, and the waiting room was cleared, Mac and Jessie were sagging on their feet in exhaustion.

"That was unbelievable," Jessie said.

Mac raised her hand and after an awkward moment, Jessie slapped it in a high five that made both women smile.

"We kicked ass," Mac said.

"Yeah, we did," Jessie said. She beamed and Mac returned her smile, thinking Jessie wasn't as haughty looking when she was happy. Maybe that was the problem, then; maybe Jessie had never been truly happy.

They were still looking at each other with new respect when Gavin came out of an exam room with a kitten in his arms. Mac looked up from the counter and felt her heart stutter in her chest. The orange tabby looked tiny in his hands and Gavin held him with a gentleness that made Mac's ovaries want to throw all of their eggs at him at once like he was the target in a dunk tank. That couldn't be good.

"Looks like we have a new housecat," he said.

"What do you mean?" Mac asked.

"This little guy was found abandoned on Route 1," he said.

"Oh, no, that's terrible," Jessie said. She held out her hands and Gavin passed the kitten to her.

While she caressed his head, Gavin looked at Mac. When she didn't respond, he widened his eyes and tipped his head toward Jessie and then toward her in the universal gesture for *What the hell is going on?*

"Oh, hey, I didn't get a chance to explain earlier," Mac said. "Gavin, meet your new office assistant."

Gavin looked at her like he'd swallowed his tongue.

"A word, Mac," he said. He looked at Jessie. "Excuse us, please."

"Take your time," Jessie said. The kitten was pushing his head against her chin and she was wrinkling her nose and making kissy noises at him. Mac never would have believed it. Jessie was an animal lover.

Gavin grabbed Mac by the arm and led her into exam room one.

"Explain," he said.

"Simple version is this. She's a business major who needs a job. You need an office manager. Match made in heaven or by the side of the road, depending upon how specific you want to be," she said.

Gavin opened his mouth to speak, then closed it, then opened it, and said, "But you hate her."

"We made peace," Mac said.

"Just like that?" he asked.

"There was some crying involved; her, not me," Mac said. "But apologies were made and accepted."

Gavin stared at her and Mac stared back. Finally, she raised her hands in the air and asked, "Well, can she have the job?"

Gavin put his hand on the back of his neck and started to pace in the little room. When he started to talk to himself, Mac leaned against the wall and let him work through it.

"She seemed to manage the office okay, picked up on the details quickly, wasn't scared of the big dogs, made the patients calm down," he said. "Doc thought she was cute."

He stopped pacing and looked at Mac. "I guess she can have the job, but I have to be honest, I had someone else in mind for the position."

"Who?" Mac asked.

Why hadn't he told her that? Since she was his unofficial trainer she should have input. The intensity of his stare made her pulse pick up and she was pretty sure she felt her pupils dilate. Oh.

"Me?" she asked.

"You," he said.

Chapter 29

He started walking toward her and Mac backed up until she felt the counter at her back. He leaned forward and rested his hands on each side of her, blocking her in.

"I bet you could run the heck out of this place," he said. His lips were just inches from hers and Mac had a hard time understanding what he was saying. His words were coming at her like so much white noise since their unfinished business from a few nights ago had her brain churning raunchy scenarios in her mind, blocking out any cognitive reasoning.

"I have a job," she managed to choke out. "In Chicago."

"Is that so?" he asked.

He kissed her just below the ear and Mac felt her legs buckle. Gavin grabbed her hips and scooped her up, setting her on the counter so they were now eye to eye.

"Yes, it's so," Mac said. "I've worked too long . . . oh, my."

He moved his mouth down the side of her neck, pushed aside her hair, and used his teeth on her shoulder. Mac swallowed hard and tried to focus.

Across the room, there was a poster of a kitten dangling from a tree limb, telling her to hang in there. Mac didn't want to; she wanted to free-fall right into a pool of hot sex with Gavin, but she knew the kitten was right.

She pulled back and cupped his face in her hands, forcing his attention away from her shirtfront and up to meet her eyes.

"While I love the idea of working here and I'm flattered that you'd want me to, I can't," she said. "I have worked too hard for too long to give up everything I've achieved. My career is in Chicago."

Gavin sighed and pressed his forehead to hers. His hands were stroking up and down her sides, making Mac long for things she had no business longing for, not now, not while she still had several unresolved situations such as telling Emma how she felt about Gavin and ending things officially with Trevor.

"All right," he said. "If I can't hire you, then Jessie can have the job. You will explain to me in greater detail how all of this came about, won't you?"

"Yes." Mac glanced at the clock. "Oh, I have to get her home to meet her daughters."

Gavin stepped back and she hopped off of the counter, already missing his nearness. She headed for the door but Gavin grabbed her hand and pulled her back. Then he kissed her and this time it was not swift and sweet but long and full of lascivious promises. When he released her,

Mac was pretty sure steam was coming out of her ears.

"Just so you know," he whispered in her ear as they left the room, "I've heard that long-distance relationships can be very sexy."

Mac dropped Jessie off at her home. There was no sign of Seth for which she was eminently relieved. Jessie surprised her by hugging her tight before she climbed out of the car.

"You've given me something I haven't had in a very long time," Jessie said. At Mac's questioning glance, she said, "Hope."

"I'm glad," Mac said.

She watched Jessie walk up the steps of the old colonial in the historic section of town, not far from Mac's family home in fact, and she noticed that while the house looked imposing from a distance there were little tells in its façade that reflected the less than perfect state of its inhabitants.

Peeling paint, overgrown garden beds, a missing shutter or two; singularly they were a mark of wear and tear but cumulatively they showed the neglect that was pervasive on the property. Jessie had confessed to dreaming of a tiny cottage by the shore for her and the girls. Mac really hoped she got it.

She returned the Jeep to Jillian at her shop and then chose to walk through town, planning to join the aunts for dinner since the wedding to-dos over the next few days were going to make any more free time for her scarce to nonexistent.

She had just turned onto Elizabeth Street when the sound of a car stereo's bass cranked to top volume pounded her eardrums with its merciless beat. She clapped her hands over her ears and whipped her head in the direction of the street to scowl at the offender.

Her jaw smacked the concrete at her feet when she saw Aunt Charlotte cruise by in a blue Dodge Challenger with a white racing stripe running over its top from front to back. Charlotte saw Mac and flashed her some sort of hand gesture that meant hang ten, hook 'em horns, rock and roll, or, possibly, up yours. Mac had no idea and she was pretty sure Charlotte didn't either.

One thing Mac did know: this madness had to stop. Right now. She was going to demand to know what the heck had gotten into her aunts. And if she had to hog-tie them to get them to talk she was going to do it.

She ran-walked the rest of the way home so that when she turned into the driveway it was to find Charlotte just climbing out of her car.

"What is that?" Mac cried.

"Our new ride," Charlotte said. "Like it?"

"What music were you playing?" Mac asked. "It sounded like—"

"Rap," Charlotte said. Her eyes sparkled.

"Where's the Volvo?" Mac asked.

"I traded it in," she said. "It was beginning to cramp my style."

"For this?" Mac felt the need to clarify. "You traded it for this."

Charlotte nodded.

"Can you even see over the dash?" Mac cried.

"Sure," Charlotte said. "They gave me a booster seat."

Mac's eyes went wide.

"I'm kidding, relax," Charlotte said. "When exactly did you become no fun?"

"No fun," Mac spluttered. "I'll have you know I'm plenty of fun, but I'm grown-up fun, not this impulsive adolescent fun you and Aunt Sarah have going."

The front door swung open and Sarah joined them. She glanced at the sports car and then at her sister. She looked delighted. "You got it? Is that our new shagging wagon?"

"Yes, it is, and I got a year of free oil changes, too!" Charlotte said.

"Sweet!" Aunt Sarah hurried down the steps to look it over. "Let's take it for a ride in the hood."

"The hood?" Mac felt as if she was going to have a stroke. "Did you hear her coming down the street? I'm surprised the cops aren't here to cite her for a violation of the noise ordinance."

As if they'd activated their twin powers the two

aunts rolled their eyes at her in perfect sync as if they were fourteen. Mac lost it.

"That's it!" she cried. "I have tried to be patient. I have tried to be supportive. But you are freaking me out! What the hell is going on and why are you two acting so weird?"

They gave her a mutinous look and Mac said, "I will call my dad and have him come here and interrogate you instead of me. I swear I will."

Sarah tipped up her chin as if daring her. Mac pulled her cell phone out of her bag and began to dial.

"I think she means it, Sarah," Charlotte said. She twirled her key ring on her finger. "We should tell her."

"Fine!" Sarah sighed. She raised her arms up in the air in a gesture of complete exasperation. "Not that it's any of your business but we're going to die."

"What?" Mac felt all of her blood drop from her head to her feet in one fast whoosh and she staggered from the sudden lack of oxygen.

"That was mean," Charlotte said. "Just look at her, you're lucky she didn't faint."

"Oh." Sarah waved an annoyed hand at her sister and then glared at Mac. "Not right now, but someday."

"Hang on," Mac said. She staggered over to the steps and sat down and put her head between her knees. "Let's try this again. You're behaving like adolescents because you're going to die someday, not tomorrow or next week or even in the next decade, but someday?"

"Exactly," Sarah said. "We're plowing through our bucket lists because we don't want to have any regrets."

Mac sprawled out on the steps. "Sweet chili dogs, I think you just scared ten years off of me. Was that really necessary?"

"It could have been avoided if you'd minded your own business," Sarah said. She stepped over Mac and went into the house.

Mac glanced up at Charlotte. "She's not lying, is she? I'm not going to find out you two have heart disease or cancer or something like that, am I? Because that would kill me."

"She's telling the truth, we're fine," Charlotte said. "But it's been a rough year. We've lost a lot of our friends lately and it's beginning to take a toll. This is our way of coping."

Mac had heard from her dad that several of the aunts' friends had passed over the winter so it made sense—but poetry slams, beekeeping, a Dodge Challenger? Wow, just wow.

"We're not wrong, you know," Charlotte said.

"About?"

"Making sure you have no regrets," Charlotte said.

The look she gave Mac was a knowing one, and Mac wondered if the rumor mill in this tiny town had already churned out tales of her and Gavin, and if so, was that what Charlotte was referring to or was Mac just paranoid?

Then there was the million-dollar question. What would Mac regret more, losing her friendship with Emma or not pursuing what she might have with Gavin? A week ago she would have put all of her chips on her friendship with Emma, but with every moment she spent with Gavin, she was less and less sure. Why did it have to be so complicated? For a nanosecond she was tempted to borrow the sports car, crank up the tunes, and drive away, taking Tulip with her as she went, natch.

They were now down to the wire with the wedding. People who had not bothered to RSVP had to be called, the final seating arrangements made, and the vendors confirmed, all while Emma and her wedding stager were logging long hours at the brewery directing the workers who were making the courtyard of the old brick building look like something out of a fairy tale.

Mac borrowed Jillian's Jeep and ran endless errands. Picking up ribbon here, dropping off payments there, badgering the florist to make sure the bouquets looked like what Emma had envisioned; it was endless. And, of course, Mac still had to pop in on Tulip a few times a day to make certain baby girl was okay. Every time she left Lester's without her dog, it broke her heart a little bit more. Every time.

On top of the chores, Emma had the wedding party booked for festivities every single night. On Wednesday, they all met at a karaoke bar, with the best man Bobby and his very pregnant wife Linda. On Thursday, it was back to just the eight of them for bowling, Linda being just a bit too pregnant to heft twelve-pound balls to hurl at pins and all.

"I think by the time this wedding is over, I will not need to see any of you for a year," Carly said.

"You're just sore because you're gutter balling," Brad said.

He and Emma were in second place to Jillian and Sam's first place. Mac and Gavin were in third with Carly and Zach dead last.

"Did he just insult me and call me a sore loser?" Carly asked.

"Yes, he did," Gavin confirmed.

"Because these shoes aren't insult enough?" Carly asked.

Mac took a sip of her beer and watched her friends. It was hard to believe that the two weeks were almost over. She realized it was going to be strange to go back to Chicago and not have this anymore.

Oh, she had friends in Chicago that she enjoyed very much, but they didn't have the life history that Mac shared with her Maine crew, which now seemed to include the guys. She had liked Brad from the moment she met him and saw how besotted he was with Emma.

She'd met Zach and Sam on a trip to Florida that they'd all gone on together over a year ago, but she'd never gotten to know them like this. She considered them her friends now, too, and she realized she was really going to miss Sam's dry wit and Zach's juvenile antics.

Then there was Gavin. Luckily, Emma had kept Mac moving at a clip the past two days and she'd had no time to think about him, or them, or his suggestion of a long-distance relationship, or anything else. Especially, anything else.

It was his hands that captured her attention now; okay, and his lips, and, oh, heck, it was the whole package, but mostly his hands. Every time it was Gavin's turn to handle his bowling ball, Mac broke into a light sweat and her girl parts ached. She didn't trust herself alone with him, sitting next to him, or even brushing by him. For the past two nights, she had done everything she could to keep her distance but her body was in complete opposition to her brain. It was exhausting.

For Gavin's part, he seemed to accept that she was not willing to go public with anything between them. In front of their group, he never made any moves on her that would be construed as anything more than passing affection. A hug here, a high five there—it was the same type of camaraderie that he shared with Jillian and Carly. But when any opportunity presented itself where he could get Mac alone, the game changed and it was smokin' hot.

At karaoke, he managed to cop a feel in a dark corner of the bar; then he sang "Can't Get Enough of Your Love, Babe" by Barry White to her. In all fairness, he sang it to all of the ladies, but it was Mac he said the spoken parts to, completely charming her stupid.

At bowling, he demanded her help in carrying pitchers of beer from the bar on the other side of the alley back to their lane. Halfway to the bar, he grabbed her hand and pulled her outside an exit door into the parking lot.

"Being with you and not being with you is driving me insane," he said. He pushed her up against the side of the building as his hands did things to her that made Mac's head buzz.

"I know what you mean," she said and she pulled his head down to hers so she could kiss him.

"Do you really think my sister will care if we hook up? She loves us both. Wouldn't this make her happy?" he asked between kisses.

Mac froze. She pulled away from him and looked him right in the eye. This was the moment. This was the moment she should tell him about

Trevor and the fact that they were taking a break but not officially done yet. Would he care? She wasn't sure. Would Emma care? Mac didn't know and there was the problem. This close to the wedding did she want to cause drama?

Chapter 30

S he opened her mouth but no words came out. "I can see from your face that you're not sure," he said. "What is it with brides and having this über huge day all to themselves?"

"Not all brides are like that, but Emma—" Mac cupped his face. She savored the feel of his stubbly chin against her palms. Man, she had gotten so fond of this handsome mug. The thought of going back to Chicago and not seeing it every day hurt.

"I know," he said. "Ever since Mom died, Emma makes an event out of everything. I love it about her even as it wears me out."

"Let's let her have her special day with no surprises," Mac said. "A perfect day that is lovely and magical and all for her and Brad."

"All right," Gavin said. "I'm a bit more interested in a magical night myself; besides, keeping this thing between us a secret is kind of hot."

He swooped in and kissed her and Mac melted against him. She had to concede he was right; stolen moments in dark corners and lonely alleys were pretty hot.

"Hey, you two, those shoes are not to be worn outside the bowling alley!" The manager of the bowling alley barked at them as he came outside for a smoke break, and Mac and Gavin broke apart.

They exchanged a sheepish glance and ducked back inside. Mac tried not to think about what she was setting in motion by responding to Gavin. One thing she did know was that when she got home to Chicago, she was going to be making some changes. For time put in, she felt she owed it to Trevor to end it face-to-face.

As for any magical nights with Gavin, that would have to wait until after she talked to Trevor. Since she was flying out the morning after the wedding, she didn't think they'd have time to do much more than steal a few moments here and there, which while maddeningly frustrating and greatly disappointing was probably for the best. As Carly had suggested, she could flirt and fool around but no more.

Friday was a blur. Mac was up and moving before dawn and didn't stop going until she arrived at the church for the rehearsal. She tried not to overthink her outfit selection but when she found herself choosing a hot red number just to see Gavin's reaction to it, she put it back and went with a more demure floral dress.

As she was leaving the house, she found Aunt Sarah trying out some hip-hop dance moves in the living room. She knocked on the doorframe to get her attention, but Sarah didn't even break her rhythm. She looked at Mac and frowned.

"If you want to have your way with that Tolliver boy, the red number is the way to go," Sarah said.

"I do not—" Mac began to protest but Sarah just shook her head at her. "Is it that obvious?"

Aunt Charlotte entered the room. "That you're in love with Gavin? Oh, my, yes."

"No, no, no." Mac shook her head. She really liked him, sure, but love? No, she wasn't in that deep, not yet.

Aunt Sarah switched off the music and gave her a look that said quite clearly Mac was too stupid to live.

"Let's see," Charlotte said. "Do you think about him all of the time?"

Mac nodded.

"Does he make you feel good about yourself?" Sarah asked.

Mac bobbed her head.

"Do you care more about him than you do about yourself?" Charlotte asked.

Mac nodded again. She was getting unhappier with each answer.

"Does he make your body hum?" Sarah asked.

"Aunt Sarah!" Mac cried. She felt her face heat up.

"Hey, it's important," Sarah said. "And judging by your face, he does."

"Excellent," Charlotte said. "I like Gavin so much better than that toady Trevor fellow."

Sarah nodded. "You two will make great babies together."

Mac closed her eyes and tried to gather her composure. "I am leaving now. Do not say a word of this conversation to anyone, or I'll delete the hip-hop from your iPod. Am I clear?"

Both aunts nodded, solemnly. Mac felt like she was leaving two adolescent girls on their own as opposed to two septuagenarians. She wondered if she should lock up the liquor cabinet and call a sitter. Honestly!

She walked to the church where the rehearsal was to take place. It was a gorgeous evening and tomorrow promised to be a picture-perfect day. She knew because Emma had her check the weather every fifteen minutes all day long.

A faint breeze tugged at the hem of her skirt and swept her hair across her shoulders. She paused to admire the pink roses that hung down over the fence around the Burnhams' yard. Mr. and Mrs. Burnham always had the prettiest roses on the street and the pink ones had always been Mac's favorites.

She leaned forward and inhaled the sweet scent that held just a hint of spice to it and the truth flared up in her like a burst of bright light. She was in love with Gavin Tolliver.

Mac steadied herself on the fence, trying to

catch her breath. When had it happened? How could she not have known?

Then she realized that it had happened seven years ago, the night he had loved away all of her pain and humiliation. That was the night she had fallen for him. She had thought it was the trauma that had made it such a soulful connection but no. Gavin had been her soul mate all along; she had just never seen it. She had been in such a horrible world of hurt, she had run and never looked back.

The realization staggered her. And then she just wanted to see Gav, to be with him, to hold him close, and to hell with what anyone thought of them together. Yes, even Emma.

Mac turned away from the roses and all but ran to the church. She was winded when she got there. She saw her friends milling around on the front steps of Abiding Savior and she raced up the steps to join them. Her eyes searched the group for Gavin but there was no sign of him.

"Mac, thank goodness, you're here," Carly said. "Emma's having a meltdown."

"Why? What's wrong?" Mac asked.

"Gav is MIA," Zach said. "He's not at the clinic and he's not answering his phone."

Mac frowned. That was weird. Totally out of character for Gavin, unless—

"Mac, you're here!" Emma cried. She looked lovely in a pale blue dress with silver trim. "Is

Gavin with you? We're supposed to start and he's nowhere to be found."

"Don't fret, Emma, at least he's not the groom," Pastor Braedon, Jillian's father, who was officiating the service, joked. "Oh, hi, Mackenzie."

"Hi, Pastor Braedon," she said. She had been worried that seeing him again would trigger some post-traumatic stress since he was the one who was to officiate her own wedding, but no. She was pleased to note she was completely over it. She even managed to smile at his joke.

"I'm sure there's a reasonable explanation," Brad said. He took Emma's hand in his. "He'll get here as soon as he can."

"He probably had a veterinary emergency," Mr. Tolliver said as he joined them. "You know how your brother is, animals always come first."

Emma nodded. "You're right. I just get worried."

"No need, he'll jump in when he gets here, and if not I'm sure Mackenzie can bring him up to speed, right?" Pastor Braedon looked at her and Mac started.

Did he know? Could he read on her face that she was in love with Gavin? Did everyone know? She felt her face heat up.

"You are his partner in the wedding, correct?" Pastor asked.

"Oh, yeah," Mac said. "Yep, that's me. Sorry, I sort of forgot my role here for a second."

They all laughed but Carly gave Mac a *WTF* look that Mac chose to ignore.

The rehearsal went smoothly as everyone practiced their parts. Emma choked up a bit on her vows, but Brad just smiled down at her and pulled her through it, her ever-steady rock. Mac felt her own eyes water up, but she blinked away the tears, refusing to give in now when tomorrow would likely be a hurricane of happy boo-hoo-hoos. She figured she'd better conserve the water.

They stood outside the doors of the church, taking their spots in the receiving line. Mac left a space for Gavin, as if he might appear at any moment. She didn't say it to Emma, but she was getting worried. Emergency or no, she knew how much Emma meant to him and she couldn't believe he hadn't called anyone to let them know where he was.

Mac's phone chimed and she grabbed it out of her purse. Hoping it was Gavin, she didn't even check the screen.

"Where are you?" she cried.

"London, you know that, babe," Trevor said.

Everyone was watching her and Mac shook her head to let them know it wasn't Gavin. She turned her back and walked to the far side of the church. She wondered how swiftly she could hang up without being rude.

There was a crisis here, after all, and now that

she knew she was in love with someone else, talking to Trevor made her feel guilty. Not guilty for loving someone else—that was out of her control—but guilty for knowing she was going to be ruining this man's week, possibly his whole month.

The thought made her shake her head. Yeah, that was telling, wasn't it? He wouldn't be heartbroken about losing Mac, but he would be inconvenienced and Trevor hated to be inconvenienced.

"Listen, Trevor, we're leaving for the rehearsal dinner," she said. "So I really can't talk right now."

"That's fine," he said. "I was just thinking about you tonight and I realized I sort of miss you. You should be here with me in London instead of that backwater in Maine."

His voice sounded slurred.

"Trevor, have you been drinking?" Mac asked.

"Just a few pints at the pub," he said. "Nothing I can't handle."

"Okay, that's lovely," Mac said. Trevor rarely drank but when he did, he got very chatty. She knew she needed to nip this or she'd be forced to hang up on him. "I really have to go now, but I'll talk to you tomorrow and I'll see you at the end of the week when we're both back in Chicago. Okay?"

"About that," Trevor said. "You're not bringing that dog back with you, are you?"

"What makes you say that?" Mac asked. She had, in fact, been devising ways to steal Tulip and bring her to Chicago, but she hadn't mentioned them to anyone, not even Gavin.

"Because I know you," Trevor said. "You have a soft heart and you probably fell all in love with that mangy mutt, but I'm telling you, it's better off with Lester."

Mac froze as all the blood in her veins went icy cold.

"What?" she asked. "What did you say?"

"It's better off with Les—" Trevor bit off the word as if just catching on that he had fumbled mightily.

"I never told you who her owner was," Mac said. "How did you know his name?"

"Oh, don't be silly, you must have," he blustered.

"No, I remember quite clearly because you hung up on me to go grease some wheels when I would have told you his name and everything about the horrible ordeal," she fumed. She felt someone move to stand beside her and saw that it was Jillian and she was looking alarmed. "So, tell me how you know his name, Trevor, tell me now."

"Look, it was for your own good," he said.

"What did you do?" she snapped.

"I might have hired someone to come and claim the dog," he mumbled. "But I did it for you, for us, with the best of intentions."

"You hired someone to take my dog?" she cried. She heard Jillian gasp but didn't look at her. "How?"

"A corporate attorney friend of mine in Boston said he knew a guy in that Podunk town of yours that he figured would do it, so he drew up bogus ownership papers and had him call you," Trevor said. "But, honestly, I was just trying to help. You don't want to be tied down to some stray mutt. You have a career to think about."

"No, you weren't trying to help me," Mac said. Rage, white-hot and blinding in its intensity, made her growl through gritted teeth. "This was all about you. You had someone take my dog away because you didn't want it in my life because it might impact your life—your perfectly ordered, carefully constructed life. You son of a bitch!"

"Hey, now, there's no call for language like that," Trevor protested.

"Oh, yes, there is," Mac argued. "How much? How much were you paying him?"

"Five grand," Trevor said.

Mac squeezed the phone so hard in her hand she was surprised it didn't break.

"I'm going to say this once, Trevor, so listen very closely," she hissed. "That break we were taking, yeah, it's permanent now. We are done, finished, over, the end. Lose my number forever because as soon as I end this call I can assure you I am losing yours."

He began to protest but Mac ended the call.

"Holy sh—" Jillian began but Mac interrupted.

"Give me your keys," she said.

"Okay," Jillian said. She opened her bag and took them out and handed them to Mac. "But the rehearsal dinner."

"Tell Emma I'll be back as soon as I can," she said. "But I have to go save my dog."

"Do you want help?"

"No, I've got this. You be there for Emma— oh, and if you could explain about the whole me and Trevor on a break and now officially broken up because of what he did to my dog thing, that would be awesome."

Jillian nodded and then smiled. "Go get our girl!"

Chapter 31

Mac was pretty sure she broke the speed limit on her way to Lester's house. Her hands were shaking. Her head was throbbing. She was so angry. How could Trevor have done such a deceitful, lying, conniving, horrible thing as to hire someone to take her puppy away from her? And why? Because it was going to inconvenience his life?

It was a damn good thing he was thousands of miles away from her because she was quite certain she'd have wrapped her fingers around his thick neck and strangled the life out of him, the manipulative bastard.

She parked right in front of Lester's house. It was still light out and she could see his Buick was parked in his driveway. Excellent.

She was not about to climb under the fence. This time she was going right through the front door. She was going to march into the yard and claim her dog. Lester could call Trevor and hash it out with him if he felt so inclined but Mac was over it.

She lifted the latch and pushed her way through the creaky chain-link gate. The grass was as high as her knees and the walkway was cracked and pitted. She could see rusted parts of old junk strewn about the yard and she felt her rage spike.

Yeah, Trevor had thought this was an acceptable life for her dog.

Mac had to force herself to breathe and calm down as she was afraid that she'd take one look at Lester and pop him right in the face. She was halfway up the walk when the front door burst open.

She immediately assumed the fighter's stance she'd learned in self-defense. If Lester wanted to rumble, she was more than ready and willing to drop him on his head. But it wasn't Lester who was charging toward her. It was Gavin, coming at her with Tulip in his arms.

"What are you doing?" Mac cried.

"Go!" Gavin yelled.

The front door banged open again and Lester appeared. He was sporting a shiner and had a baseball bat in his hands.

"You think you can come on my property and take my dog?" he shouted. "I don't care what you think you saw, she's my dog and I'll treat her however I want."

Lester lumbered down the steps. Gavin shoved Tulip into Mac's arms and said, "Get her out of here."

Mac didn't need to be told twice. She clutched Tulip close and hustled her to the Jeep. She popped the back open and put Tulip inside, making sure the side windows were down so she had plenty of air.

She heard Lester's baseball bat connect with something, making a loud thwack. She desperately hoped it wasn't Gavin's head as she dashed back across the street.

The bat was now in two pieces and had been tossed aside. The two men were squared off, fists up and ready. Lester was panting and his shiner had started to swell. Gavin was breathing normally and didn't have a mark on him that Mac could see.

"I'm taking the dog," Gavin said. "You can let us go or this can get ugly."

"You have no authority," Lester said. "You're just a vet. You can't take people's pets."

"You kicked her," Gavin said. "I saw you."

"What?" Mac cried. She started to charge forward; she was going to put a hurt on Lester that he wouldn't forget anytime soon. Gavin turned toward her and waved her off. Big mistake!

As soon as Gavin turned his head, Lester charged him. He took Gavin out at the knees and the two men hit the ground in a flurry of fists and grunts.

Mac yelped and leapt back as they rolled her way. Gavin was stronger but Lester weighed significantly more and he used it to his advantage, trying to trap Gavin beneath him. He got in a good punch to Gavin's left eye, cutting the skin and causing it to bleed.

Gavin used Lester's own momentum against him, however, and managed to roll Lester off of him. Then he rained down a series of punches to Lester's gut and chin that left him weeping and begging for mercy.

Seeing the fight was over, Gavin shoved off of him and Lester rolled over onto his belly. Mac crouched closer to Gavin to check his eye but saw Lester reach for something in the tall grass. It was a tire iron. With a roar, Lester rose and charged Gavin, brandishing the tire iron over his head.

Mac didn't pause to think about it. In one swift move, she pulled her heavy purse off her shoulder, swung it once over her head for maximum velocity, and then walloped Lester in the side of the head, knocking him out cold and sending him face-first into his own lawn.

Then she sank back to Gavin's side to check his eye. The cut was on his cheekbone and it was bleeding profusely on the front of his shirt and tie. Other than that, he appeared unmarked.

"I thought you two were supposed to call me if it seemed warranted."

Mac and Gavin glanced up to see Officer Polson walking toward them.

"Sorry, time was of the essence," Gavin said. "I had to get the puppy out of here and I didn't think it could wait for backup."

"Why?" Polson asked. He looked concerned

and he frowned at Lester, who was still sprawled in the grass.

Gavin reached into his pocket and took out his phone. He ran his thumb over the display to activate the window and then chose the video option. He hit Play and turned the phone around so that Polson and Mac could see it.

It was footage of Tulip's area in the backyard. Lester was in the yard with her, bringing her some water. Tulip was straining at the end of her leash to get to the water and she bumped Lester, spilling the water down his pant leg.

He shouted some profanity and then threw the bowl across the yard. Tulip started to slink off and then he grabbed her lead, forcing her back to him. Then Lester pulled his leg back and kicked her in the ribs, sending her rolling back into the dirt with a hurt yip.

At that moment, Mac went a little crazy. She spun away from the two men and launched herself at Lester, who was beginning to rouse. Her fists were just about to connect with his face when an arm about her middle pulled her back.

"Mac, no!" Gavin ordered. His voice was a buzzing in her ear she chose to ignore.

She pushed against the arm that held her and tried to wriggle out of his hold. Visions of grabbing Lester by his ears and bringing his face down to her knee, repeatedly, until he was just a bloody rag doll, filled her mind and she couldn't see anything else.

"Mac, stop," Gavin said. "Listen, even if Polson is on our side, if you assault Lester in front of him, he'll have to arrest you and you'll be spending Emma's wedding in jail."

"Argh," Mac growled, knowing he was right and feeling thwarted all the way down to her toes.

"Come on, for Emma," he said.

"He's right," Polson said. "Send me that video and I'll have more than enough to run Lester in. I don't want to have to process you, too."

"Can I take my dog?" Mac asked. "I'd like to have Gavin look her over and make sure she hasn't suffered any more than the one incident."

"Yes," Polson said. "And as far as I'm concerned, she's yours, papers or no papers."

Mac felt her heart lift. "Thanks, Officer."

"I will need you both to come into the station and give me a statement," he said. "If I have my way, this guy won't be going near another animal ever again."

With that he nudged Lester with the toe of his boot. Lester flopped in the grass a bit and then he began to whimper and whine.

"You saw them, Officer, they attacked me," he said. "I want them arrested for assault and battery. She hit me with that bag of hers. I think there are rocks in it. I want her busted for assault with a deadly weapon."

"Shut up," Polson said. "I saw all of it. You attacked him first, therefore as far as I'm concerned you're the only one under arrest."

"But he was stealing my dog," Lester whined.

"Yeah, about that, she's not your dog anymore," Polson said. He reached down and grabbed Lester's arm, forcing him to his feet.

"You can't do that," Lester said. "I have papers. I can prove she's mine."

Mac thought about jumping in to clarify that point, but Gavin's hand on her arm pulled her away before she entered the fray.

"Come on, let's go check on our girl," he said.

He was right. This could wait until tomorrow. Right now, she was more concerned about her dog.

Together they hurried to the Jeep. Tulip barked at the sight of them and then started to wiggle and waggle from her head to her paws; she looked giddy to see them. Her people.

They spent the next few minutes checking Tulip over. Her ribs were tender but the rest of her body seemed fine. Her spirits were certainly up as she tried to lick both of their faces at the same time. She was filthy dirty and her neck had a bare spot where the too-tight collar had rubbed her raw. Mac knew she was probably thirsty and hungry and she couldn't wait to give her a meal and a bath in that order.

"Where did you park?" Mac asked him while

Tulip licked his face. She seemed particularly concerned about his cut, which Mac kept her from cleaning with her dog spit.

"On the other side of the woods," Gavin said. "I was just doing a quick check on my way to the rehearsal dinner, but then, well, you saw the video."

Mac felt a surge of hatred pump through her. If Lester were standing in front of her car, she'd have no problem gunning the engine and running him down, she was pretty sure.

"Oh, man, the rehearsal," Gavin said. "Emma is going to kill me."

"No," Mac said. "I'm your partner. I can show you what needs doing. She's just going to be relieved that you're okay, as am I."

Gavin tipped his head to look at her and he smiled, even though it made him wince.

"You can't drive with your eye like that," Mac said. "Come on, I'll drive you home and we'll get the two of you fixed up."

Gavin put his hand on Tulip's head and rubbed her ears. "How did you know?"

"Know what?"

"That I was here," he said.

"I didn't," she said. "I just happened by and there you were."

"Just happened by, huh?"

"Yeah, something like that."

Okay, now this was really her moment. Mac

knew it. This was the grand opportunity she'd been waiting for to tell Gavin about Trevor, their former relationship, and what he'd done to her and Tulip by engineering this whole sad situation and how sorry she was for all of it—but she didn't.

As she looked at the man before her covered in blood with shredded knuckles and a puffy cheek—wounds he'd gotten while defending a dog from cruelty—she just couldn't tell him that up until two weeks ago, she'd been dating the douche bag who had caused this to happen. She just couldn't. Not right now.

Tomorrow, or maybe the day after tomorrow, when they'd gotten through the wedding, and she knew Tulip was fine—then she would tell Gavin everything. From start to finish: what Emma had asked of her, her break and now breakup with Trevor, her fear that she might be his transition relationship, and, lastly and most importantly, how much she loved him, Gavin, and how much she hoped he loved her, too.

"You okay, Mac?" he asked.

She cupped his uninjured cheek and pressed her lips to the corner of his mouth.

"Yeah, I'm good," she said. "Let's get out of here."

When Mac pulled away from the curb, she slowed down to savor watching Officer Polson push Lester's head down as he helped him into the back of the squad car.

"I'm going to text Emma and let her know that we're okay but that Tulip here needs some attention," he said. "Then I'm sending Polson the video. I want him to throw the book at that guy."

"Oh, I hope so," Mac said. "He should do jail time for what he did to baby girl."

As if she knew they were talking about her, Tulip popped her head in between their seats and braced herself with her feet on the console. Mac rubbed her face and kissed her head. She didn't care who tried to take this dog away from her, she was never going to let her go again.

Mac parked in front of the clinic. Gavin led Tulip into one of the exam rooms and gave her a thorough once-over. When it was finished, and she checked out as just fine, he grabbed some dog supplies and led both Mac and Tulip upstairs to his apartment.

"I'll feed her," Mac said. "You go ahead and clean up."

Gavin looked down at the blood caked on his shirt. "This is a bit off-putting isn't it?"

He disappeared into his bedroom while Mac sat on the kitchen floor with Tulip. As soon as she put Tulip's food down, the puppy slammed her face into the bowl. Slurps and snuffles were the only sounds Mac heard until the bowl was empty and Tulip was pushing it around the tile floor with her nose as if she could make more food appear just by willing it to be so.

Gavin appeared in the doorway. He had stripped off his bloody shirt and tie and changed into a charcoal gray T-shirt. The cut on his face was still oozing and he had clearly done a half-assed job of cleaning his face.

"How is she?" he asked.

"She's a better patient than you," Mac said. She opened the freezer and grabbed a bag of frozen peas, then she took his hand and led him into the bathroom where she put the lid down on the toilet and pushed him toward it. "Sit."

She opened up the cupboard under the sink and took stock of his medical supplies. There wasn't much.

"I washed it out," he protested.

"Not very well," she said. "You need to clean it and put some antibiotic stuff on it."

She found a washcloth and made it warm and soapy. Then she gently cleaned his cheek, turning his face so she could see the cut and make sure there was no dirt in it. Then she applied direct pressure to stop the bleeding.

He shifted his legs so that she was standing in between them and then he ran his hands absently up and down the outside of her thighs.

"You can't distract me from my purpose," she said as she dabbed ointment onto his cheek. "So stop trying."

"You sure about that?" he asked as his hands started to roam beneath the hem of her dress, seeking skin.

"Yes," Mac said. But it sounded like a lie since it came out on a hiss of air as she had stopped breathing.

He chuckled and then winced as she plopped the bag of frozen peas onto his face.

Tulip sat in the doorway, looking adorably worried, and Mac said to her, "He's fine. You should worry about you. You're next."

Mac sent Gavin out to the living room to sit with the peas on his cheek. She knew Emma would appreciate any effort Mac put in to make her brother camera ready for tomorrow's big day.

Emma had texted back that she was thrilled that they had rescued Tulip from her bad place and not to worry about missing the rehearsal dinner. So long as they were at tomorrow's brunch, all was forgiven.

"All right, you, it's your turn to wash that horrible place off of you," Mac said. Tulip tipped her head to the side as if she wasn't sure she liked what Mac was saying. Smart dog.

Mac led Tulip into the bathroom and started the water in the tub. She kept it warm, not hot, and grabbed a bar of soap that she found under Gavin's sink. Tulip did not like the sound of the running water and wedged herself behind the toilet in an effort to hide.

"Sorry, sweetie, this is not optional," Mac said. "You stink."

She shut off the water and Tulip seemed reassured by the lack of sound. Mac began talking to her just like she had on the day she found her. Soft, reassuring nonsense words, and soon Tulip belly crawled out of her safe spot.

Mac scanned the contents of the bathroom cabinet and found a small plastic cup. As if she was encouraging Tulip to play fetch, she showed her the cup and then threw it in the water. This made Tulip bark and jump at the side of the tub. Mac retrieved the cup and did it a couple of more times until in her excitement, Tulip jumped into the water.

Mac had expected her to bolt back out of the tub, which only had a few inches of water in the bottom, but Tulip was so fixated on the cup that she paid no attention to the water at all. In fact, as she tried to capture the cup in her mouth, she set the water to churning and waves crashed out of the tub all over Mac.

Mac sputtered and glanced down at her floral dress. Then she laughed. She hugged Tulip close and kissed her nose. Tulip returned the kisses on the mouth—blerg—which only made Mac laugh harder.

She scrubbed Tulip down, feeling both alarmed and pleased when the water in the tub turned dark brown from all of the dirt. Then she drained the tub and rinsed the dog, relieved when the water finally ran clear.

"Oh, now who's my pretty girl? Who is my sweet-smelling princess?" Mac asked Tulip as she got her out of the tub and onto the bathmat.

Mac knelt down and dropped a towel on her, rubbing her all over, which made Tulip wriggle from head to tail, giddy from all of the love and affection.

When Mac lifted the towel, Tulip bolted for the door. It was then that Mac saw Gavin standing in the doorway, watching them. He was smiling and he laughed when Tulip raced past him into the apartment, where she ran laps around the living room before collapsing onto the dog bed he had set up for her.

"That is one happy dog," he said. He turned back to Mac as she rose to her feet and his eyes went wide and he swallowed hard. "You . . . uh . . . your dress."

Mac glanced down. She was soaked and her dress was clinging to every curve and crevice her body possessed, leaving nothing to the imagination. She might as well have been naked. Suddenly, that seemed like an excellent idea.

Chapter 32

She glanced up to see Gavin staring at her with a heat in his gaze that she was surprised didn't leave burn marks on her skin. She took two steps toward him until she was well within his personal space, and then she turned around.

"Unzip me, please," she said. She noticed her voice was a gruff, gritty growl and wondered if he heard it, too.

"Sure," he said.

She expected to feel his fingers at the nape of her neck, instead it was his lips. He pushed aside her hair and pressed his mouth just above the fabric of her dress. It was a gentle, innocent touch that made Mac see stars as a wicked heat began to lick her insides.

Then he pulled her zipper down and the cool evening air brushed her back and made her shiver. He pushed the fabric forward and it slid down her arms to pool at her waist. His fingers insistently pushed the fabric over the curve of her hips until it landed in a puddle on the floor at her feet and she was standing in just a fancy lace pushup bra and matching bottoms.

Mac turned her head and looked at him over her shoulder. His baby blues had gone dark with desire and he leaned down and kissed her while his hands on her hips pulled her back against his erection. The contact made Mac dizzy as the rough touch of his dress pants rubbed against the backs of her legs and she grabbed onto his arm to steady herself.

Gavin broke the kiss and leaned back, studying her. One of his hands left her hip and pushed her hair away from her face.

"I think we're in that place again," he said.

"What place is that?"

"The one where you need to decide if you want to stay or go," he said. "Because the only way I am going to be able to stop this is if you go."

Mac put her hand on his chest. She could see the definition in his physique even through his T-shirt. She had the sudden crazy thought that the aunts would most definitely approve of his pecs. She also knew that they'd tell her that if she wanted this, if she wanted him, then she should go for it. What was it they'd said about living life so that they had no regrets? She didn't want to be seventy-two and look back on this night, regretting that she didn't stay.

She peeked over his shoulder to see that Tulip had passed out in the dog bed with her feet up in the air. Her chest was moving up and down. Mac listened closely. Yep, baby girl was snoring.

"If it's all the same to you," Mac said. She paused to press her lips to the base of his throat where his pulse seemed somewhat erratic. "I think I'll stay."

"Thank fuck," Gavin said. He grabbed her by the hips and hoisted her up against him.

Mac laughed as she wrapped her legs around his waist and her arms about his shoulders and held on while he strode down the hall toward the bedroom. Not even slowing down for the closed door, he kicked it open, walked across the room, and dropped Mac onto the bed.

She bounced and he pounced, trapping her beneath him in the most erotic way Mac had ever imagined, with his mouth on hers, his hands holding hers down over her head while his trouser clad thighs kept her legs pinned in place.

His mouth on hers was insistent, demanding she meet him halfway. Mac arched her back, pressing her softness against him. He groaned and let one hand slide down her side to her hip. Mac buried her free hand in his hair, pulling him closer as she kissed him fiercely.

It was as if they couldn't get close enough, be near enough, touch enough, taste enough. Mac had never felt the longing that she felt with Gavin. She didn't know if it was because she knew she was in love with him or if it was just the potent chemical mix that was unique to them.

At the moment she didn't really care. She just knew she wanted to take and be taken, to feel the magic that happened only when she was with him. She pulled her other hand free and shoved him onto his back.

He looked good against the masculine black and gray comforter, very good. Mac took note but she didn't linger on the image of him sprawled and at her mercy. She had a mission to get him as bare as she was. She straddled him as she tugged his T-shirt over his head, tossing it across the room.

When he would have distracted her by grabbing her hips and holding her hot spot against his erection, she wriggled against him once just to tease him and then she went to work on his pants, unfastening the button and lowering the zipper. When she curled her fingers into the waistband and pulled them down over his hips, she heard him hiss out a breath.

That sounded like an invitation to her, so she pulled his boxer briefs down, too, and lowered her mouth to the hard part of him that had sprung free and was desperately seeking some attention.

She worked him over with her tongue until she felt a light sheen of sweat covering his body and his hips bucked repeatedly while he groaned in a beautiful sort of agony. She moved to take him all the way in her mouth but was thwarted when he reached down and caught her about the middle, pulling her up his body.

When she was lying fully against him, he sighed as if this contact was the most amazing thing he'd ever felt. Then he rolled so that she was under him and he kissed her. Long, slow, openmouthed kisses as if he was memorizing the feel of her mouth against his, the taste of her, the way she moaned against his lips when his hand slid down her body and cupped her breast.

She was still in her bra and undies as he moved down her body, his tongue trailing a path on her skin as he tasted each and every part of her. His tricky fingers managed to remove the last of her clothing without her even being aware of it. Then his mouth was on her, tasting her, teasing her, making her cry out but not letting her come. Not yet.

When she was balanced precariously right on the brink, he pulled back and reached for protection in the top drawer of his nightstand. Mac was panting and sweating and pretty sure she was going to combust right there on his bedspread.

He slid on the condom with one hand and with the other he put his thumb right on the spot that made Mac insane. She arched her head back, and said, "Gavin."

She didn't know if it was a curse, a plea, or just the need to say the name of the man she loved, but she felt the smile on his lips when he kissed her and slid into her at the same time.

And that was it. Mac's body responded to the feel of his immediately. Her pussy convulsed around his cock so hard that he grunted as she climaxed, leaving him no choice but to come with her. A couple of deep hard thrusts and Gavin wrapped his arms around Mac and held her tight as their bodies were simultaneously ripped apart and mended by the bliss that rocked them from the inside out.

Gavin rolled onto his back, pulling her with him and covering them with the bedsheets while they caught their breath. Mac peeled herself off of his chest and gazed down at his face, feeling as if she could never look her fill of the man beside her. How long had it been since she'd felt this way about anyone? Had she ever felt this way about anyone? She traced his lips with her index finger and he nipped the pad of her finger and then sucked it gently into his mouth.

The part of Mac that should have been sated for at least a month roared to life. She glanced from his mouth, which had moved from her finger to her wrist to her elbow, to his eyes. They were dark again and she knew he was feeling the same way she was.

"Water," she croaked. "If we're going for round two, I need water."

She pushed off of him and grabbed his T-shirt from the floor. He propped himself up on one elbow and watched her pull the shirt over her head.

"Sexy," he said. Then his eyes narrowed. "Come here."

Mac felt her heart thud at his tone. He sounded very serious. She sat on the edge of the bed, but he wasn't having the distance. He pulled her over to him, and lifted her up so that she was straddling him through the bedsheet.

Her body rippled with another little burst of pleasure at the feel of him right between her legs, but she forced herself to put it aside as he swept his hands up her arms and combed his fingers through her hair.

"There's something you need to know," he said. His gaze met hers. "I would have told you before I made love to you, but I got distracted."

Mac smiled at him. Distracted was a lovely word for it.

"The truth is, Mackenzie Harris, I'm in love with you, and I think I have been for my whole life," he said. Then he pulled her down and kissed her in a kiss unlike any Mac had ever received before. Raw in its honesty, sweet in its intention, loving in its purpose, it was a kiss that was a promise of forever. She was undone.

The words *I love you, too* bubbled up inside of Mac but Gavin never gave her a chance to say them. With his revamped knowledge of her body and her response to his touch, he made love to her again and again as if he could make up for the seven years between their first time and now all in one night. Mac didn't think it was possible, but she was happy to help him try.

Sometime in the middle of the night, the foot of the bed dipped and twenty-five pounds of puppy snuck her way in between the feet of the two bodies that were curled around each other, sleeping the dreamless sleep of the happily exhausted. To the puppy, this was her new pack now and she was not about to let them out of her sight.

It was the blast of midmorning sun that woke them—well, that and their cell phones ringing as a belligerent fist pounded on Gavin's front door.

"Wake up, you two, there's a wedding today," Zach yelled through the door.

"Mac! Gavin! Brunch is in half an hour. Unless you want Emma to disown you forever, you'll answer the damn door," Carly shouted.

Mac reared back from a cold nose being shoved into her eye. Tulip! She turned away and saw Gavin asleep beside her and the stupidest, happiest grin spread over her face.

Then the banging on the front door resumed and she reached for her phone to check the time. The phone was buzzing in her hand but she ignored it.

The time read nine thirty. Nine thirty!

"Gavin! Wake up!" she yelled. "Oh, my god, we're late. Emma is going to kill us!"

"Huh? What?" He opened his eyes and saw

Mac staring down at him and a slow smile spread across his lips. Then Tulip pounced and kissed him good morning on the mouth. "Ugh, blerg."

"It's nine thirty!" Mac cried.

The banging on the front door resumed with both Carly and Zach yelling for them to get up.

"Nine thirty?" Gavin asked as he sat up. "Oh, shit!"

Chapter 33

There was no way to ignore the two people at his door; otherwise Gavin would have. It would have been especially lovely if Carly and Zach had the grace not to comment on what had clearly gone down in his apartment the night before, but they did not.

When he opened the door wearing just his pants, Carly strode in carrying a duffel bag with Zach trailing behind her.

"Whoa, nice shiner, dude," Zach said. He squinted at him. "How's the other guy look?"

"Way worse," Gavin said. "He got rocked by Mac's purse with a blow to the temple, so I'm betting he's waking up in jail today with one hell of a headache."

"Nice," Zach said and they exchanged a high five and a fist bump.

"I have some makeup that might cover that," Carly said.

"No, just no," Gavin said.

"Yeah, that look is much manlier," she agreed.

Tulip raced out of the bedroom and began to bark, clearly trying to overcompensate for the fact that she had slept through the initial knocking and yelling. Zach and Carly both bent down to give her love. They didn't seem surprised to see her here, so the story of Mac and Gavin's rescue of the dog had made the rounds.

Mac hurried into the kitchen wearing just Gavin's T-shirt and a pair of his boxers as shorts; he had to pause a moment to take that in. Then he shook his whole body like Tulip after her bath, trying to shake loose the lust that suddenly had him by the short hairs. For a crazy second, he feared he was going to shove his friends right back out the door and have his way with Mac up against his kitchen counter. Oh, boy, what that girl could do to him.

Tulip trotted to Mac's side and pressed against her. Mac put her hand on the puppy's head as she stood in front of the Keurig coffeepot as if willing it to brew faster. Judging by the way she was tapping her bare feet, it wasn't working.

Her brown hair tumbled around her shoulders and his gray T-shirt clung to parts of her that he was now intimately familiar with and wanted to be so again. Gavin turned away before he embarrassed himself.

"So, it looks like someone has been trimming the hedges in Mac's lady garden," Zach said to Carly.

"No kidding, look at her face." Carly snorted. "That's the glow of a girl who spent the night having her moo-moo milked."

Zach doubled up with laughter. "And we're

on again. Bet I know more euphemisms for lady parts than you do."

Mac's entire face went bright red. In fact, when Gavin lowered his gaze to her throat, it looked like her entire body was blushing with embarrassment. She sent him a desperate look.

"Put the brakes on, you two," Gavin said. His tone made it an order.

"Oh, dude," Zach said. His grin was wicked and he wagged his eyebrows at them. "I am just getting started."

"No, no. No, you're not," Mac protested. "Today is Emma's day and we're not going to do anything that might take away from that."

"But—" Zach argued before Mac interrupted him.

"Back me up, Carly," she said. "The bride will shank him if he goofs up her day with vaginal euphemisms, am I right?"

"Yeah, Emma will cut you," Carly said to Zach. "Probably, with a pearl-handled cake server, but, yeah, don't mess with her day. This"—she paused to gesture at Mac and Gavin—"needs to be kept on the down low. This is Emma's day and no one else's. Clear?"

"Fine." Zach sighed, obviously feeling put out.

"All right," Carly said. "We have twenty minutes to get you two presentable for brunch. Let's go."

"Make it fifteen," Gavin said.

Once the festivities started, he knew he wasn't

going to have another chance to talk to Mac, so he grabbed her hand and pulled her into the bedroom, slamming the door in Carly and Zach's faces. Tulip scratched at the door but he ignored her.

He pushed Mac up against the wall and pressed his body the length of hers. Man, he loved the way they fit perfectly together.

"We don't have—" Mac protested but he kissed her. He knew it was going to be the last long and lingering one he was going to get for a while, so he made it count. When she was clutching his bare shoulders and arching into him, he broke the kiss.

"No time to fool around, I know," he said. "Pity."

"Yeah." She sighed against him.

He pushed her hair back from her face and studied her warm brown eyes. He didn't know what he was looking for—wait, that was a lie. He knew. He was looking for regret, uncertainty, or doubt. When her soft gaze met his, however, there was none of that. What he saw made him catch his breath. He didn't think he was fooling himself. What he saw was love.

Bang. Bang. Bang. A fist rapped on the door. Tulip barked.

"Kids, we've got to go," Zach cried. "I will leave you here. I am not getting shanked by a cake server over you two."

Gavin grinned and Mac smiled.

"Really quick," Gavin said. "How do we want to play this today? Because I really don't care if anyone can tell, my sister included, that you and I are now a thing."

"Oh, we're a thing, huh?" Mac asked.

She looked ridiculously pleased, which made Gavin's own heart swell with relief and delight. After all these years, Mac was his. He was having a hard time, a wonderfully hard time, wrapping his head around it.

"Yes," he growled and leaned into her. "We're a big thing."

Mac's laugh was deliciously sexy. "I can feel that."

He almost locked the door and dragged her back to the bed, Zach and Carly and brunch be damned.

Then Mac cupped his face and kissed him ever so sweetly. "Let's keep it quiet, just for today, for Emma," she said.

He hated the idea, detested it, but he trusted that Mac knew his sister and the inner workings of the female brain better than he did.

"All right, but I'm driving you from the church to the reception and if we have to take a detour to an old secluded spot on a hill beneath two old copper beech trees, so be it."

The smile she sent him blinded him, and Gavin was pretty sure this was the most perfect moment of his entire life.

● ● ●

Mac and Carly raced into the brunch right behind Gavin and Zach. They were ten minutes late but given how strong the temptation to blow off brunch and stay in bed with Gavin all morning had been, Mac figured ten minutes was more than acceptable.

Plus, she'd had to hand off Tulip to the aunts with very specific instructions not to let her out of their sight. They were coming to the wedding later as Jessie had agreed to come over with her girls to watch Tulip, but in the meantime the puppy was on the aunts' watch. Mac tried not to worry.

The aunts did not comment on Mac being out all night, but when she was leaving she saw Sarah nudge Charlotte with her elbow and they both giggled. Mac ignored them.

Brunch was a casual affair at Mr. Tolliver's house and everyone was dressed in shorts or jeans as they went over the last-minute details of the day. The spread of food was immense, as the wedding party, the immediate family on both sides, and the out-of-town guests had been invited to partake.

Dining was buffet style so Mac loaded her plate—mercy, she had worked up an appetite—and found a table with Jillian at the edge of the back terrace. From there, they ate and watched the Tolliver cousins play in the yard while their mothers talked, pausing to scold the kids now and then before digging right back into the family gossip.

Mac watched Gavin greet his aunts and uncles with kisses and hugs. The aunts all fussed over his shiner while the uncles slapped him on the back in macho approval. He tossed the football in the backyard with his younger cousins and then he paused beside his father to chat.

The morning sun shone on his light brown hair, turning it the rich color of honey. Mac could still feel it against her fingers. When he tipped his head back and laughed, his full lips parted and showed his teeth and Mac remembered those same teeth nipping the pad of her finger and other parts as well. When one of his little girl cousins ran up to hug him, the dimple in his right cheek deepened as he picked her up and tossed her in the air, making her screech with giggles.

Mac sighed. Had he always been this impossibly handsome?

"Mac, hello? Mac?" Jillian pinched her upper arm and Mac jumped.

"Ouch!" she cried as she rubbed the spot.

"Wow, you really got shagged stupid last night, didn't you," Jillian said.

"Carly told you?" Mac gasped.

"Oh, puhleeze, you're staring at Gav like he's standing there naked," Jillian said. "If you're trying to keep it quiet, you'd better dial it back a bit."

"Ugh!" Mac lowered her head to her chest. She reached for her mimosa and took a sip. How was she going to get through a whole day of being with him but not with him?

"Be my spotter?" she asked Jillian.

"Always," her friend said. "Can I say one thing?"

"That depends," Mac said. "Is it going to damage my self-worth?"

"No." Jillian laughed. "I just want you to know that in all the years I've known you, which is twenty, I've never seen you look so happy."

Mac hugged her friend close. "I've never been this happy."

"Then don't mess it up," Jillian said.

"I'm trying really hard not to," Mac said. "But it's complicated."

Jillian swiped a piece of bacon off of Mac's plate.

"No, it isn't," she said. "Be open and honest and you'll be okay."

"I will," Mac said. "Or at least I plan to, you know, after today."

They both glanced at Emma, who was making the rounds of family and friends, with Brad at her side. In jeans and matching T-shirts that read *Bride* on Emma's and *Groom* on Brad's, they were about as sickeningly adorable as a couple could be.

"She's going to be okay with this, you know," Jillian said. "She was ecstatic when she heard you and Trevor were kaput. She loves you and Gavin. She'll be thrilled that you found each other."

"Maybe," Mac said. "But there's the little issue that she asked me to watch over him not sleep with him—oh, and let's not forget the news that I defiled her baby brother seven years ago and never mentioned it."

Jillian shook her head and her long dark curls bounced around her shoulders. "I'm telling you, it may take time, but she'll be all right with this, all of it, really."

"I hope so," Mac said. "Because I honestly don't think I can give him up."

After brunch, it was off to the hairdresser's for the girls and the barber for the boys. Then it was back to Emma's father's house to get dressed for the girls and back to Emma and Brad's house for the boys.

There was one panicked phone call from Brad to Emma when Zach managed to tear the inseam on the pants of his rented tuxedo. One of Emma's aunts grabbed her sewing kit and zipped over to the boys' house to mend the situation. She reported back that all was well and that she'd never seen such a group of fine-looking men.

Mac, Jillian, and Carly slipped easily into their Windsor blue bridesmaid dresses and then turned their attention to Emma. She had chosen a simple strapless silk wedding gown with a sweetheart neckline that was fitted all the way to her hips and then flared out around her feet.

Her hair was half up half down and the stylist had fastened her veil on the back of her head so that it draped down over the thick waves of her blonde hair to end at her lower back. She was so enchantingly lovely that Mac wouldn't have been surprised to find her growing in a flower garden as its crowning glory.

A knock sounded on the bedroom door, and Jillian opened it to let Emma's father in. When he saw her, he tipped his head to the side and two tears slid down his cheeks, one on each side.

"You are as beautiful as your mother," he said. His voice was a rough rasp and he wiped away the tears with a flick of his finger.

"Oh, Daddy," Emma cried. She rushed forward and hugged him tight. He hugged her back and kissed her head.

"Walk with me?" he asked. She nodded.

The girls watched from above as father and daughter strolled about the garden in the backyard. When Emma returned, it was clear she had been crying. Carly went into a panic, but ever prepared Jillian took Emma in hand to repair the damage.

Emma sat at her mother's vanity in the corner of her parents' bedroom while Jillian fixed her makeup. Carly and Mac sat nearby on the bed.

"Is everything okay?" Mac asked.

"Yes." Emma nodded. She pointed to the pearl necklace at her throat and the matching drop earrings dangling from her earlobes. "My dad gave me these."

"Oh, they're lovely," Carly said. "How thoughtful."

"They were my mother's," Emma said. Her eyes welled up. "She wore them on her wedding day."

"No, don't start that again," Jillian said. She fanned her face with her hands as tears filled her eyes, too. "Here, gently pull on your lower eyelids; it will make the tears recede."

"Oh, hey, that works." Emma sniffed. She took a deep breath and touched the pearls at her throat. "You know, I feel like she's here with me and I feel like she's happy for me."

"She is," Mac said. "She absolutely is."

Then Carly started to bawl and the four of them ended up in a sloppy group hug, all while trying not to mess up their hair and makeup.

Damage control took a little more time than had been allotted and it was a bit of a mad dash to get into the limo to get to the church, but the four friends giggled all the way there. When Emma panicked about not saying the right name during the vows, Carly made them laugh by throwing out ridiculous endearments that Emma could use in place of Brad's name.

"I take thee, snookums," she offered. "No? How about pickle, buttercup, honey-toast?"

Emma was laughing, so the glower she sent Carly had no heat when she said, "If I mess it up and say any of those, I am holding you personally responsible."

Carly grinned. Then she took Emma's hand in hers and motioned for them all to join hands. "You won't. You love Bradley Thornton Jameson."

"And you're going to marry him," Jillian said.

"And live happily ever after," Mac added.

"I am, I really am." Emma's voice was full of wonder.

Mac held the hands of her closest friends and felt as if the well of happiness inside of her was overflowing. Nothing could spoil this day. Nothing.

Chapter 34

Mac had seen her share of tuxedos in her lifetime, but she had never seen a man make a tuxedo look like that—a walking advertisement of hotness to make a girl swoon. Truly, she could only look at Gavin out of the corner of her eye since she was afraid a full-on look at him would render her incoherent.

Seriously, the cut along his broad shoulders, the black bow tie against the crisp white dress shirt with the black buttons, the Windsor blue pocket square that matched her dress—all of it made her want to take a bite out of him, which was not a response she'd ever had toward a man before. It was thrilling and alarming.

The music began and Zach and Carly started down the aisle; Sam and Jillian waited until they were halfway to the altar and then they began. Next up were Gavin and Mac.

Mac turned around to look at Emma, standing with her father. All brides were beautiful but Emma raised it to a whole new level. It wasn't the petite blonde thing she had going for her, although that obviously wasn't a hindrance, but rather it was the radiance that sparkled off of her like sunlight on water. Emma was in love and she was marrying the man of her dreams.

There was no substitute for that sort of magic.

She winked at Emma and Emma winked back. Then they both giggled.

"You ready?" Gavin asked her.

She nodded and clutched her bouquet of yellow roses and blue hydrangea in her left hand and put her right hand on his elbow. He put his free hand over hers as if to reassure her. When he smiled down at her, Mac forgot for a second that they were supposed to move forward. She pulled her gaze away from his and focused on the altar that seemed a million miles away.

They walked slowly, smiling at all of the faces turned toward them. When one of Gavin's aunts who had an inability to whisper said, "What a lovely couple they make," Mac had the horrifying thought that everyone in the church could tell there was a thing happening between her and Gavin.

As if sensing her stress, halfway down the aisle, Gavin leaned close and said, "You look beautiful."

Mac glanced at him, quickly. She couldn't let herself get sucked into that blue-eyed vortex again for fear that she'd forget how to walk and make a complete ass of herself.

"I thought the same thing about you," she said.

As they passed the aunts, Mac heard Aunt Sarah wolf whistle. Gavin snorted a laugh and Mac pulled him close and whispered, "Don't laugh, I think that was for you," which only made him laugh harder.

At the altar, Mac took her hand off his arm and she wondered if he felt her reluctance to let him go. He grinned at her and went to join the boys, and so the ceremony began.

The service was touching, poignant, and beautiful. The guests laughed and cried and laughed again. When Brad was informed that Emma was now officially his wife, he whooped with pure undiluted joy, then he dipped her and kissed her in a way that left every woman in the church a little weak in the knees.

The wedding party followed the bride and groom out the door and the receiving line began. Because Gavin was family, he knew just about everyone in attendance and he happily introduced Mac to them all. He kept his hand on her lower back and Mac noticed several of the guests exchanging speculative looks with one another. She knew she should try harder to keep it on the down low, but she just couldn't make herself care when she was so happy to be beside him.

After line up duty, it was on to pictures, while the guests set out for the brewery to start warming up for the party to follow. The photographer made it easy and the wedding party escaped the flashbulb pretty quickly while the bride and groom lingered.

Brad and Emma were taking the limo when

they finished the photos, so Mac went to join the girls in the Jeep, but Gavin had other ideas and grabbed her hand and pulled her over to his truck. When Zach and Sam waved him over to their car, he waved back, pretending not to understand.

"Smooth, really smooth," Mac said as he shut the door behind her and hurried around to the driver's side.

"What I lack in finesse, I make up for in charm," he said. He started up the engine and shot out of the parking lot. "Besides, I figure the sooner we get out of here the sooner we can start making out. My best guesstimate is we have fifteen minutes before anyone notices we're not where we're supposed to be."

"A lot can happen in fifteen minutes," Mac said. "Pull over."

Gavin hopped the curb and Mac laughed while he shoved the truck into park and reached for her.

"Rough ride?" Carly asked as she reached into Mac's hair and adjusted a loose hair clip.

Mac felt her face go hot. Carly laughed.

"Girl, you've got it bad," Jillian said.

"You have no idea," Mac said. She didn't even have to scan the room to know where Gavin was. He was standing with his father, talking and enjoying a cold beer while staring at her.

As if they were attached by an invisible string, Mac knew where he was at all times. She also knew when he was looking at her, because she could feel the heat of his gaze on her skin like a physical touch. Whenever he wasn't looking at her, she took advantage and gazed her fill of him. So, this was love, then. This crazy, giddy, borderline obsessive feeling was love.

It was a shock to realize that she'd never had this before. She'd thought she'd loved Seth, but looking back, it paled in comparison to little more than a crush. And then she'd thought she'd loved Trevor, but it had never been like this. In retrospect, it had been mainly a relationship of convenience. How sad.

Emma's wedding stager had done an incredible job transforming the brewery courtyard. Colorful paper lanterns and strings of white lights had been strung across the length of the open roof. Round tables with white tablecloths and bunches of blue hydrangea and yellow roses just like in the girls' bouquets decorated each table, while huge pots of yellow rose bushes and blue hydrangeas were tucked all around the outer edge of the courtyard.

Four different food stations were placed in each corner of the large space, serving everything from Maine lobster to pasta to prime rib. Because it was a brewery, there was an endless supply of beer and the wine Mac and Gavin had picked up in Portland was being served as well. A big glittery dance floor had been laid out on one end of the courtyard and the DJ had set up beside it. No one was dancing as yet, but Mac had a feeling it was only a matter of time.

She glanced at Gavin, again, and this time he caught her. He said something to his father and put his beer down. Then he crooked his finger at her and Mac was done for. She walked across the dance floor to meet him without even saying a word to her friends.

Then she was in his arms and everything was right in her world. The DJ caught on quickly and put on some danceable music and they busted out their waltz moves and danced the next three songs together, before Carly cut in, suggesting that there would be talk if the two of them didn't stop looking at each other like they were about to do the naughty.

Mac left Gavin to Carly with a sigh. When she stepped off of the dance floor, she saw Emma watching her. She had a questioning look on her face, and Mac felt her heart drop into her feet. Guilt does make for a fast elevator ride down when it hits the panic button.

Mac forced a smile, which felt marginally maniacal, and dragged Zach out onto the dance floor in a total cover-her-own-ass maneuver. Emma beamed at her and waved and then turned away. Mac sagged in relief right as Zach stomped on her instep with his enthusiastic gyrations. Karma can be a bitch.

Mac was careful for the rest of the evening, keeping her distance from Gavin during dinner, cake cutting, and bouquet tossing. The reception went on well into the night. Since Brad and the boys owned the brewery, there was no end time and most of the guests were happy to party as long as it lasted. Aunt Sarah badgered the DJ into playing the hip-hop song "Make Me Better," to which she and Aunt Charlotte showed off their grooving moves. They even got Mr. Tolliver to join them.

Mac was standing by a window in the courtyard, enjoying the cool breeze at her back, when Gavin strode out of the crowd toward her. He'd ditched his jacket and his bow tie was undone, as were the top buttons on his collar. He held out his hand to her and she took it.

She didn't bother to look and see if anyone was watching them. Right now, she just didn't care. He led her through the courtyard, now lit up solely by all of the twinkling lights and paper lanterns overhead, until he reached the exit that led outside. With one furtive glance behind him, he pushed open the wrought iron gate and pulled Mac after him.

She was in his arms before she had a chance to gauge his intentions. His mouth was on hers as he backed her up into the side of the building. Mac kissed him back, breaking away only when she had to breathe. Darn it.

"I love my sister, I really do, and I'm happy for her, I am," he said. "But can we leave now?"

Mac laughed. "The aunts are still in there bumping and grinding; are we really leaving before two septuagenarians?"

"If they were going to be doing what we're going to be doing, they'd be gone already," he said. "I know because your Aunt Sarah told me so."

Mac clapped a hand over her mouth. "She didn't!"

"She did!" he said. He pressed his lips to the base of her throat. "Oh, and your Aunt Charlotte said something about how she bet I had nice pecs."

"Oh, my god, they're out of control," Mac said.

"And so are we. Come on, I'm taking you home." Gavin bent his knees and wrapped his arms about Mac's upper legs as if he would carry her all the way home if he had to. She laughed and put her hands on his shoulders to steady herself.

"Easy there, big boy," she said. "I have to say good night to Emma."

"Ugh," he groaned.

Then he let Mac slide slowly down the front of his body, making her woozy with desire. Because she just couldn't help herself, when her face was level with his, she paused to kiss him with every bit of longing she felt.

"Mac! Is that you?"

Mac started and turned to see Trevor, staring at her in shock as if he'd just been shot and she'd been the one to pull the trigger.

Chapter 35

W hat are you doing here?" Mac asked Trevor. She pushed against Gavin's shoulders and he set her back on her feet.

"I came to talk to you," he said. He looked furious. "Now who's this and what the hell is going on?"

Mac glanced from one man to the other and back. This could not be happening. Not now. Panic made her brain shut down and she couldn't remember anyone's name.

"I'm Gavin," Gavin answered when Mac let the silence go on too long. "Gavin Tolliver."

"Emma's little brother?" Trevor roared. "I thought you'd be a pimply teenager. This? This is the young man Emma asked you to babysit for two weeks?"

Mac felt Gavin stiffen beside her. He removed his hand from her hip and she could feel his hot stare on the side of her face.

"What did he say?" Gavin asked. His voice was so soft she had to strain to hear him, which made it all the more devastating.

Mac didn't want to look at him. She knew it was going to be awful. She closed her eyes, willing the entire mess to go away.

"Mac," he said.

She turned to look at him—how could she not—and saw the two red patches of color on his cheeks. She knew from when he was young that was his tell when he was upset or embarrassed. It felt like a knife to the chest to know that right now she was responsible for that look.

"It's not what it sounds like," she said. She reached out to touch him but he stepped back as if unsure of her.

"Oh, it's exactly what it sounds like," Trevor argued. "Emma asked her to play single girl to your sad boy for the duration of the wedding, which I imagine was pretty damn convenient with me, her boyfriend, in London for the whole event."

"Boyfriend?" Gavin asked through gritted teeth. He looked like he was choking on the word.

"No, we broke up," Mac said.

"When?" Gavin asked.

Mac knew it was going to sound bad. Still, she had to tell him the truth. "Yesterday, officially, but we were on a break for two weeks before that."

His nostrils flared and he gave her a quick nod. "I see."

"No, you don't," Mac said. "I wanted to—"

"Hey, what's going on?" Emma asked as she tripped through the gate with Brad at her side. Then her eyes landed on Trevor and her mouth made a small O.

"Yeah, Mac's boyfriend just arrived," Gavin said. "Since she's not going to be available to babysit me anymore, I guess I'd better go."

He strode forward, shook Brad's hand, and kissed his sister's forehead.

"Gavin, wait, I can explain—" Emma began but Gavin held up one hand in a *stop* gesture.

"Don't," he said.

His eyes found Mac and he looked at her with unabashed hurt as if he couldn't believe that everything that had happened between them was a lie. It wasn't, but Mac didn't know how to tell him that. Gavin turned his gaze back to his sister.

"Emma, I love you," he said. "More than just about anyone, ever, and I know you love me like that, too, but you have to stop trying to manage my life. I'm okay. I always have been."

With that, he turned on his heel and strode from the reception, breaking Mac's heart with every step he took. He didn't look back and when his truck pulled out of the parking lot and headed down the road, Mac felt as if her insides were curling up in an attempt to cushion themselves from the hurt. They couldn't.

"This is all my fault," Emma wailed. Brad pulled her close and hugged her.

In moments, the rest of the wedding party arrived outside in the courtyard as if answering the Bat Signal over Gotham.

"Hello, Trevor," Carly said. Too much champagne made it impossible for her to control the curl of contempt on her upper lip.

"Trevor who?" Zach asked. "Is he a wedding crasher?"

"You might want to rethink the wardrobe if you're crashing," Sam said. He glanced up and down at Trevor's jeans and tucked in polo shirt.

"He's my ex-boyfriend," Mac said. "The one who paid Ralph Lester to pretend that Tulip was his dog, so that I couldn't keep her."

"He didn't!" Jillian cried.

"You bastard!" Sam strode forward, looking like he was eager to do some damage on the smaller man.

Trevor looked at the bigger man as if trying to decide if he could take him. Wisely, he concluded that he couldn't.

"Mac, I think that discussion is between us," Trevor said. "I flew all the way here on a redeye from London to urge you not to end things between us; I think I deserve a moment of your time in private."

Zach and Sam looked at Mac. She didn't have to think this one over, not even for a nanosecond. She shook her head, and they stepped forward and grabbed Trevor by the upper arms, holding him in place.

"After what you did to that poor puppy, I have nothing to say to you," Mac said. "I meant what

I said yesterday. We are done. Do not come near me ever again or I will have you arrested. Am I clear?"

Trevor was struggling against Zach and Sam's hold. Sam gripped Trevor's elbow, and his arm went limp.

"The lady asked you a question," he said.

"Yes, fine, I'm clear," Trevor spat. "Have fun with your boy toy, you bi—"

Whatever he'd been about to say was cut off as Zach's fist connected with his chin, knocking Trevor out cold. Zach and Sam dragged him over to a waiting cab and tossed him inside, giving the driver enough fare to get him back to the Portland airport.

They came back dusting off their shirtsleeves as if they had just taken out the trash.

"Thanks, guys," Brad said. He glanced down at Emma and asked, "Do you want us to close down the party?"

Emma glanced back at the reception. People were still dancing.

"No," she said. "But if you all would go and mingle that'd be great. I need to talk to Mac . . . alone."

Mac saw Jillian and Carly exchange worried glances. This was not reassuring. She had a feeling Emma was going to tear into her and Mac couldn't blame her. She'd asked Mac to cheer Gavin up, not destroy him.

"Come here," Emma said. She grabbed Mac's hand and walked by the caterer's truck. An unopened bottle of champagne was on the bumper of the truck and she snagged it as they went by.

Mac followed Emma around the big brick building to a tiny garden tucked away in a corner. There was a bench and two chairs and a bubbling water fountain.

"I didn't know this was here," Mac said.

"I put it here so the workers had an outdoor escape," Emma said. "It was one of my first landscape design projects."

"It's lovely," Mac said.

Emma sat on the bench and Mac sat beside her. She waited while Emma wrestled the cork out of the bottle with a loud pop. She took a long drink and then handed the bottle to Mac, who did the same.

"Okay, start at the beginning," Emma said. She looked at Mac meaningfully. "The very beginning."

Mac chugged down more champagne, clearly stalling, until Emma took the bottle away. With a heavy sigh, Mac began her story all the way back on her own abomination of a wedding day.

Emma never interrupted. She never said a word. She just sipped off the champagne bottle, pausing occasionally to belch. When Mac finished up her R-rated version, as opposed to the actual X rating, of the past twenty-four hours, Emma nodded.

"Do you have any idea what you've done to Gavin?" she asked Mac. Her voice snapped like a whip and it flayed Mac raw.

Mac hung her head. Yes, she did, because inside she was pretty sure she was dying.

"I'm sorry," she said. "I never wanted this—"

"Didn't you?" Emma interrupted.

Mac turned to look at her, but Emma glanced away. She took another long swig off of the bottle.

"I knew about that night after your wedding," Emma confessed. She stared straight ahead, not meeting Mac's gaze. "I went looking for you after everything was sorted out, and I remembered that spot was one of Gav's favorite places so I thought he might take you there. He . . . um . . . seemed to have things in hand so I didn't interrupt."

Mac blew out a breath. "You knew? All this time, and you never said anything?"

"I didn't think it was my business," she said. "And I knew you'd feel weird about it."

"Weird?" Mac snorted. "Understatement."

"I also knew how Gavin felt about you, so I figured maybe it was for the best that he got to be with you, so he'd finally get over you," she said. "But he never got over you."

Mac felt as if a giant fist was squeezing her heart in its meaty fingers, keeping it from beating and making her hurt.

"Oh, he dated and there were some short relationships, and for a while there I really thought Jane was going to reel him in, but he never looked at anyone the way he looked at you," Emma said. "Then you hooked up with Trevor."

She made a bleck face, and Mac smiled. Bleck was right. It was hard for her to imagine that she'd thought to spend her life with such a controlling, manipulative, emotionally unavailable man. Oh, sure, he helped her move on from Seth, but not really. It was more like he helped her move to the side—his side—to be whatever he wanted when he wanted it.

"So, when you asked me to babysit Gavin . . ." Mac began but Emma interrupted.

"It was complete bullshit. He loved Jane, but he wasn't in love with her, and his business will be fine, but I thought if I made you think he needed you and threw the two of you together for a couple of weeks, you'd finally see him *that* way," she said. "I was hoping the two of you—mostly you—would figure it out."

"Boy, howdy, did I!"

Emma held up a hand. "Yeah, he's still my baby brother."

"Sorry," Mac said. "But the sex . . ."

Emma clapped her hands over her ears and sang, "La la la, don't say sex, la la la."

Mac pulled her friend's hands away from her ears. She couldn't help but laugh; then she sobered up and sighed. "Emma, I'm in love with him."

Her eyes watered up because the first man she'd ever loved, the only man she'd ever fallen in love with, had just walked out of her life. Emma put her arm around Mac's shoulders and pulled her close.

"Brad and I will cancel our honeymoon," she said. "We'll have an emergency intervention with the whole wedding party and gang up on Gavin until he sees reason about this whole mess, which is all my fault, although in my defense it was done out of love for you both."

Mac smiled. She loved the idea of bringing in the troops and having all of the support, but she knew that wouldn't work.

"Thanks, really, but I think this is something I have to do myself."

Chapter 36

How goes romancing the hottie?" Aunt Charlotte asked.

"It's not," Mac said.

She stood in the doorway of the living room watching her aunts, who were zipped up in matching knee- and elbow-length wet suits, lie on their surfboards on the carpet while they pretended to paddle.

"Get ready!" Aunt Sarah shouted. "Here it comes!"

They both paddled faster and then popped—well not so much popped as creaked—up onto their feet, positioning themselves as if they were riding the waves.

"Hey, you stole my wave," Sarah yelled at Charlotte.

"Yeah, well, this is locals only," Charlotte snapped back.

Mac rolled her eyes and left the room. The aunts were planning a surf trip to Ogunquit and clearly they were practicing their surf 'tude as well as their technique.

Mac pitied the lifeguards who didn't take them seriously when they rolled up with their boards strapped to the roof of their Challenger.

"Keep trying, Mac," Sarah yelled after her.

"He's mad now, but he'll get over it, especially if you stay on his radar."

"Thanks," Mac said. "I'm taking Tulip for a walk. Back later."

She clipped the leash to Tulip's collar and set out for their daily walk down to the boardwalk. This was not a random happenstance. Over the past week, she had spent her days tracking Gavin's schedule. Some might call it stalking, but Mac figured if no point of contact had been made than it was really just familiarizing.

The Monday after the wedding, she had put in for an extended leave of absence and a transfer to her company's Portland office. She knew it was a crazy gamble and that Gavin might not give her a second chance, but she also knew that what Aunt Sarah had said was right.

The aunts were going to be gone, someday, and Mac realized she didn't want to miss any more time with them, especially since Sarah had decided that she was going to teach Mac to dance hip-hop, whether she liked it or not. How could she miss out on that?

Mac and Tulip stationed themselves in their usual spot near the outdoor chess tables in the small park that sat by the boardwalk. Right on schedule, with his T-shirt drenched in sweat and his earbuds in, Gavin went jogging by. Tulip always wanted to jump over the summer roses that separated the park from the boardwalk and love on Gavin, but Mac held her back.

She had made exactly two attempts to talk to Gavin since the wedding. Both times she had been met with a stone-cold silence. He didn't yell, or raise his voice; he wasn't scary or mean. In fact, he was nothing. He didn't acknowledge her or engage in any way. Both times Mac had stammered an apology and then fled. She was pretty sure she would have preferred it if he had yelled at her.

A few minutes later, when he jogged back the way he had come, she almost shouted his name, but she chickened out at the last second.

"Mackenzie Harris, that was pitiful."

Mac turned around to see Zach and Sam sitting at one of the outdoor chess tables. Their match was well under way and Mac was surprised that she hadn't noticed them when she arrived—then again, no she wasn't. She had been pretty fixated on Gavin.

"Hi, boys," she said.

Tulip recognized them and galloped over to greet them. Zach puckered his lips and Tulip kissed him right on the mouth. He was the only person Mac knew who encouraged this behavior. Sam patted his knee and Tulip abandoned Zach for him, wiggling all over when he found the sweet spot on her spine.

"Mac, if you want to win him back, you're going to have to work harder than spying on him from behind the shrubbery," Zach said. He looked at the board and moved a pawn to take one of Sam's.

"He's right." Sam agreed. He turned his attention back to the board and frowned.

Mac might have been embarrassed by the fact that they knew what she was doing, but she was at her personal lowest, which was ironic given that up to now, she'd always considered being dumped at the altar in front of two hundred of her nearest and dearest her rock bottom. Funny how actually loving the guy who left you made it that much worse.

"Okay, school me," Mac said. "What do I do to get him back?"

"Has he seen you naked lately?" Zach asked.

Mac frowned. "Are you suggesting I show up at his door naked?"

"It would work for me," Zach said.

"Yeah, that's because your definition of a relationship is warped," Sam said.

"No, it isn't," Zach protested.

"Loving your own reflection doesn't count," Sam said. He slid his bishop diagonally across the board and took Zach's knight.

"That was cold," Zach said. Mac wasn't sure if it was the comment or the chess maneuver that bothered him more.

"He does have a point though," Sam said. "Gav is in love with you—"

411

"He was," Mac corrected him.

"He still is," Zach said. "The only person in Bluff Point more pathetic than you right now is him, and we know because we've tried to get him out and about and he refuses to leave his sad little apartment."

Mac felt tiny wings of hope flutter in her chest.

"So, if you're going to crack him," Sam said. "You need to be an ever constant presence in his everyday. Remember, men are visual beings. If he has to see you—not trying to talk to him or win him back or anything like that—but just if he sees you constantly, he'll crack like a walnut under a hammer."

"You had to go with the nut and hammer analogy?" Zach asked. "Really?"

Sam shrugged.

"Okay, if I agree with your crazy scheme, how do you suggest I pull this off?" Mac asked. "How am I supposed to be ready to spring out at him a million times a day?"

Sam and Zach both looked up at her and grinned. "Call Jillian. With three of your Maine crew in action, the poor bastard doesn't stand a chance."

"You look like a ho," Aunt Sarah said.

Mac paused in her walk down the hallway and took the turn into the living room nice and slow. She had never worn a dress this tight or shoes this high before, and she was terrified she was going to fall and break a leg or have her dress roll up from the bottom and give the world an eyeful of her nether regions.

"A ho?" she asked.

"I meant that in the most flattering way possible," Sarah said.

"Natch," Charlotte said. "Ho is a compliment; it's slut you have to look out for."

Charlotte was seated next to her sister on the couch with Tulip wedged in between them, dead asleep.

"Thanks for the clarification and for puppy sitting," Mac said. A car horn honked and she glanced out the window to see Jillian's Jeep waiting for her. "Jilly's here. I have to go."

Mac blew them kisses and headed out the door. She had just gotten a text from Zach thirty minutes ago, telling her that he and Sam had muscled Gavin into going to Marty's to watch the Red Sox game with them. He ended the text with the words **Dress sexy.**

Mac had spiraled into a panic. What did sexy even mean? Emma was away on her honeymoon and Jillian was tall and thin and looked smokin' hot even in flannel, so she was no help.

Carly had gone back to New York after the wedding, but Mac had kept her apprised of the situation in Bluff Point. Upon receiving Zach's text, she had immediately video chatted Carly to ask her what to do. Carly had told her not to move. Ten minutes later, Carly's younger sister Gina was at the door with the dress and the shoes.

She shoved them at Mac and told her to tell Carly that she was not a delivery person. Then she stomped down the front steps in shoes just like the ones Mac wore now, the ones she was afraid to move in. Mac was filled with admiration for Gina. She didn't think she'd ever be able to stomp in these shoes.

Mac hobbled down the steps to the Jeep to find Jillian staring at her with wide eyes.

"The man is going to have a stroke," Jillian said as she took in the whole ensemble. "Is Carly trying to help you catch him or kill him?"

Mac tried to pull the dress down to cover herself as she sat down. "I don't know if I can do this."

"Yes, you can," Jillian said. "At this point, what do you have to lose?"

"You mean besides my dignity?" Mac asked.

"Dignity is overrated," Jillian said. "Ask yourself this, is fighting for him worth sacrificing your dignity?"

"What dignity?" Mac asked and Jillian laughed.

Marty's was thick with locals watching the baseball game. To say Mac was overdressed in her black micro-minidress and matching platform stilettos was an understatement, especially when Jillian was dressed in a sweet floral sundress and summer sandals.

The arch of Mac's right foot started to spasm and she envied Jillian's sandals mightily. On the upside, the extra six inches of height helped her to see over the crowd and she spotted Gavin across the room, playing darts with Zach and Sam.

Zach spotted her first and jerked his head in Gavin's direction as if Mac hadn't had a small heart attack at the sight of him.

"Courage," Jillian whispered in her ear and Mac nodded. "I'll lead. You look innocent."

Mac raised an eyebrow at her and Jillian grinned.

"I meant innocent about our being here, not innocent, because, yeah, that dress is a walking perversion."

"Gee, thanks," Mac said. "I've always wanted to be perverse."

Jillian scored a table near the dartboards, and Mac slid onto one of the stools. Her skirt rode up higher than she'd anticipated and she hopped back onto her feet with a sigh.

"Yeah, you're not allowed to sit in those sorts of dresses."

"I'm in hell."

"Maybe, but not for long," Jillian said. She gestured to the dart game behind Mac.

Mac slowly turned her head; afraid she'd lose her balance if she moved any faster, and glanced over her shoulder at Gavin. He was standing beside the dartboard looking like he'd just been conked on the head.

Mac met his gaze and then she gave him a slow come-hither half smile and a wink before she turned back to Jillian, who hopped up from her seat and said, "Okay, let's go."

"What?" Mac asked. She'd just made her move.

Jillian held up her phone. "Per Zach's instructions, dress sexy, make sure he sees you, give him a hot look, then git."

"Git?" Mac asked, dismayed. How had she missed this part of the instructions?

"We're playing the long game here," Jillian said. "Your mission is just to get inside his head and wear his resistance down, and then you can work out your issues."

Jillian grabbed Mac's hand and tugged her back into the crowd. They pushed their way through and a hand grabbed Mac's butt on the way. Without thinking about it, she turned and gave the offender a punch to the throat. He went down fast, but Mac recognized Seth as he dropped. Jerk! She and Jillian stepped over him and headed out the door.

And so it went for the next week. Zach, Sam, Jillian, the aunts, and Jessie were all pressed into tracking Gavin's every move. The man couldn't cross the street without someone sending Mac an alert.

If Gavin was shopping for produce, Mac would

suddenly appear in the melon section. If he was at The Grind for his three o'clock java booster, she would appear on the patio in a tank top and short shorts. If he was taking his daily jog, she would walk down the boardwalk in just a string bikini on her way to sunbathe on the beach. On and on it went.

She never spoke to him, but she always made sure she looked like she'd just rolled out of bed, in a good way, then she made eye contact with a wicked wink or a knowing smile and then she disappeared.

Judging by the way his brow furrowed and his jaw started clenching at the sight of her, Mac wasn't sure if he wanted to jump her or do himself an injury to get away from her. She hoped it was the former, but she noticed he never spoke to her either, which she did not take as a good sign.

At the end of the week, Mac knew that her leave of absence was ending and she'd have to report to work at the office in Portland soon. Thus, she called an emergency meeting at the brewery with her three main cohorts, Zach, Sam, and Jillian.

The brewery was closed for the day and the four of them sat outside in the courtyard, enjoying tall frosty pints and the warm summer evening. Tulip sniffed around the premises while Mac kept an eye on her to make sure she didn't start chewing on anything she shouldn't.

"I can't believe the man hasn't cracked yet," Zach said. "I would have bagged you that first night at Marty's."

"Agreed," Sam agreed. "Even my blood pressure spiked and I love you like a sister."

"Thanks," Mac said. "But I don't think I can keep stalking him or he's going to take out a restraining order on me."

"No, he won't," Jillian said. "You've got him dazed and confused, which is perfect, but now you have to go all in."

"Meaning, I should break into his house and tie him up until he listens to me?" Mac asked.

"You had me at tied up, you lost me at the listening thing," Zach said.

"Lovely," Jillian said. "No, what I am thinking is we're going back to the very beginning. It's time for you and Gavin to deal with that night seven years ago, and what better way to deal with it than to recreate it?"

"How can I possibly do that?" Mac asked. "How can I get him out to the grassy hill under the beech trees where it all began?"

"Easy," Zach said. He whistled and Tulip came trotting over to get some love from him. "As I understand it, you were doing pretty good keeping Gavin at arm's length until you had to see him about a dog, am I right?"

"Yes," Mac said. Tulip had definitely been the catalyst that had thrown them together.

"Well, it seems clear to me that the key to you and Gavin is Tulip," he said. Mac wasn't sure she trusted the mischievous twinkle in Zach's eyes, but Tulip did, which was evident when she slobbered all over him.

It was just a few minutes to sunset, and Mac was sitting on the lowered tailgate of Gavin's pickup truck, which Zach had borrowed, with Tulip by her side. She had loaded up the bed of the truck with all of the paraphernalia for a perfect summer picnic.

Fluffy comforter? Check. Basket of food? Check. Bottle of wine with glasses? Check. Music playing softly on a portable radio? Check. She was so nervous, she wondered if she should go make herself throw up in the bushes before she faced him as she was a teeny bit afraid that she might throw up on him.

She rubbed Tulip's ears and waited for the signal. Her heart was hammering so loudly she wasn't sure she'd be able to hear it when it came. She forced herself to breathe.

The grassy field under the two copper beech trees hadn't changed much over the past seven years, although when she looked up and studied the tree limbs under the darkening sky, she was sure the trees had grown up a bit, just like her and Gavin.

A whistle pierced the quiet and Mac put Tulip

on the ground. She unclipped Tulip's leash and said, "Okay, girl, let's go get Gav."

At the mention of her favorite human man's name, Tulip's ears went up and she darted off onto the trail. Zach's whistle signified that Sam had dropped off Gavin on the trail and that Zach believed he was within range of Mac.

Yes, this was their grand plan. In order to get Gavin back to the place where it all began, they had all lied to him and told him that Tulip had gone missing on the trail and they were all going to split up and search for her. Mac felt horrible about the lie but this was her last chance before she had to leave. It was their last chance for a happy ever after and she didn't want to let it go without giving it everything she had.

She hurried down the path after Tulip. Then she hid and watched through the trees as Tulip found Gavin.

"Tulip, what are you doing out here?" he asked as he rubbed her head.

He went to pick her up but Tulip pranced away as Mac hid behind a tree and called, "Tulip, where are you, baby girl?"

She peeked around the tree and watched Gavin. At the sound of her voice, his jaw clenched and he looked like he was gearing up for something. Boy, howdy, was he ever. He just didn't know it.

Tulip galloped around him and he sighed and said, "All right, princess, let's go find your mama.

She's probably out of her mind with worry."

Mac had to call out two more times to get them up to the field where she waited on the back of the truck. When Tulip saw her, she raced across the grassy field and Mac greeted her with a treat, a nice big chew bone to keep her occupied. Then Mac tied the dog's long lead to the tailgate of the truck so the puppy could lie in the grass but not wander off.

When she stood, Gavin was standing on the far edge of the field, staring at her as if he were seeing a ghost. Pretty close. Mac had styled her hair like she'd worn it seven years ago and she was wearing a puffy meringue of a sundress, which while nowhere near as full as the bridal gown she'd worn the last time she'd been here with him was still remarkably similar.

When Gavin started to stride forward, his first steps were tentative but then they became purposeful as he stared at her with that intensity she had come to love, that singular attention that let her know he was wholly consumed by her.

Mac moved forward to meet him, shyly at first. Rejection was still a very big possibility but then she thought of Tulip and how she threw herself wholeheartedly at the people she loved. Mac understood that feeling and she couldn't bear the distance between her and Gavin for another second. She began to hurry across the field. In four long strides, she was in his arms, and he was cupping her face and kissing her as if he would die if he didn't.

Mac began to cry as she kissed him again and again. He was here. He was in her arms. And she never wanted to be without him again.

She cupped his face and gazed into his eyes, and said, "I'm in love with you, Gavin Tolliver, and I think I have been for a very long time."

Gavin swept her up into his arms and carried her across the field while still kissing her.

Mac pulled away from him and clung to his shoulders while all the words she wanted to say poured out in an incoherent babble.

"I'm sorry. I should have said no to Emma . . . but I couldn't. I owed her. But I didn't realize that you . . . I never meant for this to happen . . . and then when I realized I was in love with you . . . it was too late. I never wanted to hurt you."

He stopped beside the truck and set her down on the tailgate. His blue gaze swept over her face and the look he sent her was so full of love that Mac started to cry all over again.

"Shh," he said. He kissed away the tears. "That's what I was waiting for; not an apology, there was no need; not having you spring up on me every time I turned around, although we'll be revisiting a couple of those outfits." He pulled back and pushed her hair out of her face and then his gaze met hers. When he spoke, his voice was so soft she had to strain to hear him when he said,

"All I ever needed to hear from you, Mackenzie Harris, is that you're in love with me, too."

He cupped her face and kissed her and as the tears streamed down Mac's cheeks, it felt very much like their first time together, here under the stars, secluded in the woods. Except this time, when they made love, Mac didn't leave him alone in the morning without saying a word.

This time she held him tight and whispered in his ear the words she knew he had spent years longing to hear. Words that she hadn't known the meaning of until he showed her what they truly meant, what it truly meant to love and be loved.

"I love you . . . forever," she said.

And when the puppy nearby got tired of her chew toy and let out a bark, they scrambled to pick her up. Tulip snuggled between them while they whispered about their plans for the future and marveled at how lucky they were to have a second chance. As Mac hugged her man and her puppy close, she knew without a doubt that she was finally home to stay.

Books are produced in the United States using U.S.-based materials

Books are printed using a revolutionary new process called THINKtech™ that lowers energy usage by 70% and increases overall quality

Books are durable and flexible because of smythe-sewing

Paper is sourced using environmentally responsible foresting methods and the paper is acid-free

Center Point Large Print

600 Brooks Road / PO Box 1
Thorndike, ME 04986-0001 USA

(207) 568-3717

US & Canada:
1 800 929-9108
www.centerpointlargeprint.com